ALSO BY CHARLES NEWMAN

NEW AXIS

THE
PROMISEKEEPER

A TEPHRAMANCY BY

CHARLES NEWMAN

*Divers Narratives on
the Economics of Current Morals
in Lieu of a Psychology*

HERE EMBODIED IN AN APPROVED TEXT
WORKING OFTEN IN SPITE OF ITSELF

*Certain Profane Stoical Paradoxes Explained
Literary Amusements Liberally Interspersed
Partitioned with Documents & Conditioned by Imagoes
Hearty Family-Type Fare, Modern Decor, Free Parking*

SIMON AND SCHUSTER
NEW YORK

First printing

SBN 671-20822-5
LIBRARY OF CONGRESS CATALOG CARD NUMBER: 76-139651
DESIGNED BY EVE METZ
MANUFACTURED IN THE UNITED STATES OF AMERICA

for my mother and father

Contents

Part the First

Part the Second

Part the Third

5

Part the Fourth

You er *what you is, but you can't be no* is-er
Uncle Remus

If I am I because you are you,
and you are you because I am I;
then I am not I,
and you are not you.
Hassidic Proverb

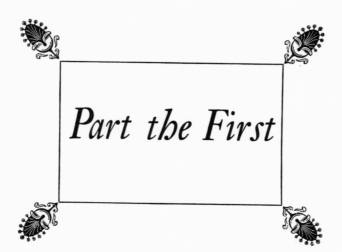

Part the First

1 · A *Thousand Ships*

"Thata boy, come on now, thata boy . . . thata boy . . . thata boy . . . *there* we go . . . thata Boy!"

The voice had been with him from the day he moved in. As it became clear that the child's toilet schedule corresponded roughly to his own, and mother's coaxing waxed superogate in the heavy mornings, he had shouted obscenities back at them— mouth pressed hard against the grille of the bathroom heating duct—but the tower's acoustics proved intransitive and his words more than likely emerged on some other innocent.

Sometimes she sang, though, more to herself than the kid, it seemed, and staring upward vacantly, Sam would harmonize until he realized that for whatever random audience he served, his was a *basso continuo* cut off from its melody, an expert tuba in a deserted cupola.

But on this hot late summer morning, neither he nor the kid would be moved. Sam got up and, holding his parts, dodged to avoid the Dott's hard stare into the living room where he had sloughed off his suit the night before.

The Dott didn't down her eyes. She wielded his sheets like sails, dark hams of arms flapping hair and sweat off the good linen while the man tied his tie. Sam Hooper mock-punched at her enomous shadow and then they embraced laughing, the Damoclean sheet cool between them.

The Dott never acknowledged Mother's voice in the bathroom, nor the occasional stewardesses or whatever might have even longer, brighter legs than Sam. She would simply come in and, drawing the bottom sheet to her chest, construct an incline to inch Sam and his relief from bed and board. She was glad there was nobody else to pick up after this morning.

"No breakfast, Dott," said Sam. "I'll eat out." The door slammed thinly.

"Worried 'bout you weight?" the Dott countered, but he was gone.

When he didn't answer she lay down on the divan and started to telephone. A few moments later, however, Sam returned breathlessly and, ignoring the Dott, began to stare conscientiously out of a wall of windows. He looked north, following the crescent of the lake until it became green at the suburbs. The opaque waves arrived diagonally at the shore. There was no division between the sea and sky. Sam folded his arm and stood silently for several minutes. The Dott regarded him patiently, holding her hand over the receiver, and then he left again, this time with his fedora, calmer.

The elevator presented itself empty and early. Sam stepped in, the doors closed fitfully against one another, the violins took up the refrain. He took it for some sixteen feet per second/per second but then pressed the emergency stop. The car jerked to like a gallows. Sam made a vulgar gesture at the ceiling and, following through, raised a fiber panel in the roof of the car. A coil of multicolored wiring sagged like entrails to his touch. He felt beyond the wires until he located the pulsating speaker, and as the fluorescent bulb seared his hand, he snatched the wiring from its solder, coiling the guts in his pocket as the music ceased abruptly.

It occurred to him that a short circuit could send him to the bottom, but the lights dimmed only momentarily, and then as the car resumed its calculated descent, Sam began to bellow the fierce mimicked Italian from an opera he loved enough to memorize but of which he understood nothing—

Di sua catena tavolta amara,
mai fu più cara libertà—

until the doors snapped apart without warning and he found himself serenading the lobby. Pushing past Dean, the incredulous doorman, he strode out on the Esplanade, hand over heart, *sotto voce.*

The Elevated stained the street with its shadows and odor. Sam gazed into the tenement windows which passed at an appropriately reflective speed. During one of those hiatuses which overtake children of Sam's precosity about the third grade, his father had taken him along to New York on business aboard the *Twentieth-Century Limited.* They had risen early to be boutonniered at breakfast by a daffodil-jacketed waiter, and then watched the Hudson sink down from its mist to become real water again. A thousand Liberty ships, anchors limp, bows aflame with corrosion, excess grain fermenting in their striped, squat hulls, saluted their entry to the city.

Farther on, young Samuel had seen his first tenements, a gallery of framed scenes, windows with shades but no screens. Not ten feet from them a child tried to crawl up the banister of some back stairs and then fell, spinning silently, dutifully, as in a dream, disappearing abruptly behind a fence. Sam looked at his father, who looked at the waiter in the daffodil jacket. He looked back at them, widening his eyes apologetically.

The Elevated went underground, the lights came on, and the passengers turned from the mirrored windows to regard each other. The train slammed round a curve and emerged on the bridge over the reversed river. The freighters were lining up at the mouth of the sanitary canal waiting for the bridge to part. Down the corridor of iridescent plashes, beyond the dredges and

13

their sullen derricks, smack on the horizon, Sam could just make out the Pumping Station, eating its own mist.

Gulls perused Sam from their favorite girders. He got off three stops before the office. He wanted to walk. It had rained the night before and it was Saturday. He was getting hungry.

Burt Street was deserted. The sun had not managed itself above the buildings as yet. Sam liked to zigzag down the street when it was lonely and rain-washed; he felt as free as if he were watching himself walk down it on television. At the end of Burt Street stood the Management Concern Building, originally the Grain Exchange, a shaft of blinking onyx and swimmy marble. The traffic was channeled through tunnels in her foundation; across her cryptoportico were ranged the names of war dead all in bronze. At street level, the bas-relief of some vintage trumpeteer, his horn turned from battle and into the impassive bayonet-garlanded faces of those he led. At the very top, the figure of a Great Lady. She gazed down Burt Street, arms at her sides, no light between her legs.

The Grain Exchange had originally dominated the skyline and still remained the only city building with something as nice as the Great Lady on top of it, but now from behind, a glittering obelisk from the lesbian sea, rose the Public Parking Place, thirty-two perfectly empty stories, only one-third complete. The Great Lady was already minimalized against it, and the new facility would soon reduce her dimensions by two within its aluminum proscenium. He was getting hungrier.

Sam felt the sheen from his seersucker on his folly as he advanced. He tripped slightly, kicking something ahead of him. It was a bird, a nighthawk, its Semite beak split like a camellia. There was apparently something in the Parking Tower's eventide fluorescence which was terribly attractive to the nobler birds. The gulls and starlings, swamp sparrows and dickcissels managed to avoid it, but each morning, the obelisk was encircled with the corpi of a hundred or so highflyers; grosbeaks, vireos, blackpole warblers, redstarts, yellowbodied catbirds, necks twisted in disbelief. A bagman in ochre overalls moved among them now, scooping the insensate flock into a pushcart with a snow shovel. Sam wasn't hungry now.

On the topmost floor of the Parking Tower he could make out a window washer in violet overalls inching his way across the facade, leaving a snail's hygienic trail as he maneuvered. Sam widened his right eye and squinted his left—in this way canceling his astigmatism at the cost of a lopsided face. In his corrected vision the snail resembled a butterfly.

"Face is so natural pretty," the Dott once said, "that you got to louse it up to save yourself."

In the higharched lobby of Management Concern, surrounded by the airy white iron filigree of defunct staircases, Sam stared up at the fresco of *History of Progress, U. S. A.* The work was divided in thirds.

In the first panel, Priests and Indians entwined arms, the Indian knelt before the Priest, the Priest-in-a-chausable held out his hands, the sun was all a bag of gold, and all about rose bearded sailors from scalloped waves to bind them together with coils of rope. The inscription was:

WITH GOLD CAME LAW AND INVESTMENT

In the second panel, at the azimuth of the arch, a Farmer, Soldier, Negro and Shopkeeper-in-apron handed each other, respectively, wheat, iron, coal and cloth, in a rather stiffly Egyptian manner. The sailors' rope had become an iron chain which grandly entangled them all, and between the links it read:

WITH BARTER CAME ENGINEERING AND EXPANSION

The third panel completed the triptych. It portrayed an amicable Man-in-a-hat joining hands with a Worker-in-a-cap and an Artist-in-a-beret. An electrical conduit joined the rope and chain in a rococo swirl. They were endorsed as follows:

15

Sam stood in the vault of the arch, its shadow casting a dull swath across the polished floor, his enormous veinswollen hands tucked in his waistband, the large face wrapped almost too far about the small but perfectly proportioned head, his lips resisting their natural curve of some obsolete disdain.

The elevator arrived and took him up.

2 · Birthday Boy

Saturday morning was "simply showcase," as Sam's better half, Wittgenstein, put it—a skeleton staff for anything that might come in off the street. They worked that shift in volunteer pairs, Wittgenstein already there in the back near the railing. The board was off, not a number or noise. Sam's eleven colleagues were off too.

With the generators quiescent, Wittgenstein had the field glasses he usually trained on the board turned on the lake. As Sam came in, passing the switchboard from which dangled the receptionist's forlorn earphones, the gaze shifted to him.

"Well, if it isn't Birthday Boy," Wittgenstein chortled enthusiastically. How'd he know that? Sam thought, blanched.

Great pear of a man, Wittgenstein could have changed firms any day of the week on the strength of his book clientele and was the last of the officers still to work the floor. Indeed, when the consolidation had been lately effected, it was he who had decided upon the present eponymous title rather than take the risk of appending his own name to the alliterative partnership of Scutter, Scoville, Whitman and Wood. Wittgenstein was "not happy" as they used to say around the old S.S.W. and W. office; he was childless, yet he specialized in trusts. But Wittgenstein had always insisted that depression must be creative, since he worked so well when he came out of one. He was an uncluttered man and hard to dislike.

Sam leaned over the railing and gazed down giddily into the silent pit. More butterflies in violet overalls were sweeping up the tapes and swapped chits. Conscious of Wittgenstein's stare, he left the railing, and began absentmindedly to rearrange the Advice Rack, filling slots where all the pamphlets had been taken, refiling others which had been mis-replaced. Then he returned to his desk, among the dozen which surrounded Wittgenstein in a semicircle, and focused his own binoculars—each lens separately—on the ground-glass walls of the office.

"Hoops," Wittgenstein had said to him when he started, "with a Purk degree and the highest Q.U.I.F.* in our history, you're definitely frontman material. Don't you never forget we got eighteen thou invested in your training program. You oughta be able to make it back for us in six months—less we hit a Creamer, a course. Still, you oughta and if you ain't a partner in record time, you can kick a turd outta me."

Sam had gotten it back, all right, but he felt he was lucky—on the contrary, they had hit a Ripper and not a Creamer and when Wittgenstein and old S.S.W. and W. had just started, *they'd* had to go through the biggest Creamer of them all. That was when they'd bought the Grain Exchange and had that foreign sculptor come over to put his Great Lady on top and the rest. He had signed his work by using his own visage as the model for the artist in the third panel, then, leaving his large family in America, went back to Carrara and shot himself in a quarry.

Hard ridges appeared in Wittgenstein's brow as he answered the phone. Simultaneously a small piercing light appeared on the auxiliary Central American board. He stared at Sam while he talked, holding the receiver some distance from his mouth to indicate that his advice was not wholly scientific. Then he gave the desk a few good raps and grinned at Sam. Sam pulled up his lips for him. Wittgenstein waved him away to better things.

Sam took up his binoculars and again fixed them on the ground-glass walls. Toward noon a shape appeared hesitantly in the hall—a woman, perhaps—in blue with red spot at her throat. She shifted her purse from one hand to the other before

* PUBLISHER'S NOTE: Quadratic Utility In-Function

18

the door. Sam rose slightly in his chair as her hand firmed on the knob, then her body turned from its profile to confront him, holding the door open with her thigh, both hands on her pursestraps as if they were reins. Wittgenstein coughed discreetly in the background.

"Forgive me," Sam said, rising.

The woman advanced a half step.

"Sam Hooper," he managed.

"*Oh,*" she blurted. "*Not* the one on TV . . .?"

"Nope," Sam said resignedly. "Just spelled the same way, that's all."

"I saw your ad in . . ." she began. "You know, 'Money is people.'"

Sam could smile again. He handled for her a chair. The lady lowered her eyes and scooted into it. She looked over Sam's shoulder as he reseated himself, noting the napiform Jewish (?) man looking at them through his binoculars from the far desk. Then she glanced down at his virgin vinyl desk. There was a sterling automatic pencil, a calendar with the corporation motto on it, *Exercise your judgment as well as your means,* and a small pyramid with *Sam Hooper* on it.

"I see by your lapel medallion, Mr. Hooper," she began, "that you're a Purkman."

"*Uh?*"

"Well, are you?"

"Well, yes. I mean I wouldn't wear it unless . . ."

"We have a son at Purk, you see."

"Really? Well, the president would like that; he's a Purky too."

"Is that so? What's his name?"

"Bins, Alfred Bins."

"Is that so? He must have been there quite a while before you."

"Well, yes, before the Big Creamer, probably, or maybe

during it. He's not really that old a man, you know. Really remarkable."

"I think that Purk is probably the finest education one can get."

"Well, they *do* work your behind off." Sam smiled and spoke in his flattest accent.

The lady with the red spot at her throat laughed purposively.

Sam Hooper had never lied to a woman in his life, though he realized that it was precisely this fact which made his seductions so effortless. Indeed, any promiscuity on his part could only be viewed as part of a larger asceticism. He knew very well that whatever people found in him, the inherent respect which he induced was generated by some very crude electricity—which if channeled properly could focus on the most profound questions of existence, but in his case had only acted kinetically to date, like those diffuse globes which illuminate nothing save the moths attracted to them. And lately he had found himself lying deliberately to mitigate the helpless charm he so detested in himself.

"So what can Management Concern do for you today, Mrs. . . . ?"

"Den-*e*-hey."

"Denehey?"

"Den-e-hay. D-e-n-e-h-e-y."

"Well, Mrs. Denehey?"

"Well, Mr. Denehey passed away last—"

"I'm terribly sorry."

"Of course, and he left me . . . some money."

Sam didn't flinch.

"Well, in war bonds."

Mrs. Denehey lowered her head. Sam smiled in disbelief at the ceiling.

"And, well, I'd like to put it to work, you see."

Mrs. Denehey slumped forward out of her stiff posture, not to examine him so much as to indicate her helplessness.

"You would, I believe," Sam began slowly, "Mrs. Denehey—" Sam did some business on his slide rule—"like to win."

"Just so."

Sam concentrated on an air vent overhead.

"There's only one thing, Mr. . . ."

"Hooper."

"Oh yes, just like—"

"But not the same, remember. I was named for my great-grandfather."

"Oh?"

"He's dead, too."

"I'm terribly sorry."

"Of course."

"There's just only this one little thing; you see, Mr. Hooper, my husband's estate cannot know. I mean, he *liked* war bonds."

"We respect our clients' wishes in these matters."

"I wish you wouldn't talk like that."

"Well, what do you want me to say? You're the one that brought it up. We'll tell 'em or we won't tell 'em. Either way you want. I don't give a damn."

"Oh, I didn't mean to intimate anything," Mrs. Denehey interjected frantically. "I'm sure you'll go far here. In a few years I'll bet you'll be in the back there with the old Jewish gentleman."

(. . . Sam saw himself bludgeoning Mrs. Denehey to death before a horrified, helpless Wittgenstein, the opaque glass walls and advice rack smeared with *gouttes* of blood, her limp body with the quail-like head twisted grotesquely beneath it flung across his supervisor's desk. . . .)

"Ah, Mrs. Denehey, you shouldn't patronize me. No, that won't do at all. There's no rank here to speak of—only specialties. I'm a frontman, will be until I'm a partner, and then of

21

course I'll still be a frontman. Wittgenstein back there is a middleman. *And* a partner, I might add. Then there are my eleven colleagues—but they're all off today, you see. And the lastmen—I'm sure you've seen them in their colorful overalls. They work only weekends and evenings, thirty-two hours in all. In many ways theirs is the best lot. Mr. Bins, incidentally, began as a lastman. But all the other partners, it's no secret, except Wittgenstein, began at the front. So I'm here to stay, you see, for better or worse."

"Well, that makes sense, doesn't it?" Mrs. Denehey beamed. "So, well, I suppose all that remains is for you to sell me."

"Beg your pardon?"

"Yes, well, tell me how you're going to make me money. And make me give it to you then."

"Well, you don't *have* to give it to us, Mrs. Denehey, that's all right."

"But I *want* to give it to you."

"Well, that's nice, but you really don't have to. I mean, we could lose it too, you know. Madness is stronger than love."

Mrs. Denehey looked more sad than suspicious.

"Look, we have only one thing to offer," Sam went on rapidly. "The thing that has built MC, such as it is, and that is, we don't press our feelings on you. We don't gloat when we win or apologize when we lose. We match your needs to their consequences, that's all. If you don't know what you need, we'll tell you that as well. I mean, in the long run, it's neither here nor there. Right?"

"Well, you've had a very superior record as I understand it."

"I gather you would care to know a little of our history. Until recently it's been rather dull. You remember all those people who lost it during the Great Creamer?"

Mrs. Denehey nodded, paled.

"Well, we got it back for them during the Ripper; that's what really made us. Not all of it for all of them, of course, but most of it for most of them. I'm not saying that was a good or bad thing, but they got it back during the Ripper—and that's the name of the game."

"Mr. Hooper, now tell me frankly. Do you think there's going to be another Creamer ever?"

"We're not clairvoyant at MC, Mrs. Denehey. Of course there will be . . . fluctuations . . . Flushes and Creamers, Rippers and Glows, you know, that's how we make our money, after all. When most are wrong, somebody's got to be right. Well, why not? But nothing real big in our lifetime probably. Too many checks and balances, you know, push-pull push-pull? Still, and this should calm you somewhat, most of our recent efforts have been directed at reducing fluctuations and stabilizing growth. In fact, Mrs. Denehey, and I can tell you this frankly, we've been through sort of a revolution—take it easy now—but making money is almost a sideline with us now. Our interests are quite complex and more humane than ever, I mean, we're almost what you'd call a 'way of life.' I'm here to see just how much rationality you can take—how much do you want to invest, Mrs. Denehey?"

"Well, I wouldn't want to tell you that yet."

"Of course. When you think you're ready, I'll be glad to refer you to one of our specialists."

Mrs. Denehey caught her breath.

"But I want *you*."

"As I told you, Mrs. Denehey," Sam said as firmly as he could, "I'm the frontman here. Christ, I don't know how the thing works, I just look out for you once I bring you in. In all fairness, I'm rather new, and there are many more experienced men here than I, be that as it may."

"The least you could do is tell me what's going to happen to my money!"

"Now look, Mrs. Denehey, if you're going to be that way about it, let's just forget the whole thing. The basic operation here is very simple. You come in here, see, browse about the advice rack, the setting for which, if I may say so, is my responsibility. The rack is divided into Political and Natural Resources, General Services, Credit, Human Fulfillment, Education, Insurance, Art, Military, and Foreign—which includes Space. Once you've looked through our literature, we'll talk it over. You tell me what you need, and I'll indicate the spectrum of probable consequences. There's no rule of thumb for this; actually, I just try to size you up and help you out. Then, once we've decided on your preferences, we fill out a slip which I take to Witty over there, and he gives it a second, personalized, once-over. If there's something he doesn't like, he shoots a reconsider slip back to me and we do—though I stress that any final decision is yours, if you can hack it, as we say. If everything is in accord, Wittgenstein then puts the order in the proper order and goes to that railing over there, and signals the pit. Some very complicated sign language. Takes years to master it. Then the pit disseminates the information and usually, in about half a minute, you get either a check or a bill. If you want to go long term, of course, it's all mailed to you. It depends on your life-enhancement policies, naturally. And if we should, God forbid, hit a Creamer, there's more bills than checks, if a Glow or a Ripper, more checks than bills. Got it? Otherwise you can depend on rather unexciting but measurable growth."

Mrs. Denehey's hair was in her eyes by this time, but with an ovulate lower lip, she blew it back into place. Sam gave her his card, which proved to be too large for her coin purse.

Wittgenstein had seen all this clearly in magnified double image, had seen her pucker and smooth her hair. Then, as the woman rose, he followed her out the door and down the hall, an elegant shade upon the ground-glass wall.

Sam turned around slowly, nodded affirmatively, and without

expression put his finger to his watch. Wittgenstein focused on the hands. It was past noon and he shrugged. Sam got up, put on his hat, extinguished his light on the board, and Wittgenstein reverentially withdrew the field glasses from his damp eyes.

3 · *The Abyss of Us All*

The child was again recalcitrant, her voice so persistent, Sam shaved and urinated in the kitchen sink. But the plumbing carried Mother's voice everywhere, and finally it was necessary to hang a radio about his neck like an amulet and plug his ears with transistors.

> *If the fire of love burns in your bosom*
> *then all is at peace in heaven*
> *and the pain of love becomes ecstasy.*
> *If the ardor of love inflames your heart,*
> *then all is at peace in heaven*
> *and the pain of love becomes ecstasy.*

His body vibrated with the baroque repeats. He found at the office that the lights on the big board moved in similar rhythm patterns. U. S. Broiler, for example, a trading vehicle due for a reverse split, moved with the metrical regularity of a Lully cantata. Lully, he recalled from Humanities I at Purk, had loved his beat so much that one day, while pounding it out with a shepherd's staff in the accepted manner of the day, he had smashed his foot so badly that he had taken to bed and died of gangrene (or rather from a single misapplication of his own true beat), the sort of finale Sam would one day wish for himself.

It was the Dott's day off. Sam did the breakfast dishes to a clumsy jig. Then, the Sunday paper blown about him like the tents of Lilliput, Sam settled back in his swivel stereo-lounger and looked out on the lake. They were racing again. Out beyond the buoys, the water was jet black. The class twos, their bright spinnakers bursting, angled away from the city. He could see all the way to the Pumping Station. He wondered how much those boats cost.

Sam turned on the TV. He participated in the landing at Normandy, a news report of an air crash, a quarter-hour synopsis of *Henry IV*, parts one and two, a class in differential equations, a Czech puppet cartoon, and an interview with the President. The more celebrated Sam Hooper, with whom Mrs. Denehey had confused him, took Sundays off.

Sam turned the set off and began looking at the lake again. The boats were completing their first leg by the Pumping Station. The Crown Prince of Norway was leading. Several seemed to shudder on the turn, spinnakers collapsing like soufflés. What was that called? *Luff* or something? Sam was extremely nervous. He had gone through a pack of cigarettes in less than two hours. And his feet were unseemly busy with their own tap-tap. Lungs blown tight with smoke, Sam readjusted the controls of the stereo-lounger so that his feet slowly rose above the level of his head. Without resistance, airborne, his feet gradually ceased their jerking. From his new position, not only did the blood flow back to his chest, the old knot dissolving, but he could see the rent-a-painting from a new angle. Allowing his astigmatism full vent, he shaped it variously for himself.

The Abyss of Us All imploded a spectrum of yellows to streaks of green and fuchsia. At times Sam thought he made out a bunch of jonquils and a hummingbird at the center, but he resisted this, knowing it would hardly be appropriate to the theme. But this new angle had decided him, and bounding from the chair, he yanked the painting from the wall, determined to exchange it at the gallery. Across the esplanade the wind caught the canvas and nearly lifted him from the ground.

He traversed the north edge of the park where the trees blunted the wind and the foreigners were playing soccer on the dew. Their improbable names gave the strangely constricted game a certain awe for Hoops. "It puts a leg on you, but often not an arm," his father said. The late Hooper, Senior, had been undefeated. Sam often watched them from his window. They looked like aristocrats and screamed like horses. He missed his sports.

The wind surprised him at the side streets, and *The Abyss of Us All* threatened to come apart in his very hands. It was difficult to see where he was going beneath the enormous rectangle.

He passed the Olde Towne In, peered in, but met only his own steamy reflection. The specialty shops had not yet opened for the Sunday promenade; the pennants not yet unfurled, the kittens not yet awake in their windows, the suds still in the keg.

Arriving at the gallery, he found himself at the tail end of an invitation-only "opening." The curtains were drawn across the windows and a lastman in organdy coveralls guarded the door. This very same reached a hand forward for Sam's credentials; Sam hesitated, then held the frameless painting before him so that only the tips of his fingers and feet were visible and the lastman was obligated to stare directly into the bowels of *The Abyss of Us All*. Moving forward imperceptibly, keeping the pressure on, Sam gradually maneuvered past him, the picture acting as a revolving door; once in, he balanced the canvas on his hip and accepted a Brandy Alexander from the tallest waitress.

Scanning the premises with his best eye, he placed the painting in the corner and picked up the celebrant's brochure, a dappled paper the size and weight of a breadboard. On the cover was a halftone reproduction of the work in the closed-off window—a horse standing against a mountain, except that the horse's head looked a good deal like a cat's, and the horse's legs were very stiff and pointed like pencils—titled *Risorgimento*. Sam tried to forget all of the horses and mountains that his own stereotyped eye had inflicted on him and quickly returned to the brochure.

FRANKLIN FRANK
cocktail preview
AMERICAN PREMIERE

Frank has created a very personal vision between the realistic and the abstract, which suggests rather than states, an atmosphere of light, shadow and texture, with technical virtuosity. Between the figurative and the prehensile, his compositional and linear strengths are predominant, suggesting the predicament of modern man; a fragmented consciousness groping in the darkness, creating an intense, illuminating and very personal vision—an allusion of affirmation.

Sam wished he'd brought his radio with him. But he strode dutifully over to the painting where the largest crowd had gathered.

The painter himself stood in the corner in a wide-wale ochre hunting jacket with his wife in long straight hair and a black tweed shift, holding each other by the index fingers and examining the floor. He looked like a perfectly nice guy. But he was very drunk, his goatee stained with the rich mixed drinks. Sam felt the artist's eyes upon him and turned with pointless sadness to the crowd of pinstripes and chiffon. The painting under discussion was called *Cave-Wave*, 42 x 108, $1,000 unframed. Sam rather liked it—the contrast of the white-and-blue wave coming out or going into an orange cave.

Hoops moved down the line. The painter was still staring at him, and this made it necessary for Hoops to examine the next picture more closely than he ordinarily would have. He tried both eyes on it, squinting in each of his sixteen possible combinations. The colors dimmed and recongealed, but still nothing happened.

"Scrambled eggs."

A large three-piece man who had not removed his hat said this to his wife directly behind Sam. His wife pulled on his sleeve so that his coat was drawn lopsided on his shoulders.

"Scraaambled Eggs."

The man whaled at his thigh with his fist and poked his wife's ribs with his elbow. She whispered what appeared to be his first name hoarsely at him. But at last she sighed, reddened, and then permitted herself a giggle as well.

Sam was aware of the painter and his wife shuffling nervously behind him, and when it became clear that the painter would not protect even his own work, Sam felt the gravity of his situation. He was proposing to exercise his most valuable faculty —that of defending what he did not understand against something he understood but did not respect.

Sam walked up to the large man and, grasping him by his shorter sleeve, rebalanced his coat on his frame. He turned as if he expected a queer or a cop.

"You shouldn't do that," Sam said, "even if you don't understand it." The man opened his eyes in wonder. "You shouldn't laugh and make jokes like that." Sam said it flatly and firmly. "This stuff is more important than you are. I mean, in the long run."

The large man's face began to take on the characteristics of *Cave-Wave*. Sam liked the picture better now. The accuser's breath caught in his throat and his wife hung on to his arm as if to a mountain rope. The large man could say nothing to the sad, perfect face. Sam gazed at him unblinkingly until the wife towed her husband silently from the gallery.

The crowd had thinned out. The painter's wife was staring at him now, snatching her hair from her face and blinking. She guided her husband toward him. He was coughing shyly. The smoke hurt his eyes.

"That was nice of you," she said. "Are you an artist?"

30

Sam retreated numbly, grasping *The Abyss of Us All* from the corner where he had propped it and drawing it partially between them.

"Oh," she said, "that's marvelous. Is it yours?"

"Well, not exactly," said Sam.

"Oh, you've sold it. How wonderful."

"No, actually, I'm the owner, not the painter."

"You've come to see my husband's work?"

"No, actually, I'm not the owner either, really. I'm sort of renting it."

The painter began to look absently through his brochure. His wife allowed her hair to cover her face again. Sam slowly drew the canvas between them.

"Actually, I'm not even the renter. I've come to trade it in, you see."

And with that, he hoisted *The Abyss of Us All* onto his back and marched to the stockroom at the rear of the gallery.

Behind a set of louvered doors, he could see someone working. He set the picture down and rippled the slats.

"Hullo?"

"Hello."

The slats partially opened. Faded cashmere within.

"I've got something for you," Sam sung-sang.

A large, heavily lidded green eye winked back. The slats closed and the door slid open.

She was much prettier than the girl who had rented him the picture in the first place. In fact, she reminded him of the co-eds who had visited Purk on weekends. Then he realized that she was simply still wearing her college clothes and that her pageboy hair style was roughly a decade old. He reflexively glanced at her hands for the ring and noticed that her nails were bitten to the quick.

"Look," he said, in the same tone that he used on Mrs.

31

Denehey, "this is one of yours and I don't think I really want it."

She laughed, a little too loudly.

"The least you could do is give me a little chitchat first," she said finally.

The girl took the canvas from him; Sam was surprised that she could lift it so easily. She carried it to the back of the storeroom and propped it up against the wall.

"Oh, that looks like a LeRoy. Cathy's always pushing him. She sleeps with him, I bet."

Sam smiled. "I'd like to see something else, please."

Her hands went to her hips. He noticed that a V of material had been added to widen her skirt above her coccyx. Standing behind her he could smell sweat and smoke in her hair. She stepped back from the canvas and covered one eye.

"That's a LeRoy, all right."

"Why do you cover your eye like that?" Sam said, intrigued.

"Oh," she blushed, "I'm nearsighted as a bat and I've lost one of my contact lenses."

"Hadn't you better get another one?"

"Oh, I can't."

"Don't you have insurance?"

"No, my husband just doesn't believe in it. It doesn't really matter. It just makes me wince a lot, that's all."

She covered her other eye and admired his face. Sam saw himself cameoed in her remaining lens. He couldn't tell whether she was urging him on or trying to beat him down. Slowly he narrowed his own weak eye.

"Aaron says they're only cosmetic anyway."

"Your husband work here too?"

"Oh, no, he's the artist in the family. Actually, he doesn't like that word—just a photographer. He says it's necessary to bridge the gap between his self and the found object. That's what he says, anyway." She winked at him several times, then held up

32

her hands for him, dipped them toward her chest and flapped them helplessly in the air. "Can't even type, myself," she snickered.

Sam then realized that she had to be a Gulley girl, and this put him on his guard, for he knew a Gulley girl who has not been able to fully exercise her Gullyness would take her toll for the rest of her life. At Purk there was some manly irony in not living up to the Institution, but at Gulley there were fewer ornamental diversions from its ideal of excellence. She blurred as Sam tried to take her in. As a child she must have been all eyes, as a crone she would end all chin—yet in her present prime she seemed somehow blunted, diffused, like those blocked-out unfinished torsos whose interest derives not from what's been chiseled but from the veil of marble they still carry—a calculated enigma, then, her face straining through its enviable softness toward character.

Sam knew all about these blondes darkening: face done with arm-length scoops, eyebrows which would grow together if not plucked, veins like a bead of water upon an amber tumbler, aristocratic ears with mismatched pearls. When she reads she bites her nails and tucks her feet beneath her buttocks. She walks slashingly, legs so tough her arms seem perfectly dispensable. When she sits, her calves evaporate and reappear in her upper thighs. She does not know the difference between education and experience, her mouth is farthest open when she is silent, she doesn't know which is her best feature, and when she lies down there is nothing like a pie.

"You're a Gulley girl, aren't you?" he stammered.

"God, gee, even two kids can't take that off you, I guess."

"You've got two kids?"

"Sure thing. You like kids?"

"Other people's," Sam said softly.

She wound her arms around herself. "You know, you really remind me of somebody." Then she returned her hands to her

33

hips. She looked at him as though she were waiting for him to turn into something recognizable.

"Why don't you try my glasses?" Sam offered.

After smoothing back her hair, she tried them on.

"Ho, wow!" she exclaimed.

"Better?"

"Hardly," she said after glancing sideways into a mirror. "They make everything so sharp I want to cry."

"Well, you should really get a pair," Sam said as she handed the frames back to him. "I mean you could fall down or something."

"I tried them in college and you know what? I found out that people don't look at you as much if you wear them. And you know another funny thing? If you don't wear them, you can't see them looking even if they do. So I decided I'd rather have them looking more, even though it meant *seeing* them looking less . . . oh lord, you must think I'm nuts."

"I've just come to trade this in."

"OK, OK, don't get pushy. Come on, take a look back here." She walked to the back of the storeroom smoothing her skirt, the V switching across her coccyx.

"You don't want any of those phonies in the front," she said over her shoulder.

Sam followed her back among the stacked abstracts.

"Just because they're up front doesn't mean they're phony," he said querulously.

"Does here," she sang back.

"Well," he mumbled, "I suppose it's just a matter of priorities." She looked at him very strangely then, closing her mouth.

"I would guess," he went on, "that your husband's work is here somewhere?"

"In here," she said curtly, "in the back."

The back room of the gallery did not have as many paintings as he expected. Posters of exhibitions, busted frames, studies of cossacks, flamingos, bridges and gorges. He felt the compulsion then to tell her his name and did so, but she had no visible reaction. Maybe they don't have a television, he thought.

The Gulley girl knelt before a beaten rattan rack and began to withdraw what was apparently her husband's *oeuvre*.

"The manager doesn't like me to bring customers back here," she said, "but I show the stuff to practically everybody anyway."

She became quite agitated as she had difficulty with the knots. Sam imagined her tieing up her husband's work with all her might. He did not offer to help.

"Somebody in *Photoculture* called him a 'Vemeer with a Leica,' " she rambled, sucking on her reddened fingers.

Finally she spread the matted prints on the table, careful to handle them by the edges. Sam squinted, glared, achieved 20/20, and moved in over the girl's shoulder.

The art of Aaron Grassgreen divided itself into two categories, respectively suited, unlikely enough, for each of Sam's eyes. He was secretly flattered to find that an artist might have the same perceptual problems as a frontman.

The first series of photos (his earlier work, which she told him she preferred) remained faithful to the touchstone of the modern—colloquial dialogue bellowed across impastoral space; in this case, improbably pert yet submerged breasts, grainy uplifted flesh waffling in vast dark waters. Most modern art, Sam knew from Humanities I, was simply the imposition of 19th-century romantic excess against a formal backdrop of the 18th century, with the resultant double juxtaposition of irony as its own subject. A paradox, this breast and its bath, picnic in a tornado. Yet, on another day, were they simply nudes gallivanting on the desert, stooping in the swamps, peeking through a web of milkweed, spreadeagled in ivy, offering fruit or a balalaika, hugging their reactionary pudenda to mossy oaks? Simulacrous microcosm of coitus reservatus!

In the last of the series, done in the Japanese manner, a young girl seated with her back just before the camera leaned into the distant shadow so that her lovely flowing buttocks became one with a small pendant breast, making a parabola, a crystalline lie that provided ample truth of her flesh. Sam jammed his hands in his pockets, starting at the touch of green-and-yellow wiring.

"That's me," the Gulley girl said indifferently. "You wouldn't recognize me, would you?"

Sam replied that that perhaps was the point.

She bit her lips and flipped more photos, but something else had disturbed Sam in the meantime, for a faint odor of his past had reached him. He sat there, bathed in it, and then it suddenly occurred to him that this was Lurleen Wilkerson's smell, or rather the way his hands smelled when he was through with Lurleen Wilkerson; it had seemed to cling to his hands and even after basketball he couldn't really get it off. As the girl was still preoccupied with her portrait, he leaned closer to sniff out this curious and sudden synthesis in his life. She did not seem to mind, indeed, she was completely oblivious of him, and at length he found that the odor emanated from her skull. When she bent over even farther to remove a piece of lint from the photo, he leaned with her, nosing down his youth and thoroughly confused sense of priorities, and then he realized that what he now smelled and had smelled of was—hair spray.

The alluring belief that this young mother of two children's skull smelled of Lurleen Wilkerson's snatch collapsed; indeed it was Lurleen Wilkerson's snatch which had smelled of this fair Gulley girl's head, and Hoops realized that the greatness of his adolescence—the substance of both his eroticism and his guilt—had been fired and circumscribed by a product he could have democratically purchased for himself.

The remainder of the portfolio consisted of several dramatic fire scenes, a dachshund with a kitten, a Puerto Rican kid with ice cream all over his face. She gathered up the photos and put them back carefully into the folder.

"I'd really like to see the rest," Sam said earnestly.

"The rest are experiments. Aaron never shows anything until he's completely indifferent to it." She winked at him reflexively. She had a debutante's voice, lips barely parted in a tone which a foreigner might mistake for an "upper-class" accent, but in fact was a nasal broad-A refutation of its own elitism, a redundant aloofness, coming around the block behind you as if to say, "See, I can put you down with my cultivation, but since I detest such even more than your vulgarity, I'll cancel even that advantage."

Sam did not say a word, but looked at her for a very long time with the same expression he used on his clients. And after covering her eye briefly, she did open the second portfolio and started to spread photos before him, adding quietly, "He says he's condensing his vision here."

The prints were larger, poster size, and numbered consecutively. Sam was not aware of what they might represent, but he knew they were not intended to be viewed this way.

"In case you don't know," she murmured, "they're walls."

"Indeed?" said Sam. He felt foolish twisting the wiring in his hands and put it back in his pocket.

"And all of them are within a block of our apartment," she added apologetically. "Aaron does not believe in the romantic myth of traveling to the found object," she recited, "the essence of which invests our everyday habitat."

She looked quite sad, more diffuse than ever, and then Sam realized she was leaning forward in the same lotus position she had assumed for her husband's flickering but seminal eye.

"Well, they're extremely interesting," said Sam hopefully, "not at all clichéed. In fact, if I had the money, and it wouldn't be an insult to your husband, I'd offer to buy them all."

She rose upright. "Interesting, you said. You mean, not like me."

"Just to be able to learn to understand them, you see,"

Sam went on, ignoring her, "I mean they really have to be lived with, don't they?"

She had risen to her knees.

"Are they for sale?"

"I don't see why not—" she blushed—"but I'd have to ask Aaron." Then she stood up gracelessly. "We've only sold a few before. And none of the walls."

"Look, why don't you rent me one in place of the *Abyss*? You can give the gallery their cut and pocket the rest. Then I'll bring it back in a few months. That'll be best for everyone. You'll get some fast dough out of it, the manager will get his profit, he'll still be able to sell the *Abyss*, and I'll have the privilege of learning something. Then I'll bring it back, and Aaron won't be the wiser. Then we can start all over again."

She had no visible reaction to this but simply said, "You got it all worked out, don't you? OK then, which one do you want?"

"You pick it," Sam said.

"That's ridiculous."

"Did he take them to be bought in any particular order?"

"Oh, all right," she sighed, "I'll *rent* you number one."

She wrapped it clumsily but cocked her head nicely when she said goodbye.

Sam took the picture of the wall back and hung it on his wall.

4 · Complections

His Monday bed was too big, his trough too warm, his body still too hard for him not to be resentful. The bed was the first thing he'd bought when he moved to the city after accepting MC's contract. The salesman who sold it to him said that it would never sag; that he would never have to "clamber out of the cleavage." Sam lay face down spreadeagled with a hand or foot in each corner of the custom bed. There was blood on the sheet but it was from his gums. Things were starting to break up a little.

He could hear the Dott doing her work in the living room, but to a strange and regular rhythm quite unlike her. He put a towel around him and walked out to find her doing situps on his slant board before the picture window. She rocked monotonously, very nearly touching her toes. Her starched white dress had slipped up her thighs, her bun clunked on the floor as she lay back. She did not grunt nor count on the upsit. It was an exercise which smacked of proscription.

Sam felt good that the Dott was sensitive enough—and indeed comfortable enough in his presence—to enjoy and contemplate nature. The lake was magnificent with September swells, divided into a tricolor of sand, weed, and deeps—a gray herringbone near the shore, a loden green farther out, and a royal purple velour on the horizon.

But as Sam approached he saw that the Dott was not watching the lake at all—but rather the bob and weave of her own filmy reflection in the window. He came up behind her reproachfully, and as she became aware of his reflection cancelling out hers, she flung herself through one final flourishing situp. Sam knew from Humanities I that man began to pay lip service to nature only when he began to see himself in it, view his heart in the world like a crow in a skeletal tree, and so he chose not to reprimand the Dott.

"How many can you do, Dott?"

"Fouah hunnert."

"You're putting me on."

"Fouah hunnert as sho as you standin here."

"Well, that's marvelous, Dott, how's about some breakfast?"

"Yeah, but I gotta leave early. Stargyle got an eye like a big cabbidge." Sam retreated to the bathroom, which was unaccountably quiet.

"Arn you gonna be late for work?" the Dott yelled from the kitchen.

"Working at home this morning, Dott, part of a new morale policy. Decentralization. 'Stay home. Keep out of trouble. Think.' That's what they said."

The Dott brought Sam the eggs Benedict as he had taught her, the sauce just thick enough to cling to the blade of his mother's knife.

"You know, Mr. Sam, I give this stuff to my Stargyle and he spit it right out. He say it louses up you eggs!"

"Did you let the eggs and butter sit for a couple of hours? Come on now, Dott!" Sam bellowed.

"Wal no sur, to tell da truf . . ." She put a palm effetely to a cheek and rolled her eyes.

It's only fair to say they loved such routines, the more precious the better, and at times the food would be lost in the manners, which of course constitutes a short history of Western religion, too much to the point to be recounted here.

The Dott slumped back into the kitchenette. "Stargyle got an eye swole like a big lettice. I gotta leave early."

"Dott, you're a wonder. *Mes compliments au chef!*"

"*You* the wondah, Muthuh. And you knows what you can do with you sauce. . . ."

"Please wait to vacuum until after I leave?"

"Y*essuh.*"

"And kindly make your phone calls from the bedroom."

The kitchen door slammed. "And next time, slice the god-damn truffle *across* the grain!"

Sam looked through the financial section while he ate. At the bottom of the exchange there was a small ad:

Sam sent Captain Fuess a postcard, put a transistor in his ear to drown out the Dott, but his concentration continued to disintegrate. And at once it occurred to him that beneath Odile's co-ed fixation and programatic bitchiness there lay an almost perfect approximation of MC's "model woman," a strain they had been attempting to perfect since that first burst of liberation in the art of loving in the 1920s. He glanced back through an old annual report on genetic projects.

Visualization of New Woman Standard

EYES: Moderately well apart; size, medium, round, bright; expression, intelligent. Color depends on other markings. Lack of pigmentation major fault.

HEAD: Proportionately broad between the ears, well defined at temples; one straight line from nose to occiput. Entirely free from wrinkle. Flat skull major fault.

41

EARS: Rather high-set; size, moderate, tapering to rounded point. Carried close to head.

NECK: Fairly long, nicely arched; throatiness major fault.

SHOULDERS: Oblique, clean, not too muscular.

CHEST: Deep, capacious; undisguised sternum major fault.

STOMACH: Resilient but distinctive. Spots major fault.

HINDQUARTERS: Clean, well-defined, symmetrical; cowhocks major fault.

TAIL: Strong at insertion, tapering to broad firm base; free from coarseness, carried with slight upward curve.

LEGS: Tough, elastic, turning neither in nor out; gait and length of stride, in proportion to size of body. Grasp should exceed reach. Endurance more important than speed.

APPEARANCE: Active, poised, alert, obedient, loyal. Shyness or aggressiveness automatic disqualification.

It appeared that Odile still had time to make it.

Sam had to force himself back to work now. The word had come through Wittgenstein; he had called Sam at midnight from some bar and told him to get started on the Christmas Memo—anything would do—just so he wouldn't have to go into the pit empty-handed.

The oboe in Sam's ear shifted from an adagio to a plaintive *bourrée*. His calves flexed and his knees pumped ominously. When his body was weaker his mind was clearer. He chewed vigorously on a pencil, whistling a counterpoint through his teeth.

Re: What Is to Be Done?
(*Notes Toward the Christmas Memo*)

Alternative defenses have different consequences, and indeed, each protective action taken, or even contemplated, seems to have equally adverse repercussions.

Sam looked down in amazement at his churning legs. Blood from his head and feet was en route to his groin. His fly was bursting.

. . . gliding past the outstretched hands he went off the opposite foot turned in the air and swished a dazzling hook over his astonished opponent . . . bracing his feet against the cool rail of the brass bedstead he buckled a squeal out of her astoundingly . . .

Repressive devaluation generated by a power grab of some regulatory agency, or artificial inflation induced by agitated cartels sheathed in hostile structures, run equally counter to our goals of full prosperity.

. . . fouled surreptitiously, they even resorted to pulling his thigh-hair, he nevertheless got the shot off this time without the slightest arc and not even touching the rim . . . each time she rebounded she lunged to kiss him on the chest, she was that short. . . .

Stimulating in advance a quantum jump of interest in the hope of altering the negative flow of needed capital is an invitation to an eventually unacceptable level of employment; on the other hand, arbitrary restrictions on such desubliminated movements are unbecoming to a world power.

. . . And take it slow and rhythmically as sheer speed and strength count for little over the long run and in clutch situations, consistency, playing well within yourself, as well as constant pressure, are the name of the game . . .

No wonder the unpopularity of aggressive alternatives, particularly since these are types of action in which no warning or cooperation are possible, and the consumer is known to discount such moves in advance.

*. . . there never was a pro who alternated styles that one can recall. But
you shoot from the floor in various ways, so why not from the free throw
line as well? . . .*

Painless at the time, perhaps, though implications for the long run
could be serious.

*. . . but anybody can be slow and rhythmic: if you've got the speed
and strength why not use it?*

Against the background of fixed relationships, the advantages of diversi-
fication, even when counter to the norms, should be obvious. Venture-
some investors may even be tempted to examine some of the more bizarre
alternatives. After all, the spread between the bid and ask is probably at
least as great as any devaluation threat.

*You'd be surprised how cool preserves the margin of victory in most
cases. . . . Now that's what I'd call eccentric!*

Nevertheless, no matter how small, reservoirs of value remain dependent
upon a prosperous clientele with sufficient excess in its members to provide
a thrust to the market.

*. . . Lad, if you do it overhand in practice then you'll tense up when
you do it underhand in a game or vice versa. You'll never be a pro if you
alternate styles. . . .*

To conclude, we inevitably seem to encounter an imponderable which
is a restraining influence on any extreme position in any direction, despite
whatever risks we are willing to take.

*. . . Twisting in, faking them out, floating, feinting, he spun in a
reverse layup. . . . Could you learn to love me?*

And as for the future, we will, of course, be influenced primarily by the
prospective developments in technology.

That should hold them, Sam thought.

You have just been through the Q.U.I.F. Like it or not, this is
how Sam's mind works. Earnest analysis extruded twixt sport 'n'

sex. Exhausting, but it's what the people want. And it's how he makes his living, after all. Think back. Minds in books are usually organs. They shimmer palpably, digest efficaciously, refer to their own workings as if they were your aunt's best spring-wound mantel clock. "Ideas" penetrate them or are spewed off, and our poor minds become circumcised by enactments of the body, as they reflect, repel, flood, creep, repress, wander, close, explode, boggle, embrace, race, spill or suck—in short, cohabit with interest and perception, as if cognition were something you aroused with a flick of your finger under your coat. Now Sam does have an organ like that, but it has its own place, its own mind, while his Head is a thoroughly modern instrument—a committee, in fact—revolving democratically, diffuse and wasteful if you're not privy to it, compartmentalized and severe if you're forced to serve, more sensitive to problems than itself, yet elusive when challenged from outside, cautious when confused, slow to take the upper hand, many-voiced though speaking as one, and lacking, by its very constitution, genius and guile, but in the end, more often than not, perdurable, fair, and on the mark.

Apart from this talent, Sam's problems were commonplace and of our time. All of his life, all the considerable love of his family and teachers had been concentrated so that he might be free to see the world as it really was—to see from a vantage point so serene and charitable, with no distortion of mind or temperament to alter his view, that seeing itself would replace the necessity of knowledge. Even will. But with his rare counter-astigmatism, even with glasses, he could rarely focus on anything: this gave his generosity, which was considerable, a rather abstract quality. On the other hand, it made his self-discipline, which would be considered puritanical in others, strangely endearing.

Sam called the Dott out of the kitchenette.

"Lookit, let's cut the shit for a minute. We've gotta talk something out."

"Oh no, man, every time you do this, ever time you serious up, we get hung down. No thanks."

"Just for a minute."

"You in love again?"

The Dott settled back on the divan, brandishing the feather duster like a bouquet. She bore soapsud bracelets about her biceps.

"Well, as you've guessed, yes, I'm into a little something."

"Oh, man, we both know what happened *last* time. . . ."

"Dammit, let me finish. This is different. . . ."

"You gonna git married, huh?"

"God, will you just listen for once? I have the feeling that this could . . . is going to . . . well . . . get really involved, you know."

The Dott nodded to the duster like a jester's scepter.

"What you got in mind? That bed may be big, but it ain't the worl."

Sam drew himself up stiffly.

"I had my doubts that you'd understand, Dott. But this isn't going to be any one-night stand, though I don't want you acting any differently than if it was. I'm just warning you that I may need some assistance."

"I knows I ain't supposed to *act* any different. What I needs to know is are you courtin' or what? Jes' what the rules of this game is, Mister? We'll play, we'll be cool." The Dott lit up a cigar. "But that don't mean we can't talk about it."

"Look, sweetheart, I don't ask you who you shack with or who you call on my phone all day. I never asked you once about even where you came from, so do the same for me, OK?"

"Maybe you oughter ask where I'm from. I knew a man like you oncet, 'cept he always had a big dog right aside him. I saw

46

that dog take a whole horse down once, grabbed him right by the elbow and pulled him off a porch. Course that horse, he shouldna been on the porch."

"See, you can't play it straight! Even once. That's what I've been talking about. You're not in the goddamn movies. I don't care if you're familiar, but just don't cramp my style, OK?"

"It's 'both ways time'?"

Sam blushed slightly and began to swivel nervously in the stereo-lounger.

"I get the picture. It's a *days* thing now, right? Days, days, eight-to-five stuff, which means she's a married woman, right? Well, that's your problem, right?"

"I'll tell you what it is, frankly, Dott, it's that this thing scares me. The first time in a long time. I mean I'm really, I was really *moved*."

"Moved? No shit. Face it, you sure can move. But you ain't mov*a*ble."

"One war at a time—you're not going to pull that rap on me, not this week."

"What you're telling me is to lay, uh, low, until you, uh . . ."

"Just be yourself, Dott. Help me out a little. If we have it both ways, it cuts both ways too."

The Dott refused to meet his eye. Sam softened.

"Look, I just want to prove a point. Can't you understand that?" But she had already shrugged and returned to the kitchen.

"OK, man," she sang. "Prove it!"

Sam was done for the day. The sun had reached its zenith and flooded the apartment with a boggling brightness. He walked around the new photo trying to interpose his shadow in such a way that the picture would become visible again. In one corner of the frame he noticed the effete scrawl, *Property of Aaron Grassgreen, Number 1*, and below in heavily looped green script, *Odile Grassgreen, TA 9-4253*.

47

He called her up when the Dott was done and she answered with a stutter.

"Sam Hooper. Your first patron, I believe." He did not like the sound of his voice.

"Credit," she laughed. Sam gave her some silence. He could hear her smoker's breath.

"I know who you are," she said finally. "I just didn't know what to say."

"Well, I thought if you weren't busy we might arrange to see some of your husband's other work some time."

"You're not just being nice?"

"Well, what's wrong with that anyway?" There was a pause. She would be winking, he thought.

"All right, Mr. Hooper. Why don't you come over for a drink this evening? Aaron should be home then. I've told him about our arrangement."

There was a childlike shriek in the background and she hung up.

Hoops signed the memo, circulated it through the extra-office dictaphone, changed rapidly into his sweat clothes.

The Dott finished a brief, curt call and began to look for a new place to hang the Grassgreen. She chose an empty shaded spot in the foyer. Her thumb spread out over the thumbtack, the nail whitening and then glowing red under pressure, but the point collapsed and the ruptured disk slid to the floor.

Sam slaps her on the behind as she bends over, but before she can smash him he's out the door. She goes to the window and watches him lope across the esplanade, dribbling the ball between his legs and behind his back, and then he is gone into the pedestrian tunnel to the park.

"Oh, Muthuh, you the wondah," she whispers.

48

5 · Stewfeet

Thou art a toilsome Mole, or else
a moving mist;
But life is, what none can express,
A quickness, *which my God hath Kist.*

Sam sang in the shower, and later in the gimping elevator. He was back on track again.

Their address was on the edge of Olde Towne, a brownstone two flat the developers had not yet reached, bearing a seal indicating participation in the League of Better Neighborhoods. The side garden was not big enough for sweet potatoes or corn or for rhododendrons, phlox, dahlias or even tulips, but it did sport pidgin lettuce, radishes, traces of a tomato vine and one dented acorn squash. The streets angled sharply across one another splintering what had been four corners into nine isosceles triangles. The largest of these triangles, surrounded by a rusted cyclone fence, had not been cleared. Its waist-high rushes pulsed softly in the breeze, spidery orange poppy-types glowed in the dusk. A single linden tree marked its center, bark gulled with soot. Beyond, a new apartment complex bore down upon them like a vast ocean liner about to beach itself on some uncharted one-tree islet.

The house presented four octagonal bays to catch the light. A knee-high picket fence enclosed a minuscule front yard of crushed gravel. The original ornate stairway had been sealed off with fiberboard to make a foyer. The door was newly painted but bubbled with the lost bristles of a cheap brush. Sam rang the

49

bell and a dulled response somehow undid the foyer door. The stairs were littered with toys, kindling, galoshes, permeated with the smell of wet clothes and animals, particularly that of a large nondescript dog who during dinner and certain lunar cycles apparently had to fend for itself in the stairwell, the blood running to that part of his body which took the lower step. Odile was waiting for him at the top of the stairs. Her sandy hair was gathered in back and two wispy sideburns were dark with sweat. A big-lipped child at her hip. "Hello, Brighteye."

She held the child tight to her so he could not fool with her breasts or anything as she held the door. She wore a violet smock. Simplicity did not fit her, nor did the hair, which was plaited with khaki rubber bands.

"Place is a mess," she grinned from her half-crouch. "Aaron's in the darkroom."

The child cowered between her legs. It was not an ugly child, Sam insisted to himself, rather simply featureless as nothing seemed either round or straight in its face; timeless in the pejorative sense. Sam always had visions of genes when he saw children—he saw the moment of conception not in mythic or physical but rather microscopic terms—in this case, Odile's genes appeared as a luminous necklace of Life Savers, undulating like a proud snake, commemorated here and there by Aaron's gray raindrops, transluscent with the black head-seed of some new scene in their shape. They did not cavort or race about each other, as they would, for example, under a microscope. It must have been more, he thought, like a slow and premeditated snowball fight, the genes backing up on and bumping one another, casually probing comparative resiliency, until imperceptibly they absorbed one another randomly, without the slightest shudder, the good gray seed chromosomatically gathering what protective plumage it could.

"Have a look around?" Odile said, giving the child a short

50

elbow. "There's stuff all over the walls, duh duh. I've got to get dinner on."

She walked heavily back into the surprising darkness of the apartment. Sam slipped off his Strat-O-Moc Grippers so as not to track up the place.

Aaron and Odile's place was very long, nearly light, with ceilings twelve feet high, but had been proportioned originally for a class who could not admit to any private functions. The useless shadowy entrance hall took up most of the center of the apartment, filled hysterically with bric-a-brac. The living room was L-shaped, the fireplace filled in with cinder block though still surrounded by a polished pine frieze of Moroccan intent. The octagonal bay was clotted with geraniums, shuttered with gray steel venetians blinds which bayed in the breeze. Off the living room veered an open alcove containing a wall-to-wall foam mattress. Above loomed an enormous abstraction done in ochre and beige, exactly the size of the mattress. There was nothing else in there, Sam saw, not a light, reading material, Kleenex, anything.

He was a little embarrassed to see that they had no compunction about leaving their TV out where anyone could see it, but this was apparently due more to Odile's slovenliness than Aaron's honesty. Sam could feel the crumbs of masticated dessert through his socks. Graham crackers and cereals were ground at intervals into the rug, the walls and woodwork smeared with tiny hands to a height of three and a half feet. Insanely responsive toys—walking, peeing, crying dolls, a driver's kit with a steering wheel mounted upon a scroll windshield which liberally revolved a topographical landscape before the driver at a touch of the accelerator, a rubber dinosaur who butted back if you should happen to punch him in the nose. The geraniums were dry and brittle, the windows opaque from mucous dots of yet unformed lips and noses too large for their faces. The blinds yipped through another gust.

Sam did not care to look at any photographs until Aaron was there to complement them, and contented himself with the library. You could not tell anything about people from what they read, Sam knew, but you could tell a great deal from what they bought to read, just as you can anticipate a man's speech from what he puts in his mouth. First, he recognized the powder-blue bindings of The Contemporaneity Book Club with Odile's maiden name scrawled in green ink on the title pages. A copy of the *Genealogy of Morals* was closely annotated in the same green ink with various stars, dashes, exclamation points, question marks, and on the fortieth page of the Gulley second-text edition, beside the phrase, "But is our ascetic priest really a physician?" there was scrawled, "Right—so Right. Ask Aaron."

Interspersed among a first edition of uncracked leathery Balzac was the *I Hate to Cook Book, Famous Dogs, Hieronymus Bosch Today*, nine dry-cleaning bills, a two-volume illustrated edition of Leibniz's *Monadology*, in the second volume of which Sam came across Odile's fertility chart, her Gulley degree *cum laude*, a photo of her parents' Colonial home, an invitation to the wedding, and a lifetime membership in UNICEF made out to Odile Odets Grassgreen.

In the Victorian Gentlemen's Library edition of *Deaths of Little Children* Sam found a signed photograph of Hank Greenberg and a lock of hair, which upon closer inspection was either Odile's or Lurleen Wilkerson's, and a letter of Odile's to her father. It predated her Gulley days and Sam realized she was several years older than he.

DEAREST DAD:

Hi!

I've been studying every minute tonight . . . but I can't seem to settle down. I'm also in a very crabby mood, so I'm relaxing and listening to Beethoven Symphony No. 6 in F Major. It's beautiful and I feel so much better now. It's just the epitome of neat music! I'm doing OK in my finals, I think!!! I decided to take an Art Appreciation course next quarter. Between Beethoven, Picasso and everybody maybe I'll turn beat!!! I heard from Jeanie that all the girls at Gulley are like that now. God, I hope they'll take me! I went to the orthodontist this morning and he took off all the top front ones except the second one in the back. To them he attached a kind of rubber band that pulls the teeth together so there won't be a lot of space. It looks icky and noticeable, but I get it off next Friday. I can't wait!

Last night the sophs gave the seniors a going away party. We all played guitars. I used Sue's sister's guitar. It cost $90 or so. Just beautiful. It was an instant success really. Everybody sang along.

I love my teeth! Just thought I'd tell you.

Can't you give me a hint about that surprise you were talking about? Tomorrow is a surprise birthday party for Linda Bennett, a swimming party. We pooled our money and got her an electric blanket. Tuff enuff . . .

I haven't heard from Mike Lupton ever. He broke up with his other girlfriend about a week ago. Thus ends my love life! This guy at Purk though, Jim Orthur, a junior, invited me to the Purk Ball, but I didn't go because he's real queer. It turned out that if I had gone, though, I would have sat next to David Ladd. Pant, pant.

Guess what? I'm beet red. The sophs had their beach trip yesterday, so hot and clear, but the water was numbing. It was so tuff. Just laying there. Once this huge wave came. It had turned me over and over and I was under it and it was pretty scary, but it was really a blast. Our spring sing is Friday. We're not really prepared, but we've got cute songs.

Saturday all the brains in the soph and junior classes and Mr. Gerinza went to a model United Nations thing. I was the delegate from the Netherlands. It was so interesting that it made you realize the problems of other countries. Our discussion was on racial policies in South Africa. "Should the UN step in." It was so realistic! These other kids came up to me and told me to Veto or else their countries would make it nasty for mine! This one from Togo said if I vote yes her country will give me financial aid. I don't know, but I felt as if the future of the Netherlands was in my hands. In the general assembly, everybody got together and debated issues. The other committees couldn't decide. It was really fabulous.

Gosh, that surprise is going to kill me, can't you give me a hint . . . ?

I'm home now, and Mom says to tell you the business news so here goes. Ed Shaw has left Y & R for a job in New York, Mike Kehoe quit; he simply got fed up, and has nothing on the fire. They just bought a new house too, so he must have been pretty disgusted. John Burnston is riding with another agency, I can't think of the name, and I can't understand Mother now. Oh, and Bob Corley was fired. Well, Mother's giving me the look so I better go to bed. I'm dead anyway. Hurry home. See you soon.

Love ya, O.

P. S. Do *you* think the U. N. should do something about South Africa?

Sam was getting nervous. He walked back through the parlor and down the dark hall to the kitchen. It was of the same dimensions as the living room except it had no windows and a large oscillating fan in the ceiling.

Odile was making a stew. Before her on a Quaker long table was a black cast-iron pot surrounded by fresh vegetables and diced meat just as in some nostalgic soup advertisement. There were new red potatoes, the orangest of carrots, great tufted sprigs of parsley, Spanish onions, celery, parsnips, tomatoes and a flank of marbled stew beef. Even a real chickenfoot. Odile whacked the meat into irregular chunks with a cleaver and then threw them, each piece, overhand down into the pot, although she was standing almost directly over it.

There was another child in the kitchen, a girl, larger than the boy and considerably more attractive. She sat cross-legged in a corner, an ivory balloon in her lap, eyeing her mother critically.

"What do you think?" Odile asked.

"About what?" Sam said.

"Why, about my interior decor, you sap."

The child smiled. Sam couldn't tell at whom.

"Well, I really didn't want to look too closely. I wanted to wait for Aaron."

"Can't venture an opinion without professional help?"

54

"I don't mind help," said Sam very methodically and folded his arms.

"Only people who don't need it can afford it," Odile rasped, and eyed a red potato.

A Gulley girl coming up with an aphorism on the spot struck him silent. He had an inkling what her trouble was. He and Odile shuffled around the table like cowboys cheating at cards. She looked at him wonderingly, like dearest Dad himself.

"Aaron ought to be out in a moment," she stammered, and then went back to throwing the stew.

After several minutes of embarrassing silence, Odile dragged a pipe chair to the door of the darkroom and motioned Sam to sit and wait. Sam did. He could hear the sloshing of various chemicals and the clink of vials and beakers through the door, as well as a monotonous humming. The doorknob was spinning.

The chair was so hard and he was so low in it that Sam was unable to spring up adequately to welcome the artist back from the interior. But Aaron Grassgreen proved to be as small, sallow and ungiving as Sam had hoped. Hairy except for the top of his head, he seemed only faintly amused by his own slovenliness. He looked very much like his son would have to. To his daughter he had given only his hair and eyes.

Sam finally twisted himself from the chair and shook hands. Later it took shaving lotion to get the stench of developer off his palm.

"I hope I'm not disturbing your dinner," Sam said.

"Not to worry," Aaron Grassgreen replied, opening a huge portfolio of photos on the dining-room table in the entrance hall.

"Odile says you wanted the walls," he said. "But that's only the beginning, fellah. How about some nice coffee beans?"

The coffee beans were impressive. Closeups through a 30 percent brown screen revealed armies on the move, fecund or desolate landscapes, fjords, rivulets, surreal jewelry.

"I got the idea from a Nuts 'n' Beans place mat," he said. "Nuts 'n' beans, beans 'n' nuts, the whole works, and yeah, here's my sea 'n' weed sequence."

This particular series was more abstract though in similar perspective: nature's patterns on the beach, spirals, arabesques, hieroglyphs, whorls which gave Sam vertigo.

"God, I've never seen it like that," Sam said.

"You don't think the ocean did it, do ya? I spent a week dropping that shit into nice-looking things. We dried it out with a sun lamp and Odile put furniture over them to keep 'em in place. She thought of the title, 'Kelp Kuts,' you know, like real mother-nature jazz. You oughta see my rocks, though."

Sam could hear Odile still flinging stew behind them. He wondered how long it would take for her to ruin Aaron.

The rocks were from formations somewhere in the West, and Aaron had typically made the air between the substance more significant than the substance itself.

"Talus-time," he muttered. "Ody thought that one up too. I'm not artsy-craftsy like that, see? Most guys take nudes against rocks, moths, big-pecker trees and like that; me, I take rocks and trees and moths and stuff *against* the nudes."

The series was particularly erotic. Naked women flung on the sand with a rock on their belly, supine in deep grass, bedded in shale, caught beneath a rotting log.

"Those aren't Odile," Sam smiled.

Aaron jostled him merrily, as might be expected from a man of insight, and Sam felt easier.

"Well, the feet are what got me first, and I'll stick with them," he said.

The feet *were* magnificent: horny, splayed, debased, censorious, grisly, preening by turns. They used their own shadows, sought their own space. They were whole things, but in each nail, vein, bunion, crinkle, were mountain, steppe, glacier, endless as the whorl of the seashell itself.

The photographer looked at him steadily.

"How much do you think they are?" Sam asked.

"Natch, I've got a Greengrass price. Haggling's not for me. But now I don't want to sound like I'm making you a deal, but since you dug 'em at the gallery, and Odile digs you, and maybe I even like you, how 'bout twenty dollars apiece? I'll mount 'em and sign 'em too."

"Fine," Sam said. "Fine, fine."

He chose two: a single silhouette of a clean foot, the toes spread in delight, Odile at her best, and a more stylized anonymous study of anxiety, two soiled feet resting against one another like druidical monoliths; only one of them Odile's—could Aaron have tripped a timed shutter on his own lumpish toes?

"And have you met the kids?" Aaron looked up from scraping glue with an inch of thumbnail. He called them in his high-pitched voice and they came into sight slowly from opposite ends of the long apartment to stand facing each other in the door of the foyer. Odile craned her neck from the kitchen door for a moment, looking beyond the children to Sam, and then went back to the stew, from which thick vapors had already appeared.

"Matthew and Stieglitz, this is Mr. Sam Hooper. Ah, Mr. Hooper, Matthew and Stieglitz."

"Hello, Matty," Sam said brightly. "From the Hebrew, I bet, 'Mattithyāh,' customs collector and storyteller."

"Nope." Aaron shook his head. "Matthew. From Mathew Brady."

Stieglitz curtsied quite beautifully. Sam wanted to pick her up but held back. The little boy was motionless, his eyes round as his hopeless mouth as he stared through Sam. Sam detested himself for discounting him.

57

"Hooper," the ugly kid screamed, "like *Sam-Bam* Hooper," and then he fled back into the kitchen.

"Who's that?" Aaron swung about defiantly.

"I don't know," Sam said, trying to simplify things. (Sam was amazed that the child was allowed to watch as adult a show as that of Sam Hooper[2], known affectionately to his announcer as "Sam-Bam.")

"Kid is funny," Aaron mumbled. "Kid is funny. Ugly-funny sometimes."

Odile had come out of the kitchen. The armpits of her smock were stained with sweat; one braid had come loose and stuck out from her head like an antenna. She flapped her apron, her dress billowing above her knees, the musculature of which caused the blood to leave Sam's head and feet.

"Soup's on. Would you like to stay for dinner, Mr. Hooper?" she asked ingenuously.

Aaron swung around with a scowl, but Sam had already declined with an affable wave.

"I want to get these home and on the wall," Sam said, picking up the pictures.

Aaron showed him to the door and gave him a tight little hand.

At the bottom of the stairs, Sam felt a draft on his feet and found he had forgotten his shoes. But Stieglitz and Matthew had bounded after him, each holding a beige Strat-O-Moc to their chests, and in the foyer the children went to their knees and professionally slippered him as he patted their heads.

Back in the car, he felt discomfort on the clutch, and, looking down, saw that his shoes angled grotesquely away from the natural curve of his feet. He switched them, then sniffed his fingers curiously.

6 · Keys to Mysteries

"Who the devil *is* that?" Sam inquired of the Dott as he brushed his teeth.

"Whaa?"

Sam spat. "I said, who *is* that out there? A friend of yours?"

"Why, that's Stargyle himself, Mr. Sam. I tole you 'bout him. His eye's better now too."

"Well, what's he *doing* here?" Sam whispered hoarsely.

"Hey, come on man, that's no way to do!" the Dott yelled at him.

Mother was petulant this morning. The Dott put down the toilet top and seated herself, muffling the heating duct with her broad back, reducing her song to a squabble.

"He's my driver," the Dott said. "And I don want you going in there and hurting his feelings neither. It's the only job he gets, and it keeps him off the street, right? An' if I were you, I wouldn' make him mad."

Sam shrugged and motioned her off the toilet. For all the good it did.

Sam usually took breakfast in the stereo-lounger, but Stargyle was there now, a small wiry man with a hairline mustache, black pegged slacks, Italian shoes, and an apricot tricot polo shirt with matching socks. He looked frightened in the deep curve of the chair and gripped its arms so that his nails were pink.

Sam nodded curtly and then was motioned out on the balcony by the Dott where a table was set with his best damask and crystal. An entire fresh pineapple was sliced on a silver

59

platter, surrounded by bewildered grapes and raspberries. His mother's knife was sheathed with a heavy tasseled napkin. Sam ate hunched over so as not to block Stargyle's view.

Stargyle nodded as Sam returned, but Sam sat at his desk with his back to him to open the mail. He was amused to find a letter from Captain Edgar Fuess, typed randomly upon a very thick paper of the sort Sam's laundry backed his shirts with. It was not clear whether this was a gross indulgence or an expedient.

TO: Mr. Samuel Hooper
FROM: Rally Point, U.S.A.
(*Evolution not Revolution*)

DEAR PARTNER IN U.S.A.:

In answer to yours of the 20th, I am enclosing *Keys to Mysteries*, one chart of all mankind, organization plan II, a first edition copy of my unfinished *Adventures*, and an arm band. We are temporarily out of lapel buttons and flags for now, but I'll forward these when your membership list is received. You'll be receiving our monthly newsletter, *The Meliorist*, to keep you up to date.

Yours for action and *now!*

With sincerity to all, I remain,

CAPT. EDGAR FUESS

P. S. Conditions good nationally and internationally to elect Captain Fuess as independent anti-Satanic administrator to President of U. S. (see *Voice of the Hour*, XVI, Number 2). Rally Point is no town or city limits, but has room for expansion (station of Burlington Railroad), free of debt and Devils.

Sam filed the letter and opened *Keys to Mysteries*, a thick frayed paperback, to the title page.

KEYS TO MYSTERIES

A VOYAGE ALONE

WITH ONE-MAN BOAT <u>STURDY</u>

Captain Fuess's International Faith

his Religion

to others a Practical Brotherhood

or sisterhood

for present or future

Each can consider it to suit themselves. A new
confraternity or panfederation, new philosophy or ecology
a new radical cooperative. No unjust sacrifices from any.

*Not written by a diplomat, politician, or member of, favoring
any other society, union or religion, than this new and independent
one founded on this voyage as a common road for all.*

*An independent international faith, anti-only BLACK ART, affiliated
with none. Your country's way to win!*

*Devices added to make the Itinerary easier to follow by the
Sole Designer, Builder, Owner and Crew.*

*Cooperation needed! I wish to get your aid in revising this
edition that it will become more beneficial and useful to a greater
number. What addition, omission or change is necessary? For it to
be a road in common with others for you? Not asking you to pay
something. What man wants is a new ideology.*

ANTI-SECRET

FIRST EDITION

REVISED

Sam turned to the introduction.

Attention all mankind: You have been so busy making a living and confused with man-made conflicts that others did your thinking. Satan has taken advantage of this to concentrate economic and cultural power in the hands of the few—and fewer hands than ever before in the history of the world (or U.S.A.). This vast new Satanic evil is not a dragon transfer of power from one empire to another, but an octopus that sucks the blood of all (See Voice of the Hour, Vol. XIV, Number 7).

We don't need Satan to create work, money, business or peace. Yet Mankind's major troubles are definitely Satan's New Ideals under many names, pretenses and camouflages, un-American, un-natural, un-just, and un-human. Satan's control is only possible with the help they get from the 1% of devils in all groups (not even members sometimes) but also from the GO-ALONGS, *who act as fronts, cliques, rings and machines. This 1% of parasites keep the other 99% divided by its messes in which they ditch, smear or wipe out the reformer and take over with the* GO-ALONGS, *the modern communication of facts and contacts which itself has overlapped sphers. This has made it very difficult for Capt. Fuess, founder, sponsor, and developer of this movement to try and stop it, nationally or internationally.*

Besides Satan? Who wants it?

1. *Would-be monopolists and dictations.*
2. *Spineless men and women willing to live as slaves for protection of their futile lives.*
3. *Millions (well-meaning) but misled to think they can buy gilt-less security with high taxes and some public works.*

Same looked uneasily over his shoulder. Stargyle was getting used to the stereo-lounger and had the TV on without the sound. Sam Hooper[2], just finishing his morning *Continuing Image of Greatness*, loomed before him. Stargyle accomplished a professional double take. Sam shrugged amiably. The resemblance was coincidental. The phone rang mercifully.

Ordinarily he wouldn't have accepted. Odile sounded strangely excited over the phone, and he had wanted to see Aaron apart from her.

"But a complete solar eclipse," she had stammered, "only once in a lifetime, Sam. You've simply got to come. And Matthew's been asking for you."

He agreed to meet them at the pedestrian tunnel. As he changed into his trunks, he explained to the Dott about the eclipse.

"It's apparently due at four-thirty. You really ought to stay and view it from here. It ought to be spectacular."

The Dott looked at him generously. Stargyle, however, had resumed his panic insofar as one so posturepedically perfect could take it on. He kept glancing at the TV, then to Sam, then back in awe to the TV.

"Look, it'll be totally dark for just a few seconds. When the shadow passes, it'll be perfectly light again. Once in a lifetime, believe me."

The Dott seemed to digest this, but Stargyle stiffened in the lounger. Sam gently swiveled him so that he faced the lake.

"When the shadow passes *what?*" the Dott called out after him.

7 · *Eclipse*

They came toward him like a Disney cartoon, *sfumato*. One improbably lovely girl accompanied by fey gnomes and other friendly forest animals, characters who are likely to start talking even before their sketchy bodies have been completed by the great animator.

Aaron marched in front in Israeli army-officer shorts, a Leica banging against his solar plexus, all thighs and no calves in thonged sandals; Stieglitz, her long black hair below her waist already tall as her father, bearer of his crescent legs on Odile's edible torso; Matthew, tiny oblate testicles hanging out of an ancient Hebrew Boy's Club swimsuit, held up by shopping twine; and Odile, in a Freedom Fighter's bikini, stomach firm as an apple, fuzzy blonde hair a mist on her unshaven perfect legs. She carried Aaron's tripod on one shoulder, a picnic hamper on the other, while the children, bumping between their parents' mismatched stride, carried contraptions of Aaron's construction through which we shall view the eclipse.

Aaron took his time in the tunnel, reading the graffiti to himself in a high monotone, feeling what he couldn't see with his palms. The children advanced toward the light while Odile, a fading starlet, walked at deliberate pace behind Aaron to keep him moving. Sam looked for alcoves off the tunnel, but there was none.

They emerged on the beach, the light off the water blinding them and the sand scorching their feet. Odile hopped up and down, a palomino Percheron; Aaron did not slow his pace, but grimaced horribly, which suited him. Stieglitz and Matthew ran

64

full tilt into the waves, the boy tripping and being dragged by his sister until he finally rolled and tripped her. Her foot smashed one of his lips. He held it mournfully.

"Oh, Aaron, take a picture," Odile wailed.

"It's the sun today, Shicksaw, no kids, no family-album crap. Go get some rays on the big white bod."

She ran off powerfully, spurting sand into Aaron's eyes, dropping the tripod in the sand. She carried the picnic hamper on her head like African wash.

"A very unhappy girl," Aaron said, apparently to Sam.

"Oh?"

"Yeah," he grinned, "she wants to be in movies."

Then he burst into a choking laugh, and Sam timed his chuckle perfectly to coincide with Aaron's convulsion.

The beach was black with eclipse seekers, bright with the aluminum shields and colored boxes they had brought to preserve their retinas. Children glanced apprehensively at the sky, their parents at their watches. Odile spread the blanket and the children ran back to roll themselves on it. The sun arched knowingly toward its newsworthy juncture. Sam sat down.

"It's the moon that covers the sun, isn't it?" Odile asked him without looking up.

"I guess," said Sam, "except I always thought of it as the sun sneaking up behind the moon."

"Any way you look at it," she snapped, "it's just that much bigger than the moon, even when they're up tight." She held her thumb and forefinger apart like calipers.

She was sweating again, this time on her upper lip and chest, as she worked at the double-hinged hamper. Sam focused on a particularly filthy spot between the thongs of her sundial sandals. It took just over a minute and a half for her self-consciousness to aggregate sufficiently so that she withdrew her feet beneath her fulsome haunch. Hoops was saddened by this; Odile's modesty had the same effect on him as Mrs. Denehey's

65

insistence. Both presupposed his motives before they had actually formed. What a terrible thing it is to be trusted to do your best, he thought. Yet he would have had no compunction about biting those doubled thighs into parting in the prescheduled darkness. How long would he have? How dark could it get? Hoops looked around apprehensively. The police were everywhere, lounging in their new summer uniforms, pale blue permacrease Bermuda shorts, off-white leatherette jackboots, and royal blue overblouse with dolman sleeves; star and number embroidered over the heart. Some fenced playfully with their riot sticks, others made scheduled duty treks with sandwich information boards suspended from their shoulders.

NO INJURIOUSNESS!

DO NOT LOOK DIRECTLY INTO THE SUN

USE YOUR EYE BOXES

PERMUTANT DAMAGE MAY RESULT

YOU ONLY HAVE TWO EYES

VIOLATORS WILL BE PROSECUTED

"What've we got to eat?"

Aaron had stomped up to them and flung himself on the blanket. The children viewed him circumspectly.

"Cold rock Cornish game hen and vin rosé, dear." Odile curled her lips.

"Cold what?"

Matthew and Stieglitz laughed spitefully.

"Well, Sam gave us that check and I thought we'd celebrate," Odile said rather too matter-of-factly.

"So look what lover got for all us kids," Aaron teased inefficiently. "Fancy chicken 'n' wine."

The children did not laugh again. Sam felt moved to intervene. Odile began to take the foil-wrapped hens from the hamper.

"Sam, will you play sommelier?"

Aaron put his hands on his fleshy hips and laughed idiotically. Sam blandly offered him the magnum.

"You want to open it, Aaron?" Aaron shook his head in pointless defiance.

"Oh God," Odile wailed, striking her fine head with the heel of her hand. "I forgot the corkscrew."

"We never had a corkscrew, baby," Aaron countered. "And we never drink wine at home that I remember."

Sam saved the day by producing his late father's penknife, and with two effortless motions sent the cork spinning across the sand. Pale rosé foamed over his knuckles. He filled up paper cups to the top and offered them to his despondent hosts. Odile downed hers in one motion and tilted the empty cup to Sam before Aaron had even brought his to his lips.

"Really savors the old taste buds, eh?" he snorted at her.

Sam noted that when Aaron snorted it was very disgusting.

Odile drank another glass and handed the foil-wrapped individual cold rock Cornish game hens around like grenades to her platoon. Aaron took his to a far corner of the blanket to watch the lake. Stieglitz demonstrated to Matthew how to disembowel an individual cold rock Cornish game hen with an index finger—wild rice and chestnuts spurted into her face—but she simply leaned down and allowed him to lick her clean. Odile watched them with a faint smile.

The wine relaxed Sam; he tore a small leg of the hen loose and the sweet husk of meat fell away from the bone as his mouth closed about it. Odile hunched over toward him. A driblet of wine ran from the corner of her mouth down her hard neck and disappeared hesitantly into her cleavage.

"An amusing little wine," Sam said, and filled her glass again.

Odile was long gone by this time, however, so Sam read himself to sleep with the Fuess.

67

When he awoke, the sky alternated violently between mustard and magenta. Odile had passed out, curled feebly about the empty magnum, the blanket littered with individual cold rock Cornish game hen bones.

" 'Bout a half hour to go," Aaron mumbled.

He was at work setting up the banquet camera, a monstrous black box with a tiny lens, burying each leg of the tripod securely in the sand. The lake was purple and smooth as slate; the Pumping Station gleamed black in the mighty distance. The kids were down at the water's edge, filigreeing a sand pylon with hen's ribs.

Odile began to roll and moan. Aaron ignored her, but between sighs and hiccoughs, she spoke:

"Help the child experience his world. Allow him outside so that he may feel the weather changes. Tell him what the different kinds of precipitation are. . . ."

Sam started. Her voice was expertly modulated, disembodied.

"Experiencing something and hearing the name which goes with it is indubitably a prerequisite to speech. . . ."

Aaron spoke to Sam without turning around.

"Not to worry, Sam. It's just the Gulley catechism again. All the time when she sleeps. Impossible . . ."

Sam couldn't speak. She was just going on in that pure voice.

"Supply his touch with variety. Inside, outside—animals that squeak, plastic rings . . . beware of styrene substances which may be poisonous if sucked indiscriminately—terry cloth, gravel, paper to crumble, paper to fold, a bit of satin, a cup without a handle . . . discarded purses give security . . . give him a paper bag and say 'bag, bag.' " Odile thrashed her hips in the damp sand.

"Mud, dough, snow, clay. Let him feel his food, too. But not his feces—instead use a deep bowl and lightweight spoon. The spoon should have a handle which will fill the child's entire fist . . . use a simple word which always means toileting. . . ."

Odile sat upright and opened her eyes.

"Eating," she blurted, "should be a pleasurable experience for every child!" Then she fell back, her breasts heaving irregularly.

"Come on now, Hooper, it's coming," Aaron said. Sam flung back his head. The sun had begun to score an alley in the clouds, distended, aerodynamic in shape, its head a clot of blood. The moon, we are informed, lay waiting indistinguishable from the clouds. Sam thought of lovely big Odile as an indistinguishable moon that he could occasionally slip up behind and bathe in blood and spectacular excess energy. She was quite pale and immovable now; her lips dry, legs ungainly spread, eyes open but unseeing, not a wink.

The heavenly bodies' parabolas had intermeshed. The children returned from the water, as if on a signal, Stieglitz leading Matthew by the hand, to lie down immediately on the blanket next to defunct mother. Stieglitz, in fact, curled surreptitiously into the curve of her palpitating body and massaged her neck. Matthew lay on his back, hugging her feet daggerlike to his chest.

Aaron handed out the eye boxes—Pepsi cases lined with aluminum foil with a pinhole to view through. All down the beach they drew similar contraptions over their faces—newspaper, stainless steel, brushed aluminum, hubcaps, corrugated board, pieplates with nail holes. They lay on their backs, senses sheathed, looking through a hole large enough for the sun and moon in conjunction but only barely large enough for the eye.

"No point in two holes because you can only see one thing anyway," Aaron said.

The sun was being obliterated. The moon bit on it relentlessly—a stupid scallop of a sun lulled in the dusk. Light and shadow were one.

Aaron lay on his stomach reading *Art News*. At ten-second intervals on his chronometer he squeezed the bulb on the shutter cable, the camera emitting a strangely unmetallic *tick*.

69

The kids lay obediently beneath their boxes, sighing occasionally; Odile was gaseous. On the pretext of getting a better angle, Sam inched across the sand so that the top of his head touched her hips as he adjusted Aaron's box on his face.

The sun was only a crescent now. Its intensity had diminished, and the entire landscape seemed only a reflection of itself. The sky, lake, and beach were slivers of a single perspective, of the same somber hue. The luminous bodies of the curious ignited like punk against nature's opacity, its contrived contingencies. The buildings at the edge of the diaphanous beach glowed brighter than their windows. Cars slowed, waves petered out, talk ceased; Sam sneezed in the constricting box. Fighting mucus and tears, he found only the black disk of the moon, a penumbra of ornamental fire surrounding it, and not darkness, but simply the palest perishable light about them.

"I wanna see!"

Sam's head was thrown rudely from the box. Odile had leapt—though that is perhaps too strong a word, since she had arrived only to her knees—but she was nonetheless staring directly into the searing eclipse.

Sam jumped to his feet looking imploringly at Aaron, who proceeded to leaf through *Art News* still squeezing the shutter bulb at the proper interval.

"If she wants to look, let her," he said hoarsely.

"But she'll burn her goddamn eyes out, you bastard," Sam screamed. "Didn't you see what the sign said?"

Odile had grasped one of his legs as a prop now and as Sam gazed down into her bloated face, he could see his own head in her remaining contact lens, a silly shocked visage crowned with fire, and he realized that it was only his skull that was protecting her from permutant damage. She looked through him into the sun, her arms and breasts lifeless upon her, swaying from her knees and repeating snatches of the Gulley catechism fitfully.

"When the child has two new things at once, he can often do neither. . . ."

"Aaron, for Christ's sake do something," Sam cried.

But there was no answer—only the perpetual lubric thuds of the shutter, until Odile herself, either stung by the light or simply exhausted, flung herself against the tripod and knocked the camera to the sand.

Aaron was up in an instant and, screaming incomprehensibly, began to beat her viciously across the shoulders with his forearms. Odile twisted away from him so she could still manage to view the sun while taking the blows on her tough legs.

Sam bent over them and again saw himself reflected for an instant in her eye's lens; then resignedly, he threw a cross body block on Aaron, punishing the wind from him, spinning him off the blanket entirely. He then turned and fell across Odile.

Aaron struggled up, choking; Sam grabbed him in a leg scissors, squeezing him between his thighs until the artist turned bluer than the very shadows, and with Aaron grounded, Samuel Hooper shielded Odile's eyes with his palms.

Matthew remained somnolent, but Stieglitz, misunderstanding Sam's intentions, began to kick methodically at his face.

So it was with some relief that out of the corner of his eye, Sam saw a policeman throw off his sandwich board and begin a sprint toward them.

Part the Second

8 · *Some Handy Background*

The following week, Sam's parents died and sent him $10,000.00 in insurance and their file of his report cards.

> *Where did you come from,*
> *baby dear?*
> *Oh, out of the everywhere*
> *into the here.*

CONDITION OF BABY AT BIRTH: Full term, face presentation, two black eyes and a bruise on jaw. Active, kicking, cried little, nursed eagerly. Frequent loose yellow stools, however. Vomiting after feeding. Complexion, fair; shape, oval. Blue eyes, blond hair. Just lovely.

FIRST WORDS: "Wee wee, poop poop"
Circumcision performed. Organs quite palpable. No breast feeding, please.
FIRST FOODS: Spinach, peas, squash, asparagus, meat broth, bananas, cod liver oil.
SECOND WORDS: "Wee weer, pooper"
AFTER BIRTH: Eyes follow slowly moving hand.
THREE MONTHS: Holds self erect. Inspects own hand.
FOUR MONTHS: Laughs. Reaches for hand.
FIVE MONTHS: Inspects other hand.
SIX MONTHS: Sits with slight prop.
SEVEN MONTHS: Speaks!
EIGHT MONTHS: Creeps. Points to radio and indicates he wants music. Can turn it on but not off.
TEN MONTHS: Pulls self to standing position.

FOURTEEN MONTHS: Walks backward.

SEVENTEEN MONTHS: Gallops, struts, jumps extraordinarily high.

TWENTY MONTHS: Skips hippity hop, hippity hop. Sings the complete Frère Jacques and ABC. High Q.U.I.F. likely.

KINDERGARTEN

PHYSICAL STATUS: Samuel is a very masculine, lithe and appealing little boy with a great deal of charm and personality all his own. He takes such pride in appearing neat and attractive, seeming to have all of those soft touches of a truly sophisticated little boy. It is remarkable what good balance and coordination he does have, and how plucky he really is, being careful but never afraid physically. It should be noted he is exceptionally good about taking care of his wraps and belongings in school and remembering to take them home. He enjoys a good lunch every day and has very nice eating habits and fine manners at the table as well as in the boysroom. He tries very hard to be "a good rester" during the rest period, keeping quietly busy with himself and asking frequently, "Am I being a good rester?" Needless to say, he is always reassured that he is!

SOCIAL AND EMOTIONAL STATUS: Samuel is a very sweet, sincere lovable little boy who gets along exceedingly well with all the children and is a favorite with all of us here at the school. He is a determined little child who is not quickly upset or easily led by other children, and demonstrates a rather mature attitude toward his least popular playmates. He is most cooperative, reliable and steady, willing to help and anxious to please, and now that he has assumed a casual and relaxed attitude toward seeing the doctor every morning, his happiness and security seem complete.

SPECIAL INTERESTS AND ABILITIES: Samuel likes to do everything at school equally well. Building with blocks, playing in the sandbox, keeping house in the doll corner even, putting puzzles together and especially listening to stories. He loves the music period too, with its singing games and rhythms (very masculine here) and plays all of the instruments equally well. He is most responsive and enthusiastic about the possibility

76

of expressing himself. I believe that Sammy Hooper is about the happiest, most contented and comfortable child that I have ever known.

FIRST GRADE

Samuel J. Hooper

School days in period: 192
Days present: 188

Studies

Other activities

Language skills:	1	Art:	2
Number skills:	2	Courtesy:	1
Science skills:	2	Effort:	2

Samuel apparently prefers reading to himself. His workbooks are done usually. Promoted to the second grade.

SECOND GRADE

A child of Samuel's determination and precocity must learn to harness his omnibus talents to specific tasks. He's had a fine record, so far, particularly after the school's changeover to the new progressive "personalized" grading system, but he can't live on it forever. If he wants to go to Purk, as you claim, he's going to have to learn to settle down, do one thing at a time within the proscribed period, and recheck his work more thoroughly. Sam can be anything he wants to be, but he's going to have to decide what it is soon and apply himself.

Development of habits in work and citizenship: *Satisfactory*
Thoughtful courtesy in speech and action: *Satisfactory*
Dependability and self-control in group situations: *Satisfactory*
Good spirit in accepting and giving suggestions: *Satisfactory*
Neatness in person, property and work: *Satisfactory*
Use of time to good advantage: *Satisfactory*
Punctuality, emission and completion: *Satisfactory*
Effort and pride: *Satisfactory*

Attention and response to direction: *Satisfactory*
Workmanship in expressing ideas in art: *Satisfactory*

THIRD GRADE

Sam has suddenly begun to go off on "dilettantish" tangents. While never lacking formal respect for his teachers, he at times shows an ill-concealed contempt for group projects. Furthermore, ever since his trip to New York with his father—which, incidentally, he refused to share with us in morning "storytime"—he has not been completing assignments. I enclose his most recent fragmentary effort, which hardly bodes well for Sam's future. I hope you will have a talk with him about this. I questioned him closely after this little display, and he promises to change his attitude.

MY SUMMER EXPERIENCES
Samuel J. Hooper

This summer I went to a restaurant. In the restaurant I went to the bathroom. In the bathroom I heard a sound. So I stood up on the toilet and pecked through a little window. There was another room behind the bathroom. In this room there was a model of the country with an electric train going around it all the time. In between his job the cook would come out of the kitchen and play with the train. Switch it? Unload and watch it go through the tuneels and up the mountains and sort the praries out. Under the table the model was on were two boxer dogs one spotted the other gray and the spotted one had a green ball in his mouth. How do you get a green ball out of a boxers mouth?

There, its out.

FOURTH GRADE

A highly strung, lithe and wily boy. Has little control unless the stage is set very carefully for him. Needs constant checking, and he gets it here. A good luncheon companion, toilets well. Sees the doctor every day.

78

However, he has, of late, shown some signs of bossiness. Very definitely wants to be the leader. Sees himself as the protector of the slower students. Because of this, perhaps, he is tense and impatient much of the time. It is surprising that children like Samuel because he does not always treat them as he should. Though capable of straight thinking, he invariably falls back on a quite ruthless charm. If he minded his own business a little more, he would find life easier.

GRADE FIVE

SOCIAL ADJUSTMENT: Means to be cooperative but the spirit is willing and the flesh is weak. Volatile imagination gets easily sidetracked. To help him work better and prevent him from disturbing others, he often has to be isolated from other children. Wants to know more about this country. Occasionally he performs a certain madness with his hands.

Wanders both mentally and physically. And, on our field trip to the cookie factory, he threw a tantrum.

Samuel's chief problem is learning to resist overstimulation. His sense of rhythm, however, is keen and in a recent pitch-discrimination test he accomplished a perfect score. Final exam enclosed.

Why I like Music
by
Sam Hooper

Music isn't just for eggheads or backsliders. It is part of the educational process and it can be relaxing also. Of all things, music is nearest us, for it has in it our very life and our hopes and our dreams even if it cannot teach us anything about them. That is really not a problem because that's everything's problem. In this way, it is probably better than books. When you're tired it can be inspiring to choose your own music or turn it off, and that is why I like music.

GRADE SIX

Samuel's dramatic proclivities have cost him repeated academic failures. Next year, when there will be, particularly in social studies, an opportunity to add some verisimilitude to his otherwise unconvincing narratives, with an improved attitude he can aim at much greater success. Samuel's work for the year has been disappointing, particularly in view of his high Q.U.I.F. His discouragement about such achievement, coupled with his great desire to be a leader, have definitely handicapped any progress. Nevertheless, throughout his hardships, even when he *felt* that he was being very unjustly dealt with, he remained constantly reasonable, courteous, cooperative. I hope that with the change in activities this summer he will gain a new perspective and a new spirit.

CAMP DRIFTWOOD FOR BOYS
Established 1904

June 10th

DEAR MR. AND MRS. HOOPER:

This was my first summer at camp, and at times, it has been a pleasure to be with your son. However, it is so very hard to be objective about Samuel. The trouble here was that there just aren't enough of those times where one wants to be objective about him. He is very strong and independent for his age, and he knows it. Samuel did give me some enjoyable moments. In a football game we played with Cabin 5, for example, it was my pleasure to organize our cabin team and I selected Samuel as our tailback, though he does not always display the competitive spirit. (For example, one day in basketball, while his team was in the process of losing, he proclaimed that he did not care if we won or not!) But back to the football game, Samuel threw two passes for touchdowns which insured our margin of victory. He didn't play flawless ball, I should say, but I could see that he did want to win. I think you'll agree with me that he should at least learn to develop a winning habit both on and off the playing fields. Ask Samuel about this game, and I think you'll find that he really enjoyed our upset win. I certain did! I should also mention that I've been on two camping trips with Samuel and although I hate to say it, he has a slight tendency to shirk his job. After our last trip, he wasn't around when other fellows cleaned the pots and pans. He offered the lame excuse that he was checking in to see the doctor. There wasn't any doctor out there! He tended to argue also a great deal over when he should and when he shouldn't paddle the canoe. He complained that it wasn't a "winning situation." Samuel needs lots of kindness but also a firm hand. You have much to be proud of. He'll be a real tough kid.

CAMP DRIFTWOOD FOR BOYS
Established 1904

August 10th

DEAR MR. AND MRS. HOOPER:

It seems impossible that time could pass so rapidly. At this rate, the summer will be over before we know it. I don't know if Samuel told you about the change in personnel in our cabin. Walter Schar, who wrote you, I believe, last time, had to return home suddenly after the trouble, and Robert Winter, the tallest man in camp this year, has moved in to replace Walter. The boys seem to like him very much. He is 6 ft. 11, 290 lbs., and really makes a picture.

I think it has now become clear as Walt told you last time that Samuel has suddenly become one of our best campers. Athletically he is unsurpassed among the midgets, and has earned awards in tennis, track, camping and nature. This gives him a total of ten awards and one honor, which is a good record, though not exceptional. We will all be interested in seeing *how many more* he gets next season. In the eight weeks that Samuel has been here he has shown great improvement in working on cabin chores and in toning his voice down.

Robert Winter just told me this morning that he thought Samuel had improved 200% in his behavior. Bob gave him a stern calling down some time ago. Finally, we have really become attached to Samuel and the other boys in the cabin, and can't wait 'til next summer.

SEVENTH GRADE

Samuel often has insights which no other seventh grader sees, but then again, he will miss relationships which are obvious to many others. He is capable of extraordinary concoctions! In spite of such struggle with fantasies, nevertheless, in three examinations this term he has averaged in the top half of the class. The fact that Samuel was one of the four nominees for secretary-treasurer of the middle school council indicates that his qualities of leadership have been recognized. Any kudos I could add would be superfluous. Samuel seems to be beginning to realize also that there are some areas in which it is better to understand what you are doing than to be farthest ahead. He continues to be admired by all the members of the group, and he makes it a point to play with everyone at one time or another. I sincerely hope that Samuel has a wonderful time at camp this summer.

CAMP DRIFTWOOD FOR BOYS
Established 1904

DEAR MR. AND MRS. HOOPER:

It seems impossible time could pass so rapidly. At this rate, our summer will be over before we know it. Last night was the annual banquet night, which is really the climax of our camping season and the point where everyone realizes we must soon return to life again. Well, all good things have to come to an end, I guess; I get to stay up here for a week or so longer, however. Samuel is an unusual boy, as I am sure you realize, but perhaps you also realize that he must have some faults as well. He tends to be playful often at the wrong time. You see, when a child is outstanding as Samuel is, winning firsts, captaining teams in the steeplechase and most outstanding with the late-season spurt earning his twenty-eight awards (a new record for both the midgets and juniors, I might add), so when he is loud and noisy they notice it more rapidly from him than the other boys and remember it. He has a certain magnetism that is going to cause him a lot of trouble later on if he doesn't learn to *use* it.

We were fortunate in our cabin this year in not having any sickness at all. Though Samuel did continue to take his nose drops and see the doctor every morning. He certainly knows how to take care of himself. I am really getting attached to Samuel and the boys.

EIGHTH GRADE

Samuel is beginning to see the weaknesses of the role of playing the fool and ought to grow out of it. Samuel is also profiting a good deal by his work in dramatics. Sure, on stage he displays some of the same characteristics he produces in class—notably absurdity. But at the same time, working on a performance does give him an opportunity to shift the cloak of a fool and assume the position of an individual with a *serious and important* role to play. Samuel has the strength, speed, skill and knowhow to be a real success. In addition, he seems to be developing of late that fire and confidence which adjust readily to fierce competition. If he keeps working and does not seek too many easy pleasures, he can plan on a success. Finally, as there are a great many permanent teeth which will replace the baby teeth in Samuel's mouth, it is impossible to foretell in what position they may erupt. Consequently, there may be some further treatment which we cannot estimate at this time. With the proper effort and discipline, Samuel can have good teeth. However, he frequently does not pay attention and give us the cooperation needed. Therefore, his oral achievement is not as strong as it could be. He seems to lack seriousness of purpose in this regard.

NINTH GRADE

Samuel has been doing better. He responds to instructions and really puts forth every effort as a competitor. But special practice in the use of possessives and contractions should be given him. He seems also to shift styles for no apparent reason. It has been, further, much concern to us that he has insisted in forcing his otherwise fine voice to a lower range, anticipating the change to a more masculine voice. This has brought on a husky quality unnatural to his larynx potential and may even permanently injure his vocal cords. His grasp of the facts is about average. He no longer plays the fool nearly so often, rather taking part in the fun of the group on a par with his peers. Offensively, he is overcoming a tendency to dance instead of run, but could still improve his open-field blocks. I would hope that he will continue to get a good rest every night, because he seems to vomit before our games.

83

TENTH GRADE

Review, turns, basics: 1
Hill parking, lane usage: 1
Revew hill parking, light traffic turnabout, diagonal parking, turns: 2
Parallel parking: 1
Expressway night driving: 1

Samuel continues to enjoy prestige of a driving leader and spirited participant in all group driving projects.

There are still holes in Samuel's knowledge, yet he has a passing understanding of just about everything. He needs to listen to direction better
and give himself Time. His attitude, effort and performance this term has
been just within honors range. Samuel was also elected a Second Class
Responsible this term and will undoubtedly be up for Squad Leader in
the next. He's beginning to live up to his potential.

ELEVENTH GRADE

Computational difficulties and conflicting interests continue to retard
Samuel's potential. We find that on occasion Samuel relies too often on
emotive appeal to put over his ideas. His record is marked by many ups
and downs of considerable magnitude. I believe he would find life a good
deal more pleasant if he could consistently keep before him the goal of
real success. His gold star book report is enclosed.

The Inner and the Outer
a book report by Samuel J. Hooper

Doctor S. M. L. Miller, *The Spirit's Environment*

Everyone has two kinds of experience, inner and outer. The first is
about yourself, the second about things. The first is harder to describe
than the second. The inner is called "the heart" and the outer "the
mouth." Dr. Miller thinks the inner and outer should be brought together.
If you can picture his mind, it would look like this:

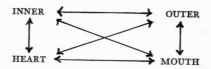

INNER ⟷ OUTER

HEART ⟷ MOUTH

Myself, I have never felt that there was any difference between the inner and outer. Some things glitter and some things glimmer. But that is about the only difference. Professor Miller says,

> "We must have a flexible and mature culture, capable of realizing an ultimate principle, and an ultimate principle characterized by an ability to give meaning to a mature culture, without sacrificing either the culture or the principle."

This seems to me relative. There are many semantic barriers here. In pursuance of the aforementioned question, I should like to point out that this is not a black or white question but a gray one. Life is basically meaningless except for struggle and search. The sad gong of death, the flute of life, these are only representative. Not a meaningful whole or a merging thing.

There is always a connection between what I cannot describe and what I can. The connection is not God or a language. It is me. And I am what holds the spirit and the environment together.

Now that we have examined and compared these two, a conclusion is necessary. It is not on one level. The Communists say we love things too much, but maybe they don't know how hard it is to love a thing.

GRADE TWELVE

Samuel has displayed a very marked ability for everything throughout his life. He has demonstrated a consistently curious approach, frequently indicating initiative, as well as a mind alert and determined in pursuit of understanding. His committee work has been unsurpassed. This, together with an interest in learning and promptness in meeting responsibility, should bode well for his future at Purk. Further, he promises to avoid the pitfalls of subjectivity when working under pressure in the future. We were, I might add, however, somewhat shocked at the sudden turn in his latest personality tests. For they indicated that while Samuel is neither haughty or familiar with those whom are clearly his inferiors, he cannot dispel a certain apprehension with regard to *their* future. While on one hand he sees no reason why he should not enjoy himself to the utmost, he also seems to bear a heavy responsibility the object of which is not clear. This manifests itself in bouts of playing the fool, alternating with hyper-ambitious and relentless attempts to organize the activities of those about him. It goes without saying that Samuel frequently knows what's better for them—as befits a boy with the highest Q.U.I.F. in school—but the trouble is, they don't know that. Given his other sympathetic attributes and talents, we are at a loss to explain how he developed such a fierce competitive spirit and desire to be first in everything.

That evening Sam began to read *The Adventures of Captain Feuss* with unusual interest.

Traveled 43,000 miles or 58,000 knots. A grand total of 101,000 miles and knots. Made one mistake throughout life—giving others, especially the organized, credit for having more brains than they had —they tried to hide THEIR defects by secretly branding me a misfit, odd or crazy.

I ask the reader to please have patience. As you will see, the writer has had little of the artificial education (schooling) and the fact that this writer-publisher is handicapped by existing organizations trying to force them to donate their original efforts to keep some outdated institutions in power, has made it impossible to hire a proofreader.

Though my mind was conducive to one line of thought, it seemed destined to be in many places. Yours probably isn't. Some brains are like stagnant pools. Others are like rushing streams, starting among some hidden rocks, too full of energy, they plunge merrily along (dodging down beneath the ground, surfacing suddenly) ever growing faster, whiter. They pass on to their fellowmen the lessons learned until they finally reach the great unknown. And I learned the hard way; it's not what is that's important; it's what happens to you there.

86

When my father ran away and died, I ran away on a voyage around the world, to become of age in the Harbor of Yokohama, Japan. I had plenty of opportunity to learn what others thought of Americans for the Nora was a U. S. ship, but there were only two, the captain and myself the ship's boy, Americans on board. In other words, the highest and lowest jobs only were American.

Not liking these long voyages, called "deep water" by seamen, I then tried the "coasters," both sail and steam. After spending a winter at deep-sea fishing on the grand banks and a spring at shad fishing on the Hudson, I decided to leave sealife. For I had learned for a man to follow the sea along has to be of the hermit type, not caring for a home, and I am and always have been the opposite of that.

No! I HAD THREE MAIN OBJECTS in my one line of thought.

FIRST: to circumnavigate the world alone in an easterly direction, the hardest way as it had only been done three times before and those were the other way.

SECOND: to show Americans are not all bluff, although we have a large percentage of them.

THIRD: to confirm the conviction that all people all over the world are fundamentally the same.

There was a FOURTH object that later proved most important, for when one tries to start something new, he is condemned by leeches that live off the old, hindering the new in ways that the average person little imagines. I got and am getting more than my share of the humbug, and so that FOURTH object was to show myself an individual, whereas the object of the voyage was Peace and Solidarity (show up prejudice and bluff) I found that I had to spend too much valuable time just being individual.

9 · *Odile Meets Sam Halfway*

The Dott opened the door and then her mouth. Sam watched her from the stereo-lounger, tipping his reading glasses forward on his nose. Stargyle, out taking the indian air on the terrace on his second consecutive weekend visit, turned in his seat; the sweat ran from either end of his mustache.

Odile stood there in an elderly camel's-hair coat, too short for her, too hot for the season, the nap dry-cleaned into a patchy blond pelt, indistinguishable from her hair, a portfolio in one hand, a guitar in the other. "I'm sorry, Sam," she said. "Do you have guests?"

Sam blanched in surprise. Had he underestimated her? The Dott glared at him.

"That'll be all for today, Dott," he said.

She goes wordlessly to the balcony and has an animated discussion with Stargyle against the sky and water. . . .

"Isn't that beautiful," Odile remarks, gesturing toward the window. "The view, I mean."

The Dott held Stargyle close. They placed their faces against the pane. Odile looked right through them, toward the Pumping Station.

Sam helped her off with the heavy coat. He was conscious of the light damp hair whorled at the nape of her neck. Like Aaron's "Sea 'n' Weed" sequence. Her Gulleyness rose to his nostrils.

"Awful hot for a coat like this," Sam said.

"I've been making calls," she said, suddenly businesslike. "It's

88

really the only presentable one I've got."

(God, she's big. Wider every place except her shoulders than me. Big and sweet. But nothing shakes when she walks. That's the new money. Only money could have kept that bulk under such perfect control. That's why the Dott shakes even though everything's hard—and maybe now, without money, Odile's going to start to shake.)

The Dott, in fact, pushed past him now, every stride the beginning of a small fall, Stargyle grudgingly in tow, digging the heels of his Italian shoes into the rug. But just as the Dott passed so humorlessly, she threw the door open, wheeled, gave Sam a big grin, and grabbing her right breast approvingly, directed it at him, giving it a few violent tugs, and then they were gone.

Sam returned to the living room to find Odile suddenly sophisticated, unwinking, legs crossed smartly in the stereo-lounger, swiveling back and forth on a 15-degree arc, smiling and holding an empty cigarette in a holder in her plucking hand.

"Can I offer you a drink?"

"It's a little early for that, isn't it?"

Sam glanced at the portfolio in her lap. "More photos?"

"No, actually, I've come on another matter."

Sam drew up the hassock to the base of the stereo-lounger and seated himself pleasantly across from her. She nervously opened the portfolio on the top of the guitar case as he leaned toward her.

"I don't know how to put this exactly. It's so hard to think seriously about larger matters when you spend all day cooped up. Well, anyway, a bunch of us girls in the neighborhood have gotten together to save Peacock Prairie."

"Oh?"

"You know, that empty triangle right across from us? With all the high grass and stuff? It's got a cyclone fence around it; surely you've seen it."

89

"Oh yes," said Sam. "I wondered what that was. It'd make a great ball field, looks like."

She eyed him disapprovingly. "Well, I can see you're not sympathetic, Mr. Hooper. I've other calls to make."

She stood up. Sam took her by the shoulders and eased her back into the chair.

"What the hell is this? Sure I'm interested. Look, just relax."

She took a deep breath and settled back into the lounger, curling her feet under her, tapping the guitar case with her smitten fingernails.

"You think I'm just one of those foolish women in search of a cause, don't you? Well what if I said I just used this as an excuse to be near you? Would you take me seriously then?"

Sam, paling, reconnoitered.

"If I took you, Mrs. Grassgreen, it would not be seriously, and I'll tell you when I'm going to take you."

She clapped her hands to her ears.

"You don't take *anything* seriously, do you?"

"See for yourself," Sam said, and got up and fixed himself a drink.

"I can twist words too," she yelled at his back, "but why should I?"

He brought her a sherry. "Indeed," he said, "why should you?"

"See," she went on breathlessly, "all of where we are once was prairie. Grasses and flowers, not old woods. It took thousands of years to grow, and now, the little that's left—what man hasn't plowed or mowed or sprayed or built up—what's left, you know, it's so beautiful, and what's more, it's a climax community, that means it's been here for so long that it can maintain itself indefinitely, if man doesn't destroy it. And that's just what *they're* trying to do. I'm so sorry about the business at the beach last weekend."

"OK, Odile."

"They want to put up a model public-housing project, they say."

"The poor or the prairie, is that it?"

"Oh Sam, you make it sound so stupid. But it's the only intact prairie left, Sam. I don't give a damn about the botanical or historical interest. It's just so beautiful. Just last week the false indigo was in bloom."

"Look, fine, Odile, but what do you want me to do? And you needn't apologize about the beach thing."

"First you can sign this petition—*People for the Preservation of Peacock Prairie*. But most important, we need a man, Sam. A front man, somebody who can provide disinterested leadership, somebody who can take charge of the campaign. Somebody who's really competitive, but whose hands are clean."

"I'm pleased and flattered, Odile, as you must know. But I've just begun this job with MC."

"But you're the only man I know who can help keep both the rich and the poor out of there!"

Sam nodded and looked at the floor.

"If you won't, who will?"

"Why not Aaron?"

"Aaron! Jesus Christ, Sam. This is serious. He doesn't give a damn about anything like that. You think because he's an artist he's interested in beauty? Well, let me tell you, he isn't. He's just interested in what's *interesting*. You know what he said to me the other day? He said he thought a used-car lot was more beautiful than a forest! Can you imagine?"

Sam glanced up at *Wall #1*.

"Peacock Prairie is for people who don't have a gimmick. People like us who don't have to use their goddamn minds like that. People who love it not because they can use it, but because it's all they have, even if they don't want it sometimes. I thought it was lovely the way you took care of me. I explained to Stieg later what you were doing."

Sam nodded appreciatively.

"Aaron doesn't have the guts, even if he believed in it anyway," she finished.

"OK, Odile, you've got yourself a president. On one condition."

"I love conditions, Sam. Just not reasons, OK?"

"Take me out there and show me what's so goddamn beautiful about it."

She bounded up, nearly knocking him over, and held her coat out for him.

They had to park several blocks away, and Odile led him at a trot through the luncheon crowd.

"I don't think Aaron really cared either. The eclipse pictures weren't ruined," she said, taking his hand.

Peacock Prairie lay in the north quadrant of intersection of three streets, an alluvial mist rising from its center. She led him through the turnstile and into the meadow. It was larger than he had remembered it, and then the prairie opened up, all of one color under the overcast, the same color as the lake at sunset, Sam noted, whatever that was. Sort of antique rose?

Immediately before them the vegetation had been trampled down, befouled by 100,000 poodles, but farther out, as the triangle grew to its hypoteneuse, the foliage grew higher than Sam himself. Across the tight-fisted bloom, newspapers floated like patches of kelp on the sea. The battered sign read:

CITIZENS 100% PRAIRIE
A Patch of Perennial Flora
The Largest Messic (Medium-Moist) Climax
Community of Forps (Grasses) Still Active.
No eating, or playing, under penalty of
Fine, Imprisonment or Both.

Odile ran before him into the grass, the foliage cleaving before her until only her tawny head was visible, then she turned and waved to him.

Hoops entered more judiciously, careful not to step on anything, and mindful of the indicator tabs at the base of each plant, the first of which read:

Nature Walk, Species #1
"Hoary Puccoon"

Do not pick or handle these plants. It took
1,000 years for them to reach this climax state.
Do not undo in your generation.

Sam made his way toward Odile, taking it by the numbers, gently pushing pink milkwort, meadow parsnip and Lazy American Vetchling aside. He found her sitting down, arms about her knees, in a patch of panic grass. She had cut across the lushest portion of the swale; various tubers, pods and split stalks, as well as a crisp hash of elbowed thistle, marked her frantic path. She smoothed her skirt, and then her head was tilted back by a heavy wet grin. Sam sat down cautiously. Up between their legs sprouted showy thick trefoil, wild madder, winged loosestrife and stiff aster.

Sam picked a sweet bugleweed and fixed it in her hair. "Princess of the Prairie," he pronounced.

"And isn't it beautiful, Sam, isn't it worth saving?"

"And I, president of the Preservation of Peacock Prairie for the People, say unto you . . ."

She leaned over and kissed him on the neck. He could feel her teeth through her lips.

"You look generally lovely today, Odile."

"I'm OK in the day. Nights I get puffy around the eyes for some reason."

"Is that so?" She was fiddling intolerably with his hair.

"Puffy, right around the eyes."

"Does Aaron . . ." Sam disguised a smile as a cough. "Does he . . . hm . . . find you interesting . . . enough?" She released his curls.

"I thought that was coming. You'd have to put it in words, wouldn't you? Well, frankly, I don't care what he thinks. Couldn't care less what he *thinks*." She actually spat this.

"He seems—" Sam waited for his inarticulateness to register its effect—"a very . . . hm . . . well, talented man."

"I no longer envy or am proud of such things," she barked stridently. But that was better than he thought she would do.

"What do you want out of him, Odile?" Sam said, suddenly taking the offensive. "You live all right. He's doing what he wants and keeping you alive. What the hell."

"I should like it," she said most softly, lightly, as if she were asking him for the last dance, "about two point eight times a week. That's just average, isn't it? You think that's aggressive? Typical? Just average, just a-ver-*age*."

Sam was had and shook his head. "Hey now, come on, don't."

"Look, you ninny, I don't expect you to understand this, but I was *giving* myself to him, see, oh, not even that, but *for* something more—"

She slumped down in the considerable grass with this, head in hands. Sam squinted his best but could take in only her paleness; her sobs seemed only a dramatic snore. A hundred years ago he would have strangled her out of pity and gladly turned himself in. Today he could only manage to smooth his sharkskin suit about a telltale and largely inappropriate reaction.

Sam reddened and cracked his knuckles. Newspaper scudded across the deranged grasses above them.

"Come on, Sam," she whispered, "and I'll show you how it's so pretty here."

Sam leaned back obediently upon locked arms, his vision

watered, aware only of her cowlick. Then his head fell back; he kneaded the grass with his fists, shivering uncontrollably. He gave no instructions, exhortations. He tried to concentrate on a cloud, but it gradually broke up into nebulae. Captain Fuess's words came back to him: "It's not what it *is*, it's what happens to you there. . . ."

Then, as our newly coronated king of Peacock Prairie could hardly get his breath, he dutifully toppled the Princess in one violent backwards somersault, her head bouncing gently on the panic grass.

Sufficiently later, as the strength returned to his hands, Sam noted they had uprooted two tufts of monkeyweed and fogfruit respectively, and he realized the prairie's existence was indeed threatened as long as Odile retained her active interest in it. The princess, however, had not closed her eyes nor achieved much character.

"Take it out," she said.

There are many different trades in the building of a boat, from the idea in the mind to the gold-leaf letters on the stern. Some claim they build a boat when they really only do a part. Although I was never an apprentice to any trade, I have always been interested in observing everything, and once I see something done, can do it myself. This is the first boat, then, which I finally finished in 1919, 800 miles from any ocean water near the middle of the United States and it was the first seaworthy vessel ever built at Lertz.

My building site was in a very conspicuous place just opposite a park, and for those who never had the experience, I will inform them that one has to get stern with the public. The workbench was constantly crowded with thoughtless sightseers and critics, giving me little chance to work, and if they get dust on their clothing, or can't fathom the plan, they tell the world that you're taking your frustrations out on them, and if you try to be nice, social and candid, they will say you're too ambitious. All the public wants is to dictate your job and give bad advice, and there's always one there who'll tell you "I'd build a boat too, but I've never got the time to sit down and do it."

The press got impatient too, afraid others would get the news first. One started calling my boat the "mystery boat," and her real name Sturdy was forgotten. She was to be unjustly known forever as a "mystery ship." I had no hard feelings. Still, it put every move I made in the wrong light until I was considered a misfit. There was no "mystery" about it. Critics just don't understand how you can build a boat without store-bought plans, or why you'd build it if it wasn't for either money or pleasure. It wasn't for neither. It was for a hard trip.

With this out of the way, I started to move Sturdy down the river bend, but the "Help" I had hired let her run away, by not using the brake enough. Some said purposely. And she turned over and over down the whole hill, causing a lot of expense and delay. It was harder to get that damn boat in the water from Lertz than it was to get all the way across the Atlantic! But we finally made it to the river. She was a schooner-type, 32 feet long, 4 feet by 9 inches draft, 11 foot beam, 8 tons depth displacement, 640 square foot of sail. But that tumble had took its toll, and she listed badly in the water.

Friends continued to warn me that internationally organized (BLACK ART) institutions would stop at nothing to make matters worse, by using their trump cards (financial rule and whisper campaigns) upon a person's mentality and morals. And true enough, the next day I come down to the wharf and there was Sturdy, only her masts showing up through the water. . . . It took some time before I felt like getting back to work.

In May of 1926, I leased a lot on the waterfront at Thunderbolt, Georgia, and started work on Sturdy II, one half the size of the "mystery ship." I built this boat singlehandedly, being the architect, electrician, sailmaker, riveter, caulker, painter, patternmaker, plumber and cabinetmaker.

I used 32 sawed frames, more difficult and expensive to make than the usual bent frames, but stronger and more flexible, so she could cut right through a wave if we couldn't ride her. I planked her one section at a time, because though most people don't know it, it's better to change around the bones a little bit and to have a tight skin than to have a perfect skeleton that people can measure, and a floppy skin. Sure, you'll say, when a boat's bang up on a beach, what's left, just the bones, that's what lasts. But I say what you got to do is stay afloat, and you got to make all kinds of jimcrack repairs to do that. When you see the bones of a beached boat what you think of is the trips it took you never saw. And I'll be on the bottom before this boat'll.

There was no Oak used on Sturdy II for in hot climates it dry rots, and in the cold it knarls and spits. Everything was of long-leaf pine except the decks and ceiling which were of cypress for lightness. I bought 5,000 pounds of lead for ballast from a friend. He offered to cast it for me, but to accept this offer would not be doing the job alone, so I refused, saying the next American that tells the world he built a boat and does not do it, I will make him eat his bluff! The small engine (for use only in ports) arrived, and being the only machinist, I had to handle it alone. This I did by unbolting and removing two timbers, rolling the engine through the port side. I should've done this before planking, but it's a better boat for it.

Then came the job of caulking. I suffered many days of sore hands for mistaking them (hands) for the caulking iron. Then I tin-lined the water tanks to keep the copper from poisoning the water. The cabinet work was next. Everything was personally designed for my purposes, and all done by hand; the stateroom ¾ locker berth, a locker seat and a small dresser with a mirror (not for vanity used, but captain would comb his hair). I expect many are wondering why so much expense was spent on the inside when she looked kind of lopsided from the outside. It was important that in the countries to be visited to have quarters any native could visit in comfort and become a partner in helping together with me in the founding and developing of a new non-secret independent service institution. Just like underwear, a good boat and gentlemen always got to have something between his self and his clothes, you might say, a membrane, that's the thing, for man is just that.

All this took much time and patience because it had to be done right and was worth doing well for even a modern boat gets a terrible beating at sea. Things are shaken loose in a way that has to be experienced to be imagined . . . but now, after years of test models and false starts, we are on our way.

10 · Churning

Wittgenstein was hung over and grouchy. He slouched behind his desk, an air jet trained directly on his chest, tie rippling like a pennant over his shoulder.

"I've got to find out about some property, sir." Sam handed him the roughed-out city plot diagram of Peacock Prairie. "Could you put it through for me?"

Sam waited as Wittgenstein went laboriously to the railing. He leaned on it heavily, and then released the paper. It glided, fluttered down into the pit, eluding the first few upstretched hands, and finally fell to the floor admist a general scuffle.

"It shouldn't be long now," Wittgenstein said. Sam seated himself on the corner of his supervisor's desk.

"You know, Hoops, old Bins has got a real bug in his ass about the great work you've done so far on the Christmas Memo. In particular, your defense of our dollar."

"Well, it shouldn't be construed as a defense, exactly."

"Cut the modesty horseshit, willya?" Wittgenstein broke off —a yellow ribbon was emerging from the visaphone. He cut it off with a pair of large gardening shears and placed the perforations against his coding sheet.

"It appears that this tract is owned by our subsidiary, Project Uplift, with ancillary rights held by MakeWay, our transportation placement division."

"So what's the picture for the future?"

"Well, it has a B-minus rating for investment potential."

"No, not its nonbuilt-property value. What are the development plans?"

"There seems to be some question about that. MakeWay wants to develop another parking tower, since that appears to be the quickest return on investment, but Uplift wants a public housing project, which of course has very little return past the initial profit, but it does constitute a built-in consumer purchasing area for a new shopping center. Not to mention getting us off the hook with the pols."

"What's the chance of getting it incorporated into the park district?"

"Don't say anything about *that* here."

"Well, how about a file on management? Who's going to win?"

"OK, just a minute." Wittgenstein batted out the code on the visaphone. "You got a buyer or something?"

"Well, yes, nothing definite. It's hard to say."

"It's difficult to tell with this particular management problem, Sam, kid. Schroeder at MakeWay is one helluva good guy. Got his finger on everything. But damn Palmitz at Uplift is a stubborn paranoid type. He was on the list in the Fifties, you know. We hired him back when the Supreme Court upheld him."

Wittgenstein flipped another note over his shoulder; it wafted over the balustrade.

"If they see me at the railing they always fight for it," he mumbled. "Rip it right up sometimes, the crazy bastards."

Sam cracked his knuckles. The visaphone sputtered. Wittgenstein decoded.

"Hey," he said. "Now that's interesting. They bet on Palmitz sixty to forty. In fact, we got a stop order in to sell out MakeWay. It looks like Palmitz is going to beat ass after all."

"Where can I get hold of this Palmitz?"

"Christ, Sam, don't go to see him directly. Get some advice first."

"Shoot."

"Why don't you go see our consulting division? That's why they're there."

"I thought *we* were the consulting division."

"Hell, Sam, the *inter*office consulting division—for personnel. You know, upstairs, top floor."

"You've never suggested we use them before. Even on the Zeus deal."

"This is *personnel*, Sam! Hell, say, if you did get to Palmitz without Schroeder knowing, it could upset the whole applecart. At sixty-forty, you know how much we could lose if Schroeder got wise?"

"That's just bookkeeping, Witty; we control both of 'em, don't we?"

"It's the morale factor, Sam, psychology. We can't have our subsidiaries thinking we're going to undercut them. Schroeder has a personal option on fifty-one percent of MakeWay. What do you think this would do to his initiative? If he loses in the free market, though, he's got nobody to blame but himself."

Sam took the elevator indifferently to the topmost floor. The offices there had not been modernized. The mahogany paneling and irregular partitioning were still intact; gargoyles hung across the windows, odd abutments featuring exquisite detail invisible from the street.

The outer office of the interconsulting division was furnished with antiques, and the receptionist proved to be an older nononsense woman, unlike those on the floor. She beckoned Sam to a seat while she got his file. After leafing through it, she looked up, obviously impressed.

"A frontman and a Purky, eh?" she said.

"Right, ma'am."

"You know, most of the people who come up to us are frontmen."

"Is that a fact?"

"Absolutely. We find that the infrastructure is such that the pressure coordinates intersect on the frontmen better than half the time."

"You mean to say we're sort of interstices of the infrastructure?"

"Precisely."

"Imagine."

"Now, of course, it's not my business to pry, Mr. Hooper, but if you could give me some sort of conceptual rundown on your problem—we could assign you to the proper man, you see."

"Well, I think you could call this . . . a . . . predictability of subsidiary management behavior problem."

"Ah. That sounds like Dr. Agapecropolis. Room 14B, Mr. Hooper. He'll be waiting for you."

The name on the door read:

DR. CHRISTOS EUTHIMIOU AGAPECROPOLIS

He sat behind a Louis Quatorze bowlegged desk with nothing on it but a gold automatic pencil. A hi-fi played somewhere behind him. Delibes?

He raised himself up, a tan balding man, narrow shoulders, impressive buttocks, and clasped Sam's hand eagerly.

"Glad to have you with them, Hooper."

"Yessir."

"Oh come now, I was an enlisted man myself. Just call me Chris. Would you like some coffee and a brioche?"

"That would be nice, sir. Chris, I mean."

"The point is to be open, open as well as deep, so we have some feeling of our self-worth, don't you agree?"

"That sounds right," said Sam, sipping his coffee.

"I believe you've just had a birthday. Forgive my tardiness, and felicitations."

"Quite." Sam was, as usual, caught from behind by his own aplomb.

Agapecropolis poured the coffee and reseated himself.

"What's your opinion of the operation here, Samuel, if I may call you that."

"Certainly."

"So what do you think of the place?"

"Well, they've treated me *very* fairly."

"Ah yes, but do you feel . . . needed, shall we say?"

"I don't want to be needed, Dr. Agapecropolis," Sam said curtly. "I just want to help, that's all. What I need to feel is that I don't need *you*. That puts me in a position to help, doesn't it?"

"Hmmm. You enjoy the role of being truthful, don't you?" A speck of brioche clung to the doctor's upper lip.

Sam looked politely at the parquet floor.

"You realize, of course, that that particular role is dependent upon an essentially neurotic audience?"

Sam looked at the soundproof ceiling.

"You see, we may as well get right to the point; management demands that we limit our functions, and we who are thus limited must play with them to realize them."

"Them?"

"With our functions. You have just made use of the dramaturgical potential of 'truthtelling.' It provides your image with a certain desirable patina—it authorizes you a performance. On the other hand, a real rebel, the man who must create his identity, it's him who will dissemble, misrepresent, throw our calculations off. But *you* know who *you* are, you see. Truthtelling can be a fun role, of course, if a highly predictable one . . ."

Sam frowned and pointed at the food on the doctor's lip. Agapecropolis understood immediately. "Wonderful," he murmured to himself. "Oh, that was a good one. Put me right on the defensive." Then he wiped his mouth and stared Sam in the eye.

"You probably think that little *faux pas* was accidental, don't you?"

Sam shrugged, grinned.

"Just a little trick of dialectic, don't you see? Already we're a mite closer. You find it a trifle vulgar, no doubt, as one whose sense of integrity will not allow him to break out of character."

Sam shook his head, trying to restrain himself from breaking the clichéed silence.

"But what's important, from our point of view, is that we make no pretense of these strategic secrets, for if we hold such things within us, we run the risk of, you know, *Black Art*."

"Doctor, I grant you all this, but I don't see what it has to do with . . ."

"Fair enough. You want to know what *my* role is?"

"Oh no, what I meant . . ."

"My job is simply to insure that you can eventually admit what is most true—namely that you need us. Establish dialogue. Of course, the trick is to keep your pride intact in the process."

"I just want to be of service," Sam fairly pleaded.

"But *helping* is *not* doing what the audience wants *done* to them, lad. It's doing what they can't *admit* they want that they want. That's a frontman's be-all and end-all!" The doctor was beaming.

"You know," said Sam wistfully, giving up his primary mission altogether, "as long as you've brought up the subject, there's someone you ought to talk to."

"I'd love to."

"Not in the firm, though, but I'd pay the outside consulting fee myself."

"I'd love to."

"It's the wife of a friend of mine."

"Wonderful. We don't get many married women up here, I'll tell you. Tell me something true about her."

"I really don't know much about it. It's mainly sexual, I'd

guess. Couldn't we make an appointment for her? I think I could talk her into coming."

"Oh that's no good, old man, on second thought, there's no point in *my* seeing her—she wouldn't tell me the truth anyway, but you will. That's *your* role, isn't it? Just come up here for an hour or so a day, you know, come up and have a casual lunch off a tray with me. You get info from her, and I'll tell you how to handle it. Then you can transliterate back to her. We can only account for female sexuality through the male filter anyway. I mean, we really don't know what *they* want out of their fathers, do we? I should say! No need involving her. After all, it would just contribute to her stressful situation. So I'll see you at lunch tomorrow."

"Well, all right," Sam said. He got up to leave. The old knot had returned to his chest and he was dizzy.

"The superior man keeps the inferior man at a distance, not angrily, but with reserve. Isn't that what you do, Samuel?"

"I suppose so, Doctor."

"And incidentally, Samuel," the doctor whispered hoarsely at the door, "I'd put my money on Palmitz."

The tantalizing and temporizing of man inconceivably by inhumane organizations is becoming well understood by men of visions, making the time not too distant when organizations and groups won't be able to work their rackets in just any place. To hasten that day was my aim and object. The nature of all this work did not leave my hands in any condition to put Sturdy very clearly on her stern with gold leaf. The breeze got more than Sturdy got on her. Though I got her to the water safely and alone, I had much trouble getting my papers from the customs house. The same hot air and humbug as with the first boat, in spite of my having made the best use of experience. Oh, I was a queer nut all right!

In early 1928 I set sail for the first time, making Charleston, South Carolina. Sturdy more than proved herself ready. But by then I was nearly 50 years old, and many years had passed since I had been to sea except as a passenger. I wanted to take no chance of failing in some foreign country. To avoid this, I made passage to New York, a one week Test Trip, not of the boat, but me. I made it a rule the first night to turn in for sleep midnight until five, leaving as much sail on as I thought safe with the helm lashed. She averaged half the speed of that when tended. When I awoke from that first sleep I knew I could make this voyage with Sturdy II.

All the leading papers in New York wanted articles on the coming voyage, their reporters interviewing me again and again, asking why and for what I was going on this trip! The main object was easily explained, but Sturdy and I had a long way to go before we could be understood. The New York Times gave a long explanation in an editorial, "Around the World Alone," and they said they might understand why, except this wasn't the time for patriotic citizens to be indulging themselves and their savings, not to mention affecting foreign exchange. They also said I was going to write a Book for Boys, and this at least was true. When explaining my book to educators, I put it in nautical words—that what I wanted was to make a book out of all the scrap of this modern world, and take it personally down the canal whilst all the people on the bank stamp and whistle, don'tcha see, right out into the bay, don'tcha see, there to sink her in style, right on the reef, just so, just so, leavin' her boiler and spar above water for the children to wonder at. Yes, I'd build that boat just to sink 'er, yes. And sink her where she couldn't be neither avoided nor salvaged—just there, to remember how far we came and where we had to stop it.

"Isn't that the very boat you've got here?" some smart young reporter in spats and derby asked, pointing at Sturdy.

"This boat here's no book," I said.

11 · An International Episode

When the buzzer continued for over a minute, he knew it was her. She was already out of the elevator by the time he unlatched the door, striding down the corridor in a shapeless green smock and sandals, a curious black ribbon about her neck. "Forgot my guitar," she said.

He took her out on the balcony to watch the lake while he got his clothes on. When he came back, he noticed that her scalp was dirty, her face puffy. The wind blew her smock up and she made no effort to smooth it. The pace of the thing was getting to Sam.

"It must get awfully boring just looking at that water," she mused. "If I had a nice apartment like this I'd want to look toward the city."

"So would Aaron, I suppose." Sam nodded gratuitously.

"Do I sound like him now? That figures."

"Things better now?"

"No, I always copy him unconsciously when I'm really screwed up."

"Odile, did you know Aaron long before you got married?"

"There was a water-ski instructor, Aaron, and you, in that order, if that's what you mean."

"Well, that's not very many," Sam said vaguely.

"Nothing bothers you, does it?" she asked.

Sam winced hopefully.

"The trouble is," she purred, "you were all about the same. Isn't that odd?"

At that calumny he had to smile.

She put her feet up on the balcony railing and her dress slipped back to mid-thigh. Sam looked out at the boring lake.

"You don't know what it's like to be married, do you?" she rasped again.

"Odile, dammit, why do you keep on with these questions? Don't you see I can't help you if you keep asking me things like that?"

"You think I need help?"

"I don't know, Odile, maybe I could, I don't know."

She stared at him, but she seemed diffuse as ever when Sam stared back.

"Look, Odile, a lot of women have this . . . problem, you know, I mean it isn't everything. Not uncommon."

"How would you know? How can you pretend to sympathize? Oh, Jesus, you're so . . . so . . . *derivative!*"

"Odile, I just can't stand it when you talk like that. It shows a lack of character."

"You have no right to be ignorant," she fairly screamed.

"Why haven't I as good a right as anyone else?"

"Because you have lived in the midst of all these things!"

"I'd like to believe that, Odile, I really would. But sad to say, it's pretty clear where my responsibility stops."

"That's easy enough to say."

"They didn't call me 'the floater' for nothing, Odile. It's just that nobody's going to pull me down."

"You realize, I'm sure, how middle class that sounds."

She had grown pale and a slight convulsion appeared in her cheeks.

"Odile, you're trying to provoke a kind of conflict that just doesn't come off any more. Honestly, you can no longer shock people, consequently you can't make them feel sorry for you either. All you can do is make them angry."

Sam did not feel guilty about transposing the little dialectic Agapecropolis had pulled on him. For the time being, he felt it

108

was the doctor's show. Who was *he* to comfort *her*? He could never imagine what women like Odile lived for anyway.

"The one thing I've learned, Odile, is the more you make your desires known, the less you'll realize them. I'm constantly amazed at how far a genuinely felt indifference will get you. These days people are attracted to what they can't understand. Ladies, particularly, must avoid credibility. Even when—" he said this softly—"they're as pretty as you."

"Did anyone ever tell you you'd make a wonderful father?"

"This is getting ridiculous, Odile, and I'm getting pissed. Why don't you play something for me?"

He got her guitar and instruction books from the closet where the Dott had hidden them. Then he brought weeping Odile out of the wind.

"Come on now, let's see what you can do."

He adjusted the stereo-lounger hassock so she could straddle it and sit straight up. Her smock stretched across her thighs like a fan. Sam slung the guitar about her shoulders and placed the fingering chart before her. She tuned the instrument methodically, squinting at the chart, flinching every now and then, not from the pitch so much as the pain in her cuticles. Sam himself sat in the lounger, surreptitiously snapping on the tape recorder as he leaned back.

She took several deep breaths, smoothed her hair back behind her large ears, and draining all expression from her face, her green eyes glazed over, began a faint banal tremolo, foot-tapping, ears cocked, forehead wrinkled, her wedding fingers bloodless from the bar chords, picking hand clawing stiffly:

> *Oh, bring me back the world*
> *Dooo unto others what they*
> *Want done unto them*
>
> *Dooo unto others what they want done,*
> *Dooo . . .*

109

Odile's fatigued fingers slipped from the strings and the chord dissolved, Sam commiserating.

"My hands just aren't strong enough," she whimpered. "I broke both my wrists once."

"How'd you do that, Odile?"

Sam leaned back in the chair and tried to free his mind of everything, as Agapecropolis had advised him.

"Diving in a too shallow pool."

"Diving, Odile, or falling?" He checked the volume of the recorder.

"Diving. Say, what is this?"

"Go on now, sing. Just sing. You don't have to accompany yourself, if that's the problem."

"What's the fun of that?"

"Just do what you can, Odile, that's what you've got to learn."

"I can never finish it, damn it. The chords get very complicated in the refrain. I've never finished it even once."

She violently undressed herself of the guitar and spun around on the stereo-stool so her back was to him. Her hair went diaphanous. Sam released the recliner mechanism and as the stool sank and slanted toward him, gravity drew her legs together, put her head in his lap. He massaged her temples.

"It's really the news that gets me, you know," she said absently.

"Hmmm?"

"He watches the news all the time. Every day he comes home and watches the goddamn news. Sam, are you listening?"

"Yes, Odile."

"Then say something."

"Odile, I . . ."

"But why does he watch the news like that? I mean he's not interested in politics or anything. Every night at six, ten and twelve, the same lousy news!"

"Odile, did you ever have it *good* from anybody?"

Her lids flicked shut. When she opened them she was all soft, nearly ethereal, past pathetic. Her guile has gone all tender. She is beginning to coalesce.

But Sam had quietly buried his opaque face in hers, fairly shouting, "You don't have to answer that! No, you needn't do anything I ask! For God's sake, Odile, don't let me push you around. Just be yourself."

"Sam, are you really fond of me? When you aren't with me, I hate you, you know."

"I try to be fond of everyone, Odile."

"But am I good for you?"

"For heaven's sake, Odile, people can't talk that way to each other any more. Why don't you try and cooperate? I am."

"Well, what do you want me to do?"

"I don't want anything special, Odile, that's just the point. For the moment, just talk. You know, make a story out of it."

The hungry lines reappear over the brief dignity as she begins nasally, her momentum buffered; Sam feels her jaws relax in his cupped hands. She chants in the sing-song she reserves for matters of vast import.

". . . Father was tall and well built with a handsome, clever face and bright blue eyes filled with fun and intelligence. . . ."

"That's fine, Odile, but let's try something else."

". . . A certain strangeness and impatience in my mother's manner struck me very forcibly. I observed her distrust of him with sad surprise. Her bitter and ironic smile, at all events, showed itself too plainly. She seemed to wander about without aim or object, always in a state of perturbation. Despair eventually overmastered her soul. For her, I perfected a meaningless little smile. . . ."

"Oh, let's get on with it, Odile."

"Frederick, my brother, enjoyed the deaf-mute next door who allowed him to take liberties beneath the privet bushes. Once he

111

made me hold it in my hand. . . . 'You'll be seeing a lot of these,' he said. He was wrong. . . ."

"That's right, Odile, get it out of your system. Tell it."

"The family, so admirably suited, it seemed, to deal with the contingencies of American life, was nevertheless uncommunicative in that very special sense which separates a community from a mere regrouping of convenience. . . ."

"Excellent. Where's Aaron fit in?"

"When she first saw him a pall crossed her heart. Despondent, those dreadful eyes, the hysterical laugh, ungiving to the point of hilarity, she sought in him what all her family's love had never been able to provide her—a vocation. . . ."

"That's a girl."

"Yet she sensed, especially on those heartbreakingly clear autumn mornings for which Gulley is noted, a peculiar ambiance in her attitude toward him. Was this a maternalism so refined—as befitting those girls who are perhaps the last gentlemen of our culture—that it allowed her to ignore those problems of sexuality which she had postponed for so long? Or was this a quite permissible vagueness which corresponded to a genuine inner need, a quest for originality, conviction. . . ."

"Oh, come on. For chrissake."

"His father then was a pharmacist in Brooklyn or perhaps a pharmacologist. They lived over the drugstore in a thin, dark apartment and his mother tearfully ran olive hands through her blond hair when her son presented her with a cheer belying their tradition. . . ."

"Remarkable."

"And when she was surely pregnant, the rabbit test in her purse, both sets of parents agreed to an abortion. . . ."

"Slow down, now. Think."

"Their relationship thus given a new edge by their progenitors' ill-fitting modernity, they were resolved to be married, which in fact took place on a hillside in Rhode Island, a nondenominational ceremony with a prolegomena of Buber and Kierkegaard, and six months following, Stieglitz showed her sleek, bruised head, courtesy of Mt. Sinai. . . . My father, reduced to his natural sympathies, encouraged Aaron to change his family name in the interests of the children, but he could manage only to reverse it. . . .'"

"Hmm. I think that should do it."

"And she would often say to the girls who occasionally come to share her homemade bread in the late mornings after the children had been sent to school that she had had to 'use all her wits to hide all her wits. . . .' "

"OK, Odile, done. Done. Good job. Fine. That was *very* good, I think. Now promise me that we shall never have a little scene like this again."

"All right, Sam. Which approach did you like best?"

"They were all rather the same. Isn't that odd?"

"Oh, you're just trying to get back at me."

"On the contrary; you must realize that your quite banal sufferings as expressed through your case history have analogues throughout human experience. Moreover, your references to your 'past' have nothing to do with your 'problems,' which are functions of the present. And to talk about it in the way you invariably must, to make a story out of it, is simply to take advantage of other people."

"Yes. *And?*" She was nearly tearful.

"And that if I am to help you, we must agree never to speak in this manner again."

"Yes. God, yes!"

"All right then. Go to the bedroom, I'll be right with you." Sam turned up the recorder to full volume, angling the chair toward the bedroom door. Odile got up from the chair wearily and did as she was told.

When Sam emerged naked from the bathroom, he found her

lying on the bed, smoking, staring up at the ceiling.

"Sam, will you undress me?"

"No, no. Just lift your dress up."

"Sam!"

"Do as I say. What have you got to lose?"

She said nothing, but did squint as he strung her gimbals with a single flick.

Ah. First they were chaoses; then they were carcasses. Their eyes a single violet transplant between them. Sam's pillows were covered with cigarette ashes. She turned on her side and traced an O in the sozzle.

"Well?" he asked, brushing the spume into his hand.

"Better," she said. "You're really incredibly strong, you know."

"Better? Jesus, Odile, let's just say it was different."

"Oh, Sam—" she bounced up, for some reason cupping her breasts in her hands, not one line in that pleasant face—"oh, Sam, I love you."

Sam returned to the bathroom with the ashes, where he pounded dramatically behind the closed door.

"God, Odile," he whined feverishly, "when are you going to learn? Oh, you're going to be so ashamed for that."

He drove her home at dusk. They stood for some time at the gates of Peacock Prairie, a hard wind blowing spores of the last climax community in America about them.

After twenty-four hours of real hard going in the heavy rain, squalls close-reefed us before we got east of Nantucket point. But in spite of the fact I had three men's work, navigator, sailor, and cook, I did much especial thinking, comparing experience to mankind's great need of a practical non-secret international brotherhood to take the place of the ancient racket of groups getting control and dominating the whole. Nature was non-secret but still not with us, but Sturdy and I were un- afraid because out there we were the natural thing. I talked to Sturdy slow and easy through these first storms, coaxing her through the worst of the swells, and I imagined there being rays projecting from my words, going out to my brothers in America. But I thought, what if my brothers aren't in America, and I asked Sturdy about this. Then the rays don't hit anything, she said.

12 · An Admixture

Impacted against his brain as the bloated tongue of a starving calf, marinated with moulted messic forps, Sam's sinuses extruded a steady viscous stream into his lungs. He rolled in the bed like a gaffed kingfish when the buzzer did.

Dean the incredulous doorman spoke hesitantly over the intercom: "I'm sorry to get you up on your day off, Mr. Hooper."

"You didn't get me up, Dean baby, I've been up for *hours*."

"There's a man here, a gentleman to see you, Mr. Hooper, says he knows you. Name of Grassgreen?"

"A *man?*" Sam sniffed.

"That's right, and he's got cameras slung on him like a bulldog got hickeys. You wanna good camera, Mr. Hooper?"

"No thanks, Dean, he's not selling. Send him up."

Sam opened the door, undid the safety chain, put coffee on, took four antihistamine, and slipped Mother's knife into his bathrobe pocket. Then he went to lie as innocently, vulnerably, as possible in the stereo-lounger. He heard the elevator cough open with a glissando of a rewired "Some Enchanted Evening," and Aaron knocked shortly thereafter.

"Come in," said Sam, clearing his throat.

"Morning, Mr. Hooper," he began cheerfully.

Sam's fist balled in his pocket as he regarded the artist quizzically. "Morning, Mr. Grassgreen. Out taking pictures, I see." Sam's voice was as low as he liked it, but still sticky. "Like some coffee?"

"Kay. Sure."

Sam turned his back deliberately upon the artist, giving his adversary first shot, as his father had taught him. The late Hooper Sr. had been undefeated.

"My wife said you might, could, help me out." Sam wheeled about, ready as ever. But his voice was miles off.

"Yeah, she said if you weren't too tired or something you might be able to help me, since you kinda like my work, you know?"

Sam heard himself whimper something like "What is it she thinks I can do for you, Mr. Grassgreen?" He hands him a cup sharply. Aaron's bright eyes are down.

"Well, you're a pretty big guy, right?"

Sam shrugged.

"Good shape?"

"Fair to middling."

"Well, I gotta up my production, see? Odile thinks so too. You know a guy can get so involved in his work, so full of himself, that he ends up never finishing it the best he can. If a line ain't a measure, it's nothing, right? When you start thinking of something very special, in a way, you don't even have to finish it, you know?"

"I guess so, Aaron. I have to do something every day, though, just to get through it. Even Sundays. So I wouldn't know."

"Izat right? Well, I oughta try that too. I gotta step up my production, like I say, I gotta get a lotta stuff ready. Or I'm never going to make it."

Those black eyes which Odile had found intolerable were pupilless now.

"Look, Aaron, what can I do? I don't even have twenty-twenty."

Sam tipped his glasses toward him. The artist's figure slammed forward, then blurred to a fine haze along his sightline.

"And anyway, my line of work's got nothing to do with yours."

"All I know, Hooper, is Odile said that if I wasn't 'developing

117

at my own pace,' that's how she put it, that I might do better at yours. Maybe you know what she's getting at?"

"I can't imagine what your wife had in mind, Aaron, I—"

"Well, you're a big fellah, right?"

"I believe we've already ascertained my size and relative prowess."

"So the only way I can step up production is to work faster, and lugging all this crappy equipment around just beats my ass. I need somebody to carry this stuff and keep me on schedule."

"You want me to be your bearer?" Sam coughed.

"Just helper, Hooper. Helpmate, you know; Odile thought of it."

They emerged from the pedestrian tunnel and headed north along the lake, Sam balancing the banquet camera and the tripod on his shoulders, the other equipment in a mountain pack and a bandolier, stepping cautiously around the alewives washed up in the night. The bulldozer crews had taken the weekend off, and the wind was blowing in. High waves spew white against the Pumping Station, but for Aaron and Sam, protected by the serpentine breakwater of the yacht basin, the lake merely lapped nervously at their side. The yachts were parked in their slips, a party on each, the basin discolored with remnants of brunches. An older couple were dancing on the flying bridge of one of the boats. Sam had heard that Sam Hooper[2] kept a cruiser here he never used.

Aaron led him along the edge of the edge of the promontory. The swells and stench increased. The asphalt ended and they began to clamber over the enormous granite cubes of the breakwater. At the end of the corduroy rocks, he could make out a group of boys swimming nude in the protected waters.

"We can start with that," Aaron commanded as they arrived, and Sam wedged the tripod in among the stones, holding the camera against his chest as Aaron tightened the stanchions.

Sam had always been surprised at the bodily meagerness noticeable in the progeny of lastmen, etc. This had been first brought home to him when as a thirteen-year-old member of a timid private recreation department, they had run roughshod over a football team of color from the inner city. He recalled stepping on the face of one stocky, heavily bearded youth twice his size, and the childish scream of terror he emitted. He realized that no one got his head stepped on in an open field unless it was someone who was destined to do so. He was later and likewise amazed to find in the enlisted men's barracks such degree of pointless ugliness and weakness, and to discover that the poor were neither tough nor revolutionary, that listlessness and feigned ignorance were their best defense, and that he harbored more potential outrage within his laconic protectorate than any army of lastmen. For violence, as Sam's kind find out early, is simply failed aggression.

The lads varied in their monstrousness. The most reasonable facsimile among them, a tall angular Pole, perhaps, his skin already shot through with varicose lesions, stood sullenly waist-deep in the lake, his parts floating and bobbing before him like a meal of leftovers on Steuben glass. A black boy, well built in the shoulders, sporting a glutinous maximus twice the size his frame could bear, flung himself stomach first upon the six-inch waves. A wiry spic picked absently at rather distinguished-looking sores, a large tortoiseshell comb in his hair. Another kid of indeterminate origin sported pubic hair which completely submerged his genitals and rose in an unbroken fountain up his stomach to form a handlebar mustache on his breastbone.

"There's a collection for you," said Sam under his breath.

"They gotta *do* something," Aaron countered aimlessly.

Sam advanced upon the suspicious bathers.

"Hi, fellas."

"Hi." The spic spoke warily for the group.

"Look, we'd like to take some pictures but we don't want to

119

bother you. So just keep doing what you want to do, OK?"

The foursome looked at each other but said nothing.

Sam returned and looked over Aaron's shoulder. He had the Negro upside down in the lens, but the boy just kept pushing his stomach into an occasional wavelet and biting his lips.

The others stood as before, staring down at themselves or looking nowhere in particular. The spic resumed his scratching hesitantly. The Pole sloshed water against his hips, softly cursing something he had stepped on.

Sam was getting irritated and went down to the edge of the water again. The Negro turned swiftly, his buttocks roiling the water.

"What you want now, Mose?"

"Well, look, couldn't you guys swim or something? We're trying to get some shots."

Sam could hear Aaron tramping the stone impatiently behind him.

"Canna swim, Mose."

Sam was incredulous.

"You mean none of you can swim?"

The Negro laughed, protruded his stomach before him, and slapped it harshly. The others held their noses and submerged themselves dramatically, their short breath bubbling up crystalline to Sam.

"Hey now," Sam implored. "Can't you just dive off a rock or something?"

The Negro wrapped his arms about himself. "How much, Mose?"

"How much? Christ! Can't you just have some fun and dive a little?"

The spic buried his head in the water and exposed his cumbersome scrotum.

Sam returned to Aaron. "The son of a bitch wants money," he said under his breath.

120

"So, you got any?"

"Christ," Sam yelled, "you mean you'd actually pay them? What about all this 'integrity of the found object' crap? The thing-in-itself! What in hell are you talking about?"

Aaron shrugged wistfully and fiddled unconvincingly with the lens. Sam went back to the shore. The spic had grinned and stretched.

"OK, here's a dollar," Sam said. "Now dive."

The spic took the bill back to his pile of clothes, then climbed uncertainly on the top of the highest rock, where shivering and holding his nose, he jumped feebly into the lake, his legs coupled beneath him like a bazooked vulture.

"Get it?" Sam yelled up to Aaron.

"Get what?" said Aaron. "He went down like a goddamn stone. He's gotta dive, jump, leap in the air. This about *divers!*"

Sam turned away in a fit.

"All right, goddamn it. I'll show all of you something, dammit."

He walked directly into the water in his shoes and socks and grabbing the spic in a hammerlock, dragged him back out of the water, careful not to close off his throat, the lad's heels and buttocks banging on the striped stones. When he got him up to the top of the rock, Sam lifted the kid above his head and as he swung him, whispered in his ear, "Hold your breath now, baby," and then flung him far out into the lake. The boy contracted into a frenzied ball, but at the last moment he desperately arched himself flat and slid headfirst into a wave.

You must do to them what they cannot admit they want, Agapecropolis had said. *People all over the world are the same,* Fuess had set out to prove, *but you have to get stern with the public,* he found out soon enough.

"Great!" Aaron called down.

The spic surfaced, sputtering.

"Got t' water up my nozzles," he blurted, and then in shallow water he urinated convulsively, foam encircling his knees. The other boys were now making panickily for the shore, slipping on the smooth stones, but Sam reached the Negro as he stumbled and, mounting the rock once more, spun him out to deeper water. He also caught and flung the darker of the other two, who simply gave up giggling, but nevertheless inscribed the weekend air with unique gyrations.

Aaron danced clumsily behind the camera. Finally only the Pole remained, and he, after combing his hair, climbed on his own initiative up to Sam.

"You throw me too, mister?" he asked timidly. Sam was trembling.

"That's all the art for today, kid," and he climbed wearily down to Aaron.

Aaron could not contain himself on the way back up the promontory. He bounced ahead of his bearer on the cubes of granite, clasping Sam's free hand and slapping him on the stomach between the equipment. Sam's sinuses flooded his chest with the secondary stench of rotting fish.

"I don't know how much longer I can take this, Aaron," he said.

"Odile said you'd probably get tired," Aaron whined enthusiastically. "But you're goin' great. The divers was her idea too." He blushed.

The promontory did what promontories do when they join the land, and they headed for the tunnel across the park. Suddenly Aaron stopped short.

"Holy Moses, Sam, look at that."

Sam squinted through the haze. The park had opened up into a vista populated with basking couples and enormous elms. Beyond the last line of trees heat ribbons rose from the expressway; the skyscrapers seemed to be made of gelatin.

"A little eighteenth-century, don't you think?"

"Not the *whole* thing, man. Look, you gotta learn this. What's the most impressive thing out there? Now look careful."

Sam looked again, focusing each eye on each couple, but could still find nothing exceptional within the landscape's oblong scene.

"Sorry, Aaron, I guess I just don't have it."

"Look," Aaron said, "just to the right of the flagpole—the man lying down."

Sam pushed his glasses against the bridge of his nose until it stung. Finally he made out the dark man, napping on his back, his face covered with newspapers.

"So what, can't even see his face," said Sam.

"Oh, man," Aaron whined. "Look at his feet. Look at *it*," he said.

Sam focused again. The dark man's feet were large and bare, but . . .

"Come on," said Aaron huskily and, yanking the telephoto from Sam's pack, started to run across the sward. Sam put the rest of the equipment down and hurried after him with an easy stride.

Aaron dove prone in the grass some twenty yards from the figure, cursing while adjusting the heavy telephoto. Sam looked through the binoculars. The man was apparently listening to a radio, for his feet were methodically tapping the air, causing him to scrunch his toes periodically and thus keeping time, twitch out of range.

"No good," whispered Aaron. "You know what you got to do. Go ahead, do your stuff."

Sam didn't move, eying his interlocutor quizzically.

"You know," Aaron whined. "Hold 'm still. Do what you have to do. Just don't block the foot."

Sam was suddenly overcome by a strange and necessitous excitement. Recalling the nauseous kickoffs of his youth, he loped in a low crouch toward the man, weight initially balanced equally on the balls of his feet, but accomplishing the last few yards on his stomach. Upon drawing near the prostrate form, he gathered himself for one final surgical effort, then draped his weight painlessly about our subject. The newspapers flew up and the dark man let out an unforgettable scream; Sam pinned his shoulders down quickly and lay across his torso.

"Don't move a muscle," he whispered in his ear. "Just for a sec, then I'll let you go."

Our subject's breath smelled of rum as he pressed a whiskered gray mouth against Sam's chest and groaned. Tears welled up in his bloodshot eyes. Then he went rigid.

"OK, gottit, OK," the distant cry came.

Sam jumped up and hauled the man to his feet by his insignificant lapels. But his legs immediately buckled and he went to his knees, gasping long and hard. Sam began to brush the grass clippings from the dark man's hair, but soon Aaron had taken him firmly by the arm and led him back to the equipment. The man toppled over onto his face, his immortal feet splayed in the grass.

"That'll complete it, you'll see," said Aaron. "Just like an alligator, that foot was. An alligator jumping for a butterfly."

Back on the sand, the stench of the alewives more formidable than ever, Aaron was still ebullient.

"It'd be nice, you know, if we could work together more."

"I suppose we could, Aaron, but I'd have to go into training."

"Naw, too bad, maybe once in a while, but—"

Sam was slightly hurt by this.

"Well why not? I mean you seem to make use of me well enough, and God knows what *I'm* getting out of it."

"Aw Sam." Aaron said, showing uncharacteristic compassion, "It's just your *connections*, you know what I mean."

"What the hell are you talking about?"

"It's well known," Aaron said firmly, "that MC has a vital

interest, you know, in Black Art."

Sam was thoroughly confused. First Fuess, then Agapecropolis, now even Aaron had alluded to this . . . Black Art?

"I just don't know what you're getting at."

"Aw, let's forget it. I know you're not free to talk." Sam was too tired to pursue it any longer.

He put Aaron and the equipment in a cab and then went home to sleep through the remaining day and evening.

After a week or so I got tired of talking to Sturdy and I got out the phonograph and had an arty duet with John McCormack, there being no-one within hearing distance to stop me, and the captain liked my part well as he sat at the wheel. Then I shaved and washed the salt out of my eyes. There was no one to see me, but it freshens you and makes the world look brighter. On trips to foreign lands before I used a self-taught system of language in each country visited. I never got to speak the language, but could get something to eat and give the natives many a laugh, and this was accomplishing something, for anyone can make them cry. And between sings I practiced my languages finding this kept me from fear better than talking to Sturdy and was almost as good as singing. But you got to be in the mood to sing and then you got to have a companyment and use up valuable lectricity, it can get to be a kind of drug. Alone at sea I'd rather have one word of spanish for spar or spanker in my throat than a whole rag band balling on the poop. . . .

13 · *Deflections*

The Dott was giving Stargyle a bath when Sam got up. They too were subject to Mother's serenade. Stargyle, sporting mutton-chops of soapsuds, searched the ceiling for the anonymous voice. "Hi-fi?" he asked Sam hesitantly. The Dott just smiled to herself and scrubbed his purple back. Everything still smelled to Sam of fish.

Anticipating Agapecropolis' free large lunch, Sam skipped breakfast, and, for the first time he could recall, beat Wittgenstein to the office. The lake was pearl at the shore, mauve at the horizon and a little turbulent beneath the haze. The dictaphone scanner light fluttered from his short breath in the early morning.

THE CHRISTMAS MEMO: II

(*The aesthetics of economics, the economics of aesthetics*)
RE: Proposals for Maximization of Human Fulfillment Program
FROM: Hooper (Front)
ATT: Wittgenstein (Rail)
BLIND COPY—Agapecropolis (Infracon)   No. 18973.043

Given the sullenness and withdrawal symptoms now prevalent in the artistic community, it is no longer sufficient for us merely to employ humanistic rhetoric, but rather take concrete action to improve our image. For our very efficiency, it seems, is treated as a cause for alarm in more desperate quarters.

As we all know, art is a proper surrogate for channelling revolutionary impulses. And our task, traditionally, has been to organize the material environment in such a way that "individualistic" impulses might be expressed with a minimum of antisociality, according to the hypothesis by which we ourselves have prospered; i.e., gross private acquisition (self-expression), pursued independently, results in net public profit (culture).

We should note, therefore, that the artist's prerogatives, though he calls them forth in the name of Beauty, do not differ in the end from our own, and while their kind are historically inclined to be disestablish-mentarian, we increasingly monitor them in our beneficence. Therefore, I should like to make a three-pronged proposal:

I. To bridge the gap between current intellectual dissent and positive objective production, I propose the creation of a fellow-ship program the purpose of which would be to enable promising young artists to produce works of art to become the sole property of MC, replacing the neo-Creamer artifacts now in such pro-fusion. We would offer to buy all such works produced during the term of the grant at par value, thus stabilizing the potential market and ascertaining a fixed bargaining level. Sufficient grants over a period of time would allow us prime influence within the art commodity index and any related debenture offerings.

II. To offset the impression we are merely calculating, to legitimize our operation, as it were, I suggest that a humanistic rebate, some nominal amount, be made to all our clients. This check would be presented with a personalized note to the effect that we have discovered a computer error in our accounting pro-cedure and that all clients are due this amount. This would not only create the impression that *we too* are human, but also that we are sufficiently efficient to ultimately control our machinery in the best interests of the consumer. While this would likely in-volve an expenditure of several millions in this fiscal year, it could be written off as advertising (retroactive tax loss), for this is truly a people-to-people venture of explicit diffusion and optimum impact.

III. As a morale booster to younger members of the firm, and to forge a stronger bond with the artistic community, I suggest the formulation of a "Challenging Horizons for Creative Man-

127

agers" program. For truly, professional management has developed into an especial art. A first step in this direction might be a Nobel Prize for creative management! I hope this idea captures your imagination as it does mine. This might best be implemented by increasing our Swedish holdings as preliminary strategy prior to direct intercession with the king.

Sam played the dictation back, surprised as always by his hard-won prolixity, but finally he shrugged a guffaw away and pressed the distribution button, reserving a photocopy for Aaron.

At noon on the dot Sam knocked on Agapecropolis' door. The doctor was sloped down behind his desk, a pyramid with an amber eye at its apex before the bright window, reading from a large book, A *Million Random Digits with One Hundred Thousand Normal Deviates*. The opaline blue food cart had arrived, burdened with a jeroboam of 1934 Mouton-Rothschild, a bouquet of Caribbean freesia, decrusted finger sandwiches of vegetarian pâté, and individual bowls of fondue. Sam sat down before he was asked to.

"How are you doing today?" the doctor asked.

"Fine, I guess."

"Did you find out anything?"

"Oh, just the old story. Here's the tape. It's all there. For what it's worth."

"Like what though?"

"Just the same old stuff, I tell you. Gulley girl, usual upbringing, Mother mean, Daddy nice and weak, Brother grabby, delegate from the Netherlands to model U.N. a decade ago, married the poor if talented son of a Brooklyn pharmacist—or was it pharmacologist?—after getting you-know-what before, two kids, one of them pretty nice-looking, married for art's sake, which she regrets, I'm sorry to say, wants to be more creative herself though, feels her vagueness may be permissible if it corresponds to a genuine inner need, husband watches the news too much, and she hasn't ever, you know . . . finished."

"On that last point . . ."

"Quite sure, Doctor."

"So what about the dream?"

"She doesn't seem to dream much; that's the problem, maybe?"

"No, *your* dream."

"I didn't have no dream, Dokker."

"The one you had last night. Come on!"

"I tell you I didn't have one."

"I can see it in your face, Samuel."

"Then my face is the liar."

"Oh come on now, Sam kiddo. Before the wine gets to you and you have to make one up."

Sam swabbed the last of the fondue from his bowl.

"Oh, for Christ's sake," he sighed, "all right. How's this: I'm on this elephant, see, a kind of mahout . . . I know that because I've got on this sort of breechclout."

"Don't you ever use a synonym with me, Sammy boy."

"And well anyway, I want the elephant to go faster, but he won't. He just keeps walking along very slowly, swinging his trunk back and forth, sucking up corns or something."

"Color of gold?"

"Yeah, and I kicked him and cracked him a good one behind the ears, but he never went any faster. Just kept swinging his trunk back and forth picking up those corns . . ."

Agapecropolis was regarding him very tolerantly.

"Well," he said shyly, "I guess I *am* a little elephantine."

"What makes you think it was you?" Sam shot back. "He was a lot bigger than you."

At this, Agapecropolis reddened as though with apoplexy, an

incipient smirk cut off by half an eclair. His mouth locked open for air, stalactites of custard dropping from the roof of his mouth. His eyes white, wine spurting from his nostrils, he hacked timorously into his napkin, the laugh uncharacteristically softened by the occlusion.

Sam began to gag in spite of himself but he was determined to hold out lest the consultant accuse him of missing a cue. Still, this particular instigation seemed a little rococo to Sam; the doctor continued to gag into his napkin, his feet pounding the carpet, his convulsive eyes locked wide in a perfect mime of fear, until *A Million Random Digits* slipped from his lap to the floor. Sam saw this as particularly significant, but out of some perverse stubbornness let the book lie. Either the doctor was trying to offend him, provoke him into some gratuitous insult, or he wanted to see if he could trick Sam into coming to his aid, clap him on the back, admit that he had indeed envisioned the doctor as an elephant. At all events, the strategy was working, for Sam was becoming rapidly as sick as the doctor. And finally, furious with himself for not being able to fathom such obvious intentions, Sam was forced to retire to the restroom, where, in the unattended silence of the beige-tiled chamber, he fought successfully to keep his sweet lunch.

Regaining control, he saw no reason to continue the dialogue on the doctor's terms, and as the market had closed, upon return to his desk, he went home early. The other eleven gazed at him fretfully as he packed and bolted.

The Dott and Stargyle had left early as well, but leaving a note.

DEAR MR. HOOPER,

Things I put away. 1 hat, 2 brushes, 1 shoe polish, 3 cuff linx, shaving things, money—$3.16, 1 pair shades, 7 tea shirts, 8 pair schocks, 4 shorts, 1 book. *Things I took home.* I took home a glass of whiskey to make me some medicine. I took home two old magazines—The Meliorist—about the worker's way to win. I also took some candy.

Oh yes, I also took some pensils so I could do hard reading.

Dott

Sam drew a bath and took some cigars and the latest issue of *The Meliorist* in with him. The latter was devoted entirely to recent unsettling events in the nation's capital.

THE AMAZING FAILURE OF PARLIAMENTARISM

a smashing and indisputable document

CAUSE: Moral wealth worn out:

Never before have our managers been so unesteemed. The most serious questions of national and moral gravity are being faced with the most challenging insensibility. Many sinecurists are participating in partial debauchery, the vilest of factional motives, venal and bribed. Historical and religious inexactness have come into circulation, the people are under a primitive ideological confusion, even the most special have been supplanted.

EFFECT: Panorama of Mobocracy

When a nation faces its citizens with indifference it should not be surprised when they dream of transgressions. Not following their usual activity they become obstacles. Youth, for example, has been derailed. The genuity of their plans defeated by their own propulsion. Educationing has lost its bases. 40 millions of school books have been pulped as inappropriate. Puberal liveliness has been exploited, and their theories get repulsive in action. They changed the capital into a robbery town, carnaging it. They broke windows, used ironed things, and ignored the district attourneys. Even the football ground was subject to the people's madness. The FACTS shows Defamations up 36%; Deceits up 19%; False accusations up 24%; Insults, Threats and

131

Resistances, up 56%; Ravishment up 46%, Other Defalcations up 24%.

CURE: A new big ideal

It would be nice to see their purposes changed to reality and cover their creative ideas with success. We could start with educational excursions to historial places with speeches by expert scientists to make American reality believable. And alot of things could be managed in the area of entertainment as well. If this was done obligately from childhood, lavishness and scandel could not get started and partial passions would be left aside. For even more than an ascending economy, or the sanitation of state functions, the biggest problem now is one of onomatology.

Yours for action, and NOW
Edgar Fuess, Capt.

Sam noted that the good captain was becoming quite obtrusive. Could this be the same man who wrote *Keys to Mysteries?* As he settled back into the soapy water he wondered what the Dott would make of all this. Then he was asleep, resolving to dream the captain at his best.

October 13th, 1928; at dusk anchored Tangiers, Morrocco. 44 days, 9 hours and 45 minutes from New York, average of 77 knots per day. The native port and police officers came aboard and arranged for to show me the city in the morning. All Nature was going to rest. The Moorish homes on the hill had lit their lights. I, together with Sturdy went to rest. God spare us from misleaders, misnomers, misrepresentation and misunderstanding.

At dusk, even at bath, the familiar knot appeared in his chest and Sam went to the closet for the basketball. The pedestrian tunnel was lined with frost, falltime whisking like acid across the prairies. The court was deserted in the violet sky; in the peripheries of his gone sight splotched the blood-red of the barberry, the peach of the peony root. The lake was all of bronze, the last of the sun searing a fiery alley upon him. The buttock-shaped clouds sent reversed mates to the still flat lake.

His pores open, relaxed in the cool breezes, Sam pumped several long shots wishfully at the basket, but the wind defied him, the ball knuckling in the air as if it were oblate.

But then he stepped to the line and underhandedly deposited one hundred and forty-two consecutive freethrows, setting a park record, though he did not know it.

14 · Dreamingup

Sam Hooper[2] hove into view on the tube at 21:30 hours a week later. Sam[1] finetuned the stereo-lounger and finished the bottle. Hooper[2] was at his charming best, professing ignorance, grinning knowingly, playfully punching his guests across the banquette. His *Continuing Images of Greatness* format had been much imitated but never duplicated, and his only competition in prime time remained reruns of his earlier shows. It was as if the only thing left for him to conquer was the artifactuality of his own past, and that was the secret of his appeal, no doubt. With a ratio of his two live appearances a day to one taped rerun, he was outdistancing his initial self with increasing velocity. And in thus preempting prime time, he was building such a formidable backlog of the present that the question of his death had become as irrelevant as wherever he came from. He had cast the accumulated past into the present so fast that the discrete moments did not even have the opportunity to perish in time. (Yet, in the arched eyebrow of his all-night stoicism, the fact that he exists *only* when he is seen allows us to conjure up for him the possibility of a secret life. The transistor of all stories save his own, maintained by vast self-control, not to mention expense, he comes to us like heroes used to, not impressive for the public acts which gain them posterity, but for arousing in us democratic access to the myth, to wonder if, off the screen, *how much he is like ourselves*—Did Charlemagne masturbate before a battle? What's *your* story, fella?—and such a man, in this way, becomes indispensable.)

On this redundant evening a movie actress was explaining a

senator who was sponsoring anti-gun legislation, a night-club comic was relating his early summer-stock experiences to a well-known publisher, a Lebanese field-goal specialist, and a pessimistic psychic. The actress was saying how she was giving up the theater to set a record for transoceanic-flight-for-women-in-a-single-engine plane.

"Well, what *is* the record for Leningrad–St. Louis?" Sam Hooper[2] inquired.

"For men it's thirty-eight hours," she beamed, "but there is no women's record." She was very lovely. The senator cupped an ear to hear.

"You mean to say even if you don't break the men's record," Hoops[2] interpolated, "you automatically set a women's record?"

"That's correct," she said, crossing her legs.

"That's just great," Sam[2] said.

"I can tell you, you'll make it," the now happy psychic said.

After a commercial, she continued. "See, day after day, I went back to my room to memorize my scripts, but every time I went out on the street I'd see all that stuff wasn't really involved with the sources of life, as it were, that in this society people don't really need art any more, because they've got everything in life, you see. They're *living* creatively. Oh, just walk out on the street any night and look at them. Some people with the straightest clothes imaginable, and people in all different sorts of costumes, people who have eaten the finest food in the world, people who have eaten garbage, thought great thoughts, thought nothing, high and low on every kind of stuff, able to buy whatever they need for the moment, so how can you justify just going back to your room to memorize? Nobody needs that any more. They get their kicks otherwise. So my husband, he's my agent too, he said to me, 'Why don't you take up flying?' "

Shortly after ten, the phone rang twice and Sam dropped it twice before Odile's voice came through hesitantly. "Sam, are you alone?"

"Well, sure."

"I've got to have a drink. Aaron's just being impossible. Can you meet me at the In?"

"What's wrong? Specifically?"

"I don't know, I'm just upset. Just keep me company, OK? No more stories, I promise."

"All right, Odile. I'll see you in about half an hour. I've got to finish something."

As Sam entered Olde Towne, the actress appeared to have something. Women brushed him as he walked, couples of every conceivable intent groped each other randomly in the halos of street lights, suburban matrons minced among the young toughs smiling, searching out the produce. A Clone girl, not more than sixteen, in slacks, a man's shirt open to the waist and a gold bell about her neck, stopped directly in front of him. She looked him over with complete detachment, smiling and brushing her hair back. Something Odile had once said to him came back now. "I don't want to tell my Stieglitz not to screw," she said laconically. "Then I would be a seductive mother. I just want her to choose good men." The girl continued to stare at him. Sam let her watch as a singular thought crossed his mind—hide Odile in the bathroom and let *her* watch, him and this Clone. It would serve her right. . . . And then it occurred to Sam that this was precisely the secret of his appeal; that whenever he indulged, it was as if he were performing for some third party, that this curious rite was enacted for *their* benefit (or perhaps discomfort) and that for all comers he performed with the zeal of a man who was keeping a promise at all costs. The nature and beneficiary of this promise was hardly clear, but most of Sam's obsessions were equally inexplicable. That he felt their presence was sufficient. The only thing that concerned him was whether this was private or shared information. How, i.e., would Odile react? The substitution would be easy enough; the problem was whether she would comprehend her new position on the triangle and could be equal to its honor—what more can a lover do than place his love at the Archimedean point of his own potency?

Sam had thrown back his head and laughed so outrageously that the Clone girl started. No, he didn't have the guts to bring it off. He began to rationalize; the Clones were notorious for their diseases, they were frequently under age, and some were known to be police stakeouts. But the truth was, he just didn't have the guts to face Odile with that. Imagine the guile of a man who would straddle his woman, and upon hearing the inevitable and redundant "Why this, why me?" reply in the profound shorthand which centuries of artifice have hopelessly disguised: "Because I've promised somebody something and they're watching."

So Sam passed on to Odile with the sad realization that he would know neither lust nor manners in his lifetime.

The In was packed and Odile was in back with the menfolks. "I didn't think you'd come."

Sam was aware of the long tables of expertly coiffed men listening.

"Odile," he began softly, after ordering drinks in sign language from the sweatshirted bartender, "did it ever occur to you that I've got hangups too? I mean, did you ever think that *you* could do anything for me?"

"Of course not," she said in a rather hectoring tone. "I wouldn't chase you like a dog unless I thought you were strong enough to put up with it. You don't think I want to marry you or anything, do you?"

"No, I didn't think so."

"Look," she said. "Even if the children didn't exist, I probably still wouldn't leave Aaron. At least not for someone like you. You'd make me pay the rest of my life for being the weak one. Aaron still stands for all the reasons I married him for. The

137

reasons just aren't mine anymore. *He'd* have to leave *me*, then it might be OK. I love your big dick because it's a luxury and my punishment for having thought everything out in a half-assed way, but don't think I'm after you."

She went on talking here but Sam was hypnotized by the gum she twaddled betwixt her archaic smile. She had on false eyelashes and a portable beauty spot, wearing that worried more than open "don't-fall-in-love-with-me-for-your-own-good" look which he detested more than anything in this world: yet he was fascinated by her matter-of-factness; her sham, his fetter. "Why the gum?" he was going to ask but suddenly she broke into hearing again.

". . . Oh I know what you'd do to me all right. Every time I started to put myself together you'd do something to break me up again. You don't *want* me to develop, do you? Just like the other afternoon, letting me pick myself apart like that."

"Odile," he said quietly, "this doesn't sound like you at all."

She was winking very fast now, whipping her head back and forth.

"At least with Aaron I know where I am."

At this point, however, she for no apparent reason ceased agonizing, changing to a quiet and admirable defiance.

"My life's gone, you're my fun. OK?"

Sam wanted very much to ask her how she'd feel about being that Third Person, but she seemed to anticipate him and cut him off with a ludicrously inappropriate grin. "For God's sake, don't just sit there looking so responsible."

Then she leaned closer.

"Keep it in your pants, honey, this show is just starting."

But before he could answer she had put a finger to her lips and shushed him quiet.

There was a poetry reading every Friday midnight at the In. A long, circumspect man in a velour V-neck blouse mounted the small bandshell as the bartender slammed for quiet with a mug. The poet introduced himself affably as George Stablefeather. "I've heard of him," Odile whispered. "He's the guy who got the Government grant for an art workshop. Aaron says he's a real asshole."

George Stablefeather introduced his work by saying that in times such as these it was incumbent upon the poet to speak out—for between the mendacity of our public figures and the apathy of the middle classes, it was the obligation of artists everywhere to unite and provide civilized leadership. Then in a voice choked with breathy caesura, he read:

> the great whooping crane
> is rather extinct
>
> it's not shot at much in
> its flyways, it simply
>
> builds its nests (ovaform
> or curvetangular) in spots
>
> exposed to predators.
>
> for every chunklike crane
> brought down in flight then
> 2.8 lithe ones are punctured
> by weasels, owls, or adders
>
> not shot down commuting
> but eaten up at home
>
> bitten in the bowels, not head
> if not up in the air, then
>
> assuredly in bed.
>
> the world succeeds by such comfortable ratios
>
> nearly three times
> better are we
> than the weasel

the great whooping crane's
problem is in his knees
they are backwards, they
are for walking on water.

he does not know if they
are landing-gear or ailerons

he only knows that he must
put them in a nest at night.

3:1, the colon's a beautiful
shape. it reminds me of the

crane's clean eyes when he
perceives the balance of
natural forces.

cranes fly not with their wings
as much as against their gravity.

the great whooping crane
has had a long history. once
the Germans, they put several
millions of cranes away. (a

standard confusion between
nest & flyways) once

the Turks, they drove the thirsty
birds into deeper water once

the Mongols, they treated
several nations of crane like

geese (a Confucian perversion)
and once, my irretrievables,

once the Americans, once they
burned up the nests to get at

the Weasels. (it wasn't their
fault the cranes weren't flying that day.)

dismal equalities, divine ratios
are what preserve us. (the

Lisbon earthquake, for example,
was not as bad as no rubbers
in India now.) it could have

been worse. the Turks were better
than the Mongols, and the Americans

were better than the both of them put
together. if it weren't for the

Germans, though, we could all be in trouble

those who kill cranes in the
air *are in the minority.*

it is those with feathers
in their mouths who are guilty!

it's the nest-drubbers who will go to prison!
those snakes who try to fly.

The rule at the In was no more than two poems per poet, so George read an American Koan about "Alternate Layers of Slush and Grit" and then relinquished the platform.

"Well, what did you think?" Sam asked.
"Oh, I liked the last part." Odile smiled. "Real resonant."
Out of the corner of his bad eye Sam could see the poet making his way through the crowd toward them.
"Yeah, but what's it *about?*" Sam hissed. "Quick, he's coming."
"He means," Odile said thoughtfully, "that we're the most dangerous society in the world—" but as usual, Odile had no chance to finish. The poet stood before them smiling, a lock of wavy prematurely ashen hair on his high forehead.

"Excuse me, you're Mrs. Grassgreen, aren't you, Aaron's wife?"

Odile struggled to her feet like a man. Sam remained seated, noting the poet's heavy canvas shoes with their sawtooth sponge-rubber soles. Odile held her throat and introduced him as a Mr. Hooper, a friend.

"Not *the* Sam . . ." the startled poet began, but Sam had already shrugged him off.

"I'm glad you could come, in any case," George said. "I was afraid there wouldn't be much of a crowd. I wish Aaron could have made it."

"He doesn't like that verbal stuff too much, you know," Sam interjected.

"Oh, I see, and are you a visual artist yourself, Mr. . . . Hooper?"

"No, I'm Odile's psychiatrist."

"I see, a busman's holiday, then."

"Actually—" Sam began, but Odile had butted in.

"Sam's with Management Concern. He's very interested in Aaron's work. He's working with him on a project. He's helped us a lot."

"Very good," George said, "very good."

"We enjoyed the reading," Sam said inadvertently, "but we were wondering, Mr. Stablefeather, if that last part really meant that our society is the most dangerous in the world?"

"As a matter of fact—" the poet smiled—"I do happen to believe that we're a violent nation, but, of course, my poems are just about themselves, you see. I believe that poetry must relate finally only to itself, the dynamics of inner creation, and not to any protest, necessary as it may be. Hamlet is not a person, but a mouth. I am not Stablefeather, but a voice."

"Then that wasn't what you meant?"

"If it meant that to you, I'm flattered."

142

Sam signaled for another round of drinks.

"Well, I think you're right in a way."

"About violence, you mean?" George nodded quickly.

"Yes," said Sam, "If that's what—"

"We really are a terribly dangerous country, aren't we? I mean anyone who works for MC is aware of that, I should imagine."

"Yes indeed, Mr. Stablefeather. But we at MC believe that Management should stick to what it does best. We're not in the business of protest, necessary as it may be."

"Oh this is getting ridiculous," Odile interrupted, clacking her wedding band nervously against her glass. "For God's sake, let's not. . . ."

"Perhaps you misunderstand me," Sam continued evenly. "I know very well—better than most, perhaps—just how much other people's words affect one's life. That's why I don't take your poetry lightly, not at all, Mr. Stablefeather. But let's get one thing straight at least. Are you talking to those people you're reading to, or are you not?"

Sam gestured at the perverse bar. The frieze of bodies was instantly annealed. Liquids, gestures, propositions, discourse came to an unremarkable standstill.

"To be honest," George remarked thoughtfully, "they seem rather threatening."

"Ah, so that's the crux, is it? But, Mr. Stablefeather, don't you see—" Sam's head was spinning from drink—"it's *we* who threaten *them?* My tremorless demeanor, for example, unnerves them. As does, to a lesser extent, your agonized public voice, as do, in their proper place, Odile's presumptuous tits. Label us what you will, my friend—bourgeois killers, practitioners of Black Art—but *we* remain the point of reference. Everything else must take us into account."

As Sam finished this he slammed down his drink and the bar came alive with a collective flinch.

143

"I think you may have taken my work too personally," George managed.

"I found it—" Sam paused thoughtfully—"I found it, how do you say? jejune." He rolled the word in his hearty mouth, "Yes, that's it, *je–june.*"

The poet was abashed. Odile tugged on Sam's trousers beneath the table, begging him to desist.

"Oh, don't take it personally," Sam hedged. "I mean I just liked the sound of that word, was happy that I thought of it. No, you couldn't call it a just criticism."

"Perhaps you might define the proper aim of art for George," Odile interrupted sarcastically.

"That's easy enough," Sam said brightly. "Just have a look around. Well, the art of our time must address itself to this question: Just *who* is threatening *whom?* We really can't go on until we make up our minds about this."

George Stablefeather put his hands in his pockets and stared wonderingly into his lap. Sam bowed curtly to a miffed Odile and, after putting down the tip, excused himself.

"I didn't know your friends were interested in politics, Odile," George said, slightly hurt.

"He knows there's a war on, if that's what you mean," she cut him off brusquely.

George pressed one of Odile's concupiscent knees between both his beneath the table.

"Keep it in your pants, honey," she said softly.

Sam was now available on commonplace terms, but the young Clone had cut out. Back in the apartment he mixed a desultory nightcap, dialed the stereo-lounger to an odd-numbered Shostakovich symphony, opening the side vents for maximum reproduction. The room wheeled about him but he found no interest in the music and opened the *Adventures* pretty much at random.

I noticed a thing in Morrocco which suggested to me how one could get out of the label Secret Fixers put on you. I had seen tattooing on the foreheads of many of the natives, and this had been puzzling to me till I learned there was a famine in Algiers in 1903 and some of the Christian churches gave out food to their members. Nonmembers had to join to get any, and it was well known that hunger would force many to be hypocrites and deny that they were Baptized afterwards, it being offensive to their own religion. So with the Baptizing went the tattooing of a cross where it could not be denied on their foreheads. To get over this difficulty when the famine was over, the people had much more tattooing done around the cross until it was lost in the new design. Thus we all elaborate and beautify our labels as best we can. Sturdy and I had been through enough weaving and bobbing so that our cross was lost in the wash too. . . .

Dutifully, Sam opened the channel to the extramural dictaphone and began. His lips were blue with ideas.

THE CHRISTMAS MEMO: III   CONFIDENTIAL
(*The aesthetics of economics, the economics of aesthetics*)
To: Wittgenstein (For your information)   #18973.0414
cc: Agapecropolis

Despite the proposed increase in our humanistic rebates, the costly conflict between Manager (or so-called Bourgeoisie) and the Artist (or putative Bohemian) continues to retard social progress. I suggest a three-pronged program for amelioration of the situation:

    1. *Finding common ground:*
    Emphasize that our current differences are largely rhetorical, stress common nineteenth century heritage, in which both economic and. aesthetic industries insisted that to insure the supremacy of the best final product, the respective processes

which produce them ought not to be subject to outside interference.

II. *Forgive but not forget:*

Though we will always be indebted to those of the older Top Management who endured the days of the "aesthetic cartel," their continued resentment, however justified, is no longer serviceable. It took much patience, of course, to stomach the claim that the "forces of material production" ought to be managed in a "manner responsive" to "public" needs, while "artistic enterprise" remain "free" of (any such) coercion. But given time, and bitter reconsiderations, it has become clear that the aesthete's self-indulgence carries its own seeds of destruction. To take only one index, the mean percentages of the divorce, felony and suicide rate of artists surpassed those of the managerial community in late 1946, and this trend continues unbroken. We lost a battle but we've won the war.

III. *New ideology demands cooperation:*

We have come full circle. The ideal of a self-generative homogenous process has replaced the obsession with final product, and our mutual interdependency is reinforced through a new ideology. Management has become an art. And art is no longer therapeutic except insofar as it is experienced in the marketplace. Managers are no longer measured arbitrarily by *what* they manage, but how, as managers, they *live*. Artists likewise have been relieved of terminal judgment of what they produce—the new process has made it possible for them to *live* like artists.

In this new CREATIVE LIVING lies the greatest market potential this nation has yet seen. Our obsession with products will ultimately wither away and die, profit and savings become one in the same, new bonds of fellowship will be forged in serving one another's chosen life styles. Life will indeed become a matter of *taste*; shared wants, satisfied immediately by information retrieval systems, will make class, vocational and national differences irrelevant.

Radicals of the last century (Marx and Freud, say) were

notable for their separation of art and life; as the new revolutionaries, we shall be remembered for making them indistinguishable.

Semper Ceterius Paribus!
Vere magnum habere
Fragilitatem hominis
*Securitatem Dei!**

As Sam channeled the memo for distribution he became slightly nauseous, but gradually he was aware of his jaw muscles tensing, the frontman coming through in spite of everything, and at last an enormous unreferenced grin filled his face. Shaking his silent head in disbelief, nerves charged with the clowning and self-abuse, he heaved a sigh and pressed the release button, reserving a predated carbon for George Stablefeather.

A day of belching, farting, vomiting and diarrhea, otherwise uneventful. Amazing how many voices a man's got at any one time. You'd think they were moved into him makeshift after he was made. Put in a cove on the south side of the island where it is said the Apostle St. Paul was wrecked in 58 AD on his voyage from Syria to Rome. It is interesting to note the manmade intolerance in a creed only fifty-eight years old when head office finally allowed him to proceed after trying him for improper procedure. Then I got muchos sick and was forced to put in in the main harbor. HMS Royal Sovereign was anchored there and several midshipmen invited me aboard. Society Dames may pick on my grammar, but right there I showed my ability as a social climber. They offered me paint, rope or any help that we might need. I told them we greatly appreciate their offer to help our undertaking, but that I could manage and that England had enough to do to pay the USA their war debt.

* *Publisher's note:* "Always all other things being equal. True greatness is to have in one the frailty of a man, and the security of a God."

December 1st, 1928: Started down the harbor at 7:00 AM. As we passed the Royal Sovereign, I was completely taken aback to see all officers at attention and saluting on her foredeck. As we passed, the Captain stepped out of line and called out, "Goodbye, Captain Fuess, Goodbye." This gave me a chance to do something, so I shouted back, "Goodbye."

15 · Contingencies

For the next several Fridays they began to meet obliquely at the In, coming and leaving separately, resisting George Stablefeather's advances by their sad silences, trying to hear the poetry above the graying fags' harangue.

"Do you think he'd tell Aaron?" Sam wondered out loud. "He must figure."

"Not as long as he thinks *he's* got a chance." Odile smiled impressively. "Anyway, we're not doing anything anymore. What's wrong with you anyway? You got somebody living with you or what?"

"Why don't you try it with George?" Sam murmured. "Couldn't hurt."

"Sam, why are you such a shit?"

Sam drank fast to catch a grin short.

On one occasion they returned to Peacock Prairie but the fronds were wet and reams of toilet paper had been spooled throughout, so they simply walked about the triangle, she holding Sam's index finger like a child, gazing through the rusted cyclone fence, their shades preserving the molting grasses from the shadowgraph of that fence's web. Sam had to admit that the chances for preservation didn't look good.

And then, on the second Sunday of October, the Olde Towne Autumnal Art Fair brought them together again.

The streets about the Prairie had been blockaded and artists and craftsmen had set up their booths on the sidewalks. The clarities of Indian summer had turned the locust trees to a hurricane green, suburban families moved amoebically through the streets, children running in locked circles about the martial couples. Peacock Prairie had become monotone, goldenrose, the lake had rusted achromatic. And the Pumping Station wound bright with pastel crepe.

From the high stoops of the surrounding brownstone rooming houses, the Clones watched sullen, disdainful, immobile. It was cool and Odile had on her mother's postwar Persian lamb coat.

"Hey," a Clone screamed from a fire escape, "grab the tourists come to look at the freaks!"

Odile blushed and let go of Sam's arm. He was tolerably confused. None of them were big enough to fight. Naturally he sympathized with their lassitude, their blurry penance.

"Hey, motherfuckers, a bird in the brain's better than a foot in a sprain."

As each year he had inched away from the certainties his psychic privileges afforded him, he had begun to wonder if the expensive matched luggage of his training might not have been put on the wrong flight. He respected that they were perhaps the first of his country to fear the right things, but he doubted they could envision the ferocity of the counterattack they might provoke. Already, in the offices and lavatories of MC, the string of unending jokes at the Clones' expense was reaching hysterical and momentous proportions. The customary leer of the pros was approaching a snarl, certain surgical measures were being recommended. You can strip a pro of everything except his cynicism and still live with him; but once he has nothing to fall back on except his own repressed decent impulses, he becomes a foe worthy of any challenge. So beyond his own impotency and generous concern for their strategy, the only clear emotion that Sam felt for the Clones was that peculiar scorn which the middle classes once reserved for the idle rich—with all their advantages, why weren't they more effective?

"I should have run away to something like this," Odile

muttered politely, "only there wasn't anything like this to run away to when I was ready. I would have had to be some fat man's mistress."

"You'd've probably died of hepatitis or VD before you were of voting age." Sam laughed briefly. "I'll bet you were a great adolescent, Odile."

"I'd be afraid to take any of that stuff now," she went on. "I don't know what I'd do. I'd probably kill somebody."

"You really think so?"

"Sure. But it would be instructive to see *who* I would kill. Aaron, myself, or the kids."

"Not me?"

"What would be the point? I'd be afraid you'd get me first."

"I would, too, Odile. You wouldn't have a chance."

She walked on, too gravely for the moment.

"Have you ever taken any of the stuff, Sam?"

"Oh sure. But I always throw it up, every time. I just can't keep it in me. Isn't that strange? Even in the service I couldn't keep it down."

A Clone with a great purse passed, jouncing a bell at them, skin sallow in its shroud.

"They really hate us, don't they?" Odile said wistfully.

"They're not supposed to," Sam said.

They had stopped before one of the crafts booths in which a small tanned woman, her hair pulled into a taut bun, was accomplishing modernistic jewelry upon a miniature anvil. A coil of gold piping was looped around her neck, and she drew the end of this slowly through a piercing blue flame and then beneath her tiny metronomic hammer. She plunged her completed designs into a cup of surgical spirits and displayed them on dental gauze. Sam bought Odile a pair of abstract earrings. She would wear them on her last night.

"It's funny to think you might be one of the last girls ever who couldn't . . . you know," Sam said.

Odile regarded the golden spiral in her palm.

"Now I've got to have my ears pierced."

It was then Sam felt the first mucous dot on his neck and another sodden on his hat. He turned toward the brownstones to see a cloud of debris descending upon them. The gabled windows were crowded with vacant faces, the families on the sidewalk aghast. Shaving cream, deodorant pads, keg beer, concentrated orange juice, sharp-cornered packets of frozen kitchen cut vegetables, detergents, leftovers, and the loveliest orifice filler of any description rained down upon them. A banner was unfurled from a rooftop:

ART IS DEAD—MAKE YOUR LIFE THE QUOTIDIEN

Valiant fathers and mothers threw themselves upon their children, various garbadges and cosmetics streaming from their foreheads. Artists stepped in front of their canvases and a few of the crowd broke ranks to assist them. They draped their aimless bodies over the works of art, choosing what was nearest and loving it in retrospect. The viaduct was clogged with spectators.

Sam was strangely exhilarated as the barrage continued to chunk into the locust trees, ricochet along the curbing. The crowd, now all prone, was not amused however; cuddling their children in mimes of courage, they squinted to determine the source of the fusilade. Odile began to cry. A pot of rotting marigolds crashed down not a yard from them. A lipstick glanced off Sam's temple. He held Odile close inside his overcoat, pushing her into a gabled doorway. Garbage oozed into sight from the rim of his fedora, the gutters glowed with refuse.

At the end of the street, in a cul-de-sac, Sam could see one of the larger Clones scratching frantically at the pavement, trying apparently to make himself a cobble. But the sleek seamless asphalt resisted his every attempt, and his nails were bloodied for nothing. Finally, in desperation, he threw himself against the nearest car, intending no doubt to begin a barricade. But the immense obdurate auto only swayed gently against his weight, the grill puckered in a feline grin. He could not budge it an inch, and was last seen sobbing up a stoop.

Meantimes, the lady in the jewelry booth had slowly slumped forward, and Sam gallantly zigzagged at a low crouch through the missiles to her side. Her skull was halved, the pink brains already graying in the air.

Another bullet shattered the display case and Sam dashed back to Odile and pushed her through the doorway. He continued pushing her up the stairs to the first landing, where they flung themselves to the floor below the level of a shattered window. A Clone threesome were crouched petulantly in the opposite corner, a giant-size can of shaving cream beside them, glancing fearfully at Sam and Odile.

"I told you this would happen," one said to the others. "The fuzz've gone berserk. They're going to kill everybody now." The others pointed at Sam fearfully, putting fingers to their lips.

Sam drew his coat closer about Odile, pulled the rim of his fedora copwise over his eyes, and stared them down.

The gunfire gradually grew more sporadic and then ceased altogether. Sam looked at his watch. It was three-ten exactly. Then they heard the sirens. At first only police and ambulances, but soon these were joined by the deafening all-clear of civil defense.

Sam doffed his hat to their companions, who were certain they'd been fingered, then got Odile out the back entrance. They ran along back alleys for ten or so blocks and then cut with normalcy across the park. Through the blighted elms they could make out coils of smoke, families hauling themselves from the ground, the surgical blue and red strobes of cops 'n' docs on the scene.

153

Sam wanted to get back and see it on television, so he got a cab for a breathless Odile and then walked as fast as possible back to the apartment. Running, he figured, would have been too suspicious.

Dean the doorman slunk out from behind a pillar in the lobby as Sam passed. "They mean business, don't they?" he said tremulously, but the elevator door cut him short.

Sam opened his door and not much to his amazement found Stargyle on the floor. At first he thought he was cowering in fear and searched the window for the concave opacities of errant shrapnel. But Stargyle was lying menacingly, as for example he could never *sit* menacingly, at least in the stereo-lounger. Then Sam saw his turban.

"Where did you get that, Stargyle?" he asked, but his ward's ward could only smile helplessly. Then Sam squinted and saw the Lucarno-Wesson 30-30 cradled in his anemic arms.

"How . . . how . . . could you do this to me?"

Stargyle looked as absorbed and abashed as a dachshund.

"Aw, come on, Sam."

"Jesus, Stargyle, I make you welcome, give you the run of my apartment, lend you money, and then you do this to me." Stargyle hung his head, said nothing. "And don't call me Sam." Stargyle's lips quavered in some secret litany.

"Look man, what's the point?" Sam took a different tack. "You know who you got out there today? An old lady jewelry maker. And at best, a couple of kids. Where'd you get that thing anyway?"

Stargyle handed him the weapon without a word. The muzzle was still hot, and Sam could feel the shell casings imbedded in the heavy nap of the carpet as he walked.

He turned on the TV for Stargyle, and bade him sit.

"There," he said.

There was some short circuitry, the lounger began a redundant rubdown as the set warmed up, but ultimately the picture skittered into view.

"Mrs. Mina L. Loy of 7677 North Rogers was shot in the head today," the man-on-the-spot was saying, headphones like babooNears, eying the monitor furtively, "as she worked in her booth at the Olde Towne Art Fair Annuale. The bullet, after destroying her brain, severed her medulla and lodged finally in her lower abdomen. She was killed instantly."

"See," Sam said. "See? See, I saw her."

Stargyle had folded himself stiffly into the lounger and adjusted the fine tuning knob as the chair subtly pummeled and kneaded his new lifelessness.

"Shortly after three this afternoon, as families were taking their Sunday stroll, shots rang out in the Peacock Prairie Triangle area. The parameters of fire converged on the art display, where Mrs. Loy was managing one of the booths, and was, in fact, a founder of Art Day. She leaves her husband, Bernard, a sister and two grandchildren."

"See," Sam said. "See!"

Cameras panned the row of brownstones.

"The Clones who largely inhabit this area responded by using whatever they had at their disposal in a counterattack."

"Ha," Sam snorted.

"And it will please those of us who were somewhat anxious about their antisocial conduct that there were many instances of individual bravery noted. The children generally provided a protective screen of refuse and gave of their lodgings freely to those under fire."

The camera panned the street again. Artists were to be seen putting their wares up, indignantly dismantling booths, porkers were interrogating Clones who shook their furry heads funnily.

"Commissioner, who do you think is responsible for this catastrophe?" A heavy, cowled face filled the screen.

"This infamous attack was clearly a premeditated conspiracy of the first order. We have determined that the fire was triangulated and came from as many as fifty different sources. We have made no arrests as yet, but we have mounting evidence in a mythoplastic pattern."

"You infer, Commissioner, that the fire was triangulated in a paramilitary manner. But is it not true that the area under fire was triangular in shape?"

"We have determined, as I said, Bob, that the fire was triangulated on the triangle. It does not bode . . ."

"Do you see any significance in the fact that Mrs. Loy was the only casualty? Do you have any information why she should be singled out?"

"Mrs. Loy did not avail of herself in any of the normal civil defense procedures. She refused to move out of the line of fire, and did not practice any of the measures we've prescribed. Bob, I don't know how many times I've stressed this through our great public media, but citizens are their own first line of defense. I'll reiterate this once more for your audience. If you hear or see gunfire, or have any suspicion of it, you should drop where you are and cover your face in your hands. If you are in your own home, put on protective clothing and draw the blinds. If in a public place, follow the shelter signs until the all-clear sounds. I just can't help feeling, Bob, that if Mrs. Loy hadn't lollygaggled, that if she had taken the appropriate measures, that she would be alive and kicking today."

Sam was sufficiently absorbed so that he did not notice Stargyle's departure. He had left the door ajar.

The station shifted to a commercial. Sam noted that the weapon had cooled. He took out the magazine. It had five shells remaining. He glanced once more at the screen and then gazed reflectively out over the city. The sky was outrageous. The buildings swam in the lowering sun. The lake was stone. The gun sweated profusely in his hands.

Sam switched channels, turning the volume of a quiz show to maximum, then walked circumspectly out on the balcony where he fired five times into what seemed to him a single puff of tearful air.

The wind was now against us, making us heave to off island of Lemnos. At Dardanelles, 16 vessels of different flags were waiting for the wind to let up. It was difficult to tell if they were enemies, or just wanted through too. One of the unbecalmed pilots came aboard and pointed out where the ancient city of Troy was located. (Just another dominating empire and its millions who went through hell and wars to build (700 BC) and millions more went through hell and Alexander to conquer (334 BC) and then still more millions went through hell for Rome to conquer (187 BC) and today, what's left?) Naturally we of the USA have our faults and should drop them, but we have been unjustly criticized for things like this. Other countries have had the trouble, then we're judged by some conspicuous fault out of History. There is no good reason why we cannot get together on this and educate or choke our own. The wind did not let up for several weeks and Sturdy and I forgot the Black Sea route to India and determined to take the easier route via the Red Sea, one of the most important changes in course for the whole voyage.

My health was getting worse. Did not know if it was the food, climate, water, keeping the course and the Book for Boys, but my nerves were under a great strain. Unpacking trunks brought from home with me, found both chronometers in bad shape, however. This proved they had been opened in transit. Was it friend, neutral or foe?

Second night out after wind stopped, sighted Ashrefi light and anchored for the night on the great Shaab Ali reefs. There was plenty of room to lay Sturdy up there, miles of it and no one to object. Slept heavily until daylight.

October 12, 1929; through carelessness and/or fixers, Sturdy II was lost by fire. I hated for us to part, but I had left no stone unturned in trying to save her, and friends, on reading this, will understand. The remainder cards for the Book for Boys went down with her, and there on the Shaab Ali reefs is the book as it was meant to be written.

In writing this book, I have used we and us as much as possible to avoid the objectionable I. But now I knew the we and us part was gone. There was only I, a captain without a ship. Rode in the small emergency skiff to Ashrefi lighthouse. The keeper was black but spoke English and wondered where I had come from in so small a boat, which I gave him, then, to go fishing in, as I would give it to you.

16 · A Cold Buffet

Sam went immediately to Agapecropolis' office the next morning. The doctor had not come in as yet, but his secretary made a luncheon reservation. He worked unsteadily for less than an hour, feeling Wittgenstein's binocs on his back, then took a walk along the breakwater. Instinctively he sought out the place where Aaron and he had produced *The Divers*. It was now deserted; too cold to swim. The water bore a thick fringe of green scum. A large pike, a lamprey hanging from his stomach like some fantasmaniacal penis, drifted, eyes popped, offshore. The yachts were berthed and being dismantled for winter storage. The alewives had been collected and ground to decent fertilizer. The lake was dying. A cold mist hung on the horizon like a sausage, but through it, Sam could hear the drone of the Pumping Station—as loud as he had ever heard it work.

At noon he was admitted to Agapecropolis' office, where he told him what had happened the day before.

"Well," the doctor said cheerfully, turning down the hi-fi, "what do you think it all means?"

"I wouldn't know," said Sam. "I guess it means that I want to kill somebody but I don't have the guts to do it."

"Do you think the shots were directed at anything in particular?"

"If I had to choose, Doctor," said Sam, "I suppose it would be at just everything in particular."

"Did you shoot in *our* direction?"

"Nope," Sam said. "My apartment doesn't face in this direction. If it did, I would have probably shot here."

"Are you going to report this?"

"No."

"Why not?"

"Hell, man, I'm an accomplice. You want me to lose my job?"

"Oh dearest Sam, institutions like MC were built precisely to keep men with Q.U.I.F.'s like yours *out* of trouble. The very stability of our society is dependent upon the fact that men such as yourself preferred wealth to gut power, self-aggrandizement and prestige to simple authority. There's a tacit agreement, you know; you get your money and stuff if you leave politics to the people. They'll get what they deserve; they always do. 'The people are a river,' as Alph Bins says, 'we're the bridge.' You better start looking out for yourself. A prince shouldn't harm anybody, except fatally, as they say. And you're not getting paid to act on your common impulses, my boy. Shit, friend, this could get out of hand!"

Agapecropolis sighed and reoriented his bulk so that the sun shone directly over the top of his head into Sam's eyes. "Well, no use crying over spilled milk. I assume as a start you'll not again welcome this individual in your home."

"Fair enough," said Sam, and hung his head convincingly.

Agapecropolis then offered him a pimento-cheese-and-datenut-bread sandwich with a cup of bouillon. A sliver of marrow, cut in the shape of the MC medallion, floated just below the amber surface.

Sam was curious about what the doctor would do for an encore.

"I'm sorry about not getting the drift of your . . . intentions the other day," he said slowly. "Just how was I supposed to react?"

"Oh, that technique's about run its course, I should think. Too schematic, probably." Agapecropolis finished his soup with exaggerated care. "The time has come," he began, "to discuss your politics."

"You can't be serious."

"Everyone has a politics, Sam," he said. "They represent the basic infantile experience. We just learn to express it later on, that's all. Think back now and tell me a story: the first thing you remember, politically speaking."

It was no trouble for Sam to remember:

"OK. Well, I'm in a darkened room, after a nap, I guess, because it's light outside, and I can see by the clock that I'm not supposed to be finished with my nap yet, but I'm crapping slowly in my one-piece pajamas, and when the clock is right the maid comes in and pats me there and laughs. . . ."

"You needn't go back that far actually." Agapecropolis put down his bouillon, faintly nauseated.

"Well, how about this? On our very first field trip, our fourth-grade shop class is taken to a cookie factory. In this cookie factory, at the very end of the assembly line there is this old woman turning the cookie boxes around. The conveyors don't mesh properly, and she has to give each box a quarter turn so that they can start on a new belt toward the final packing. Half of the class thinks this is inefficient, the other half thinks it's too bad that anybody has to do something like that all day. So already, it seems, everyone has made up their mind, and you could tell from then on how they would vote. Our predispositions in these matters seem to be formed quite early. . . ."

"No, no," Agapecropolis cried impatiently. "Now you've gone too far the other way. Now look, this is the sort of thing I want. Now listen, this would be *you* talking:

" 'Well, Doctor Agapecropolis,' " Dr. Agapecropolis began, perfectly imitating Sam's heartland manner, " 'my politics are like an older happily married and distinguished man being in love with a very young girl, if you know what I mean. The man knows that he doesn't even really like the girl, she's superficial and egocentric, she dyes her hair perhaps. He knows he will grow tired of her in the same way he is presently tired of his other long-standing responsibilities, so he knows that in the long run he won't be any happier. But he can't resist, you see, this throwing away of everything, resist the predictability of his life, reassert himself. He's old enough to know that nothing is going to change, rationally speaking, but that it is necessary either to accept this risk or give oneself up. It's the last resort of our starved selves, so to speak. The last chance nature gives to those who've discovered they're dying.' Now that's the sort of thing, you see?"

"You want something more artistic, I guess," Sam said.

"If you like. For example, do you conceive of yourself as dying, Samuel?"

"It's beginning, Agapecropolis. Yes, I can feel it."

"You are then, by your own definition, sir, a danger."

Sam tried to hang his head again but found he couldn't swallow.

"When did you first become aware of this strain of, uh, violence in you?"

"Oh, I've had it all along. I thought it would be serviceable once. It's just lately that I've been able to control it—or at least thought I should. See, I learned the conservative things first, and the liberal things second. You know—to make it good for somebody else, you got to suck your own balls up. Lately I've been trying to love whatever's nearest."

"But why such half-assed violence, this . . . playing at revolution? Why don't you go full out, like you're capable of?" Agapecropolis pounded his soft fist upon the desk. "This way, you're just *asking* for *it*."

"Simple. Because I've seen that with everything I got going for me, I'm still only barely making it—I mean personally, not professionally speaking—so I've become afraid of losing *any-*

162

thing. I feel sometimes that if I knew *one* less thing than I do, then I'd blow up. If I ever forgot a single thing I've learned, that I'd be done for. . . . Doctor, what I want to say is what this country needs is *more* dead bodies, a lot more! But I can't say it. I just can't."

"Aside from that, what's worth remembering?"

"Oh, easy. Just a couple of nights ago, for example, I had dinner in a restaurant, alone as usual, you know. All of a sudden, this man came in and started to play the flute. It was wonderful, really very good, some Basque thing probably, and afterwards he passed his hat. But after he got some money (and he deserved what he got) he didn't leave. He just put on a big camel's-hair coat and went out to sit at one of the tables on the sidewalk. He ordered dinner out there, right in the weather, dumping his hat's collection into the waiter's apron. He ordered steak with a 'warm interior.' I heard him say 'warm interior' several times. The waiter was freezing out there and nodding with his arms wrapped around him. The man buttoned up his collar and put his flute down next to his knife, and when the steak came, he put his whole fist down on it hard to see if it had a 'warm interior,' like this . . .'"

Sam put his fist down hard on a pâté sandwich; the filling squirted out on the desk.

"And see, if I hadn't seen that, or if I'd forgotten it, well, I might not be here today."

"Hmmm," the doctor said, daubing his napkin in Sam's tiny mess. "Well, in any case, Samuel, as unexemplary as that is, I think you ought to know that, in a sense, I admire your attitude."

"Doctor, what in heaven's name *are* you doing here? And what do you want out of me?"

"Hooper, only you and others like you can tell me that. I act only on the accumulated data of my investigations. My job is quantification, Samuel, because *that* is what spares our feelings."

Sam helped the doctor scrape the extruded pâté back on the plate.

"Let's try again, dear Sam, before you get sick and run out again."

"Politics again?"

"Well, let's attack it more tangentially this time. You're obviously threatened by the obvious—uh, let's see, well now, how about some dreams? When you have sex in dreams, what do you do, eh?"

"I don't have sex in dreams, Doctor, that's the whole point. I always wake up. Even in the service I woke right up. Like I told you, I'm trying to control myself."

"Well, what seems nice to you? Obviously you're not always running around just firing out of windows in your fantasies. How about falling or other defenestrations?"

"I do remember," said Sam, trying earnestly to apply the doctor's format, "a rather recurrent dream that really made me very happy. But it was very simple. I'm just bending down, you see, and there is this girl and I kiss her heavily, is that the word? Maybe it should be 'hard,' except that's what she is, 'hard.' I mean her lips are pursed, not defiantly, but sort of ignorantly like she's bracing herself, but I'm not excited or offended. . . ."

"Oh God," groaned Agapecropolis.

"Bad?" said Sam.

"It's not what I'd call ideal," said the doctor, "but knowing you, it's got to be something more."

"Well, that's all there is to it, more or less," said Sam. "But it's not a fantasy, you see, I mean the girl doesn't excite me all that much. I don't even remember her from dream to dream, except for those odd lips."

"It's almost as if," the doctor's voice quavered, "she were—a child?"

"Yes," said Sam, "rather like a child."

"And that your politics, then, if I may extrapolate, resemble your indifferent kiss on that unsuspecting mouth?"

"Fair enough," said Sam.

"That's lovely, Mr. Hooper, I'm proud of you. You've got something there, you know. Remember, every political act is a repressed erotic wish. Life may be language, but language is not life."

"What makes you think I didn't just make it up?"

"If you didn't enjoy the truthteller's role so, I'd be suspicious," the doctor said. "But this is something unique. No question about it."

"You're making me feel better," said Sam.

"Well, stay away from these rebels for a while, Mr. Hooper, and I think we'll be ready for some routine tests soon."

"I always did very well on tests, I warn you, Doctor."

"Good. Here's one to take home with you then, and also here's a little portfolio to help you with our Mrs. Grassgreen. I've listened to the tape several times now, and I think you'll find everything you need there. Anyway, none of it can hurt, I'll bet. She's a real winner, isn't she?"

"Thank you, Doctor."

"And I'll be interested to know what happens with this child-woman, Sam. Somehow she's the key."

"You think so?"

"We've got to find out why you're fascinated with her, Sam, to see if you're really dangerous or not."

"It's really neither here nor there, Doctor."

"Well, I've got to run now, but just what do you think that this recurrent young sweetie means to you?"

"The one in the dream?"

"Surely."

"It means simply that she accepts my presence, Doctor."

"Does it not suggest a superficial relationship? Is it not one without initiation, without responsibility?"

"No. I feel very old in the dream, Doctor, and nothing can

165

corrupt me. I know exactly what I should do, what the situation calls for."

"You are, then, all-powerful?"

"No, I don't have to use my power. It's as if I don't know which of my impulses is strongest, but I know which are worth following. I don't feel pressured at all. Like I told you; it's weird precisely because power doesn't enter into it."

"Do you believe in this, Samuel? This acceptance without power?"

"Of course not. It just happens. It's not a concept that's easy to put in words."

"Would you give up your life for it?"

"Probably not. I know what comes of that."

"What would you do if you kissed her in the dream and she died?"

"That happens seldom, Doctor."

"But how would you *feel?*"

"I wouldn't be surprised. After all, I wasn't surprised when she showed up in the first place."

"Are you quite certain she wants you to . . . touch her all over like that?" Agapecropolis shifted uneasily in his seat.

"I wouldn't have created her if she didn't, would I?"

"You create her, yet you have no responsibility?"

"You killed her off, Doctor, I didn't."

"How do you justify all this, dammit?" The cords in Agapecropolis' neck had tightened, become violet.

"I keep it in proper perspective, Doctor, I don't get those things mixed up. I never did. I mean it's just a dream, right?"

"You don't feel cheated?" the doctor queried huskily.

"People like me never feel cheated, Doctor. Only guilty sometimes. We know exactly what things cost. There are only two ways you can be now, Doctor. Sweet or tough. But I feel sweet *and* tough when I kiss her and she feels sweet *and* tough to me. I'm just describing it to you how it is. It isn't going to bust my life up."

"People must be attracted to you because of your self-control, Sam."

"Maybe that's why the girl in the dream is a kid. Because they're so vulnerable to power, you put it aside, you become a presence, and you know you're healing yourself by not using it on them."

"The only trouble is, Samuel, do they know that?"

"It's hard to say."

"How do you feel, then, when you kiss this wife of your friend?"

"The one *not* in the dream?"

"You know, dammit, the one whose *role's* been vitiated."

"Ah, now, that's different. She *wants* all that power, you see, intensified to the point where it's almost inhuman. You know what I mean. I've often wondered about that. When I kiss her she feels all my muscles, and she says to me how hard they are, and you know how much harder they really could be. I think I must swell up like an animal when she does that. It's really beyond nerves or sex then, it's as if I'm impenetrable. A 'proud professional,' you might say. It's kind of a throwback, I guess. But I feel so silly afterwards, I'm incapable of taking it seriously anymore. To blow yourself up that way, a big bag of strength and stoicism. It's really very disgusting."

Agapecropolis seemed exhausted. He slumped in his chair, tapping his automatic pencil against his teeth. Finally, he seemed to regain his composure and, raising his eyebrows, leaned forward.

"It's amazing, isn't it," he said softly, "what people will do just to feel alive?"

Sam shrugged.

"Ah, Samuel—" the doctor leaned back—"why such self-hatred? Just relax. You've got the equipment. You shouldn't worry so much about what other people think of you. Don't you see, you're unique. You are both phantasiemensch *und* burgher!"

Sam murmured something the doctor couldn't pick up.

"What do you want, young man? You couldn't be in a better position." Sam knew now a little of how Odile felt. He cupped his face in his hands.

"To have a secret life," he said inaudibly. "That's the thing. That's what I want most."

"Oh, you just want more mystery. That's an old . . ."

"No! What I want is to get the mystery *out* of it. Completely out. Just once. Then . . ."

"If you get the mystery out of everything *else*," the doctor said evenly, "then, Samuel, by definition, *you* will be a secret. Right?"

They look at each other across the table without speaking for several minutes. The sun disappears behind the doctor's shoulders.

Then Agapecropolis shook himself severely and looked his patient in the eye.

"Well, Samuel," he said, "you better shit or get off the pot."

The Dott had thoughtfully laid a fire for him, and after a stiff drink Sam enjoyed that undifferentiation of the flesh as the nervous system finally manages to accept itself for the day; the *corps* returning to the *corpus*. Good and loaded, Sam got to work on the doctor's true or false:

1. Do you almost never feel hurried? Or are you uncertain?
2. In your life so far, has there been anything which created a special problem for you?
3. Are there things about your present circumstances that you might like to change?
4. Do you find it difficult to ask a favor?
5. When discouraged, do you pull yourself out of your "low feeling" in about average time?

6. If time and money were no issue, would you rather be a skindiver or a novelist?
7. Do you sometimes lose yourself in experimenting with an idea that has no presumed practical value for anyone else?
8. Does it seem to you that you are forever having to weight values and make a choice between them?
9. Do you feel that people sometimes expect too much of you?
10. Do you think people are likely to take advantage of you if they can?
11. Do simple, usual things often seem mysterious and exciting to you?
12. Do you get a lot of fun out of dabbling with the out-of-the-ordinary?
13. Could you get more, if you wanted?
14. Do you feel the ordinary person is likely to be unreliable?
15. Are there times you feel it necessary to make someone else afraid?
16. When you are working with your hands, do you tend to forget everything else?
17. Is it true that your best work is the result of inspiration or planning?
18. Are you inclined to worry about things which are not quite clear?
19. Do you give considerable attention to preparing yourself for emergencies?
20. Do you feel there is an unseen force which will operate through you if only given a chance?

To spare you the details, Odile showed up before Sam was up the next morning, the Dott admitting her to the bedroom indifferently. "Prove your point yet?" she muttered.

Sam resumed his work on the questionnaire as Odile pulled her smock over her head.

I better shut the door, she said. You know I'm a screamer.

Sam nodded as she crawled in beside him.

I've been thinking a lot, she thought she said.

Afterthoughts?

I haven't slept since the fair.

I haven't worked since the fair.

Sam? He did not look up. Sam. How can a man as cultivated as you work for something like MC? I'm not trying to put you down. I just don't get it!

Odile, don't *you* understand? You want the same thing from me that MC does. You hate that sort of power in the abstract, but you want it on the sly just like everybody. And I give it to you as I give it to them, as it was given to me—for no particular reason that's worth discussing.

Why are you so cynical? Is it just a tough pose, or what?

. . . .

Nothing really happens to you in the office, does it?

Nope.

She tries to wedge herself beneath the questionnaire. Her irises are different colors.

You're . . . you're just the best thing that ever happened to me, that's all.

. . . .

But I don't know anything about you at all! How old are you, anyway? Where did you come from?

Between eighteen and thirty-five.

What do you really think is wrong with me?

You are a borderline paranoid-schizophrenic complicated by my reticence. Or you want to fuck your father but you don't like him. Or you want to like your father without having to fuck him. I don't know, Odile. Lay off, OK?

You're *such* a smartass. What are you afraid of?

. . . .

For God's sake, talk to me. Tell me anything! When did *you* get to be *you?*

Will you please keep your voice down? The Dott . . .

And who in the hell is the Dott?

All right, that's enough. OK, roll over.

She stiffened as he dropped the questionaire and hooked a leg about her.

I wake up crying, she said crying, as soon as I wake up, I start crying.

I thought you said you couldn't sleep.

170

She grabbed him as the bone rushed into his blood, then paused.

What do you look for in my eyes, Sam?

My face.

Aw, Sam, cut it out, just once, be tender too. . . .

He licked the salt from her ears, the brine from her eyes. She whistled through her nose and bit her tongue.

You're so good to me. You take me places I've never been.

She arched and lifted him so that all his elbows and knees were airbound: *He raised a mortal to the skies/ she drew an angel down.*

It was almost like the stereo-lounger as she began to yell her lyric. The Dott found it necessary to turn on the TV, vacuum cleaner, dishwasher and kitchen exhaust fan.

Sam stood nude at the window while Odile dozed. The lake was hidden in a sulphurous haze, but the rising sun refracted off the water so that the poisonous air seemed an Edenic green, rather like the concatenation of Odile's iris beneath her remaining lens. Maybe through all that gop, he thought, those uneven eyelashes, those slightly serrated teeth, the sun is finally coming up.

You're beautiful, Sam. She was soft now again. You're really beautiful, just to look at.

. . . .

Do you think of yourself as handsome?

He folded his arms.

I'll bet you've got women after you all the time.

. . . .

How can you do it so long?

I'm somewhat repressed and programatically tender. It also helps to drink a lot.

You are an incredible prick!

Don't push me, honey. I'll cut you off in a second.

171

Anyway, you're helping me. I feel some days I could do anything now.

I was *lib*erated a long time ago, baby. I'm trying to find out how to love. You're still hung up on what's worth loving. Each time you hope it will be better, don't you?

You can't liberate yourself *by* yourself. . . .

. . . .

Do you know you've never once treated me like a person? You put all kinds of absurdities in my mouth. You've never acknowledged the *real* me.

Odile, now listen. You're very nice, but you're simply unconvincing. You never said a thing you didn't pick up somewhere else. You couldn't tell a story straight if you had the book right in front of you.

She rolled over and spoke sibilantly into the pillow.

Is it always the same for you?

Pretty much.

Why do you do it then?

. . . .

I feel you're judging me, she went on and on. That you're watching me.

I'm watching you.

You make me feel so self-conscious. Then I think about it and I feel inadequate and then I can't do it.

. . . .

Do you think maybe I have a low sex drive?

How am I supposed to tell? I mean, maybe you *are* finishing. How do you know? Is that what being a woman is?

I'm afraid, she said, more than thoughtfully. I'm afraid that if I let myself go with you . . . maybe then I'd be completely dependent on you . . . you know?

. . . .

What are you thinking about?

. . . .

I'm afraid, too, that you'll get bored fucking me.

Don't push so hard, Odile.

She was combing her hair violently, strands jerked out with the comb.

At least tell me not to be afraid of you.

Don't be afraid of me.

Oh, what a *clever* bastard.

I'll hurt you only necessarily.

Fucking words again. We should put this on tape.

Sam shrunk. If it wasn't me, it'd be somebody else.

That's *really* insulting.

. . . .

At least tell me not to be afraid of you!

You want me to force you, to beat the shit out of you? Is that what you want?

Odile was up in a fury now, and stalking to the bathroom she proceeded to dash the three available water tumblers in the sink. The shards exploded about her most impressively; the dull powp of distant artillery, the light dry rain from the bunker's ceiling.

Sam got back into bed disconsolate, staring at his long, bare feet as the glass exploded about the bathroom. She was wailing. He wished he had his Strat-O-Mocs.

All you want to do is fuck me, she wailed.

That's not true, Odile. I really don't care about that.

Oh . . . I hope you . . . *die*.

Sam pulled the covers over his nakedness. He was also worried about the mirror shattering in her face.

Now, just think about it, kiddo. I could've got everything I wanted without promising anything. I mean I don't have to go through this to get laid.

She came out then and threw her smock back on, cramming her girdle and bra in her purse.

You're not as bright as you think you are.

Sometimes, Odile, I think you lack awareness.

She was standing by the window now, hands rammed in her coat pockets.

Are you using me? Experimenting with me somehow?

No.

Aren't I good for that?

Yes.

Don't you know what you're doing to me?

No.

Don't you really care?

Yes.

Do you have to be of two minds about everything?

. . . .

OK, fella; she put her hand on the knob and turned with the horsey grin of an unconvinced madwoman. Sorry about the mess. Then she smiled him prone. I really do appreciate being treated as a . . . sexual object. And sorry too I'm such a screamer. The first door closed hard.

OK, brighteye, but next time, listen; don't fake it!

The second door slammed.

Sam stayed in bed until he heard the Dott leave. It took him most of an hour to sponge up the glass. Then he collapsed into the stereo-lounger. Rivulets of condensation were forming between the double panes of the window. Spying her guitar beneath the coffee table, he opened the fiberboard case and slung it into his lap. It was a commonplace instrument, with some surprisingly fancy inlaid fretwork and the basic chords scratched on the sounding board. He laid his bad hand soundlessly across the gut.

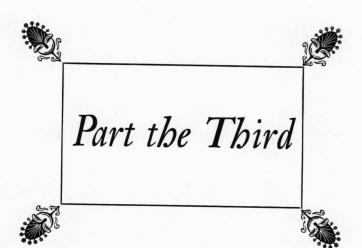

Part the Third

17 · A Good Dinner . . .

"I can't use 'em; take some of your wayout friends out."

Sam called Odile immediately to convey Agapecropolis' generous offer of tickets for the ballet benefit.

She said great but what about the kids?

Sam offered the Dott to sit.

When he ask her she say sure thing.

The doctor had grinned churlishly upon handing Sam the tickets. *I trust you'll let me know how you liked it* he said more mysteriously than nicely.

Let's go out for dinner before, Sam suggested later that afternoon.

Let me clear it with Aaron.

Aaron called back. Sam assured him that the tickets were free and it would be all right to wear a turtleneck.

I practically had to beg him, Odile was thinking.

Aaron is dressing up and likes it.

Sam goes out into November to prepare the car.

Let's get on with it.

. . . he brought the car up from the underground and picked the Dott up at Dean's door. She clambered into the back seat, but before she could shut the door, a short man darted from nowhere and flung himself into the front seat. He proved to be a strictly unsympathetic wiry fellow with a large birth blotch on his tightly stretched forehead. Tugging inquiringly on the deluxe armrest, he demanded, "This come with the car?"

"Sure," said Sam ceremonially.

"I had a nice little car just like this oncet," he said nervously, "and it didn't come with mine."

The Dott was speechless.

"Floor mats too? You get the mats too, *with* the car?"

"Afraid so," Sam said earnestly.

"And Jesus, look at this," he yowled, striking the dashboard, "I got some crappy crackle finish, you got leatherette. Soft too."

"It just came that way, sir."

"But *mine just came that way* too," the short man whined, and banged his head on the dash. "You sure you didn't get this stuff later?"

"Positive," said Sam. "Got'er right off the floor."

"Didn't cost you nothing? For all this?"

"Not one penny extra, my friend." Sam's bad eyelid was fluttering imperceptibly.

The man with the tight forehead gazed at him in disbelief, and then, bowing, bounded from the car and out of sight.

The Dott did not choose to comment.

Stieglitz met them at the door in her father's pajamas, back-cracking out of a facetious curtsy upon seeing the Dott. Aaron at the kitchen table kept his back to them; Odile craned from the bathroom and sung she'd just be out. Sam deposited the Dott in one of the sling chairs from which she preeminently ignored the children as they circled her suspiciously. Sam noticed the bed in the alcove was not made, felt the familiar glutinous texture of wonderbread underfoot.

The couple had by now, however, appeared together in the foyer like children being introduced to grownup guests—the real children behind them in nightdress, mocking their parents with their casualness, emerging genitalia pressed against the pale flyless flannel—Aaron self-conscious in a prewar double-breasted pinstripe suit and the aforementioned turtleneck, the pinstripes no longer parallel, Odile magnificent in an inherited black velvet Empire gown, a jet ribbon in her upswept hair, and, somehow, lemon elbow-length gloves. In her hand she held a preset 300 millimeter 3.8 telephoto lens.

"You both look lovely," Sam had to admit.

Aaron shuffled miserably, Odile beamed. The Dott twisted around in the chair to get a load of Aaron, mouth aflame with awefull grin. Sam hauled the Dott from the chair and introduced them. She pulled her forehead out of its knot and smiled. Shuffling and nodding, Aaron shifted his insignificance from foot to foot. But Odile stepped forward, gave the Dott a hug and a peremptory kiss upon the now reknotted forehead, and whispered some no doubt practical advice into a saffron ear.

The Dott stared all the while over Odile's shoulder at a shrinking Aaron. Sam opened the door as a hint. The Dott was reseated but she stared Aaron right out the door. Matthew, doubling his legs under him, however, leapt without warning into the Dott's lap, she emitting a manly grunt.

"Hey, you could hurt somebody that way," Sam warned him.

"Not around here," Odile whispered as she slipped by him, and followed Aaron down the stairs.

As Sam shut the door, Matthew became invisible in the Dott's arms.

Aaron was afraid of cars and insisted upon sitting in the back, Odile braving the death seat.

"What was she looking at?" Aaron asked plaintively.

"She wants your bod," Odile smirked.

"Come on, you two, let's not start that tonight," Sam said curtly.

Sam took them to the International Club, presented his MC card at the door, and Leonardo led them past the chromium

179

butcher's counter to the gleaming table, where he pulled out a captain's chair for Odile—into which Aaron swiftly slumped, providing as it did the premier view of the lake.

When drinks came, Sam proposed a toast to Aaron's art, and Odile cried out in response. Aaron took the olive out of his martini and put it on Odile's butter plate where it revolved until she popped it into her mouth. Sam and Odile then drank, but Aaron remained with his finger in his drink.

"What's wrong, honey?" Odile put her hand on his.

Aaron was gazing morosely at the other diners. Their skin stretched ripely over their skulls and rotund diaphragms, the wives' bodies younger than their faces, and husbands' faces younger than their bodies. Odile and Sam used their respective good eyes on the crowd.

"How come we're eating so well lately?" Aaron asked.

"We're celebrating, Aaron," said Sam. "Don't you see?"

"What?" Aaron persisted.

"We're celebrating," said Sam. "The fact that Dr. Agapecropolis could not attend the ballet; secondly, the event that I have the good fortune to know you; and third, the supremely important fact that you were available this evening."

"Here's something to celebrate?" Aaron said.

"It's all there is, I'm afraid," said Sam, and ordered another round.

"Good God," said Odile. "No philosophizing tonight, please!"

"Don't get drunk again, Odile," Aaron said, "or you won't be able to see the dancers."

Sam immediately felt Odile's thigh against his. He kicked at her vulgarism, and Aaron knocked over his drink.

"Sorry," said Sam, "very sorry," and placed his napkin over the stain.

"What'd I do?" said Aaron.

"My fault entirely," said Sam.

Leonardo had noticed and quickly replaced Aaron's booze. The photographer gave him a remarkable grin.

"Ya know," said Aaron, the second drink bringing a strange flush to his face, "who shouldn't mind having dinner here every day? I'd get sleek and fat, and Ody could dye her hair, and every day we could come up here and get shitfaced."

"Aaron," Odile cried, "what can you be saying?"

"That could get pretty boring," Sam affirmed.

"No, I mean it. Look at all the Jews in here. I got the best-looking wife in the joint. Why should I beat my brains out?"

His head sunk on his chest.

"Take it from me," Sam said, "that's no way to live."

"Certainly not," said Odile sharply. "Where's your integrity, Aaron?"

"There's not a man in this room who wouldn't trade places with you, Aaron, if he had the talent, including me," said Sam.

"My father used ta tell me," said Aaron slowly, his eyes glittering, "that I shouldn't trust nobody who told me I was well off. Because that meant he was doing something to me from behind."

"Oh God," moaned Odile. "Can't we just enjoy ourselves?"

"You think I enjoy what I do, Hooper?" Aaron said from behind his small pointy teeth. "You think I chose it freely or something? You think I like having you pay for my dinner?"

"Aaron, what you're attempting is far more important to society, and more self-satisfying, than what most of the people who can afford to come here do."

"What you will not understand ever, Hooper—" Aaron drew himself up surprisingly straight—"is that people like you can't ever make people like me happy. You think because what we do might make you happy that maybe you can reciprocate. That's a big lie, though; no matter how much money I make, it's *you* will

181

always be taking *me* to dinner, and no matter how fat I get, or how thin you stay, it's only *you* who will enjoy it."

"I'll have the fillet," Odile interjected harshly. "Is that all right, Sam?"

"Aaron," Sam continued in his calmest, most Purkified voice, "there's only one trouble. According to you, Odile's in my boat. She can't make you happy, but you say you can do it for her. Well, you dumb bastard, have a look at her!"

Odile was sobbing behind the menu.

"My wife is cursed," Aaron said without hesitation. "Neither one of us can do anything for her. I'll have a hamburger, well done."

"The ground round steak *trop cuit?*" the waiter intoned.

Odile asked to be excused.

Sam grabbed her hand as she passed and dug into his pocket for a quarter. "There's probably a maid in there," he whispered. "You'll have to tip."

Sam and Aaron contemplated each other over another round. Sam's good eye was not as playfully defective as the other. Aaron moved in a wash of pastels and glints, the guests mere chrysoprase and porphyry.

"Aaron," said Sam slowly, "you can respect yourself all you want, but you've got to do something about Odile."

"It's outta my hands," Aaron said. "She's gotta help herself."

"Somebody has to prove to her that life is worth living," Sam insisted. "You have to do that with women, you know."

"Maybe it isn't," Aaron said evenly, "for her."

"You mean it's hopeless?"

Aaron downed his drink and looked up. "Even for you," his accent slightly slurred, "it's hopeless. That's why I'm not afraid of you anymore."

Odile returned, her face scrubbed red, hair combed, pupils enlarged, a quarter the poorer, as the food arrived.

"What were you two talking about?" she asked.

"Oh nothing," Sam said, "Aaron's just promised to explain to me about this Jew business some time."

"I can hardly wait," she said as she sat down.

Aaron severed his hamburger in half and picked at it, holding his fork in his fist. Odile glanced at him, leaned forward, frowned, but then lost herself in the fillet. She cut across the grain with a butter knife and marveled at its pinkness. "God," she murmured, "just incredible."

Sam thought for a moment he could spend the rest of his life buying girls like Odile some steak. But then, disgusted with himself for this, he fed his dry but not unexpectant mouth.

A few bites later, however, he looked up to find Odile staring at him mercilessly. At first he thought she had simply lost control and, stimulated by the meat, was about to embarrass them all with some suberotic commentary. But she had eyes only for his food.

"Is that lobster?" she inquired tonelessly.

"Sure, would you like some?" said Sam.

"Hardly," she said.

"You don't care for shellfish?"

"I seen her eat it before," Aaron offered.

Odile reached back over her chair and took a menu off the server, glanced at it again, then flipped it back.

"Just as I thought," she said evenly. "South African. It says so right underneath. You couldn't have missed it. 'Genuine South African lobster.' Flown in today, it says; I'm very disappointed in you, Sam. Really."

Sam hovered in mid-bite, staring down at the rosy carapace on his plate. Aaron seemed to smile as he picked at his certified meat.

"After all, Sam, there are other things you could have ordered." Sam repacked the bite inside the shell and closed up the cavity with his fingers. Then he turned the lobster on its back.

"You'd think you could give up just a few things for the sake of solidarity."

"I'm sorry, Odile, it just didn't occur to me."

Aaron had begun his salad ravenously.

"I'll call the waiter back."

Odile gasped, "Oh, God, don't make a scene, Sam, you've already paid for it, the money's already in their coffers!"

"Well, if you'd been here when I ordered, perhaps—" Sam began.

"And now it's *my* fault," she wailed. "Can I help it if you're so indifferent?"

"It's all right, Odile, I won't eat any more. Please, let's try and enjoy ourselves."

But she had dissolved into tears once again, putting her hands to her face. "Oh, I've ruined it again!"

Aaron quietly slid the remnants of her fillet onto his plate and finished it along with several rolls. Then he combined both their salads, swallowing convulsively as the waiter cleared the dishes.

"The *langouste*, was it not good?" Leonardo inquired of Sam.

"Oh, it was very good," Sam said. "It just wasn't right."

The waiter hesitated only for a moment before whisking it back to the sea.

18 · . . . An Evening at the Theater . . .

They approached the trans-opera-office house in the rain:

The Theater formed the lobby of a skyscraper surrounded at street level by a staggering colonnade of derivative Egyptiana, its travertine loggias giving off to free elevators and endless slate lavatories. Custom-built in the Big Creamer to the specifications of an enterprising meat heiress, it was so designed that the rent from the high offices might subsidize opera-in-the-lobby in perpetuity, but subsequently, upon the discovery of antitrust violations (packing-house's price fixing of porkbellies) the heiress's trust officer and confidant was sentenced to an extended term in the penitentiary, the building fell into receivership, and the soft underbelly of *l'opéra* accordingly suffered a lengthy dyspepsia. Despite a decade of energetic pump priming, hot lunches for ersatz stagehands, it took the war before the house fully recovered its old momentum, functioning admirably as a bowling alley for intransit servicemen. And the best was yet to come, for the spate of mergers generated by the Whiz made it possible for the tough-minded but benevolent management of Scutter, Scoville, Whitman and Wood to assume directorship, and, after restoring the theater to its former coral-and-fuchsia glory, they imported a series of outstanding international attractions, even after commissions, turning a large enough profit to make up the increasing deficit of office rents, as the oak-and-onyx office space and commodious slate lavatories had with time become uncompetitive on a dollar-return-per-square-foot basis; and thus it could be truly said that commerce now rested firmly on the stooped but regilded shoulders of a thriving pay-as-you-go-culture. Or at least this was how it had been explained to Sam.

Agapecropolis' seats were excellent, Odile's fresh hair foiled the plush perfectly. Aaron adjusted a monopod between his legs and screwed the telephoto, which Odile produced from her evening bag, into his infrared Hasselblad planer R.

Odile was flushed and silent, her eyes set deep in pools of teared mascara. Sam saw in that face the quintessence of Gulleyness, the openness and excitement of simply being part of a defined audience, the spectacle itself unimportant, an audience whose courageous function it was to witness with equanimity the absolute impossibility of its own renewal.

Sam opened his program between them. The lights dimmed as a stout tuxedoed man announced to dispirited sighs the necessity of a stand-in for the male lead.

"He's Latvian-born, it says here," Sam said for their information.

"Don't read about it, just let it happen," Odile whispered scornfully, biting his earlobe for good measure. It actually occurred to Sam to smash her in the nose for this—the blood foaming on the plush, the ushers trying valiantly to stave off his flailing attack, Aaron faithfully recording it all, the headlines: "Frontman Punches Out Jew's Wife at Ballet."

As he submersed his shy grin behind the program the curtains parted, and Sam withdrew his pencil flashlight, intending to take a few notes for the doctor.

The stage was bare, brightly lit, perspectiveless, save for a large monument of indeterminate function. Sunney (the Latvian-born stand-in) *wrapped tight in Everyman's gauze*, according to the program, is carried onstage by eleven colleagues, paying as they are tribute to his coming of age. They are joined immediately by Sunney's old mentor, who *despite his corpu-*

lence is still capable of performing the *hilarious tankard-dance* amongst the congregation.

"The strings are questioning the oboes with a plaintive note of impending tragedy," Sam reads for Odile.

"Shush, Sam."

'A Grand Satrap enters with Sunney's mother,' Sam scribbles. Between them *with gracefully syncopated demi-entrechats they spool the lad from his carapace.* The crowd, which is now complete—gelded Nubians, neglected urchins—applauds this *sly* virtuosity. 'Sunney, however, seems somewhat disenchanted with this . . .' Sam writes, then copies from the program, *Tour de force, and exemplifies his contradictory nature with a remarkable* échappé soussous réléve en dehors.

The crowd responds characteristically with folk dances, artists and peasants present their wares, but Sunney indicates that his coming of age is hardly an occasion for levity. His mentor thereupon collapses in *a darksome stupor.* The Grand Satrap, *sensing a fiasco,* organizes the pretext of a hunt to divert the Prince's mind. Darkness falls abruptly. . . .

"The mysterious and doomful theme," Sam points out again. "Hear it?"

"Hey buddy, keep it down, will ya?"

Sunney nevertheless cannot dispel his apprehension with regard to the morrow. He stares dully up into the proscenium, its lengthening shadow absorbs him, a spotlight is turned upon him and he covers his face with enormous veined hands. . . .

All rush off into the night.

With the conclusion of the first act, Sam left Aaron and Odile to deserve each other. But, unable to recognize a soul in the high-columned lobby or spacious slate lavatories, he returned peremptorily with two cartons of lukewarm orangecrush.

"How you liking it?" he asked hesitantly.

187

"Oh, I just loved the—" Odile began.

"Modern, just modern," Aaron interrupted.

But the lights had dimmed, the curtains parted, and Aaron busied himself adjusting to the new light conditions. "God how I hate transitions," he mumbled.

"The music continues to develop its theme of strange foreboding," Sam read in a whisper, but Odile cut him off with a short elbow.

The ambience is watery pastel, a lake *made with mother's tears*, a single blowsy tree, and a precipice which looms in from the wings like the prow of a Jap destroyer.

Sunney and his colleagues hasten to the lakeside where they make out something in the distance which *gives them pause* . . . i.e., the most beautiful and certainly the biggest bird they have ever seen. "Sunney moves quietly, lest he disturb her," Sam writes. 'She seems terrified, he promises to help. . . .'

Laying down her lyre at which she had picked so unconvincingly, the Biggest Bird in the World *pauses motionless in arabesque* . . .

"Whilst the music informs us of the pathos of this gesture," Sam recites.

Odile gives him a furious slitlipped stare and even Aaron seems fairly disconcerted. Someone behind lays a hand on his shoulder for an instant.

She gestures toward the glade, he is abashed, their eyes melt and fix, Sunney is taken with his own reflection. . . .

Odile leaned over to whisper in Sam's ear, "Wasn't that just great?" and Sam loses track of the action momentarily. "You think I'll have as good a figure as that when I'm that old?" she persisted.

"Don't know, Odile. I won't be around when you're old," he whispered hoarsely. Much shuffling behind them.

. . . lover, love her, never love another, Sam reads, then writes, 'Then she will be saved?' The harp sounds a series of arpeggios, Sunney tries to make his way to the Bird, but she always glides just beyond his reach, until, spying the Sorcerer crouched on the precipice, she throws herself onto Sunney's back, driving him to his very knees. The Sorcerer extends a hideous foot into space and begins a stuttering stalk. . . .

But Odile had broken Sam's interest for good; in a fit of pique he snatches the telephoto from Aaron, who merely shrugs, gazing at the topmost edge of the proscenium. Sam focused initially between the hips of the Miss Julie Rowen to whom the part of the Biggest Bird had fallen this evening. He could not understand why Odile had thought her elderly—indeed her face was utterly childish, if impassive, and her sinewy pelvis seemed altogether delightful, though oddly cleftless.

A solo violin took up the romantic theme of the adagio—an old man in front of them attempted to disguise his cough by awaiting the most stirring chords—Sam could make out the bruises on her bare midsection, courtesy of this inexperienced emigré stand-in, no doubt. A rivulet of perspiration ran between her breasts, her makeup was gutted . . . then Sam noticed that the ballerina was staring at him as fixedly as he was regarding her. Was she using his large and open face to spot her turns? Sam smiled. She seemed to grit her teeth in reply.

Meantime, a chorus of birds has appeared *à la serpentine,* fluttering among Sunney's colleagues.

'The latter seem eager to slaughter the birds,' Sam writes. *The Valse Aparte begins.* The Big Bird bends low, her quiet body stirring expectantly. Sunney stiffens himself wistfully. . . .

"The idyllic nature of the dance has become luminously clear," Sam explicates innocently.

"Hey, how many times do ya have to be told . . . ?"

189

And now her love supports her as she accomplishes a slow pirouette. With some woodwinds gently hopping, she extends to her full height, palpitating with *petits battements.* Sunney is all obeisant love. Big Bird balances for an instant, then, holding her pose, falls to the side—at the last breathless second caught by her suitor. *Such distanciation achieved, a faint flush of light heralds the new dawn.* 'The Sorcerer now reappears on the precipice,' Sam notes, 'Big Bird is drawn irresistibly toward him, she is apparently helpless and must obey.' Sunney finds that he cannot rise from his knees. A pair of calculated cupids throw themselves at his feet. The Grand Satrap *commiserates in the new dawn as the birds are dispersed in it.*

The second intermission was brief, half-lit, no refreshments were to be had. But Sam stayed in the lavatory until the last possible moment, not wishing to face Odile's critique. He reflected that Purk had hardly prepared him to appreciate such art. He made his way back to his seat just as a trumpet flourish announced the ballroom scene.

'Griefstricken self-relevatory chords,' he wrote, 'Sunney appears aimless and solemn, scarcely looking at his guests.' *They are dismayed by his indifference, but cannot display their displeasure too markedly for fear of embarrassing their host.* Suddenly, a crash of cymbals announces the arrival of unexpected guests: it is of course the Sorcerer and the Big Bird; the latter returns Sunney's stare with a glance of cold but passionate interest. The crowd will not be denied their preparation for the banquet. They break into small groups, dancing only for each other, the ladies elaborating the basic positions of the classroom, the men's étude a simple competition of stunts and leaps, the children and ministers of the court joining in at their peril, while on a raised platform a dream banquet is pantomimed. But the Big Bird soon exerts her dominance, however, and choreographs the crowd as static couples to give dimension to her entrance. A gross tiara flashing on her head, she displays her cunning and guile with an unbelievable series of *échappés ménage de petites tours*, balanced, self-sufficient, ethereal. Sunney is clearly infatuated and performs thirty-two *fouettés* on his knees. *His fate hangs in the balance.*

'The music hesitates, and ignoring the Grand Satrap's advice, he takes some oath.' But at that moment, a crash of thunder brings him to his senses, and only then does he notice another (?) bird fluttering helplessly in the highest window of the palace. He has been deceived! Bird^1 is not Bird^2. The body in the window is wracked with sobs. The Sorcerer and phony bird exeunt with a flourish. The corps resumes its existence elsewhere. Sunney, *in an agony of guilt, ponders his quest.*

Sam was too embarrassed to fight his way out of the row for a record third straight time so stayed put. He urged Odile to read the program but she adamantly refused. Aaron ignored his genial questions. Then it was dark again.

All is hard and brittle in the moonlight. *Onset of a fierce storm.*

The birds yearn for the return of their leader, who enters forlornly, the Sorcerer ominous above her on the precipice. Sunney appears at once, frantically searching for his real bird, for Big Bird has secreted herself among her own kind. He is about to abandon hope when the birds bend down to reveal her. 'Sunney asks forgiveness but it looks like it's too late.' *With tears streaming down her smiling face, she eludes his spasmodic grasp and dashes headlong up the precipice.* . . .

Aaron was enraptured, his mouth open, the telephoto lay benignly in his lap.

Sam dropped his notes and took up the lens without apology, following Miss Julie Rowen as she leapt into the lake. He saw her disappear, plummet behind the scenery—and then, for an exquisite moment, her foot reappeared above the horizon as she rebounded from the trampoline. (A vision of Liberty ships, plunging through green waves, grain steaming from their funnels and portholes, swept over Sam momentarily.) As Sunney struggled to copy his love, however, the cheated Sorcerer caused the lake to recede, 'thus making his deathwish at once both impossible and superfluous,' Sam noted.

Clouds of steam rise from the stage, and Sam can see Julie Rowen make her way to the wings, there to lean nonchalantly against the stagelight control board. But Aaron chose this moment to wrestle the glass back from him, and as his program had slipped away in the confusion, it was necessary to readjust for the *dénouement*.

At first Sam thought the curtain had broken, for Sunney remained straining and frozen in a difficult *port de bras*, lost in the trough of an *entrechat royale*, not lovely but truly uncopyable, somehow redeeming his mediocre partnering in this— while the orchestra held its lusty chord for some minutes. Gradually, however, the dancer ceased to regard himself, and the audience, its collective ear canal jellied by the chord, realized finally that his eyes were not for but upon them.

Suddenly Sunney clasped his hands to his face, emitting a terrifying sigh which clunked the house as still as a mote. Sam could not tell whether his agony was due to a missed cue, physical pain, astute upstaging, or simply a final flourishing note of calculated modernity. But the orchestra was running out of breath and finger tension; the chord began to waver and roll, as if caught in the last groove of a recording, when just before redundant madness, the stylus was mercifully plucked free.

In the flooding silence, the Sorcerer descended from the precipice as the Bird entered from the wings, and each taking one of Sunney's hands, relieved him from his spectacular but untenable positioning. Rather than strutting toward the applause, however, they *bourréed* as one backwards until, upon nudging the set, their buttocks on the far horizon line of the defunct lake, they unclasped hands and assumed hands on hips, an untheatrical indifference. Sam noted that their detached passivity was perhaps the highest proof of their love.

The same stout man who had announced the necessity of a stand-in now returned, the spotlight trailing him fitfully, to ask, not without some disdain, that the audience turn to the last page of their programs. Sam located his beneath the seat.

IN THE INTERESTS OF A FULLY PARTICIPATORY CULTURE, THE CONCLUSION
OF THIS PERFORMANCE WILL BE DECIDED BY MAJORITY VOTE ON THE SEVEN
POSSIBLE LEGITIMATE CLIMAXES. KINDLY DETACH BUT DO NOT FOLD THIS
REFERENDUM CARD. CHOOSE ONE (AND ONLY ONE) ENDING WHICH YOU THINK
OR FEEL MAKES THE OCCASION MOST WHOLE, AND DEPOSIT IN THE CANISTERS
WHICH WILL BE PASSED AMONG YOU. DO NOT SIGN THIS REFERENDUM CARD.

[ ] A. TRADITIONAL APOCALYPTIC   (ALL DIE)

[ ] B. CLASSICAL APOTHEOTIC   (ALL DIE, BUT SUNNEY AND BIRD GO
                                        TO HEAVEN, THE SORCERER NOT)

[ ] C. AMERICAN PICARO   (SUNNEY KILLS SORCERER, LEAVES BIRD)

[ ] D. ENGLISH ROMANTIC   (EITHER SUNNEY OR BIRD KILLS SELF
                                        AT THE EXPENSE OF THE OTHER)

[ ] E. FRENCH REALISTIC   (BIRD KILLS EITHER SUNNEY OR SORCERER,
                                        LEAVING OTHER TO OWN DEVICES)

[ ] F. RUSSIAN CONTEMPORARY   (NO ONE DIES AND ALL MAKE UP)

[ ] G. INTERNATIONAL ALEATORIC   (SORCERER KILLS ONE OF THE TWO, THE OTHER
                                        RANDOMLY RECIPROCATES IN HIS FASHION)

But before Sam could exercise his birthright, Aaron was up and slamming down the row, minks' head and tiny deboned paws jumped upon the shoulders of those whose toes he interdicted. His telephoto swung a cruel arc from his pelvis, knocking the canister from the hands of the pert usherette, scattering the ballots upon the scarlet carpet. Sam with Odile in tow apologized profusely down the scandalized row, hustling after Aaron up the aisle.

A wind had come up, creating a vacuum in the columned lobby. They could barely open the revolving glass doors against it. It was the first time Sam had ever seen Aaron out of his slouch. They caught up with him at Burt Street, where he turned north toward Olde Towne, away from the Great Lady, now like a green gladiola against the tuberose sheen of the completed Parking Tower.

"Culture," Aaron yelled over his shoulder, "is just what hurts artists most."

"You could have at least let us see the end," Odile blurted, puffing so hard she couldn't push one cry.

"The end. Screw the end," Aaron was screaming at the top of his lungs now. "You can't just pimp the old stuff and call it new. The bastards are just marking time, busting up everything—if you fuck over the old stuff you just copy it—like a reverse negative."

Sam was speechless at this outburst, so amazed in fact that he did not even regret his own silence.

Yet he was not particularly disappointed to have missed the end. For he had detected in Sunney's mood—though this was no doubt attributable to the shallow mimesis of the stand-in—the promise of his ultimate capitulation. That in a sense he was fated to succumb to his own misappropriated strength. Not that he was nothing without the Birds (one or the other, what does it matter in the end?), not even that he was to finish unforgiven and without dignity, but simply the small knowledge that a single concession to her kind of weakness would be sufficient to destroy him. Sunney was getting monotonous, and he would have to go.

Sam and Odile took up their places at Aaron's side and escorted him north, across the river. The river emptied into a rectangle of white night at the lake, in which was framed the Pumping Station, glowing from within, its tiny derricks limp, a brooding chapel in the middle distance. Once he thought he heard footsteps behind him and turned only to see the Parking Tower, a formation of Canadian geese zonking serially into it, its V-formation becoming U.

They passed Peacock Prairie without a word, and it was there that Odile took her husband's arm, almost tenderly.

"Well?" She brightened. "Which end would *you* have chosen?"

Sam revered them at this moment—for Odile retained all those impulses which in Sam had become blunted, complected through his modicums of success and what we might as well call knowledge. Her meliorism had remained embryonic and on display like a fetus in amber, an artifact of fundamental decency, neither misdirected nor achieved, just stumped. As for Aaron, Sam no longer envied his talent, that German 10-forward-speed transmission and that little Monocoque Jewish chassis, but simply the absence of guilt in the man. So at last Sam felt that density which must have occasioned their first encounters, those nights on the linoleum in a Brooklyn pharmacist's kitchen; he scorned a life so large and distracting that it could absorb the full strength of their repudiation, package it and feed it back to them in bite-size morsels until appetite itself was ritual. Suddenly unable to help either, he could love them both.

"But which *one?*" Odile whispered at their door.

Aaron ascended the stairs slowly. Sam remained in the foyer. Odile stumbled in her high heels in the dog smell between

196

them. Aaron spoke softly without turning around.

"Look, folks," he said, "art's just a zoo. And that's what's nice about it. But what makes a zoo in the end is the cages, not the animals. And the cages are built with the looker in mind, not the animals. The buffalo's is bigger than the salamander's maybe, but then again maybe it suits the buffalo to put him in a box so's he has to kneel and give the salamander more running room than he's got strength for. But you don't ask who's treated better, do you? 'Cause they can't talk, even when you throw them a marshmallow—just sigh or growl. The whole thing depends on the keeper—whether he can make you forget about if whether they might be happier somewhere else, but just make you certain—and if he's good, glad—that they're there at all. Now if you've got a cheetah who can run a hundred mph, you've got a problem. If the people who pay wish he was back in the jungle, then you've screwed up—but if they say to each other 'It's a shame he's not where he can *really* run,' but are secretly glad he's right here so they can afford to say something generous like that, then you've made it. You've done your duty, and I say fuck the cheetah. 'Course the truth is nobody moves much in a zoo, probably 'cause they don't eat much. Not even the vultures eat much at the zoo. But still, why do the people go? Well, the main thing they hope for is that maybe something will get out of those cages, isn't it? That's the keeper's job too, to help them think it's *possible* even though everything's locked up tight, so's they can always come back, whenever they want, watch them slipping on their shit, eat and sleep and hide and even die. . . ."

Aaron's voice had become only a murmur as he fumbled with the door.

"Gee," said Sam, genuinely impressed, at the bottom, in the dark, "with a little education, Aaron, you could have made a great manager."

Odile glanced repeatedly but without conviction up and down the stairs.

The Dott was asleep on the mattress in the alcove, Matthew curled in the arc of her haunches. He woke up suddenly as they entered, eyes white with fear, and Odile brusquely carried the boy back to the rear bedroom. The Dott rubbed her eyes, stretched insouciantly and walked heavily to the foyer. Aaron paid her out of a piggybank filled with change, and as she deposited it in her coin purse, she grabbed his hand up to the wrist so that he cringed, but then she was gone down the stairwell.

"I guess she likes you," grinned Sam on his way out.

"She knows I'm worse off than you, that's all," Aaron muttered.

"But she likes me too, Aaron."

"Why shouldn't she? You're her meal ticket. Well, thanks for the show."

"You think you got anything good?"

But Aaron had already shut the door to the darkroom. Sam yelled back to Odile. "How'd you like it, kiddo?"

She did not answer immediately, but just as he shut the door he heard from the kitchen, "You've taught me not to have simple reactions like that."

Sam gave a sigh like Sunney's as he backed out.

In the darkened stairwell the Dott grabbed his hand and whispered, "Man, you oughta see what he's got in that lil ol' darkroom!"

"Yeah?"

"An'," she added, much too loudly, "you oughta see his unnerwear!"

As they reached the street, Sam snapped his fingers in dismay.

"You know what, Dott?"

Her eyes widened expectantly.

"I believe I've lost my car."

19 · . . . *And a Late-Nite Snack*

Sam accompanied the Dott halfway on the subway and was home himself before midnight. He finished a bottle of Scotch and two heavy Morocco lids to the sound track of *The Crazed Bird*, opening his side vents for maximum brilliance and reproduction. The room wheeled about his body, a nest of light filled his brain, the phone rang—an offended neighbor—he hung up on the programatic scream, disconnected the phone, tuned the stereo-loungerspeaker to its last decibel.

Then he stripped and went to the bathroom, took his several vitamins—B^1 through B^{12}.

Sam Hooper took unabashed and detailed account of himself in the mirror. He had lost an inch or so on his calves, he supposed, even more in his thighs, particularly in the hamstrings which had tightened in deference to his commutings, so that while his buttocks had not actually enlarged, they appeared so in relation to the diminished thighs. There was a small inexplicable fold of flesh above his pubes, and his kidneys had begun to balloon slightly over his pelvic bowl. His arms remained heavily veined and sinewy, though the biceps were no longer startlingly convex, and the scars on his forearms had disappeared save for a small gray dot where he had broken a pencil off into himself during that eventful third grade. His once bony shoulders had filled in nicely, however; the broken collarbone had knitted—all this on the plus side—but he was disturbed at the way his nipples had begun to converge toward each other slightly, indicating a collapse of the lungs, a weakening of the diaphragm and a deterioration of the foraging muscles. He was oblivious to these pectoral mutations, but even that was not true—indeed he was honoring them—but he proceeded after several warmup *demi-pliés* to extend his punting leg, first horizontally to his body, and then finally, after more pain than the average man can stand, into a reasonably graceful and fully extended *developpé*, assisted by bracing his foot on the shower-curtain rod, achieving perhaps 166°. He balanced there taut in the mirror, the loose grin of a gentle head set in a body trained for victory; then, removing his numbed heel from the shower rod, he launched into bed.

October 19, 1929: arrived at Port Tewfe where Sturdy and I had put in nine days before. Told them of my plans about building another boat, and they said I should stay and build it in their canal shops. No doubt some were sincere, but I was also getting other talk from behind my back.

October 27: took the train for Palestine on a whim. A high official of a church there asked me, "do you believe in God, Captain Fuess?" And when I answered "yes" he said then, "I am surprised that after the way you have been and are being treated that you believe in any kind of god at all." The Jews are small of stature but seem to be of good nature.

Traveled by rail some 450 more miles south to Luxor (?), traveling second class so as to spend the day among the natives. On asking among them why-how a religion on which a great empire had been built can completely disappear was told it was only one of God's multitude of stepping stones, leading mankind to something better. That seemed fair enough.

I was much impressed by the ruins built by Ameno the third, where it hit me like a flash-of-light. I had sat down on a stone that had fallen from the ceiling inside the temple and the truth seemed pretty simple. The King of Luxor, like the carpenter of Nazareth, was unable to have a child. The queen was embraced by "God" in this room and had a "Virgin Birth" of a naturally future king. This was recorded by the Temphramites who scratched their divinations in the thick ashes of the ruined temples of their civilization and who were then blamed for both ephemerality and blaphemy. As Sho-Mar has said, "they out-brillianced their own brilliance," but they knew what to write on, if not exactly what.

I came out of that damp, semidark room a wiserman. It's not what is, it's what happens to you there!

"Shoemaker," I said to myself, "stick to your last!"

Sam could not concentrate on the Fuess, however; the good captain's voyage seemed to have lost its momentum. Guiltily, tentatively, he switched on the TV. Sam Hooper[2] was just completing *A Continuing Image of Greatness* review:

". . . It cannot be said that this production was a total failure, and, in fact, if one was to judge by audience reaction alone, it might well be termed a moderate success. On one level, it is the usual girl-meets-boy story—girl meets boy, girl loses boy, girl gets boy, and both are lost; on another, it presumably relates to some European legend, but such references are incidental to the choreography and the wise spectator is advised not to pursue any such analogy too far. But having placed the production in intellectual perspective, we should move immediately to a consideration of *this* performance, though as we shall see, there is no escape from some reductive, comparative analysis. After all, it isn't the *first* time I've seen this ballet.

"Let it be said, initially, that the conducting and the score triumph over any of the characterizations; above all, this is a work for the melomane. As such, it was not surprising to find the corps work rather muted; the story, of necessity perhaps, unfolds against a picturesque if static tableau of immobile bodies which take part only peripherally in the action. Nevertheless this is not just an assemblage of bits and pieces for their virtuoso aspects but a unified work of art, realized with strangely loving care, by an all too invisible choreographer.

"Act I is little more than prologue and rather overweighted with mime, but its *allegro vivace* pace is endearing and the variations were well conceived. Nevertheless, I felt that it did not properly prepare one for what was coming.

"Act II, justifiably famous, departed from the original with its heavy emphasis of the subplot, and made extensive use of choreography taken from other ballets. It smacks of after-thought, tries to pack too much in, and initiates a progressive fragmentation from which the production never really recovers. Furthermore, the *scène d'action* between the two principals was not sustained, only on one occasion achieving genuine poetry.

"Act III is too long—though perhaps only for those who know it well—consisting of the usual complement of independent eclectic character dances, though it must be admitted that the final *grande révérence à la queste* is both a brilliant foil to and summation of the rather arty, erratic and involuted exercises which began the act.

"The well-known final act, while perhaps best from the intellectual standpoint, has no special dance interest; indeed, it is curiously unresolved in this production, over before you know it, and at one point the action and tempi slowed almost to a halt. I did not stay for the final tabulation.

"But enough of mere story summation: for the peculiar characterizations here should bear our closest scrutiny. All of them, these personages, bear some relation to the real world; strange things may happen to them, but they live finally within predetermined conventions. If I understand the director's intention, we are presented with perfectly nice, normal, fleshed-out people, who, rather than developing according to his dictates, gradually strip eachother of personality, losing their dimensions in the process, as from stereo-organism to sculpture to bas relief to fresco to afterimage. What prevents this from being merely agonizing is the character of the girl. For in the world of sky and water she is at home, but where romance is possible she is irretrievably lost; her love for a worldly prince is doomed from the start. But it is not the quality of her love which attracts us; *her fear is what stirs our passion.*

"Alas, in Miss Julie Rowen, we have a well-intentioned but mechanical performance; her schizophrenia is rather too stylized to sustain our interest, though there are those, I'm sure, who would insist that this is the very point. Nevertheless, this most arduous of dual roles, in which down and bone must never be confused, can only succeed when it exemplifies those "thousand little touches" which can be gained only from hundreds of performances, under varied conditions, and in this day and age our performers are simply not exposed to such thoroughgoing experience.

"Her lack of confidence was not helped by her partner—a stand-in, albeit. His strain was quite apparent during the great majority of the lifts—as anyone knows, he should lift her high and laugh as he does it. Strong and graceful perhaps, but lacking that ultimate stature we associate with true virility. He can manage, I should say in his defense, to stay up in the air longer than any male lead I've had the pleasure to see, but his getting up there can be rather grotesque. Making up for his lack of both height and concentration, he at times overcame eclectic style by getting way up into the air, feinting, floating. Nevertheless he failed to grasp his role as Prince, acting extraordinarily uncomfortable with those who were clearly his inferiors. In this sense, I'm afraid this Sunney is a poor vehicle of expression. He was forever staking out an ambivalence when he could have been engrossing. After all, the trick is to show that Sunney is sick of his own story without making *you* sick. A workmanlike, honest and truthful performance, then, but here we need something better than the truth, something beyond the technical perfection of this Latvian aviator.

"And surely, the most disconcerting of all, was the rather strange conception of the 'villainous' Sorcerer, which was played with such an ambiguous combination of animal talent and calculated lethargy that one not only questioned his capacity for evil but wondered what profit there was in his putting the Bird under his spell in the first place. If there's a mean streak here, it's Sunney who has it.

"We would also be remiss not to note that the role of Mother was excised from the third act and a lengthy pantomime introduced in her stead. And also, to comment on the shoddy quality of the borrowed sets: the precipice sagged and the abyss bounced.

"So, all in all—attractive though it is, requiring considerably precise execution, and filled with the most heartbreaking recapitulations, lyrical digressions which abate without warning, accelerations which obliterate all contingencies—its exuberance seemed, at least to this viewer, somewhat out of keeping with the serious mood dictated by the theme."

Sam was by now asleep, however, and shortly he reenacted the dream he had so palpably concocted for Agapecropolis, finding himself in the interstices of domed hallways, being introduced to a dainty chick of definite pubescent disposition. They joined hands without a word and walked out on the balcony of a minaret which overlooked a plaza of the very best neofascist persuasion. A colossal statue of a togaed trumpeteer dominated the deserted plaza, and at its furthermost edge Sam could make out other marble-inlaid plazas multiplying into infinity.

They wound down the spiral staircase to find each rectangle ankle-deep with clear warm water, the mosaics perfectly visible but their geometricism pleasantly plastic in the sunlit eddies. Each rectangle took on the hue of the mosaics which made up its floor; the waters spilled silently from fluted corners to the next level.

They walked hand in hand, wordlessly, she in a short tunic the color of which changed to match the water in which they waded; upon reaching each horizon Sam would jump down to the next level and then, reaching up with one arm, swing his companion down, her tunic caressing his face, her pinched thighs sliding the length of his lubric body, until her impassive face passed his and she was beside him. He refused to kiss her, curious about her reaction, but she seemed in no hurry. Sam, seeing no end to it, awoke purposively to a twilight sleep, his mouth death dry.

Then, leaving her petulant upon the highest ledge available, he drifted down again, into one of those better dreams in which he often specialized, both observer and participant.

. . . Give me one reason why I should have recognized him. He looked just like any one of those shortish ugly successful old men from whom we all make a good living serving. What am I going to do? Ask him where's his tie like some lady *maître d'?* Provide him with the lumpish house sportcoat last worn by the poloshirted son of a Dayton impresario? It's not for me to hide his collarbones. His agent knew we couldn't afford to care.

I showed him to a corner booth, the one where converging mirrors splinter the diners appropriately into mismatched halves for other spectators, and didn't think any more about it. As far as I know, Leonardo accomplished his usual no-nonsense serving. And it certainly wasn't the food. Yet, after the gazpacho, steamed turbot and zabaglione, I brought them the bill. And right there, before my eyes, the agent took a silver laundry pen from his vest, and handed it to the old gentleman who proceeded to scrawl all over the tablecloth. It was pretty illegible, but it said PICASSO. Then they both pushed past me, grinning horribly.

They certainly didn't anticipate anything like that in Purk

Hotel School *Case Book*, I can tell you. I think I had read something in the papers about great artists like him not paying for things like that. But I never thought it would happen to me. Well, I ran around the serving table just in time. They were almost to the coat rack when I intercepted them. The agent tried to push by me but I gave him a short elbow. He crumpled exaggeratedly against the coat rack, managing his best lawsuit stare. Picasso, though, just stood there in his hot-shot Riviera sport shirt smiling pleasantly. He wasn't "screeching hysterically in a foreign tongue" or anything like that. I'll give that to him. The agent caught his breath, hissed, pointed dramatically at me.

"Christ, buster, don't you know who this is?"

I replied that I had indeed heard of M. Picasso.

"That signature is worth ten of your lousy meals right now and more than that in publicity," he averred.

I allowed as that might be so, but that I really could not accept anything more than the advertised price of the meal. Under the strained circumstances, however, and for the sake of international goodwill, you could say, I would not charge for the tablecloth.

The agent fell back quizzically, groggily. Picasso shrugged and wrinkled. I seemed taller than either of them. The agent and I exchanged baffled glances for several minutes, Picasso intermittently admiring our collection of celebrity photos.

The agent put a limp hand into an inside coat pocket. "OK," he muttered. Draping a polyethylene sheath of cards over his forearm, he selected one and waved it wearily at me.

"I'm afraid we don't take credit cards," I said. "It says so right on the menu. That particular one, as a matter of fact, involves a kickback of some thirteen percent."

Then it was the agent who began to "screech hysterically in a foreign tongue." He yelled at Picasso and pulled on the delicate lapels of his sport shirt. Picasso produced the insides of his vaudevillian pockets, blushed and grinned at me. Neither had a cent on them.

"I know what you're driving at," the agent gasped, "you want *more*, don't you? You wanna pretty picture! Right? OK."

He shoved Picasso back to the table and made him take out his pen again. Working recalcitrantly, his whole fist about the cylinder, he put ears on the *P* and changed it into a goat. He made a crucifix out of the *I*, and a pig in heat out of the *C*. Then he stepped back hopefully. The agent nodded but I didn't. Leonardo had a silly pleased smile on his face. (Our people work on a salary basis.)

The agent held up the tablecloth, flourishing it like an Arab for my better knowledge, which I disdained. Picasso shrugged and added a garland of flowers about the edge of the cloth. I didn't bat an eye.

It was getting along in the afternoon and nearly all of the guests had left. Leonardo was putting the unused pats of butter back into the cooking crock. They both had sat down again, disconsolate in their booth. Picasso seemed calm enough, but the agent looked as though he might make a run for it any minute.

"Look, Mac, what is it that you want?"

"Why, a fair price, sir."

He sunk in a glower.

"Free gifts don't go very far these days, you see." I tried to be polite about it.

Picasso nibbled on a salt stick and kept doodling away on the tablecloth. The agent watched him sadly.

"You're getting a goddamn masterpiece," he sighed.

"If he hadn't signed it," I said, "I could take it home and put it on the kid's bedroom wall. He could figure it out, then, lying on his back at night, and see it when he got up in the morning if he had time. But now you're making it what it is. I couldn't take it. Just pay for your meal and get the hell out of here. If M. Picasso liked the food, he'll be back."

The agent stared sullenly.

"Go ahead, ask him if he liked the food."

The agent translated.

"He liked it OK, I guess."

"Just OK?" I said.

"Nope," he admitted, "he liked it a lot."

"You see?" I said.

I folded up the tablecloth carefully, cheerfully, and presented it to them. Then I relaxed and sat down in the booth with our clients.

M. Picasso has his art all right, but it's people like me who make or break civilizations.

"It's getting on toward dinnertime," I mentioned later.

Picasso was dozing in the corner of the booth. He looked like a newborn baby, and, as he snored, little puffs of fog appeared on our converging mirrors. I supposed he was especially comfortable in his beltless white trousers and sport shirt. The agent and I then had a long discussion about the war, his recent surgery, and several marriages.

Leonardo dropped some dishes in the back, and M. Picasso awoke inquisitively. He stood up, stretched and began to putter about the restaurant, returning eventually to the gallery of celebrity photos we had inherited from the previous management. He seemed delighted with Frankie Crosetti, Wilbur Shaw, J. D. Salinger, Edward R. Murrow, Constance Bennett, Charles E. Wilson, Billy Graham, Emile Durkheim, Vincent Price, J. C. Penney, Lionel Trilling, Harry Hopkins, Van Cliburn, Ludwig Erhardt, and the rest of them.

I kept the agent hostage with a patient knee. Picasso asked Leonardo for a butter knife, who obliged him with a bow. Picasso then began to pry the celebrities from their frames, taking care not to mutilate or fold, stacking the prints neatly upon a Sèvres serving platter. Leonardo brought him a chair so he could reach the highest ones, and *cher maître* took off his pointy shoes so as not to crush the plush.

At the very top, he took down the signed profiles of Ernesto Gallo, Solly Hemus, John K. Galbraith, Walter Slezak and A. Krishna Menon. Then he called for a thick béchamel sauce, which he spread with a spatula into the frames, larding here and there with an adhesive mixture of Bel Paese and crème Chantilly. He didn't spill a dollop, and very soon the wall was solid with white béchamel, each empty frame geometrically distinct.

In the upper left-hand panel, with pastry guns and skewers of pistachio nuts, he began to construct an elephant of sweetbreads, low. The elephant proceeded clumsily through a bas relief of pecan palms and liver pâté boulders. For perspective, he built a crenellated wall of transparent prosciutto, with battlements of snow peas and flying buttresses of green snap beans and Mrs. Mangle's Louisville lime pie. A bite-sized boy of vanilla extract with a skeleton of allspice proudly carried the head of veal roll giant toward the city. Picasso spoke sharply to his agent.

"David returning with the head of Goliath to Jerusalem," it was translated.

Picasso shrugged and went on to the second of the twenty-eight available panels. A cornstarch-and-watermelon-rind Jehovah exploded from a macaroon sun upon a scene in which a marzipan boy was crushed beneath a cart of *papillote* laden with lingonberries. The bulls drawing the cart were of striped sea bass, their craven aspic drivers prodding them with gaffs of celery stuffed with red caviar. The cart's wheel was emendated with spokes of crab and frog. The onlooking evangelists were of tamale and rhubarb, respectively, cloaked in artichoke. And above, around and all about cruised multitudinous cupids of apricot mousse. The Lord held a miter of banana *rhumbé*, his coriander eyeballs fixed apprehensively upon his own proscenium: in this case, a decorous foliage of sculpted tongue and quatrefoil zucchini, dotted here and there with niches in which fey madonnas of guacamole with childs of tartar conducted business as usual.

Picasso spoke sharply again.

"The Reliquary of St. Zenobius," the agent translated.

Picasso went on working while we got things ready for dinner, Leonardo keeping an eye on the agent for me. When he was finished, however, and the twenty-eight panels gleamed with the whole of our kitchen, Picasso turned from his work and instructed us to sit. We pushed butcher's blocks together in the kitchen, laid our various uniforms over them and put on the best service. It was at this point that Norman the chef became hysterical, opining that there was no food left to serve the clientele, much less ourselves, no matter what the significance of the occasion.

Picasso seemed to understand. He spoke at length to the agent, who summarized:

"This is the most outstanding of my works. I labored at it with the utmost ardor and technical attainment, completing it with all possible artistry, sense of proportion and knowledge of art. Let's eat."

Picasso started to sign his name at the base, but I gently took his hand and beckoned him to the table. Then we all carried our plates to the gates of paradise and helped ourselves. Dishwashers and waiters, saladmen and pastrywomen, honored guests and employees, our heads banging against the pans and servers as we sat to our buffet. And at either end of the table, *Purk School of Hotel Management*, Ithaca (B.S., M.B.A.) and *Academia de Bellas Artes*, Barcelona (no degree taken).

I myself gourmandized the wheel of the *Zenobius* reliquary, topped with the raisin eyes of the evangelists, and the curried pluvial of our Lord. Picasso had the bulls on their backs, angels of minced quail and the pepper and pimento abyss from the *Apocalypse*. Our agent had only a section of meringue quatrefoil, feigning nausea as the first fork punctured the masterpiece. I would have had him eat the whole of it for his better knowledge, holding his nostrils the while.

After dinner we returned arm in arm to have a last look at the gates of paradise. They were nearly stripped, of course, the frames obscured by our hasty serving; bits of garlic sausage remained, as did clouds of sesame, caraway, anise. A whole uncooked beef tenderloin which had served as the *Catafalque of St. Felix* sagged from its skewers; a film of blood had turned the béchamel to the dusk rose of transubstantiation.

"A new period. A breakthrough!" screamed the agent.

Picasso and I exchanged weary glances and began to put the photos back in place. We squeezed them into their frames, he deftly cleaning whatever sauce oozed from behind their glazed faces. He took particular care with the profile of Frankie Crosetti, as the remains of the panel distorted his face.

The restoration took longer than the creation. Leonardo had had to turn away a dinner crowd at the door.

When everything was back in place, Picasso took the agent firmly by the arm and asked if I could recommend a place for a late supper. . . .

Sam's eyes clicked open. He had forgotten to pull the drapes and was terrified to see Odile twenty-seven stories up, banging and barging against his window in the moonlight like an enormous seabird. She held her arms out to him imploringly.

He leapt from the bed and just made it to the bathroom, where in dreamy convulsions he vomited the lobster *et al.* Without a single thought, he lay on the cool tiles the rest of the night in his own and various fluids.

20 · *Partner of Her Doubleness, or Domesticity*

Sam had lost his patience and was about to really give the Dott hell for once, but Dean's introduction light interrupted them. He managed to press the release mechanism in spite of her obduracy.

He was purely relieved to see Odile. Since their "celebration," he had called in sick to the office for two straight mornings—spending long unproductive hours in his echo chamber—he was beginning to sense just how full of life he was, and how much it was being wasted for him. Furthermore, he knew Agapecropolis would expect a full report on the ballet, and in all honesty he didn't know quite what to make of it. Indeed, he had found both Aaron's and Hooper[2]'s postcommentary more interesting than the performance itself, and this militated against everything Purk and Humanities I stood for. All he could really recall the morning after his "iodine" poisoning was how much he'd like to break that little bitch Miss Julie Rowen's proscenium, turn all her impassiveness to an ugly moan, give her something real to get her tail wet for. For once, his lycanthropy was neither charming nor serviceable.

Odile had been done another way. Had bought a new dress, a crimson stretch shorty, with panels cut out exposing her hips. Her hair swept into a kind of horizontal bouffant, eyesockets sprinkled with sequins, lips tumescent, fried and frosty. In one hand she carried an enormous strapless alligator wallet, and in the other, lord love her, a mandolin.

"I'll bet you feel like a new woman," Sam said.

"Aaron's gone to New York for an exhibit or something. The kids are with the folks. I can stay all night for once." She was winking furiously.

The Dott was not disarmed and got out of there fast.

"Actually, I'm glad you can stay," Sam said, swiveling the stereo-lounger to receive her newness. "This fellow at the office has given me *quite* a little package, the latest thing, he claims, and I think we ought to go over it together."

Odile smiled secretively and seemed to be in a reasonable mood.

"Have you eaten anything within the last four hours?" Sam inquired.

She shook her head pertly.

"Good, well, shall we have a look then?"

Sam took the fat envelope from his attaché case and flipped it into the bedroom. The Dott had just put on fresh striped sheets. Odile undressed with her back to him as if she were in a movie. Her skin was oiled, the whorls of light hair along her spine were iridescent in the sunset. Against her body the lake was burgundy. She backed toward the bed and snapped the sheets over her. Sam got in beside her and opened the packet on his chest. Then he began to read matter-of-factly:

INSTITUTE OF DYNAMIC SYNTHESIS
A Systems Analysis of Sexual Reciprocity
by Dr. Karla Carmel, M.D. Ph.D.
• a Doctor and a Mother •
Circulated in conjunction with Management Concern's
Living Authors Program
Christos E. Agapecropolis, General Editor

"The Buddha, it is said," Sam continued, "died from eating a piece of spoiled meat, for he was too polite to complain to his host. It is such well-intentioned affectations that the modern conjugal couple must avoid if the Christian institution of marriage is to be saved, nay, revivified. Yes, our aim is nothing less than refulgent, dappled meeting of all the senses for joyous purposes. . . ."

Odile had begun to cry.

Sam put his arm around her, cupping a breast.

Our narrator skipped the sections on "The Panther's kiss," and "The Coital Boomerang," but he could not resist the packet which fell from the centerfold onto his stomach.

Aphrodisiacpak: Take one fresh carp, scald in a mixture of its roe, add one ounce Gizend, one ounce vanilla, two elxologarum pods and this packet. Let the whole macerate for fifteen days, to which add forty grains pulverized musk and three drops of rose essence. Strain. Boil in pure spring water and serve with the wine habitually drunk (Remember, California is making some good wine these days).

He opened the packet, took a whiff, and then placed it carefully on the bedside table. In the packet there was also a small recording, *The Sounds of Love*; the first band, "Low Moans," the second, "Gentle Oohs and Ahhs," and the flip side, "Exquisite murmurings." Sam put this on the stereo-lounger and, turning to Chapter Seven, or "Gita Govend," dogeared by Agapecropolis, began to read against the stylish grunts:

"It is not *Know* thyself, friends, but *Be* thyself. Pure expression in the pure embrace—*Yab-Yum* the noble *Yab-Yum*—for it's such sex that frees man from desire itself. . . ."

Odile was still crying. Sam hugged her close.

". . . Only ignorance can make you feel pain. Only misguided intelligence can prevent you pleasure. The end is when *each is both*, and then truly, the whole universe is *Play*. The old, old tenth-century Prayer of the Sweethearts is relevant here."

Bhoga Worship

I love you for the confusion
Of your intentions, the
Hopelessness of your persistence

Oh, how I love to see myself
Reflected in one who will end
Even worse than I

The ache of invisibilities, gross
Need so dignified, for as snakes
Are souls, so our bodies seek communion

Where each is both, a natural love is that
In which woman kisses all manliness away,
And he will be partner to her doubleness.

Odile had stopped crying and simply sniffled.
Sam continued:

The Seven Vesicles of Liberation
The First: The quad-o-grotus (originally marketed as the Memphis Extension) a medical science breakthrough.
  A two-piece appliance, carefully manufactured by American craftsmen of the foam and latex industry to rigid government specifications, designed to rekindle dormant emotions. Guarantees more concise friction between those neglected zones which more than likely do not make adequate contact during normal or adventitious congress. If you really are going to be a partner to her doubleness, then you must have this dual-response simulator.* (Available in flesh or ebony)

Odile had again disappeared beneath the covers sobbing like an engine.

* *Publisher's note:* We strongly advise the man with large endowment or minors not to use the Memphis extension.

"For God's sake, Odile," Sam barked, "relax. Take it for what it's worth. There six to go."

She kicked viciously at him out of her fetal position. He wiped his grin away.

"Look, I'll just give you this little test, Odile, now just lie still and quit bawling. Now," Sam read: " 'If you just met me, and you thought I was trying to make you, and I said, *Look, why don't we go for a walk in these lovely woods*, what would you say?' Hm?"

"Yes," she moaned.

" 'Now, what would you say if, on the other hand, I said, *Let's go to that lovely hotel over there.*' "

"No," she moaned.

"See, there you are. A breakdown in urban communication. You've been conditioned to get your attention from denial. You've pitied people who've tried to get in your pants for too long. You've got no style as a result."

Odile poked her head out from under the blankets, emerging loving and tender, *ad majoram gloriam*, incapable of pursuing the discussion rationally. Why, it's Miss Odets, Sam thought. She drew her clutched thighs along his hip, kissing him on the chest like a child. Then she looked to him, every feature softened with incredulity.

"Sam, what are you trying to do to me?"

"We have to try every angle, Odile."

"I will *not* let you use that thing," she said finally.

"It says here:

> The truth's, Madam, you would not even know it there
> And pray, perchance you *didst*, thou *wouldst* hardly care."

Odile lay back rigid. Her makeup had begun to congeal, sweat pearls appeared on her throat and heaving breasts.

"Well, look here," Sam continued affably, "here's the Appendix. Now take a look and see if you've thought of all of these."

The Appendix was abstractly conceived but nevertheless ingeniously constructed. On the left-hand pages, there the ladies bent, rocked, lay radically supine, appearing to accomplish complex but innocent Yoga-like exercises. Legs kicked the air, hands grasped ankles, backs arched explosively in a multitude of positions . . . but whoa, wonder of wonders, upon applying the right-hand-page tissue overlay, a platoon of menfolks by the same great animator hove into view, pragmatically catching the ladies at their solipsistic tricks. Their respective eyes and nipples were indistinguishable. Truly it could be said that *each were both*.

Odile had stopped crying altogether and casually flipped through the colloquim, working her ring from finger to finger. At length, she began to giggle and bounce.

Sam was discouraged now and lay back, dozing off. He tried to reconjure the girl in the plaza, but she and the water were gone. The mosaics burned his feet.

FITS IN POCKET OR PURSE

COMES APART FOR EASY CLEANING

When he awoke, he saw the book shredded and balled in every corner of the room. But Odile, her lensed eye bright as a lapis, the other slitted, still held two pages triumphantly. By taking a page at random from the women's section, and an uncorrespondent overlay from the men's, she had succeeded in creating a daring collage.

The couples swirled about each other, flying, prancing, woofing, their discrete little bodies defying recognizable *acts*, but conjoined by strain and intent, balancing precariously upon eachother's wrists, the edges of their hollow bodies intersecting, leaping quite through eachother, each rare juncture defined only

217

by the other careening pairs on the page. Incongruous, yes, but for once not isolate; and in these weird wingings, the absurdity of their tangents, those same nipples and eyes now gleamed with fire . . .

Ah, innumerable mismatched sets *in vacuo*, poorly programmed but not dispirited, unbearded angels, your genitalia sketchy due to the second *rush* edition, contractless, weightless, tell us how to hover without premeditation, Odile's ideal, how, with eyebeams twisted, we may all ride together there. If not on the same page, in a large enough volume of transparent vellum, so that one man's plunge is relieved from its deadly omniscience by his double of the second part, his counter in the codicil; not precisely orgiastic, but with reference, index and perspective. Only in the sight of eachother's vicious humping shadows are we not animals. . . .

Moved beyond himself, Sam took her heavily. She cried out again and again incoherently until the walls rang from distraught neighbors amidst dessert, and it became necessary to put a pillow over her face.

"Yab-yum, yab-yum," she gagged obediently.

Sam kept at it for half an hour, more or less, following the injunction of the *Second Vesicle of Liberation.*

"Yab-yum, yab-yum," she groaned hoarsely until her voice gave out.

"See?" he said later. "That's what you have to do to accept yourself. It doesn't matter what you say or think. What happened anyway?"

But Odile had gone to rest, her eyes and nipples at one. Sam covered her as with a shroud and then reclined naked in the comforting coldness of the stereo-lounger for the remainder of the night, occasionally switching on the short-wave police calls, watching his body become itself again.

21 · *The Result*

November 22

12:30 P.M. Boarded the *Imperial Prince* to return home taking
drawing rules and paper. The Chinese steward took my things to
a stateroom and the captain installed a desk for me. Naval
architecture is a real science and I took great pains with the
smallest detail for the first and second *Sturdys*, but now I had no
time. I just needed a replacement to finish the voyage with.
Design above water might look the same to you, but propulsion
arrangement was changed to insure power-at-sea and 4500 knots
tank capacity; faster, but again smaller. Who could piddle
around now?

The weather at sea was beautiful, so much so that a pencil
never rolled off the drawing board. Nature had finally seemed to
realize I had troubles enough. The plans were finished by the
time we passed Gibraltar and material lists ready to mail on
arrival at New York.

Went back to Lertz to find a proper place to build, saving
time, money and trouble, and got this time the use of an old
building to build in. It was a big help as I would not be delayed
with bad weathers or the bloody public. Left plans with the
railroads to make sure the finished boat would not be too bulky
for them to carry to the coast when finished.

Arrived in Lertz December 16th, 1929, only two months and
four days after leaving *Sturdy II* on Shaab Ali reef, and right
smack in the middle of the Big Creamer. After a few days,
though, I had the boat construction started. It was evident there
was to be no help from friends, who'd been changed (and were

going to get worse). They gossiped that my morals weren't any good and it had served me right to have plenty of trouble all around the world. All this, with many people preferring evil to good and the tendency for the less people know about a thing to talk more about it, led some to saying I was *really* crazy now.

The press had been fair, but amusing the public to sell papers was their business. They had under my latest ad, SKIPPER SEEKS BRIDE, the following:

"*Captain Fuess, 51 years of age [I was nearer 52] made his last pile in the building business. He became famous for his movable office. [This was true enough.] An American who has followed the sea all over the globe, he has also demonstrated that he can hold his own with landlubbers. He wants a bride 30 years old, with courage and fondness for travel, who has some knowledge of shorthand and the typewriter, for Captain Fuess has something to write about.*"

Publicity turned out to be the wrong kind. It was the old curse of the secret fixers again, sending the police to break up the interviews I held in my hotelroom. This made it impossible for me to trust anyone from then on. I was satisfied that there was no group in existence to give people of goodwill a chance to contribute their good to mankind as a whole. Yet I still had a *Book for Boys* in me, and not long after the police left, into the lobby walked *The Result* of my ad, and I signed her up on a trial basis. We would wait and see, I said. She said she was 30, was dark, and quiet, claimed she had the proper knowledge.

On top of all this humbug, the railroad notified me the boat was too tall to go through the tunnels so she would have to go by way of Chicago to avoid the mountains. (Fixers would stop at nothing now.) So they put a 50 foot flat car by the shop where by using rollers and tackle I loaded *Sturdy III*, and made arrangements for the flat car to be spotted in the principal cities she would pass through. After making three stops, in Cleveland,

Buffalo, and Albany, *Sturdy III* arrived at New York, hugging the Hudson, having safely completed the 1400 miles around the mountains to the coast, and there was rolled onto a 50 ton float and brought alongside the SS *City of Batavia,* lying at Busch Terminals of Brooklyn, where she was hoisted aboard and securely lashed to the deck.

July 15, 1930. 6:00 A.M., we left the dock, *Sturdy* now replaced, and WE can be again used to avoid constantly using I in narrating a voyage in which I was the lone maker and lone rider. The *City of Batavia* not being a passenger steamer, *The Result* and myself were signed on as stewardess and steward, respectively.

July 27, passed Gibraltar and on the 3rd August arrived in Port Said, ending *Sturdy III*'s 3,000 miles on the steamer deck as planned. But three months later than I had intended.

The Harbormaster was on vacation so his little daughter could not christen *Sturdy* as I had hoped, so the 13-year-old daughter of the British Vice-Consul, Miss Annabelle Erskine, did it to us. I had brought a bottle of water from an American river for this christening. When it was broken, it stunk. The secret fixers may not have had anything to do with it, but that river don't stink. People the entire length drink its water.

Then on September 1, 1930, almost exactly two years after leaving New York with the original *Sturdy II,* we took authorities for a trial sail on *Sturdy III.* Captain Froge decided to give us 800 pounds additional iron ballast, telling some friends behind my back he would rather give us ballast than life preservers.

September 3, left at 6:00 A.M. when it was light and with the help of new power made Ashrefi light at midnight, and turned in, letting *Sturdy* tend herself. Early in the morning we left through the Straits of Jubal, the light to starboard and Shaab Ali reef to port where the original *Sturdy II* was laid up 11 months and 23 days before, and what a mountain of work and expense I had waded through since then, what hopes, what disappointments, and *what* humiliations.

The sea made up fast, and coming from aft, was afraid she might broach so took in the main and fo'c'sles. By 7:30 P.M. took in jib, running her under bare poles. There was no phonograph on deck that night. I had my evening songs just the same. And such times forced more straight thinking on me in spite of the fact that my mind was dull from loss of sleep. Nights were so sultry that sleeping was impossible, and I continued having my usual sing at the wheel during the long night watches. *The Result* stayed below.

There were then 420 knots between us and Colombo, India, and the worst time of year to make it. But what an ideal condition for adjusting impressions and meditations. One case that touched me was a pair of exhausted birds trying to continue their journey. One soon tired and kept returning for his mate, trying hard by chirping encouragement to it, but it could not get off the deck. Finally its mate scolded and picked at it. This kept up for some time, but the stronger bird finally had to continue alone. Its mate crawled under our small dinghy, and while scrubbing the decks next morning in the scorching sun I found it dead. It was not lazy or possumy as its mate had thought, but had given its all. Yes! We have to die to be believed or appreciated. And then even when we do, they don't.

Other visitors that amused me much was the flying fish, who fly three to five hundred feet through the air or tilt their wings toward a light. At times they would hit the sail and fall on deck and we would have a fish for a change.

The religions of Ceylon being mainly Buddhist, the most important stop was Kandhi, where at the temple of Tlooth (580 x 40 ft.), I had a long talk with the priest who enlightened me about the essences of all religion.

First: keep from sin.
Second: get virtue.
Third: clean your own heart first.

We were heading to clear a rocky point, then all of a sudden what looked like a swell about to break on the end of a reef ahead, wasn't. I tried to tack, but with little wind and a heavy swell, *Sturdy* damaged her rudder on the rocks. I let the port anchor go but before it got ahold we were on the bar. Daylight saw that the wreck as always was caused by a simple thing. I had mistaken the buoy off the end of the point for a breaker, for its paint was covered with bird lime (secret fixers). But we were luckily near port. It was an interesting all-day journey, limping slightly but persistently towards Bangkok which I found a crowded city of 450,000 agreeable people. *The Result* stayed on board and missed the fireworks, funeral and other celebrations.

Their dances were clean, sincere and instructive. I will describe a professional one held under some trees: The women think they are birds and dance that way, and the men think so too because they try to hunt them. But it turns out that an evil Buddha has only dressed them up like birds, because he thinks they look better that way. So the men finally find out that they are really women. They go ahead and kill them anyway.

July 25, 1931. We are halfway around the world, just east of the Japanese island, Yomikosima, and I bet *The Result* that the last half of this trip won't be half so hard as the first. The wind was with us, nature natural, and time was speeding up.

July 29; in midafternoon entered Yokohama Harbor where 31 years before I became of age and saw the beginning of the light that has been growing brighter ever since. I was then the least important of a crew of 38 in a sailing ship of 1500 tons. Now I

223

was the whole crew of one in a ship of one ton! They would not let me ashore as I had not gotten my visa renewed. But *The Result* decided suddenly to "see the Orient" and was gone for several days. I could hardly realize Yokohama was the same place. No sailing ships at all, like when it was I got my first impression that people were different in color, language, religion and customs, but as a whole, the same. But now, after voyaging 30 years and seeing nothing that changed this impression, I knew that *I* was different!

The second day out from Yokohama I started the engine as usual and found it burned out. Not only was the wiring changed but the brushes were ones too narrow and too thin. I now remembered in settling my bill, the Japanese had assured me he had the best help working on *Sturdy* and an American had worked on the starter. I hope on reading this the Japanese will not judge all American mechanics by him.

August 23rd: crossed the 180° meridian. My day was 48 hours long and I made a record of 215 knots that day. This made me the first man in all history to circle the earth, going east, alone. (And still, I could not tell friend from foe.)

September 28; arrived in Honolulu with an impression that will always give me pleasant memories. Spoke to the young men's Buddy Association, then at once sent for a typewriter and a dictionary. I leaned back and started to dictate, but before I even got a few words out, *The Result* giggled and admitted she couldn't type. (Probably couldn't read neither.) I now realized that the *Book for Boys* was lost forever, and I saw that in a way I had been lying to myself about it. I saw that the only thing I'd ever get my name on was a damnfool logbook like this, but a book that would be an example to future lads was out. Because every time I tried to think up what *they* wanted, I only ended up

224

writing about myself or *Sturdy*, who was really just another part of me, and so what I was going to end up with was that most accursed of man's inventions, a book about a book. You can bet I was pretty low by then, even though the trip was almost over and I had done everything I said I would. But the fact that I couldn't think of anything to tell the lads, that seemed kind of shameful.

That night I put *Result* on a black freighter bound for Cuba, and eased *Sturdy* out of Pearl Harbor. The only thing that kept me going then was the necessity to finish the voyage and *prove my point*, though the voyage was actually finished, except technically.

The moon made it as bright as day, and towards midnight I could make out a monsoon making for us. *Sturdy* began to buck and roll, and I went out on the foredeck to check the headstays, which were becoming a real worry. I'd used up all my wire long ago and only had twine left now.

Halfway up the mast I was when the storm hit. It was some peculiar torture. That mast whipsawed me back and forth in that too-light night until my chest was black as the *Result's* poop, and I don't mean her stern superstructure either. I was factually bleeding from my armpits, but every roll I hugged her all the tighter. All of this while I was trying to work with one hand and hold on with the other. A mile a minute—aloft! Only room for one foot at a time on the ratlines. The mast seemed to be trying to jerk my arms from it. I wondered if *Sturdy* herself had had enough and was trying to beat me to the bottom. Maybe we had gotten too small and too fast not to hate ourselves in that big striped sea and solid air. The tighter I held her the worse it hurt me, but I wasn't going to die when I was down and out and not on *her* account, for she was built to live for. So I wrestled her through that storm, even though the mast was right level with the waves at times; she had to learn what my whole weight on top of her tiniest point meant. By my bruises she'd be heeled. And I didn't mean to be shaken loose when I was only 400 knots from Frisco Bay.

It was very strange to manage her from the exact point where I least controlled her, where I was almost dead if you like, but could still hustle her through the storm.

And when dawn came out, and that 'soon was gone, I gave her a last bear hug she'd never forget and she righted herself respectably. The moon and sun changed places just like that, and a fish smell then came out, not like the one *you* get when you go to market or read about, but like all the fish were coming up for air and huffing into it, a *delicate* fishy smell like those Bangkok ladies with licorice or whatever on their breath, big smoking sharks hiccoughing, little female squid afarting. I was satisfactory exhausted. But *Sturdy* and I were never more together.

When that fish smell came out though, I knew what kind of a disillusion I'd been under. It was the idea that I had some kind of life that could be passed on like a mystery ship that just floats into somebody's bay out of the fog one morning with the table all set for breakfast but not a captain or crew in sight, with the logbook open to the last page, "Taking water. The crew is taking it like a man to a man . . ." or some fool such. I'd always thought of living as making something that would carry on after you, and now that the book for boys was gone I was angered for all the living I'd given up for it. There's no moral to that; I spose it's a rare man who can hug both his book and boat hard enough to know the difference. And just then I remembered that big sign outside of the old Lertz Yacht Basin—you can't miss it coming in. It just says, CUT DOWN INTAKE. Well, I reckoned that's all the future was likely to get for me, and now that my life and its story were never going to get together, I had better start livin' with the fact, just setting the course and keeping our position. So this voyage what originally looked like a race against time was actually just making up more and more of it. Like this, for instance.

October 27: Sighted Faralon light and at daybreak passed through the Golden Gate.

Now what could a lad learn from that?

22 · *Separating the Men from the Boys*

November 23

The domestic board was down. *Speed-Packaging* was divesting itself of its Liberian timber interests, and the Marines had been dispatched to insure a non-nonsense transfer. Mrs. Denehey had called three times, Sam assuring her that the market drop would be discounted before noon, as in fact it had been. Odile had also called, "Just to talk."

"Well, what about?"

"Oh, I know I'm bothering you," she said. "But you think we're going to war again?"

"Heavens no," said Sam. "Where did you get that idea?"

"Aaron. He's very upset. He's done nothing but watch the news since he got back."

"This is just a security probe, Odile. Don't worry. Wittgenstein would have sold short or something if it were really serious." Sam gave a wink for the other eleven, who were always grimmer than he.

"Sam, what I really called about was—"

"Odile, I'm sorry to interrupt but I've just remembered something. You recall the night we went to the ballet?"

"How could I forget, Sam? It was marvelous."

"Well, good. Do you have any idea where I left the car?"

There was a short harsh silence. Then he got the phone down just in time to cut the obscenity off.

"A hot one," he confided to the other eleven in his best locker room complicity. He put the phone on "very busy" and gazed out on the obsidian lake. He was hoping to sneak out early but

Wittgenstein had sidled to the fore.

"Everything's dead for the day, big boy; let's take the rest of it off."

"Great," said Sam, flattered at the attention. "Where'll we go?"

"Why don't you take me to the Purk Club? I sure never been there. Challenge you to a handball game."

"You know I can't do that, sir."

"Why? Because I'm Jewish? Come on."

"Of course not. Because you don't have your degree."

"OK, buddy, I'll take you to *my* club then."

"I don't play handball."

"Don't matter," he said, "I'll show ya."

Wittgenstein's enormous car was brought forward. It had a police radio and a telephone in it.

"Listen to that." Wittgenstein flipped a switch. "Leningrad." A frenetic cello in midadagio came through the static.

"How do you know?" Sam asked.

"11.67 cycles," he said. "It says so right there." Wittgenstein tapped the dash nervously. "11.67 is Leningrad. I always listen to Leningrad."

He drove effortlessly through the heavy traffic.

"Sam," the big man asked timorously some time later, "did they teach you to hate suffering at Purk?"

"No." Sam thought for a while. "No," he said slowly, then brightly, "No, but they *do* teach you to hate the people who *don't* hate it. . . ."

Wittgenstein grinned and accelerated.

"When are you going to let me know about the Peacock Prairie deal, anyway?" Sam demanded suddenly.

"When are you going to start fighting for it?" Wittgenstein countered. "You're just asking for a favor. You ain't giving up nothing."

"Christ. So what should I give up?"

"Oh, I know your kind. You think it's all just part of the same pot." Wittgenstein squinted through the sun glancing off the black lake. "But you gotta show that you're *willing* to give up something, see?"

"It's not a question of pride, believe me, Witty. Just tell me *what* to give up. I'm that big. This isn't something to be all that tough-minded about."

Wittgenstein sighed hoarsely. The car wandered on the broad road. He trained the ventilator on his perspiring face. The unlikely sun was frying his chrome:

"It used t' be," he said softly, leaning forward into the jet of air, "that you could get away with stuff like this with no sweat. You could move into an issue and get out before they could ever check your account. You could come out better than the guy above you, because it was bad form for him to even talk to you. If you didn't care what they thought, you could do what you wanted. They assumed that what you had was what you were. They knew that the more you made, the more they would. You know what I'm saying, why I'm staying? I coulda retired comfortable when I was forty. These last years, I just wanna see if they can *get* to me. If I'll convert on my deathbed. You're a college boy, a Purky even. You know what that means—hell, Sam, together, in the old days, it woulda been you and me *against* Palmitz and what's his name."

"We wouldn't have been together in the ol' days, Witty."

"You think?"

" 'Cause I woulda wiped up the street with your flat ass."

Wittgenstein howled hilariously. As a mark of respect he passed on the right. "Shee-it," he glowed.

"It's bad in a way," Sam said, "that you're my only friend."

The old man sucked his lips back:

"You just know," he said from the deepest part of him, "that nothing you can do can hurt me. That's all. That's what you young people like. Someone who's impossible to hurt. Then you can warm up to them. But you're making a serious mistake, son, you think there's enough now to go around without fighting for it. What you'll learn is that it's just the fighting that makes it enough."

Sam's nails dragged across the leather seats. Their folded and stitched gray contours reminded him of deoxygenated brains.

"Why don't we try it this way?" Wittgenstein went on. "Let's make it look like a trade. Show them you're ready for a compromise. Give up one for the other. Which do you want most? The Prairie deal or the art grant business? Preserve the past or hedge on the future?"

Sam switched off Leningrad to think. "I guess the art grant," he said finally. "It isn't so abstract."

"You got somebody in mind?"

"Oh sure, a lot."

Wittgenstein leaned back. "Sam," he asked slowly, "you really think we can buy these guys off as easy as the lastmen?"

"That's not exactly what I had in mind. . . ."

"Sambo, I don't get it. What do you want? What are *you* getting out of this?"

Sam tuned Leningrad back in.

"I really haven't set my price yet. I'm still sort of devaluing. What I'd really like is to simplify my own position."

Wittgenstein pulled the car up next to a large gray building near the docks and derricks and taking a large brass key from his fob led them up the back way. Sam could smell leather and antiseptic, hear the shouts and stomp of games above him. A problem on one of Agapecropolis' questionnaires occurred to him. "Which do you prefer? The smell of leather or of perfume?" He couldn't remember his answer. It should have been, he reflected, "I like them both, but leather probably a little more."

"You know, Sam boy, you're really coming on strong," Wittgenstein said on the stairs. "Even that asshole Agapecropolis thinks so. You're going to have my job pretty soon, except for you, that's just the start. You're really going to have some power. Not like me."

"I don't want that much power," said Sam sullenly. Wittgenstein blanched. "I mean," Sam said, "look what you did with it."

The old man snatched his gym suit from his attaché case and Sam followed him up the stairs. At the top in a padded booth, he signed in and signed out the equipment they would need. The attendant smiled shyly as he handed Sam his gloves. He gave the ball to Wittgenstein.

Wittgenstein's belly, let it be said now, covered his genitals completely. And yet he had no buttocks whatsoever. He led Sam to a court and, placing a coin in the meter, shut them in.

The bright ball jumped off the wall, Sam jammed his fingers diving for it. He was a blur against the slothful pear, floating up the walls to return impossible placements. But the wily broker's strategy proved incontrovertible. Wittgenstein stood his ground, rarely moving more than a step to either side, the ball coming back to him continually, magically. Sam retrieved everything he hit off the wall, but Wittgenstein drove him gradually into the back corners of the court with power drives, then penultimately dropped a reverse spin shot that died upon impact. This strategy never changed. Yet Sam's quickness could match it only one in ten. Hopelessly behind at match point, Wittgenstein blocked Sam off with his body, the ball skipped by them and Sam drove a knee into the old man's lower back, sending him to the floor. Wittgenstein did not try to break his fall, merely turning aside his face just before impact, hitting with an ugly resigned smack. Sam rushed to help him. The old man was dry. Not a drop of sweat, even in his armpits. Sam dragged him to his feet.

"God I'm sorry."

"That wasn't necessary," Wittgenstein said softly.

"I know it. I said I'm sorry."

"See," Wittgenstein said, "you use your advantage when you have to. It's just that nobody's pushed you yet."

Sam looked shamefully to the floor.

"I'm very sorry. It was just a reaction, frustration."

"What kind of gutless wonder are you?" Wittgenstein bellowed. "You gotta be behind before you play hard? If I was you, I woulda cut me down the first time I tried that."

Sam tried to open the court door but it was locked.

"We got the court for an hour, fella," he said. "The meter won't open up till then. You're in here until we see what we've got."

Sam took off his gloves and squatted petulantly in the corner. He could taste his lunch, his hands were swollen. He looked about the cubicle; the white wall streaked with the black ball. He wondered how many games it would take to blacken every single square inch of the court. He calculated there would still be some white left over at the end of any era, that you would have to precisely and alone *aim* the ball to surely blacken everything. The court would lose a little whiteness with each shot as the series progressed, until they would find themselves in a bright black room, the ball the same color as the wall, and the perfect game, over forever.

"If you quit," Wittgenstein was saying, "you'll never know if you can take me."

"I don't care about that," said Sam. "I really shouldn't . . ."

"You'll have to, one of these days and soon, old buddy."

"You consistently bring out the worst in me," Sam muttered into his new yellow gloves.

Wittgenstein practiced his drop shot till time was up and the door clicked open, whence he led Sam back to the locker room.

"Take off your trunks and take a shower," Wittgenstein said. Sam did as he was told, and was then led huffily to the pool.

233

"It's usually quite crowded this time of day," Wittgenstein mentioned casually.

The pool was indeed full of laughing naked young boys, packed so tight one could not see the water. They dove and slithered among themselves like eels, paddled brief distances, dogs aping fish; the aqua tiles reflecting their bright bodies, the heavy air imparted them.

"Go on," said Wittgenstein, "take a dip. I'll be waiting." He shoved Sam forward.

Sam gently but deliberately wedged his couth body into the happy maelstrom. He was poked and splashed playfully; he wiped the water diffidently from his eyes. He used his elbows to keep their bodies clear, but they dove beneath him. Their ribs against his thighs kept him off balance. Foam in his face. Grope at his flesh. Their peters are all up like gherkins. The Second Vesicle of Liberation comes into its own as a defensive measure. Sam kicked out once or twice but the viscosity of the water made his proud gestures only playful and his high arch met only resilient flesh. Finally, after being dunked from behind, Sam escaped under water, threading his way amongst the milling legs and feathered groins, bobbing up for a breath when a mote of light appeared between the bodies.

Sam was numb; the water eddied just below his chin, the bathers blurred as chlorine filmed his retinas. He was no longer conscious of his body beneath the water nor of his breath in the humid air. He began to relax, sink, the massed anonymous flesh enfolding. . . . A hand grabbed him by the hair. He looked up to see Wittgenstein kneeling above him at the side of the pool, his breast-stomach sagging like a bitch's.

"Nice, huh?" he said, strangely calm now. "Let's get out now." He offered his hand to Sam and with amazing strength pulled him from the bathers. Then he disappeared, beckoning, though a stainless-steel door. Sam found his peter had shriveled completely from sight, his scrotum tight as a green plum.

In a redwood room, two masseurs were waiting for them, a septuagenarian gent in a pince-nez, breechclout, boxer's nose and Socratic dugs, as well as a beautiful sullen Slav, skin of chamois, torsoed as a javelin thrower. Igneous rocks glowed like sautéed kidneys in a brazier in a corner which illuminated a large bronze bas relief *Trumpeteer Upon a Crag*, curved bone horn to his lips, hounds in a fury at his feet.

Wittgenstein waved him generously to the handsome one. "Take good care of him, Wilmer, he's the hightest Q.U.I.F. we got," and lay himself down on the further table.

But it soon became clear that Wittgenstein had taken quiet advantage of him again. The old gent bounced around the broker like a hummingbird, kneading and pummeling so rapidly and expertly that the old broker was a blur of gradually raspberrying mousse, while Wilmer desultorily ran his fingers up and down Sam's shin, concentrating on the contractions of his own forearm.

"You're in pretty good shape," Wilmer drawled.

Sam nodded. Wittgenstein was groaning from his pummeling.

"We don't get many athletes up here, I'll tell you," Wilmer said, dropping a sheet over Sam's now negligible crotch.

Now he was kneading Sam's feet, which was actually somewhat enjoyable. Then he moved up front to work on his trapezius, leaning down to whisper, "They're mostly like fats over there."

The old gent was popping the broker's joints as if he were uncoupling freight cars.

"Yeah, you've got a real nice body here," Wilmer went on. "You really don't need a rubdown."

"I wouldn't say that."

"Yeah, a real good body. Almost as good as mine. Your legs look better maybe, but you're bony up in the shoulders." Wilmer sighed, expanding his *lattimus dorsi*.

Sam tensed his neck and trapezius, challenging Wilmer to

235

relax him. The masseur gritted his teeth until the veins in his forearm glowed royally, but he could make no indentation in the muscle whatever.

"Are you there, Wilmer?"

"Say," the answer came. "How'd you get that scar?"

"Oh, it's an old . . ."

"Boy that's really something. A bayonet, betcha? What's your story anyway?"

. . . .

"I never seen a scar that long and curvy before. Must've hurt, huh?"

"It still hurts, Wilmer."

"No kidding. Why didn't you tell me? I could've given you a local." He opened a jar of salve and began to spread it with his index finger along the purplish seam. "Look, I'll even show you so you can do it yourself at home. And I'll give you some of this stuff free. The scar'll go away in a couple of months. You watch. You won't even know it was there."

Sam looked at both his secret hurt and Wilmer in disbelief.

"You're just like all of them, aren't you?" Wilmer muttered. "You think just because I'm interested in your body that I don't have a mind."

"On the contrary." Sam flushed.

"Well, you ought to see the bodies I got to work on. Think they mean anything to me? Big hunks of flab and hair. I can relax 'em, sure. Better than their wives, I'll bet. But you think they give me any credit? Nah, they think I'm some kind of machine."

"Look, Wilmer—"

The old gent had Wittgenstein in a full nelson now, pinging his vertabrae like a slipping rachet gear. The broker was sighing in that funny zone between pain and delight.

"Yeah," Wilmer went on, "you work and slave all day and then they come in here and flop down and you think you can get

236

a word out of them? Not on your life. Oh, don't tell me they had a hard day too, when you try to be nice you'd think you could get at least a civil yes or no."

Wilmer was beating a faint rat-tat-tat upon Sam's sternum.

"Here's these men, running the goddamn country and you think they'd ever discuss it with you? They think because I work with my hands I don't think. Well, I do. I'm trapped in his hot room all day and got time to think a lot and when I've got their neck in my hands, I got my rights, you better believe it."

(Sam was sizing Wilmer up. He'd probably go for a right lead and then he could catch him in the kidneys with a short left, and then with a neck chop as he doubled over. Wittgenstein would like that.)

"See, you're just like the rest of 'em. You won't talk to me neither. I'm just a body to you."

"Wilmer, you seem to be confused. I'm *the body* to you."

"But *I'm* a total person too."

"You shouldn't be ashamed of working on bodies, Wilmer; think of them as . . . problems to be solved!"

"Easy for you to say."

Sam had pulled himself upon his elbows and was about to put both Wilmer and the mind/body problem to rest when he saw Wittgenstein grinning at him from beneath the sheet. His face shone like a mango beneath the ultraviolet; Sam realized he had just been treated to a perfect if benign model of MC control. So conscious was he of Wittgenstein predicting his behavior that it mattered little whether Sam confirmed or refuted him— punched out Wilmer or kept his cool. The strategy was simple as it was effective:

1. Define the situation in terms of complicity or rebellion

2. The subject is vulnerable the moment he accepts such a situation

3. The subject's actual response—resistance or no—is irrelevant since:

237

4. If the situation is reduced to two alternatives, the predictor will be right at least half the time which more than suffices.

It was what had made MC great.

Sam grinned sheepishly and threw up his hands. Wittgenstein arose and headed toward a far door. Sam wadded his sheet and threw it to Wilmer, who recoiled.

"Well, the only thing I can say, Wilmer, is that you got to rub awfully hard before you deserve to be listened to."

Wittgenstein held the next stainless-steel door for Sam. Steam seared his eyes, nose and throat. He groped about the mucous marble until he found a seat. Wittgenstein sat opposite him in the mist, drawing a blue towel about him. There was no sound in the room at all save the hiss of the compressor. A canvas hose dribbled a cold jet of water over his feet. A single bulb gave off a putrescent glow. All of the men in the room were very old, older even than Wittgenstein. They sat silently, feet and buttocks splayed on the marble. Flesh hung from their throats, breasts and thighs, their scrotums were hairless and discolored, organs no longer palpable. Not a pisser in the lot.

Sam glanced at Wittgenstein, but his eyes were closed in reverie. An octogenarian next to him, his gray, warped feet crossed over one another, perused a newspaper, but the news got soggier as he turned the pages, absorbing the lymphatic air, and at last the paper disintegrated into his redundant lap, leaving him holding tufts of margins in his fists.

To Sam's left, another shaved, in direct violation of the rules above the door, clearing a corona about his collarbone where the white hair of his pinched chest apparently stood a chance of spoiling his collar line. He had difficulty drawing the skin sufficiently taut to receive the razor.

Another man, every bone and artery visible, peeled a tangerine with a long yellowed thumbnail, forcing its segments one at a time between his teeth, not masticating, but simply allowing the weight of his skull to crush the pulp within the vacuum of his jaws. His larynx did not quiver once, the juice had no place to go but down. He dropped the rind, a perfect scarlet spiral in the steam, into a sodden paper bag between his feet.

Suddenly Sam grew uncomfortable. He squirmed on the marble, gestured frantically to Wittgenstein, but it was too late. His cock had sprung out and hovered about his navel. The man with the razor dropped it. The man with the tangerine covered his pubes with his paper bag. The man with the newspaper gathered his loins and tottered hysterically to the door. Wittgenstein was blurred with laughter, his stomach uncreased itself spasmodically. No . . .

Finally, Witty raised himself and led the doubled-over, blushed-out Sam from the steam and provided him with a towel.

See?" he said. "That's why you got to fight." And then he moved out of Sam's sight, his shower clogs crackling on the tile.

Wittgenstein dropped Sam at the Elevated, but Sam did not go home. He hailed a cab, in fact, and headed for the Purk Club, where the open mahogany foyer reassured him. Wives and dogs were waiting patiently in their enclosure, not permitted beyond the lobby. The maze of mail slots were uniformly empty. He took the elevator to the Panorama Bar where the buffet had begun.

The bar was bereft. The lake was at its best; purplish as the sun sank into it, brown and blue thereafter. Sam demanded a dry martini.

"One needn't specify 'dry,' sir."

"Quite," said Sam.

He felt weak on the stool. His flesh still tingling, but his musculature enervated. He ordered two more doubles and perused the decor.

Above the bar was featured the great disputed crew race between Purk and Grandiver, two shells caught in mezzotint as they entered a fog bank in the spring of 1911, the coxswain's megaphones turned toward one another parabolically, equidistant progress mirrored in the still water which divided the respective washes, their bodies' unison patented, patinaed, themselves the only horizon, *ni fleuve ni l'air* . . .

The number *five* man in the Purk boat had caught a crab. By squinting variously, Sam could make out the grimace hidden in his mustache. Below, framed in fruitwood and velvet were the *Letters of the Crew*; conflicting testimony as to what actually transpired at the finish line in that aged fog bank:

Whatever the fated outcome, wrote the then Admiral Sharpe some forty years later to the then President of the Republic, *we have put the lie to the canard that oarsmen are short-lived, for all of the Purk boat, which you stroked and I captained, save our number five, Roger Griffin, who was lost over France, are still very much alive and persuasive . . . the togetherness of competition remains the only worthy training for those whose charity springs from the willful control of their superior strength and* [*undecipherable here*]

His senses dulled, his parts settled, free from steam and viscous waters, the old fog in his face, Sam's pectorals tensed as he recovered his buddies' rhythm and stroked home.

The Dott had left the Fuessbook open again.

Time to think now in the Pacific and God knows we needed it for we now had hundreds of organizations against us and I WAS ONLY ONE WITH ONE HEAD AND ONE LONE EARTHLY FRIEND, STURDY: AND SHE HAD NO HEAD. Tied up on the eastern end of the Panama canal. Though at sea for only one week we just made it. The machinist found the bearings all ground up as if. sand or emery had been put in them. This was typical of the secret fixers to systematically wound their victims in such a way that it looked like they did it to themselves. It looked like the showdown.

We put to sea at three P.M. December 21, but making no headway against a headwind, turned back to the port. This was the only time in the whole voyage that we turned back after leaving a port. One blow followed another for the next eight days. This accounted for the report in the press that we were missing, for we did not really leave until December 29. If you're in port these days, you're missing.

June 17, 1932. But after five weeks more to think at sea and prepare myself for enemies, I tied up at the quarantine dock in New York, six years and six months after starting to sew the sails for the first Sturdy all by hand on the deck of my houseboat at Lertz, and I had proven that not all Americans are bluffers and fourflushers.

23 · If It's Not Worth Saying, Sing It

Later that very evening, Sam "could stand it no longer"—
dodging the dog-do, punching the broken buzzer, lonely, seeking
concrete family, he rented a flesh-tinted Chevy with reclining
seats and was up the stairs three at a time. Here is stolid little
Matthew blinking at the door.

Sam whisked the child up with the intention of setting him
atop his shoulders, but he had misjudged his space, and as
Matthew's head crashed against the doorway's fluted cornice, he
let out a fearsome scream. Stieglitz ran from the rear, her black
hair settling as if in the first moments after electrocution; Aaron
emerged presently from the darkroom scowling. Stieglitz tried to
hoist her brother back to bed, but he lay where Sam had
dropped him, coiling and whimpering about his Strat-O-Moc.
Stieglitz then dropped to drape herself about the other. Aaron
laughed mercilessly at our pinioned frontman.

"You sure got a way with kids, Sam."

Sam stooped to inspect the boy's skull. His pink flesh shone
through the light hair like a rabbit's, an ugly clot rising to the
surface among the follicles. He massaged the kid's hair and
patted his wet face. Matthew stopped crying but grasped his foot
more intensely than ever. Stieglitz undid his garters.

Odile had not moved. Sam could see her long legs extending
from the bed alcove. She was practicing again, a new song
apparently:

> Ah, you ache just like a woman
> But you break
> Just like a little girl

"Hey, you're getting better, Odile!" Sam cried.

"No shit."

Aaron returned to the darkroom, slamming the door. Sam tried to move but the kids had him locked up tight. Nevertheless he managed with great effort to pick up first one foot—Stieglitz was raised off the ground, clinging terrified—then slowly its mate passed her, burdened with Master Matthew screaming; Sam proceeded across the living room with Brobdingnagian strides until he placed the squirming passengers of his appendages before Odile.

"Foot-bus, foot-bus," squealed Matthew.

"Sam is the best foot-bus ever," sighed Stieglitz.

Odile did not look up, fingers reddened from the chords, legs crossed now, skirt hiked up around her hips.

"What's wrong with you today, Princess?"

"Nothing that a little *yab-yum* wouldn't cure."

Sam blushed, glancing at the darkroom door. It was closed.

"How can you talk like that with the kids around?" he whispered hoarsely.

"Oh Sam, go away, can't you see I'm practicing?"

"Funny," he said. "The one night I need you, you have to *practice*."

"I'm *very* sorry," she snapped. "The kids have been *just* impossible."

"You know what I like best about kids, Odile?" She looked up briefly. "They eat when they're hungry."

She strummed and strummed, regraduating her instrument.

"And you know something else?" he went on furiously. "I think I've got you figured now. And the trouble's not what you think. It's because you don't have enough passion to try and lie. You've mixed up sincerity and honesty for so long, you think being shitty is being upright, and because you've never been caught lying, you don't know who you are!"

"You can't talk that way to me," she said under her breath.

243

"What've *you* ever done for anybody?"

"Cut your fucking pretensions, Odile," Sam said, hoarse now with rage, "and take care of your kids. They could care less whether you're *sincere* or not. Look at 'em, they're filthy." Matthew was indeed spooling snot about his fingers.

"Booger," said Stieglitz, mocking a retch.

"Booger," corroborated little Matthew.

"Stoppit," screamed Odile.

"Booger, Booger, Booger, Booger!"

"Booger you, kiddo." Sam pushed the kid away.

"Foot-bus, Mr. Foot-bus," Stieglitz sang out and hauled herself farther up Sam's leg.

"Oh, foot-bus, Mr. Foot-bus," Odile chorused, improvising a run in her instrument, "oh, foot-bus, Mr. Foot-bus, how come your foot's so strooonnnggg!"

Sam was surprised to find that Stieglitz was actually hurting him, sinking, as she did, her nails in his calves. He reached down quickly, and, unlacing his Strat-O-Mocs, sent them skimming into the hallway. The kids released him and charged after the shoes, falling upon them laughing, wiping their noses on the shoes' genuine sheepskin tongues.

"Keep it up," strummed Odile, "now the socks, Mr. Foot-bus."

Sam could feel the food in the rug through his stocking feet. In his blurring vision, the kids pummeled each other with his shoes. Aaron popped out of the darkroom again.

"What the hell's going on?"

"You talk to him, Aaron, I've had it up to here."

Odile plunked an atonal chord to emphasize her pointless pun, resolving it deftly as she caught Sam staring at her. Then her face went incorrigibly soft.

"Aw, is Mishter Foot-bus lonely? Oh, we's sorrhy! Come on down and have a sing with me, Mishter Foot-bus."

Sam did as he was told. He realized that he could kill the entire family now, wipe them right out and it wouldn't make any difference to anyone else, that he would never be caught.

(Yes, first the biggest butcher knife clash in the top of Aaron's head, right up to the hilt, the faintest trace of lymphy blood, Odile too dumbfounded to move, then one quick slice at her throat, her head hitting the floor like a melon, the undone hands clutching at the guitar reflexively [would she finally finish like a man who's hung?], then the sparing of the kids, their conventional indebtedness and lack of reaction perhaps embarrassing. . . .)

Aaron in the meantime busied himself with the children, throwing Sam's Strat-O-Mocs down the stairwell so they would no longer distract him. He went back to the darkroom momentarily, returned with some colored papers and spread them on the floor before them.

"OK," he said, sneering only slightly. "Is what color?"

"Blue," Stieglitz, Matthew and Sam chanted in unison.

"You think so?" Aaron snickered.

He took other strips of manycolored paper from his pockets.

"You and your names," he hissed playfully at Sam. "I'll show you just what kind of memory *you've* got."

He placed a yellow strip halfcovering the blue and moved it from side to side.

"What's the bottom one now?" he said.

"More green," roared Stieglitz.

"Redder," said Matthew gravely. Sam blinked unsteadily, attempting to refocus.

"Nothing more deceptive than the colorful," Aaron laughed at Sam.

Odile coughing impatiently thrust a mimeographed sheet into Sam's limp hand. It bore the lyrics of a new song and the chord positions for her fingers.

"You be the chorus," she said.

Odile sang the ballad slowly and flatly. Sam mouthed the chorus carefully.

ODILE: *I wanna do what they think I am.*

SAM: Dew-wha-deoo.

AARON (Takes a red circle and instructs Stieglitz and Matthew to stare at it for thirty seconds while he taps his foot to the song): "Simultaneous contrast the cause of all deception," he recites, smiling smugly at his cantatrice and her singular audience. "Hooper, this is what you're doing to Odile."

ODILE (fiercely): *I want 'em to see just what a little package is.*

SAM: Dew-wha-deoo, dew-wha-deoo.

AARON (Now swiftly substitutes a Chinese white circle for the kids to look at.): "What do you see *now?*"

STEIG: Green moons.

MATT: Blue diamonds?

ODILE: *Oh yeah, I've learned a lot.*

SAM: Dew-wha-deoo, dew-wha-deoo.

AARON (Suspends a piece of orange paper in front of the kids): "Now what?"

STIEG: Purple worms.

MATT: Hurts . . .

ODILE (*agitazione*): *But not as much as I could've.*

SAM: Doo-doo-doo.

AARON (Turns on overhead fluorescent light): "What you call this now?"

STIEG: Here, there . . .

MATT: Owww!

SAM: Doo, wat, doo-wat.

The performance trails off. Aaron shrugs and packs away his tricks. The kids rub their eyes. Sam can "stand it no longer," drops the music sheet and goes to Aaron.

246

"My turn now, friends."

Aaron cringes. Odile starts.

"Been practicing the exercises like I showed you?"

"Oh God," Odile says from the mattress.

"Some," Aaron says sadly. Stieglitz shakes her head gravely behind her father's back.

Sam kneaded the photographer's shoulders. The flesh was enfolded and substanceless as ever.

"Like hell you have," he said.

"But look," said Aaron, and promptly did seven pushups, an ugly vein creasing his forehead.

"Blue," pointed Stieglitz.

"Ma-gen-tah," countered Matthew.

Sam lifted Aaron to his feet.

"Watch his head," warned Stieglitz.

The photographer's underarms were slick, he was breathing heavily, black eyes gleamed wide, imploringly. Sam realized with considerable disgust that the world was still ultimately his own for the asking—and that Aaron existed only by his good graces.

"You know, Aaron," trying desperately to inject some humor, "did it ever occur to you you might not have a collarbone at all? I mean, that might be the problem."

"Now there's a thought," said Odile.

Sam felt the photographer playfully about the chest. The neck was intensely if unconventionally muscular, but it sloped precipitously and without differentiation into his trunk.

"We've just got to do something about your shoulders, Aaron," Sam said. "It's the key to upping your production. I can't always follow you around."

"I did what you told me already."

"OK, OK, I can feel some real progress." He suspected for the first time that perhaps this self-absorbed pathetic man was providing Odile with precisely what she deserved.

(. . . to put the collarboneless bugger on his shoulders to act

247

as his eyes. Himself would play the body of this terrible dis-
jointed animal that could terrorize the earth. The vision of this
gruesome twosome, the lower half ravishing Odile, the upper
half recording it for posterity, running amok in the offices
of Management Concern, overturning and smashing the computers, uprooting the files with its indestructible black horn. . . .)

He put his hand along Aaron's sallow cheek. The artist
reciprocated, but Sam started as his tough pat seemed to become
a caress.

"What do *you* get out of all this anyway?" Sam whispered.

His wide gesture took in all assembled.

"I really need to know."

Aaron's eyes only widened, blackened more. Sam nodded.

"It doesn't mean a shit either way, does it? You'd be the
same, with or without 'em. That's the secret, isn't it?"

But Aaron was of little help. "I'm going to a movie," he
announced huffily. "I'm depressed."

"Take the kids with you," Odile chanted, strummed.

Sam slumped into the sling chair. Aaron got the kids dressed
and hustled them down the stairs without a word. Sam stared
down at the colored paper scattered on the floor.

"That was fun," he said. "I wish they'd have stayed; you don't
know what I've been going through lately."

"Oh God, Sam," Odile said, "I've just *got* to get out of here.
Take me for a drive please."

She had forgotten all about the car. She took him for granted.
"I'll be dressed in a minute." Odile drew a shower curtain across
the alcove.

*I will here again repeat as when I was among you, the secret fixers;
good, bad and indifferent, on both sides of the fence, went to work
again. I soon saw it would be a hopelessness, but the experience and
impression worth seeing through. We sighted a bulging steamer ahead.
They drew alongside and the officer shouted my name, and then urged*

me to stop my Peace Voyage right then and there and go home with them. How they waved their arms! "No!" I said. We continued east. . . .

Odile had put on a short pleated skirt, a sleeveless nylon jersey, no underwear, sandals, and tied her hair back. Sam wondered if Aaron had ever tried to hit her. He was finally certain of his contempt: This would be his last visit. He recovered his Strat-O-Mocs in the stairwell and did not open the Chevy's door for her.

"I liked the other one better," she said.

They headed northeast on the expressway, the luxury apartments reflecting themselves in the lake like the brief bejeweled fingers of an amputated potentate. Odile moved in next to him, laying her head on his shoulder. He was aware of the kitchen in her hair, but the warmth of her body relaxed him and started his engine, arrummmm.

Her bare arms circled his waist and dropped into his lap.

His stomach muscles tightened, his knuckles whitened on the wheel.

He switched to the passing lane, braking and accelerating jerkily. The apartments grew smaller and less glassy, the land worth less per square foot; the drive curved to the breakwater's edge, and then swept back in, permitting a crescent beach here, a missile defense system there, guns and butter, buttered guns.

Odile pressed her full weight upon him. Sam locked his door. He noticed Wittgenstein's apartment house against the sky. It was all lit by spots, a luminescent white. On the roof there was a party to which no one he knew was invited.

Odile was making it difficult for Sam to be disgusted with himself. But he did his level best in the far left lane.

He told Odile to watch for cops but she only tongued his ear.

He noticed that when he took his hands off the wheel they had about two and a half seconds to live.

He recalled the impressive brilliance of Aaron's eyes as they swung around a dawdling cab. He realized, not without admiration, that Aaron had mastered her in his own fashion, circumscribed her vacuity, that his very indifference was what gave her season and shape.

The lake receded and the buildings shrank. Savings and loan institutions intruded themselves. The roadside inhabitants became older, wheeled to the doors of their depositories to watch such as Sam and Odile accrue the night. DRUGS LIQUOR FILMS embossed the neon air. The city in its period: beyond St. Clone's Cemetery glowed the exclusive one-family dwellings, taking the lake unto them. The place to build your cash cushion.

LAST CHANCE TO FILL UP: The sign appeared above them. Sam swung off the road to the pumps and washing station. They swabbed them down and filled them up. As they rinsed the windshield, the attendants gazed down at Odile's legs. He was handed a voucher with his change and then waved forward. A corrugated iron door rose as they broke an electric beam signal. A lastman scurried down the ramp toward them, sponge and chamois in hand. A chain was attached to their undercarriage; he was told to cut the engine, rolled up the windows upon instruction.

Suds engulfed them, marbled shadows spread across their bodies. Odile swung over Sam, her sinewy back arched against the wheel. Sam stared first into her sweatstreaked bosom, then quickly at the perforated soundproofed ceiling, vaguely aware of the vibrations from the lastmen massaging their flanks. Odile moved above him ominously, her teeth embedded in his lips, the horn bleeding from her syncopated presumption.

She canters down into his seat, he's glad he's got the wheel to hold. The reclining seat mechanism jams. Screwed again. Demand refund. Odile recites in Sam's ear in rhythm to her bouncing. She likes the dirty words, but only in conjunction with, and whispered. The horn sets up another shaky blast. She regularly bites his forehead, her jaw working against his skull, and her cries are frozen in a little balloon above them. "Sum," she sighs, "Sim, Soom."

Sam could "stand it no longer."

The rinse floods them visible again. He grasps her hips and twists her free. She smoothes her skirt over her kneecaps, patterned now with the Gleneagle plaid of the seatcovers. The lastmen step back in awe.

Compressed air dries them. Water beads on the hood and is sucked away. Outside, the first frost of the year is settling in. Christ, she's nuts, Sam thinks.

Odile fixes her hair and switches on the radio; the chain is removed from their undercarriage and a few lastmen indifferently touch up the chrome where the machines have missed. The lead lastman refuses their voucher with a disbelieving grin of all creation, they are turned round in the direction they have come, restored to their own power, as the chances of their getting lost grow more and more remote.

Trying to hang on, I sold or was fleeced of everything; navigational instruments, flags, tools, spare sails, even some ballast went. I was in the final fight with Black Art to the finish. And soon, it was, a day came when I had to let my last friend Sturdy go, and all I got for her was $1,000 when the materials alone, not counting a penny for my labor, was at least $6,000. I was still in hopes that I could buy her back later, but it turned out that The Result had worked with the enemy as their agent while I was working for Mankind. Again, much time wasted in just being individual in my task to prove all men the same. Seeing I might be even further delayed in jail awaiting trial, I took the bus back to Lertz. A friend there let me use his office, where I slept on the floor and went to work getting material together for the Chart of All Mankind. It was now necessary to make public record of my aims and objects of my new non-secret Movement, while still protecting the interests of my friends in all parts of the world.

The librarian of Lertz was very helpful. My plan was to have every race and nation represented in their native costume on my Chart of All Mankind. An art school recommended a lady who could draw and color from the pictures I picked, but what she finally did was not what I had in mind. I was unable to use it so cut it up, keeping the figures only, and drew the world myself, rearranging the figures on it.

Saw an Armistice Day parade with disabled veterans, some having to be carried from hospitals to automobiles provided by public-spirited people. There were Gold Star Mothers who had given their all. The Hearses in the parade forcibly reminded me of rows upon rows of markers like I had seen in France, but again, gave me an idea for possible jobs in the future. I'm not ashamed to admit that my eyes were wet long before the boy scouts passed, manly little fellows in every land, marching behind their flags.

Yes, I knew, it was time to start the Land Voyage of Sturdy.

Amidst great difficulties and behind-my-back scheming, moved headquarters to proven fertal ground west of town, exact center of this USA, this Rally Point, arriving with bad leg from being thrown from a truck on the way with a bundle of Practical Brotherhood literature on my back and thirty cents (30¢) in my pocket. It was the TWILIGHT of the DAWN of my international faith, but I was resolved to test Sturdy a new and translate my 39 years of insight into MAN MADE HELL.

Suffered from cold, heat, and inconvenience but compleat over-all plan was being formed. Built a special makeshift mast and began on Sturdy IV, more or less a model, incorporating all the changes from her sisters, smaller true, but again with a special trailer constructed from movable Office plans, faster. For I didn't have much time left and couldn't piddle around now. Though Sturdy IV was itching to set sail, the building went slow. Satan's inner cross-currents had made it necessary for Capt. Fuess to live and work alone, but needing more income to continue Peace Voyage, he went into new business for himself in town.

All who want to help this movement stay free and independent, kindly cooperate in keeping OUT of this township all who will not fit properly into this Gigantic task. . . .

24 · *Leptokurtosis, or The Final Analysis*

Agapecropolis handed Sam a tunafish canapé and then stretched out on his couch, divagating a persimmon with his ΦBK penknife.

"And how'd you find our little performance?"

Sam was quite prepared.

"Oh, it was most enjoyable and we're grateful to you. Myself, I found it, for the most part, oh, risible." Sam rolled the word in his mouth. "Yes, that's it—*risible.*"

"That's not what I'd call empirical observation, Samuel. Come on, I've got a little surprise here if you tell me something more."

Sam had gone somewhat pale. He could no longer feign detachment.

"Well, to tell the truth, it seemed . . . more complicated than compelling. Here're my notes anyway."

"You don't say? Well, we won't go into how you voted today. Oh, I promised. Here's a free gift."

Agapecropolis flipped a set of keys across the desk.

"What for?"

"Just a new car, that's all. Be a little more careful with this one, eh?"

"I don't know what to say."

"Why sure you do."

"I'd forgotten that I'd lost it."

"Be that as it may. You can pick it up at the tower this afternoon. Now not another word about it."

Sam had seated himself seriously. The keys were hot in his pocket.

"Doctor, I need to know something. Why do you indulge me? I warn you, I haven't been working well lately. Not at all. What do you actually expect of me?"

"We're just interested in seeing what becomes of you, m'boy! I *have* had the feeling that you've been a bit distracted of late, and your work has been, shall we say, scattershot?"

"So you know I'm not working up to potential. You don't *really know* what I might do then? If I'm at all unpredictable, for God's sake tell me!"

"Didn't I explain all that to you once?" The doctor rifled nervously through a box of index cards on his desk. "About the predictability of your integrity? I thought for sure that I—"

"Oh yeah. You said that I could be a nuisance only when I gave up my pride, that you'd made 'arrangements' for my life-style, that I would end up needing you. It went something like that."

"Yes, yes, of course. I thought I had . . ." He finally found the card and refiled it. "Whew, for a minute there I thought I was slipping."

"You still haven't explained why you're going so overboard . . . to help."

"That's your bag, my friend. I never said we were *helping* you."

"That's true."

"Look here, Samuel, if men like you did not *think* they were free, they wouldn't act in predictable patterns, and then where would we be? Probability would just go out the window! It's the man who thinks he's *pre*determined that you can't trust. So the fact is, the freer everybody thinks they are, the more they will act like eachother. It's the main artery between Democracy and Liberty. The end of competition is not a superior product but rather to regularize behavior and anticipate it. That's what our founding fathers meant when they said: 'Give us free men to manage.' Our challenge, then, is to organize life so that error as we have known it is virtually impossible. Only then will the market be able to take correspondingly greater risks, and only then will we be able to measure and contain them."

"You mean to be free of you, I'd have to give up my old notion of freedom entirely?"

"Oh God, you Humanities One people make me sick," Agapecropolis growled. "You think because you can play with the language of indeterminism that you really can cut it. A little Kafka, a *soupçon* of Kierkegaard, a dose of Einstein and Heisenberg perhaps, something nice and pat like the second of thermodynamics, and you think you've adapted yourselves, that you can be modern too. Well, cutie, those aren't metaphysics; whatever they are, they aren't that. A Humanist is a man who thinks that anguish is a frame of reference. You're not going to get around us that easy!"

Sam cracked his knuckles, flexed his pectorals.

"The next thing you'll be telling me," the doctor continued scathingly, "is about pushing some stone up some goddamn mountain just to see it roll down again because life's in the pushing, not at the top. Well, I've been in this business a long time, and I've yet to see the man who could live on that. That's just sentimentality—no matter how tough it sounds, just the ass end of the old idealistic horse. No, you'll really have to suffer some, friend, before you will have a right to your little profundities. You can get it out of your head right now that you *stand* for anything, you have no constituency; no, you're going to have to go a little farther than that if you're going to put *us* off the scent."

This outburst was uncalculated no doubt, and later Agapecropolis himself would admit regretting it, but Sam was surprisingly benign, as it was clear that, for the first time, the doctor was near vulnerable. After a thoughtful pause, Sam murmured, "Why is it that we think suffering deepens us, Doctor, gives us passage, dimension? From what I've seen, it only thins us out, knocks our edges off; we've all become shadows of our little strengths. And yet, you tell me that the pain is just beginning, Wittgenstein says I got to pay my dues, and the other night, I lost control and said much the same sort of thing to Odile."

"Ah, Mrs. Grassgreen, that reminds me." Agapecropolis made a steeple of his fingers and leaned back prone, breathing heavily. "I'm glad you brought *that* up. I've been going through her tapes again, together with your tests, and providing you haven't abdicated your truth-telling role, I believe I've diagnosed her problem."

Sam maintained respectful silence.

"Let me put it this way," the doctor ambled, seeming quite sure of himself now. "The changes in the logarithms of value over any period in this lady's life constitute an equally distributed ensemble, with a standard deviation proportional to the square root of the length of the period."

"You know I don't understand that crap," Sam complained. Agapecropolis giggled in assent and threw up his arms.

"You see, Mrs. Grassgreen is what is known in the trade as a Pseudo-schizo. In layman's terms, she *thinks* she's two different people—an ethereal sort which is in conflict with a practical post-bourgeoisie—but in fact, she's a single personality, uncompartmentalized, perfectly integrated, *common* even, as they used to say. The only problem with Mrs. Grassgreen is that she would like to be someone else, but doesn't have the imagination to bring it off."

"But what about the . . . finishing . . . business?"

"Finishing is when you stop, son. Stop *is* finish. By definition."

"But I don't see how—"

257

"Oh, don't play meek with me, moonface. Mrs. Grassgreen resents herself because she can predict herself. You above all should understand that."

"But with me, she said it was getting *better.* . . ."

"A man with your Q.U.I.F. can hardly afford such presumption. Particularly," Agapecropolis's eyes hardened, "particularly when they avail themselves of certain . . . certain Dynamic Synthesis methodologies."

"I didn't use it, none of it!" Sam yelled, slammed his fist down.

"In any case," the doctor resumed gaily, "your experience with her is based upon an extremely simple chance model. The truth is, son, you just can't maximize two variables at the same time. No one index corresponds to another. So how are you going to measure—?"

"But her being *afraid*—surely that's genuine?" Sam was a little panicky.

"Ah, individuals act in ignorance, it's true, but people know what they need and they usually get it. Now, Mrs. Grassgreen's getting more than most, I'd say; it's a nondiscretionary strategy to be sure, but what do you expect? Fear, you say? Ah, but that's a constant variable. The cost of new information is very high and she simply knows she can't afford it. She may be lovable for all I know, but she's not worth pitying, I'm certain."

Sam's peristalsis had doubled. "Are you trying to say that *I've* got nothing to do with it?"

"Most normative work in utility approaches, I'm sorry to say, now appears to be obsolete."

For the first time in his life, Sam's rage was not calculated.

"You have the gall to sit there and tell me that I'm *not* a factor, that I didn't help?"

"There is no evidence in Mrs. Grassgreen's situation of imbalance large enough to permit a technical correction by you or anyone else. Can't you see, it's all the same?"

"But I swear she seemed to be improving, I mean, sure she had her down spells, but generally she was progressing."

"Your judgment might proceed more soundly if you foreswore analogues with physical processes such as tides or waves." The doctor was very severe now. "You would be more to the point if you treated the Grassgreen phenomena as infinitely divisible, and equally distributed over the long run. What you see may have the look of cycles, but they are not. When such trends are observable, they are simply observations after the fact. There are no facts knowable today which can be used in evaluating such behavior."

"It's hard to believe," Sam mumbled, patrician calm evaporating, "I mean the way she hopped around, cried out and all, you'd have thought she . . ."

"It's quite simple, my friend." Agapecropolis could hardly contain himself. "It all tests out. Our Mrs. Grassgreen *wants the world*, you get me?"

Sam shook his head. Rare fusion of sport 'n' sex had extruded no quickie analysis for the floater this time.

"Yeah, that's right." The doctor was squinting. "She wants it from everybody. As many as she can get. And anonymous too, I'll bet. You're just as far as she can go without losing everything else. You represent the everybody else she wants, but can't admit to. She's been led to expect some kind of *intrinsic value*, and there's only one cure, Samuel. She must enter the market randomly, just like a little roulette wheel, and in the long run, who knows?"

Sam was fairly desperate: "But what if I could show you that, *with me*, it was getting better? Wouldn't that . . . ?"

"Any information of that sort, my boy, would be disseminated immediately, if not discounted. This sort of temporary leverage is illusory, I assure you. It's quite universally adopted. If you don't believe me, why don't you test it out? Arrange for her to enter the market randomly for a bit. Why, *I'd* even take a crack,

259

if you like, then check her out and see if she's any worse off than she was with you. I'm afraid that with any decent sample, you'll find no meaningful distinction between your efforts and those of the indubitable majority."

Sam had slammed the desk again and stared the doctor down.

"Are you saying that she'd be just as far right now as if she'd just 'guessed,' with anybody? Are you trying to tell me I'm not a . . . professional?"

"Isn't it just too much?" Agapecropolis grinned, raising himself from his couch.

He resumed his place at the desk, noting with some disdain the frontman slumped before him, then he leaned back in his chair until only the top of his gleaming head was visible. Behind him the window was frosted blank. Suddenly Sam brightened and lunged forward.

"Waitaminit. Maybe all this, maybe this is just your perverse, obverse way of telling me . . . I'm fired."

"Hell no," Agapecropolis laughed savagely. "It means we need guys like you more. than *ever*. Your kind of pride isn't easy to find these days, boy, it gives people that 'good feeling.' So keep the stuff movin', Sambo," he bellowed. "Keep autocorrelating your information, keep your advice rack clean. Tell 'em it's *you* who are responsible for that uptrend, sell 'em America!"

"Is that the kernel of your advice, sir?" Sam was truly weary.

"Well, there *is* one more thing. You ought to think about having a family. It'll take your mind off things, and you won't be so abstracted all the time. You won't make much of a husband, but you'd probably be a pretty good father."

Sam was so depressed he did not even want to hit him. Phlegm had appeared predictably at the back of the doctor's good mouth, he began to choke and fumble for the wastebasket. But this was apparently involuntary and not part of some larger technique, for the doctor sensed his uneasiness and, holding his throat, motioned Sam out the door, which, to the acute discomfort of the receptionist, Sam slammed on the gales of congested laughter.

Sam returned to his desk without a word. Wittgenstein and the other eleven gazed quizzically after him. But he soon became nauseous, the stomach cramps increased, and then he was dashing through the lobby to the restroom. The lastman of the lavatory had a bloody time changing a five-dollar bill as Sam squirreled and shuffled on the tiles. Then finally, plunging a dime into the slot, he wheeled himself down.

Surrounded in the cubicle by the attempts of nonprofessionals to rise above it, smudged dutifully by the industrious lastman before the information could be properly disseminated, Sam squinted through the haze of erasures on his walls. A palimpsest of the middle body; phone numbers, times, places; exhortations, specificity of desires, contretemps; technicians, fundamentalists, feed thy zoos. Was it possible that over a given time, in such a place, if you provided a wall, encouraged speculation and reward, rationalized all possibilities, you would get the same information as if it were simply left to chance? Would not throwing that ball against the wall blacken it more thoroughly than merely, gamely, batting it?

Sam glowed in the afterimages of his predecessors, moribund. Then slowly he withdrew his silver pen from his coat hung before him, and not wishing to admit it was a new day, wrote Odile's name and phone number on the door.

He banged out of the stall at a brisk pace; the lastman had the faucets running tepidly, standing by the basin with a towel over his forearm. But Sam, jingling his change, brushed past him announcing, "I don't shit on *my* hands," and bolted into the lobby.

Wittgenstein was right; he would have to fight. He'd have the good doctor at his own game.

261

At home, Sam had a drink, ate nothing, searching out the passage in Fuess's *Index to the Meliorist* which occurred to him in the restroom. He had not marked it, but finally came across it again:

In 1909, I went into business for myself in Lertz, knowing that I would have to accumulate a lot of money to finance Peace Voyage. But by the time I had started to really save, these United States was entered into War I, and not wanted in the army, I went to work nights at the munitions factory. It was there that I became first aware of Molasses Futures and figured a way to guarantee myself a living wage (for one man, one boat) by puts and calls on the Molasses market. By keeping a chart, unaided, in the logbook, by use of a very simple mathematical formula, I found that I could predict the rises and falls of this market. Had I more Capital and less ideas for Peace, I could have become a billionaire. By this means I was able to finance myself in enterprise beyond subsistence for many years, even during the Big Creamer, though a dollar doesn't buy what it used to, I have never taken a handout and wouldn't, you never know if the trend of molasses or anything else is going to peter out. . . .

Sam got out his best stationery and wrote the good captain.

DEAR CAPTAIN FUESS:

Your candidacy-at-large for Anti-Satanic Administrator to the President of the U.S. has recently come to our attention. It is heartening to see that Patriotism is not a lost virtue for some of us. I'm writing you, Captain Fuess, to reintroduce myself as well as the firm I represent, for I'm sure you're aware that the most well-intentioned and NONSECRET candidates traditionally have made their financial statements public. Inasmuch as you have made your living, by our own admission (*Index to Meliorist*, pp. 74–75 ff.), from investments, it would seem proper for you to make your logbook, income tax, speculative assessments *and* formulae available to a reputable firm such as ours, in case any Secret Fixers should press conflict-of-interest charges as the campaign progresses.

We would, of course, hold such information in our data bank at no cost, and make it available only to authorized inquiry.

Do let me hear from you.

With sincerity to all,
Yours for action, and now,

SAMUEL HOOPER
Account Executive
(Front)

Smoked out, exhausted, Sam dials the stereo-lounger to Sam Hooper[2]. Tonight he is discussing new ways of testing out idealistic philosophy. To normalize his nerve endings constricted by nicotine, Sam[1] drank a good deal. And soon the show was nearly over.

Sam[1] spoke sibilantly, evenly, nose to tube. There were two Sam Hooper[2]s before him to receive the best Purk had to offer:

"What more is there to get, Sam-Bam? Or what is there to give up?"

For the first time on record, Sam[1] outlasted the late show, and as Sam[2] signed off and his image faded, Sam[1] found himself conversing with the telltale blitzing snow of pure energy.

25 · Sitting

During the interregnum, Sam was relieved only once from total
self-preoccupation, taking up Odile's request to sit with the kids.
Aaron didn't like the idea at first, but was glad in the end to save
the money.

"Every little bit helps," he announced on their way out,
" 'cause *we're* going to the International Club."

Odile was in black again and silent. Aaron told her to take his
arm on the stairs. She affected, one could only say, a fantastic
demurity.

(Somebody one day is going to make a lot of money out of
this, Sam reflected. He was thinking about going into business
for himself, a sitting service for and by his sort, those specialists
in bred charisma, last of the gentlemen, first of the new mothers
by default; this Q.U.I.F. corps would be freed by statute to
reflect on weighty issues of public concern during the day, and
then by night fan out into the city, taking over the ceaseless
progeny of careless weary middlemen and autistic artists, to rear
them better than ever. . . .)

It was indicative of his degeneration, Sam knew, that he had
lost all sympathy for his friends, that his one remaining concern
was for their neglected children.

Stieglitz broke his reverie in the sling chair; putting a foot on
either point, she straddled and asked him: "Where'd they go?"

Sam stared at her feet, so reminiscent of her mother's. Had
Aaron discovered or dictated their remarkable qualities? Would

Stieglitz also be laying querulously for up-and-coming frontment? Or would she join the Clones? Of Aaron's mark, all she bore were his eyes. They inquired of him now, moving into that brief range where his astigmatism did not fracture her person.

"So where'd they go?"

"Your mother and father?"

"Mother and Aaron."

"You shouldn't call your father by his first name."

"I call you Sam, don't I?"

"I'm just your friend."

"I like you better than Aaron."

"That's neither here nor there."

Stieglitz settled cozily in his lap. The vinyl sack of the chair groaned with their weight. She kissed the back of his hand. Her body smelled of rosemary, her pajamas riding up her brown body.

"Stieg," Sam said nervously, "what do you want to be when you grow up?"

"Like you," she said softly.

"Come on now."

"Yeah, like you."

"Well . . . why?"

"Cause . . . cause, you don't make anybody ever tired."

Sam thought about the possibility of an endowed scholarship for Stieg at Purk: the first bird on their stones. She wound her brown legs about his.

"But you can't be like me, Stieg."

"Why not? Mother wishes she was. I heard her say so in a fight."

"You don't understand, Stieg, neither does Mother. I'm not a good man. I'm just in a position where I don't have to be mean. If I wasn't, I would be. And it looks like that time may just be coming. . . ."

"But I'm not going to be like Mother."

"Of course," Sam said, hugging her. "You must want to be yourself."

"No," she said slowly, "now I'm making myself pretty. Like *that*." She pointed to an Etruscan vase from a *Life* cover which she had cut out and taped to the wall. "Just like you," she finished. Sam could not make out the frieze, only the uterine shape of the vase.

"Stone?" he said. "That's neither here nor there."

"A pitcher," Stieglitz corrected him, "a big pitcher. A big pretty pitcher with people running around it. That's what I want to be."

"You're pretty big and very pretty right now," said Sam, wishing very much at that moment for the comforting distraction of the stereo-lounger.

"I'm not *that* pretty yet," she mused, "not even as pretty as Mother was."

"You think Mother has gotten less pretty?"

The child began to bounce and bob as she talked.

"Her mouth is still pretty and her nose is still pretty and her hair is almost as pretty, but her eyes got darker and went back in her head."

"Well, *I* still think she's pretty."

"All I said was I'm going to *stay* pretty." She jumped from Sam's lap and stamped her foot. "Like you."

"I'm not supposed to be pretty, Stieg. Come back here. A man's supposed to be a man and a woman's supposed to be pretty."

"It's neither here or there," Stieglitz mimicked, and flounced back to the bedroom, hiking her pajamas up.

Sam went back later after a drink to check the kids out. Stieg lay face down on the lower of the double-decker, holding the hips which were just beginning to swell forever, brown toes

266

turned in, white soles without a wrinkle, crying into the proverbial pillow; and in the upper, Matthew punctuating her sobs with a whistley minisnore.

Sam sat down on the side of the bed and massaged the small of her back. He felt a snort behind his ears and looked up to find Matthew staring down at him.

"OK, kids, time for a little bedtime reading before the Mr. and Mrs. get home."

Sam produced his battered copy of *The Meliorist Index to Keys to Mysteries*, lay back on the lower bunk, doubling up his legs, bundling Stieglitz into one arm, Matthew clambering quickly into the other, keeping a well-rubbed eye on him.

"All right, kids, this is from the adventures of Captain Fuess."

"Captain who?" Stieglitz asked.

"Captain Crunch," Matthew murmured.

"No, both wrong, fellas," said Sam. "It's Fuess, Cap'n Ed Fuess, Big Ed they used to call him, sort of rhymes halfway between peace and mess. Anyway, your Uncle Sam thinks he's got a lot to say."

"Right, *Uncle* Sam," Stieglitz said in a disconcertingly bass voice, while folding her arms.

"Promise you won't interrupt me? I'm only reading this part for the first time myself."

"Right, Sam, you're the boss."

"Well anyway, here goes."

Sam opened to the page marker. Above him, on the bottom of Matthew's mattress, he was aware of a damp, dark stain.

. . . *in the Consulate library in Cairo (from which Cairo, Illinois takes her name), I came across a book which I read while Sturdy was getting her bottom scraped. This book, the name of I can't remember, is about a whole family that comes to no good end. But at the end, two real characters, a boy and a girl, are getting set to run away to*

America. The boy has been accused of a murder. His father, as I recall it. He and his girl are going to run away to America instead of being sent to Siberia (they are Russians).

They boys thinks there still bears and red indians in America, and they can live here on berries, do their work and learn our grammer. WORK AND GRAMMER!! All right. But once he gets them you know what this Ruskie wants to do? He wants to go back to (Mother?) Russia to die. He thinks he'll get disguised with a warts and lines from one of those "wonderful" American technical doctors, and with their long grey hair grown from work and grammer, he and his girl, they'll be able to go back.

Well, what if we said the same thing! They'd say we were exploiters! And after taking all that Work n' Grammer from America, the only thing he can think of is to go back home and die with it!

You've got to give him credit though, for putting his finger right on the problem. Nobody, see, wants to admit they'll die in America or of it. All that Work and Grammer . . . made here, to speak and do like everybody, and then leave her to die! Well, I'll go away maybe, but I'll die here (there at home) not in some damn foreign land (precautions taken). That's the "I will" spirit.

But so, this Ruskie saw that everybody comes here to get their Work and Grammer and then just takes it away to die when they do, someplace they thought they began of. Sometimes I think this country is made up just of people waitin to get in and then waitin to get out from under, like some fancy privy, with shamed people waitin their turn on one side and smartasses comin out the other side—oh, don't they look embarrassed while they're waitin, hoppin up and down on one leg or pullin an ear, but when they're done, when they take that one prize dump, they come out and look around a little depressed, their eyes don't track right, but then they walk around like anybody else who's still waitin is crazy or worse, and then before you know it, you see 'em goin off down the road, hitching up their pants and scratchin. Nothin ever gets passed onto anybody . . . what disappointments . . . What humiliations . . .

"I'm hungry," said Matthew.

"Don't interrupt," shot Stieglitz.

"No, that's all right," said Sam, "I'm just as glad he did. What do you want?"

"Captain Crunch," said Matthew.

"Well, as long as *I'm* sitting you're going to get better than that," Sam said.

Matthew shrugged, but old Stieg was listening. Sam went out to the kitchen and started to rifle through Odile's cookbooks. The spines of most of them were still stiff; occasionally, he found a recipe circled (i.e., Roast brisket of lamb basted with cream of mushroom soup; no watching necessary, 1 hr. 45 min.). Finally, in one of the more useless wedding gifts, an illustrated, uncracked *Larousse* (the Book Club Edition number carefully razored out), he found a recipe for *Boeuf fondue*.

"OK, mates," Sam announced. "*Now* you're going to see something."

He set Stieg at dicing a T-bone, while he concentrated on the dips. Odile had a good spice-and-herb rack, many of which had never been opened. Well-trained Matthew set the table somnolently.

"Try the green; that's shallots and amali and yoghurt."

"That's pretty good too," she said. "Was *your* mother a good cook, Sam?"

Sam hesitated a moment. "I've really nothing to judge her by," he said curtly.

Matthew was the last to finish; his belly was distended to the edge of the highchair tray.

Their sauces had become mixed together, becoming all of one puce.

"How'd you like it?" Sam asked.

"It was the best thing I ever put in my mouth," said Stieglitz.

"I'd ruther have nine meats and one sauce," Matthew said.

"OK, everybody back to bed."

"Who's going to wash up?" asked Stieglitz.

"We'll leave that for the Mr. and Mrs.," Sam said.

Sam picked up *The Meliorist Index* from the bunk and tucked them in.

"Shall I finish it?"

Matthew said nothing, Stieg pulled the covers up to her nose, her eyes bright as Greek olives.

"OK then."

. . . *but his girlfriend set this boy straight in the end. She told him he wouldn't make a very good martyr and that she certainly wouldn't, and that it wasn't necessary to Jesus-like throw your self away for that "other man" in America or to become the "other man" there.*

Because all which was necessary, I remember exactly the way she said it, all which was necessary for him was to remember the "other man" always, remember him always and that would be enough.

So I guess he died there after all, though the book ended before it got to that. He didn't have to come to America and become that "other man." But maybe if that Ruskie had come to America after all, he would have liked it here, would have got to like his new disguise so much that he would have died here too.

Well, I know how he felt all right, because I've put up with the hermit life too, even though it's again my nature, and my daddy left us fore I could kill him, and I had to run away to see . . . and maybe, if I'd had a girl like that I wouldn't have put all my Work & Grammer into a Peace Voyage.

But now that I have, I've got to train myself to remember that "other man," the man I might've become, back in America, remember him always. And I'd say that's a full time job right there . . .

Matthew was asleep again, Stieg's eyes just slits.

"Who's that other man, Sam?" she asked dreamily.

Sam flipped back through the pages for a specific name, but she was asleep before he could find one.

By midnight, Sam was getting nervous. He wondered if Aaron had taken enough money with him. Out of liquor, he paced the foyer as much as it would permit. His weak eye ultimately fell on a shelf near the door. A bulky letter, slit across the top, postmarked the previous day, addressed to Odile in a frenzied hand, was wedged among the whatnot's bric-a-brac.

It proved to be from George Stablefeather and contained carbons of his latest and lengthiest work—the *Odile* poems. There was no correspondence, only manuscript, of which Sam digested the last page.

> *numb from your*
> *furious lulls*
>
> *waves suck*
> *as much as*
> *they spew*
>
> *lave your*
> *irregular*
> *archipelagos*
>
> *your salt*
> *your sand*

Odile had dated the manuscript and also annotated it in her familiar green Gulley hand: *pithy, but lacks resonance. Despite increasing clarity and unique diction, could be more effective.*

So George is after a little too, Sam thought, pacing up and down before the darkroom, and Odile is finally getting some mileage out of her degree. He was aware of a brief surge of the old competitiveness, but resisting the predictable, he forced it down, pleased at his control. As the old knot formed about his heart, he wondered at Odile's casualness in leaving such things around. As usual, he did not know whether to attribute this to honesty or indifference. The knot was taking over his entire

271

trunk; he dropped to the floor to do a hundred push-ups. From his new vantage he noticed the darkroom door ajar. He lay before it in a mild sweat for some time. Finally, against his best intentions, he entered the darkroom and put the red light on. The filmstrip of the ballet was threaded in the enlager; he put his good eye to the viewer and focused.

Sam saw then that Aaron had made it, fulfilled his own injunctions, why he had seen fit to take Odile out for dinner and celebrate. Each frame illumined a perfectly composed close-up of the dancers' bodies, but in a manner as to isolate them completely from the dance—the pure solid, shadow and space of some wondrous psychological asphyxiation.

Totally inexplicable and yet surprising; not unlike a sudden series of offstage arias in an opera of an unknown culture, in which the simple beauty of the voice obliterates any necessity of plot, action or libretto, and even the principals are pointlessly transfixed, loving their artificiality, having become themselves their best audience. . . . But even this was not true, for the works implicated no other medium. Their power derived from their resistance to any possible commentary. Indeed, by the use of some acid emulsion, Aaron had made it difficult to tell whether they were photos, engravings, or even acrylic. The utter lack of perspective also made the distance of the observer from his subject and the nature of the instrument impossible to determine.

Only through the fact that Sam had been permitted to share the lens at the moment of inception could he label them, and only, as a result, could he alone tell us that the small dark ovals shimmering in one corner of the fourth frame were in fact bruises from the blunt fingers of a Latvian-born stand-in on the bare sweatstreaked midriff of a Miss Julie Rowen in the second act of a benefit performance of the *The Crazed Bird* in the city of ——— in the year of our Lord ———. Sam resolved that no one should ever know the purpose, angle, macroscopics or f-stop of these shots. He wanted only to love them as much as their terrifying integrity would allow.

So Aaron was up to zero. He had rediscovered that line definitive where human sense apparatus finds its limit and technology begins, that margin of the ancient brain where all perception has no name but is only an endless jelly-electric commentary on itself. And here, in this foul unlikely room, Sam finally understood the meaning of Black Art. Fuess's scourge, Agapecropolis's opiate—this was Aaron's very impulse carried beyond playful self-regarding curiosity and institutionalized— first in Humanities I and penultimately in Management Concern. Black Art was simply the honorable—and for that very reason most heinous—confusion between the tasks of transmuting human nature and that of managing it.

Sam was also saddened, however, for he saw in the oblique eroticism of these works the hopelessness of his and Odile's condition. Aaron had joyfully reversed every assumption they took seriously; for to "finish" required, as this work testified, and as Sam Hooper[2] would explicate in his review of their display the day before Aaron's hasty departure for Rome:

. . . the willful reduction of instinctive pride, the willingness to experience segments of the mind and body, to break down all compromised integration into their constituent parts, reduce organic matter to inertness, celebrate the distance between and disintegration of all definitive faculties. . . .

They had not been taught that.

Sam went back to have a last look at the kids. The windowless room smelled of baby oil and hairspray.

26 · Questing

On what for present purposes was the following Monday, an untidy bundle, packaged in the glutinous covers of *The Meliorist* and bound with chicken wire, awaited Sam on his desk. The other eleven feigned indifference as he opened it.

Rally Point
(*Evolution, not Revolution*)

DEAR PARTNER IN USA:

In answer to your last, I enclose all "Keys to Mysteries" I can lay my hands on now including Mollasses log book and latest *Voice of the Hour XVII*. I have a whale of a job but am waiding through, luckly, I have an agenda in the ruf. I am not surprised you have found many interested in my life and literature, Satan's 1% has America on the spot, their artificial misnomers are at the throat of all mankind.

Sturdy's truck exhibet is almost ready for the road. Then give the calf more rope and . . .?

Remember about enclosed information, all have a right to criticize me and my work and I have a right to criticize all and their work (anti-ism). This is good and wholesome for all. That is why all must keep free and independent under their own won names. I never was a sissi and no one should be, I never was a bully and no one should be.

Yours for action and NOW!!

Sam did not trust Wittgenstein's curiosity with the material and so, for the first time in his tenure, bypassed his mentor, taking the spiral staircase to the pit.

At the bottom a middleman lounged insolently within a booth by the bolted door. He appeared amused by Sam.

"You're not going in with *them*, I hope?" he said.

"I need to give this stuff a pattern analysis," Sam said evenly.

"A frontman in with *those* pigs?" he said, smoothing his hair. "You'd never make it."

"Listen," Sam said, balling a fist in his pocket, "this could be of the utmost importance to the very existence of MC. If this is what I think it is, and one of our competitors got ahold of it—"

"You're pretty young to be a frontman, aren't you?"

Sam's bad eyelid began to flutter. "Look, what's your name, buddy?"

"Larry."

"Well look, Larry, I mean what do I have to do? This is too important to go through normal channels."

"You got an authorization?"

"Christ," Sam nearly screamed, "*I'm* the guy who gives the authorizations in our—"

"It must be nice working up in one of those big bright offices, dealing with the best people. Not like down here, a door's width from those swine."

The clamor on the other side of the metal door had in fact increased, like a storm coming up or the sea beyond the mountains. Sam decided to change his tack.

"Boy, it really must be hard to deal with them. I mean anybody with any sensitivity, and then all those stairs. I got vertigo just coming down here."

"Well, it's not so bad," Larry said, relaxing, tugging at his ascot. "They stop bothering you when they know you won't stand for any foolishness."

"But those stairs, wow!"

"You've just got to decide you aren't going to let things like that bother you," Larry sighed. "We are, all of us, put upon."

"Well, I guess I had better start trekking," Sam said. "I've got a lot to wade through myself. When do you think you all might be ready for me?"

"Look, uh, why don't you give me that stuff? It's an off day anyway. If it's only pattern analysis you want, I'll run it through when there's an opening and give you a ring."

"That's awfully sweet of you."

"You'd do the same for me, I'm sure."

Sam disentangled the log book on the molasses futures market and handed it over.

"Careful with it now," he murmured. "It doesn't look like much, but he's probably one of those eccentric millionaires, you know."

"You fellows up there really meet the most interesting people, don't you?"

"Oh, you'd be surprised at the sameness of it all, the airlessness. It's not all the glory it looks. And I'm rather savagely impatient with the detail. It seems so nice and quiet down here. If it wasn't for all those stairs. But to think that on the other side of that door, well, that's real life, isn't it?"

"You would find it incredible, I assure you. One just has to harden oneself. As President Bins said at last year's Christmas party, 'Management is just one damn thing after another.'"

Sam chortled knowledgeably. "Thanks much, I'll look forward to hearing from you." He wheeled and took the stairs three at a time.

"Hey, Mr.—" Larry shouted after him but to no avail— "why, he didn't even give his name. . . ."

Inside an hour, the intramural phone flashed for Sam. He took his feet off the desk and answered it deliberately. Larry's high voice had the pitch and tone of a motor scooter.

"Hey, why couldn't you tell me who you *were?* I've been running you down in the directory for half an hour, jesus you can't just come down *here* and expect a guy to know *where* everybody *is*. But I got what you wanted. I'll say this is *really* something. There's a pattern here sure enough and *holy* mother what a market imperfection it *is*—a positive serial correlation of successive changes from 1909 to the present, and this old coot's formula had it *pegged* exactly, every rise, every fall. If he'd a had more capital he coulda had the world by the balls this guy *wow* this throws the whole random theory up for grabs they'll go asswild in the pits when *this* gets out. But maybe we shouldn't move too fast, the pols'll be all *over* our backs. Christ, I had the *devil* of a time finding you, what should we . . . ?"

"Thank you, Lawrence."

Sam hung up on him and could not resist a full swivel in his chair, a mechanical but still triumphal survey of the other eleven and Wittgenstein, the last time in his life he would ever have to be accountable to any of them. The knot in his chest disappeared, evaporated into his body, renewing it.

Only the calculation of logistics remained. The first step would be to threaten Larry into a pregnant silence; a short chop across the mouth in the dark of those spiral stairs should be sufficient warning. Secondly, should he take Wittgenstein into his confidence? Between them, with such leverage, they could finish Agapecropolis for good. But he could not gauge whether the old man's long-standing bitterness would still be strong enough at this late date to overcome his accretion of loyalty. He resolved to present the situation hypothetically and test his reaction—it was such an unthinkable coup that he would not be suspected in any case. Finally, there was the question of how much he should take personally from the first inevitable Whizz. He could no doubt play the market alone, unknown, with his own modest resources, making enough in several weeks certainly to sustain him for life, but then undoubtedly he would be fired for cause, banished from the management community forever, and he, like Captain Fuess, had no desire for the "hermit-life," circumnavigating himself endlessly, even as a millionaire. What

277

would impress Bins more? Threaten him with creating a rival to MC unless a partnership was forthcoming immediately? Barter with him for stock options and a no-cut contract, in return for a ninety-nine-year lease to the pattern? Or would it be more sanguine to place the Fuess Formula dutifully in their hands, stressing their not so long but still privileged association, counting on the old proud Purk solidarity and corporate guilt of the fathers, to provide "that unspoken prestige which accrues to those whose humble diffidence in the face of absurd success only obviates their power"? Hmmm. Yes, he would bet on their fear of his inexplicable loyalty; for his control would be then grounded in their guilt and not their beneficence.

Sam then began to make up his Christmas list. The Dott would be pensioned for life, an educational trust fund set up for Agapecropolis' children, free lifetime psychoanalysis for Stieglitz and Matthew, the preservation and extension of Peacock Prairie, funds enough for Fuess to get the land voyage of *Sturdy* under way without further delay. Wittgenstein would take over for Agapecropolis, Larry would have Sam's old slot, Wittgenstein's former post would be abolished as no one of the new generation could possibly fill it, Aaron would have his grant and then some, and as for Odile . . . what for Odile?

The phone made our Sam jump. He stared at it for some time and then picked it up, as one might cautiously overturn a seashell. Larry was nearly in tears:

"Oh jesus Sam that's your *name* isn't it? The *bottom's* fallen out of the son-of-a-bitch the fastest I *ever* saw it! As soon as the info got disseminated the market discounted it quick as a *whistle,* the old coot's lost everything . . . the pattern's gone, we can't *even* get a pro*jection* on the son-of-a-bitch now. Can you *imagine?* Sixty years of strict predictability and now *blooie!* Of all times this has to happen, it's a burden on us oh I know its a burden—"

"Hold on there, Larry boy, there'll be other times."

278

But Sam Hooper's comfort was as mechanical as his triumph: Agapecropolis had warned him; the information had been disseminated, universally adopted, then discounted. And what would become of the good captain now?

Sam left right then and there, thinking, I really can't take too much more of this, but shortly after midnight, the old smoke again like a fine cheese in his lungs, he got out the maps and set a course for Rally Point.

He arrived at the Parking Tower before dawn, and just as he presented Agapecropolis' keys and his credit card to the attendant, a powerful foreign sportscar hurtled down the ramp, its tappets like a thousand crystal goblets breaking. The interior was all of veal and smelled of oregano. He could not get it out of second on the outer drive, but as soon as he hit the expressway south, he took the Cordon Blue to an effortless 120. The blurred landscape suited his astigmatism perfectly. "They can say what they want," he mumbled, "but I love this little car."

Actually, Sam had tired of searching where he came from. He had complicated it so much, and started at it so early, it was simply easier to consider himself a professional orphan. And there are distinct advantages in advertising as historyless.

He had convinced himself from the beginning that the profuse blue baby book which Mother kept in her dresser and had subsequently been enclosed with her insurance was nothing but a painstaking ruse to convince him of some credible link with others. There they were, pasted firmly on manila, a series of little photogenic strangers, each infinitesimally larger and wiser than the last—his props, Irish mail to English racer—documents, genealogies, inoculations, deportments, adjustments, certifications—corroborative detail, locks of saffron hair, inky wrinkled footprints, waxen seals of state, first steps, first words— tricks of perspective, a standard handout to create the illusion, as

279

we look up from our most recent strafing, that we were all somehow shot from the same gun.

It took half the day to find the town postmarked on Rally Point correspondence. It had not prospered. The grain elevators tottered for miles across the incised prairie—hollow Chartreses at once glorifying and devitalizing the land. In the newest purple plastic silos, in aluminum cylinders, in concrete capsules, in wooden cribs, or just in rotting piles, the corn was ubiquitous. Not one forp in *those* contours.

Sam opened the MC *Route Guide* which had been thoughtfully chained to the dash.

for the curious-minded:

Rally Point, originally named Lertz for unknown reasons, and scene of the notorious "bloody" riot, is also notable for demarking the furthermost penetration of the great glaciers, so that to the north one finds rich flat republican loam, and to the south, wrinkled democrat basalt, sinks, bluffs, ridges, pockets of coal and quartz. . . .

Sam looked about. The captain had settled right on the lip of the old ice. The corn came to an abrupt end north of town, the mine shafts began on the other.

Most of the houses are equipped with the primary regional architectural innovation—the front porch—and the purist will, upon close scrutiny, note remnants of the first asbestos sheeting used in the territory, in a few cases, cunningly disguised as brickwork.

Unfortunately, the courthouse with its fine pilastered arches, cryptoporticos, and consoled balconies was torn down some years ago in a road-widening project. The majority of the chestnut trees also met a similar fate, for although giving an appearance of rustic calm, they actually militated against the fully majestic view of the open spaces. The motorist, in any case, will now find little to complain about. . . .

280

Sam drove slowly into town. A leafy railway spur crept in from the corn alongside him, only to be tarred over in the main street. The two-story façades of the one-story stores had been buttressed with neon. Sam parked on the deserted square—a small park circumferenced with concrete-stuffed walnut trees wound tight with iron hoops. The trees were further protected by a kneehigh fence of leftover hoops, the arches of which mirrored the crescents of the telephone wire that sagged from one newly lacquered pole to the next, alternating as they did with the walnut trees.

In the center of the park, slightly off plumb, hulked a small deserted band shell, and before it the war monument, a shoulder-high figurine of a Civil War soldier, putting to his lips and cradling on his sinewy chest what appeared to be a French horn or battle tuba.

The original inscription on the pedestal read:

Super cuncta, subter cuncta,
Extra Cuncta, intra cuncta

but across this a plaque had been bolted:

SOLDIERS, SAILORS, MARINES
NINETEEN-SIXTEEN—NINETEEN-EIGHTEEN

and below this a medallion

1941–1945

and finally at the very base of the block was etched

50—53

The names of the deadest heroes had been inscribed about the frieze of the pedestal, but gradually they had run out of room and filled all four faces of the stone, abbreviating the first and middle names to initials, typeface progressively reduced, utilizing every square inch of space until the white marble was utterly black with inscription. Across these names, in penknife and chalk, were scriven the pledges of young two-fingered lovers, and across these in a heavy block stencil Sam could make out

DEFACEMENT OF OFFICIAL MONUMENTS IS FORBIDDEN

A Koolgas station now stood on the site of the courthouse, a blue-and-yellow cantilevered glassy trianon. Blue-and-yellow cans of oil were piled in perfect pyramids in each arcade, nine blue-and-yellow pumps stood in serried rows of three. In the garage a blue-and-yellow wrecking truck was being washed by an attendant in blue-and-yellow overalls. Sam was near empty and eased in. Told him to fill it up and asked him how long he'd been around. Said he'd had his franchise for a year. A quick, lean lastman from the middle South.

"There used to be a courthouse here," Sam inquired nonchalantly, "didn't there?"

"Sure thing. Big'n. With fancy grillework on the roof, y'know. It was a good'n. Big as a bahn. Company bought it, blacktopped the front yeard. Guy befo me worked outa the parlors. But it looked pretty funny. Big white house with gas pumps in front like that. So they toah it down. I got one of the old mahble fireplaces out back. Can't burn nothin in it though. Goin' to put it against the wall on my frontporch. Why?"

"I'm looking for a fellow name of Captain Edgar Fuess. A remarkable man."

"That right?"

He finished up wiping the windows. He wiped them all, on the sides and in back, scratching away at the stubborn summer bugs with his fingernails. Then he returned to the trianon to make change. When he came out he had a sheet of blue-and-yellow stamps.

"You can keep those," Sam said.

"We got fer hunnert and twenty-seven stations in thirteen states," he countered. "An thas quita cah you got theya."

"Thass all right," Sam said, "you jess keep 'em."

Trying to persuade, Sam had already lapsed into the lastman's affable accent. He gunned the mighty Cordon Blue to go. The attendant folded the stamps, taking care they did not stick together, and slipped them sadly into a blue-and-yellow breast pocket. Then he shrugged and counted out the change, popping the bills a few times like a shoeshine rag before handing them over.

"Come back and see us, heah?"

Sam was hungry and circling the square found a DINER/DINER/ DINER. Ordering spareribs, he asked the waitress if she knew about Fuess.

She surely did.

Then, noting her suspicion, he announced mendaciously that he was the nephew of Edgar Fuess and the waitress threw up her hands.

"Oh, get Twitch," she said to the countergirl, and the latter ran off into the kitchen and from what Sam could hear the back door as well. In five minutes she returned with a stocky scrubbed old man, fine brown veins in his face and fingers.

"Your name Fuess?" he said, holding his hat.

"No, but my uncle is Captain Edgar Fuess, of Rally Point, U.S.A."

He sat down in the booth and took Sam in as he finished the spareribs.

"You eaten?" Sam asked.

"Twitchell."

"Sorry?"

"I'm Twitchell," the old man said, "Faragut Twitchell."

"I see."

The old man nodded again and slipped some paper napkins into his pocket.

"Yep, Fuess," he began, "Fuess was a corker all right. Got the bodies out in the riot."

"Was?" Sam said.

"Was what, lad?"

"You said he *was* . . ."

"Was, is, so what, lad."

"Is he *was?*"

"Was the only man ornery enough to touch 'em," Faragut went on. "We all thought they had the ague, y'see."

"Ague?" Sam chorused casually.

"No Ague. Just niggers."

"They were Negroes?"

"Yhep. And Ed Fuess was a big little man, yes sir, and he thought a lot uh me."

Sam tried another tack.

"Did you help him with the bodies?"

"Had to. Drove for him. Took his word for it."

"And nobody got the ague?"

"Course not. Twenty-eight got shot, though. Mostly niggers."

"The bodies were Negroes?"

"Yep. . . . Say, you sure you're related to Ed Fuess?"

"I told you, I'm his nephew."

The old man raised his eyebrows and nodded more. Folding another napkin in eighths, he hid it away in his vest and began again.

"You probably heard all about the riot then."

"No," Sam feinted, "the family doesn't seem to know much about Uncle Edgar at all."

Faragut nodded again, got up and walked unsteadily but purposively out of the diner. Sam hastily tracked him. The waitress beamed and whispered to the countergirl as he left, "*That's* Cap'n Fuess's nephew. He sure a good-looker."

Faragut was halfway down the alley when Sam got outside.

He ran to catch up but the old man suddenly stopped in front of a garage.

All your life, you run to catch up with people and when you finally do, they stop without warning and you knock them over.

This old man dodged, nevertheless, and choosing the correct key from a ring of fifty on the first try, he opened the double doors of the garage.

"I still got it," he said, "it's bout the only thing ah hain't sold."

Sam didn't know what it was at first. For your information it was an old horse-drawn hearse.

"Bet you never seen anything like that!" Faragut Twitchell paused and ran his hand over the seat. "Got the isinglass and genuine leather just the way she was. Even got the tassles still. Here's what we put the niggers in. Your uncle and I slung 'em up by the hands and feet fore they got bloaty and flied all over. Didn't make a penny offen it neither."

"He mentioned something about undertaking once in . . ."

"Surely was. Good'un too. Didn't take to it much, under-takin', but he did it. He was a stickler he was. Those niggers probably be layin' there still 'cept for him."

"I'm lucky to have found you," Sam said reluctantly. "I want to know everything about my uncle."

Faragut smiled a little more and walked through a beaded curtain into the rear of the garage.

He lived there. An enormous black maple bedstead, a washing stand with a swivel mirror, a kerosene stove, and a Tiffany lamp. Tables piled high with corded bales of magazines, newspapers; parts of a hundred bicycles. "Tell me everything," Sam pleaded.

Faragut looked at Sam steadily. His hair was absolutely white and had been brushed until it gleamed with the waxen glow of lilies. He went to his rolltop desk slowly, picked up something

285

between his fingers, and held it to the light.

"Here's an interestin' objek," he said.

Sam took it from his hand and stared at it politely for some time.

"That there's a three-lobe tribolite, member of the Pal-eo-Zoic era." Faragut took it back, rolling it between his pink hands. "I found 'er right west of town in a gulley."

"Tri*lo*bite," Sam corrected him.

He placed the shell back on the desk exactly on the spot from which he had taken it, then stooped below the drawers and dragged out a lady's hatbox. He removed the lid, rummaged about, and came up with a daguerreotype.

"Guess who that is?" he spoke triumphantly. "None other but the former Mrs. Fuess," he continued. "A real gentlewoman, a lady of color, if you knows what I mean." Across the muddy photo was written, "All my love forever, Result."

"She left him, I guess," Sam opined ingenuously.

"Never talked much bout his women," Faragut said, but he was already looking for something else. He found it in a lower drawer.

"Bet you don't know what that is neither." Sam didn't.

"Just a Jap ashtray from the World's Fair, thas all. Picked it up on my way back from Texas, an ashtray of the Japs."

"You're from Texas?"

He looked at Sam intently for some time before answering.

"With your uncle," he said evenly. "He stayed on a while after I came back. He was a corker, all right."

Sam did not recall any reference to Texas in *Why I spent $38,000 going 100,000 Miles Alone in 64 Years.*

"Jesus, I didn't know he was in Texas."

"He said to me he said, 'Twitch, I think a lotta you. I'll give you a farm here and you can try it, and if it don't work out you don't owe me nothin', and if it do then all the better for both of us.' And I told him right then and there I said, 'With all these

286

niggers and Mexicans and alligators, I'll be goin' right now,' I said, and I surely went. He came back a course, in a couple of years. Some say a millionaire."

"Was that from portable office or molasses?"

"Ed Fuess was a shrewd'n," Faragut said, "as shrewd as they come."

He had exhausted himself for the moment and sank into a Ulysses Grant rocker. Suddenly he lurched and snatched a bottle from the dressing table.

"Got this from a feller in St. Louis," he said. "Betcha you don't know what was in it."

Sam shook his head.

"Bear oil," he nodded vigorously, "bear oil."

Sam was getting angry.

"And looky this." Faragut produced a document from a ring binder and floated it through the rank air to Sam.

To all whom these presents shall come, Greetings.
WHEREAS, Socrates F. Fuess, by taking part in the late Rebellion, has made himself liable to heavy pains and penalties;

AND WHEREAS, the circumstances of his case render him a proper object of Executive Clemency;

NOW THEREFORE, be it known in consideration of The Premises, and Divers other good and sufficient reasons thereunto moving that he be pardoned and all real property and constitutional rights restored unto him. . . .

"You mean," Sam gasped out, "he was a slaver . . . ?"

"You might say his father were. But Ed Fuess was a shrewd'n. Cause of what his daddy done, he had to go round the world. And he did it." Ignoring Sam's grimace, he continued. "And that. Lookit that." He fondled a paperweight. "Section of the first Atlantic cable. It broke, y'know, and they sold it in two-inch slugs for a quarter apiece. So's they could put another one down, I guess."

Sam got up, began to look despairingly about the room. He tried to read the newspapers that plastered the wall, but they overlapped too often for him to get more than a paragraph of each. When he turned around again, Faragut was casually affecting a large sombrero and had balled his fist into a varicose pink-and-brown mock pistol.

"Whoa there, partner, Tom Landry's hat is here," he announced noncommittally. Sam sat down heavily.

"I'll bite. Who's Tom Landry?"

"Why, foreman of the Phelps Mine. You *sure* you Ed Fuess's nephew? He's the one who brought the niggers in, strike-breakers from the South. They brought 'em in in boxcars, had built a stockade for 'em right in the old Indian burial grounds. The miners lined up though and shot 'em like cattle as they rode through. 'Cept the niggers on that train, they had guns too, we found out soon enough, and old Tom Landry took one through the throat. I picked up his hat on the street that very day. And we threw him right in the hearse with the niggers. Old Cap'n Ed got a boot outa that."

Faragut grinned and poked a pink finger through the hole in the crown of the hat.

"That's only thing what a good man can do, son. The way things are, he can't catch nobody while they're fallin'. All's he can do is stay free 'n clear, and pick up the bodies afterwards."

"Look," Sam said, "can't you tell me something specific? I mean about Edgar Fuess personally?"

"I know," Faragut mused, "I knows. And your Uncle Ed was mighty good to me. Remember now, he had an old bitch oncet. I traded him a spaniel puppy for her. I knew she weren't no good, but I never could abide pups. The bitch weren't no good, I

288

thought, but I fed her anyway, kep her in the barn with the other dogs. One day, I thought I'd get me a pheasant for dinner, and I don't know why but I took that bitch along to the river with me. Well now, a big cock went up from the bank and I got him with the first barrel. And that bitch dog was by me like a blue streak, and pretty soon she brought that bird right back to me. Reckoned I had something then. And pretty soon that old bitch flushed out two more, hens this time. I got one goin' up the river and the other goin' cross it. The first'n fell in some reeds but that bitch she went right after it. So I started to go for t'other but she beat me there too, sure enough. She had *both* big hens one and two in her mouth. Knew I had somethin then. Ever see a dog could carry two hens at oncet? Well, I took the birds home and I took that bitch out of the barn away from the other dogs, and I gave her the hens' heads and wings to eat, and a cock's foot to sleep with, and made her a special bed in the washhouse. Well, the next morning I got my gun and got down to the washhouse early, and you know something? That old dog was frozen plumb stiff." Faragut rolled his eyes and leaned back. "Your uncle was a shrewd'n all right."

"You know something, Faragut, I don't think you ever knew my Uncle Edgar!"

Faragut stiffened and began to dig in a pile of magazines.

"Don't, huh? Well, lemme get you a li'l proof. But I get *your meaning*. Left us all, didn't he? The old son-of-a-bitch. . . . Wal anyway, looky here." He pulled out an ancient rotogravure section from the Cleveland *Plain Dealer*. "Never heard of *Our Lady of Akron*, did ya? Well, I was pretty good with my hands in those days and my friends was going to work on this dirigible, they seemed to think a lot of me and asked me to come along. But my mother, she said no. She said, 'If you're going to build that thing, as sure as I'm your mother you're goin' to want to fly it.' Well I didn't go. And the next year she blew up over Akron and killed all my buddies. They made the gas from pouring sulfuric acid on steel, ya know. If they'da used helium, they'da laughed at the world."

There was a picture of a blimp and seven men in knickers standing before it with their arms around each other.

"I'm fourth on the right," Faragut said. "Your Uncle Ed, he took the picture."

For a moment, Sam wanted to hit him. Faragut's past had outdistanced pity.

(So they'd find him stuffed in his own hearse, pink old face not pink at all, his body one flooding bruise, each major internal organ mashed to pâté, the brown blotched stringy fingers wound about some artifact. . . .)

"Where's he at? I'll get there by myself."

"Surely. Two hundred and forty acres west of town. I hain't been out there since the Stokes boy got into the bear pit."

"Rally Point, U.S.A.?"

"Your Uncle Ed, he had a bear pit and brung up bears from Arkansas to eat the garbage. I told that boy to stay away from the pit 'cause they were slaughtering pigs that day and there was an odor in the air, y'know. Well, we heard a turrible screamin' during supper and your uncle he went in after him with a marlin spike but it weren't of no use."

"I believe you, Faragut. Have you got a map of the land?"

He turned and opened another cubbyhole in the desk, bringing out a heavy scrapbook. He opened it to the center and from between several pressed flowers withdrew a canceled postage stamp and handed it over. There were five sailors on it.

"The Rogers boys," he sighed. "All of 'em went down with the *Delaware*. Post office remembered them with that." He was near tears and buried his head in his arms on the work table.

Sam grasped the quivering shoulders, but the old man shrugged him off.

"The Wynadotta Expedition," he exclaimed. "You never seen arrowheads?"

290

Sam grabbed at him as he rummaged in a trunk. "Where's that land? I've got to go."

"Go west on County K. When you come to a creek, it's his land aside it," Faragut muttered and went back to his trunk. "You'll see the signs more likely 'n not."

"Fine. Thank you."

Sam edged to the door but as he turned to go he heard music. He wheeled to find Faragut playing a Sousa march on a xylophone.

"My brother got yellow fever in the Cuba war," he said solemnly. "After they let him out of the hospital he done killed his self. He was a real artist."

Sam sagged in the doorway. "Sir," he mumbled, "I gotta go. Sorry."

The old man nodded understandingly, laid the xylophone carefully on the bed, then he shuttled sideways across the room to a table where he removed a bell jar from a tray.

"A chip from Lincoln's cabin?" he asked.

Sam shook his head.

"I bicycled down there when I was fourteen. . . ." he continued, but Sam was already out the door.

"Hey," Faragut yelled. "Young fella!"

Faragut's voice had changed; it was sharper, menacing, bitter or forgetful, Sam didn't know which. But he stopped. Faragut drew himself to in the doorway, steadying himself by hanging from the frame, with his new scowl looking very much like an aged pink gorilla.

"You," he went on, glowering, "you don't even know about Emily's biscuits!"

He was so severe, Sam feared for his health and let him finish.

"Wellsir," he said, smiling solemnly when he saw he had him, "there hain't much to it." He eased out of the door frame where his gestures would be freer. "It's just that when we came out here, your uncle 'n me, and pretty little Emily, God rest her soul, we had nothin' to eat in the wagon. I mean nothin'. Somewheres in Ohio I think it was, we come across this big hoofprint in the road. We were gettin' mighty hungry so we dumped the last of the meal in that holler place to mix us up a biscuit. But we didn't have no water, so your Uncle Edgar, he called for Emily. 'Dearie,' he said, 'we're needin' some water for our biscuit.' So's Emily she jumps right outta the wagon, comes over to that holler place and hikes up her skirts . . ."

"That's disguisting," Sam said blandly and raced for the car, Faragut howling and slapping his thigh in his wake. Why is History always ending up like that?

It was near dusk when Sam left the square. The Teens were in from work on their rods, cruising the war memorial, looking around. The Koolgas station's arc lights were on and clouds of gnats attacked the glow. He found County Road K by the railway spur and followed it out until the tarmac veered away into the fields. It was dirt but smooth and he took it over sixty. Soon all he could hear was the vortex of the car billowing the corn. It grew right to the edge of the road, its pointless ripeness bent toward him from every side. The land was fine, without a rock or ripple to cant it, and when the wind came across the field, the corn turned black like the underside of a wave. It was long past any possible harvest.

Sam drove for a long time before he finally hit the creek. It ran at a diagonal to the road, the banks coarsened from hogs; beyond, CORN/CORN/CORN. He got out and standing on the hood located a roof in the center of the field. It was fawn and brittle as the corn itself, settling like the rusted turret of a gunboat in the shallows. Sam jumped down and ran into the field, darting between the stalks, knocking ears off as he ran. Adrenalin softened the knot in his chest.

The first sign he came across read:

The next:

Your Countries Way-to-Win Project
CAPT. EDGAR FUESS'S INDEPENDENT INTERNATIONAL FAITH
A common road for all, affiliated with none
His religion, to others a practical brotherhood
Each can consider it to suit themselves
Its only support is Free-will help.

Next:

THE NEW WORLD IDEOLOGY HAS SEVEN DON'TS
The most important four are
1. It *don't* rely on passing the buck, and ridicule.
2. It *don't* rely on small men and henchmen tinkering.
3. It *don't* rely on Europ's recent game that uses conceit and weakness in people to get them on the spot to double-cross.
4. It *don't* rely on Extremes; each extreme that gets in power has to become a bigger tyrant controlled by more beasts than the one it got human help to oust.

Sam ran on. He could see the house now, the corn growing within a few feet of its stoop. Adjacent was an open flatbed trailer, its wheelless axles on two-by-fours, proclaiming in hand lettering:

Land Voyage of
Sturdy
One Man, One Boat
Your Countries Way to Win

Inside, her masts foreshortened but otherwise intact, lay *Sturdy IV,* her bleached teak deck encrusted with chicken droppings. A mother hen stared imperiously at him from the fo'c'-

sle. A chart of *Sturdy's* course from Lertz to The Spot in the Red Sea where Satan's Servants had forced abandonment had been painted on the cabin. Above, a *Chart of All Mankind.* Below, a fragmentary prolegomena referred the tourist along the high point of the voyage.

1879—Born
1886—Left School
1889—Minded the store, studied comparative religion
1897—Father runs away to die so do I.
1898—Dawn of new international faith
1900—In Yokohama studies take a more realistic turn
1902—Went into business for self
1904—Changed name
1909—Invented movable office.
1916—Work in munitions factory for duration
1917—Discover Molasses truth
1919—Completed *Sturdy I*—32 ft.
1926—Starts *Sturdy II*—18½ feet
1928—Begins Foundation Voyage
1929—*Sturdy II* lost by fire
1930—Starts *Sturdy III*—13 ft.
1931—Yokohama revisited
1932—Foundation Voyage Compleated
1933—Compleat Over-All Plan Compleated
1934—Moves to Rally Point (~~Evolution, not~~ Revolution)
1935—Starts *Sturdy IV*—9½ ft.
1936—Chart of All Mankind Compleated
1937—Goes into new business in town for self and charity
1938—Launches Land Voyage Campaign as Anti-Satanic Administrator to President of U.S.

Sam left *Sturdy*[4] to inspect the house. His heart was beating more anxiously than he had ever supposed it could. How would he begin with the old man? He wrung sweat from his palms, loosened his necktie. His jacket would not stay straight on his shoulders. Unsightly blotches appeared at his handsome pectorals.

The house was of hand-molded brick with irrelevant ionics supporting the porch, from which the corn in the wind looked like the sea in the sun.

Sam caught his breath, planted his feet and tugged at the door. It appeared to be nailed shut. Suddenly hysterical, Sam yanked with all his strength, and one by one the nails tore free. The hinges spewed rust . . . the door swung open . . . several golden tons of shucked corn toppled forward and enveloped him.

The information had been disseminated.

Abstracted, Sam accompanied his final knowledge back to the car. Behind him, rivulets of corn cascaded from the porch into the cornstalks. From the car the house now appeared as a beached freighter, broken on some soft, uncharted isle, its cargo come home at last, mingling indistinguishably with the sand. County K was clear and he sped north smoothly on Koolgas.

He passed pungent smells and griping crickets, a gnarl of kittens in a ditch, staring cattle, sleepy farmers with resin in the corners of their eyes, cypress-lined drives, the bluish-green vapors of synthetic dung. He swerved to avoid combines and idled behind trucks of bellowing crated hog and turkey. He passed windowless churches and the friendliest college in America. Miles of telegraph clothesline sagged with cumbersome underwear. In the rear-view mirror the tall white houses stood like fangs in a food-emaciated mouth.

Sam pressed the embroidered accelerator until the Cordon Blue's very carpeting sighed. The speedometer circled swiftly and without hesitation to maximum 140, then passed on imperceptibly, shuddering until it closed in again upon zero.

To blame himself for Fuess's demise at this late date could only be self-indulgent, Sam saw. Edgar Fuess came and went like glaciers, leaving different things in different ruts. He made his living speculating and kept the bodies off the streets for charity. In between, he made a Peace Voyage. That's not a bad good life. His only mistake was, he never broke his word, and things, for that, seemed to die around him all the time. And Faragut Twitchell, if prolepse, wasn't daft. For your information, Edgar Fuess *was* dirigibles, riots and expeditions, Jap ashtrays and simplified xylophones. His were the remains of niggers and sailors, bear oil and yellow fever, tribolites and Atlantic cable, underestimated dog and his own patented biscuit.

Whether he was their sum or they were his chaff didn't matter. Whether he found plenitude or the void didn't matter. Whether the Peace Voyage was finished or not yet begun didn't matter.

There was no longer any question of substituting one world for another. Between these two, only the fear had been passed intact—the unique and indigenous fright of the frontier—that one day, in a clearing, you will come across a man whose soul and expertise are exact replicas of your own, that he will recognize his brother, the smile tear over, the knife drop from his side; and you realize you must either eliminate him or cease being yourself. One would rather have to love the world entire than deal with such another.

He was home before dawn and the onset of a fierce storm.

The stereo-lounger vibrated him awake at noon, and on some strange impulse, Sam calls the Purk Club, instructing them to make reservations at their New York branch and leaves straightaway for the railway terminal in time to catch the 5:30 express. He was surprised upon arriving to find the familiar red carpet gone and the Twentieth-Century Limited disbanded, though he was assured by a Balkan-looking conductor it was after all the same roadbed and schedule. The meliorist in him was secretly pleased to find that there were no longer porters available to carry one's luggage, and as he struggled smiling down the platform, he knew finally what he missed about his youth—the only thing, in fact, that he had ever missed—and this was the pleasure of direction. Not a sense of movement for its own sake, or even destination, but simply that if one went east or west, up or down, it somehow mattered. He had given up the escalator approach to life out of a mixture of goodwill and contempt for his struggling contemporaries, only to find that disorientation was the largest cliché of all.

Sam boarded the last of the slumber cars and found his bedroom by himself. He put his Strat-O-Mocs in the shoe locker, pulled the shade, and lay down to nap. Both his bare head and feet were pressed against steel.

He woke with pain as the train pulled out smartly. The carriage seemed to be sprung, he was rolled from side to side 180°. He decided to go to the observation car for a drink, but upon opening the shoe locker he discovered that his Mocs were already gone. He nevertheless padded diffidently down the corridor toward the diner. In one compartment a conductor was asleep with his suspenders down, head buried in hands. The coaches were nearly empty: an occasional priest, a few sailors, a carney Indian in full headdress; mostly railway workers themselves in their striped coveralls, a few foreign tourists in trenchcoats and berets, eyes like hornets against the mudstained windows.

His stockinged feet burned on the steel floor of the vestibules. The train's velocity seemed to increase only laterally. There was, however, no wait for dinner. The daffodil-jacketed waiters, the chef and the purser were playing cards. Sam seated himself at one of the least gravied tables. Eventually a waiter took his order for a double Scotch, but had difficulty coming back up the aisle, banging painfully against the table corners, the purser laughing at his clumsiness. Sam looked down into his drink. The ice cube appeared as a tiny parachute in amber. He could feel the telephone poles whipping by the gauzed periphery of his bad eye. Telegraph wires furled their predictable crescents like the graph of some blue-chip public utility against the trees and blinking crossings. Like Fuess, Sam discovered he hated the very medium that his passage defined, and more, that somehow all those who had once been placed outside the train to be celebrated, observed, were now on board and sullenly touring the space which they had, with so little complaint, once measured. The scenery was simply unfurled, a tiresome dramatic convention, against their equipage's slipstream. The waiter's bad teeth in the window's reflection blotted out forest and factory, field and stream, and this was perfectly just, for looking down into his drink, the ice was now a limp sliver, a body falling away from him in sulphurous eddies, and Sam realized he could never again bear to look outside. Each rail's weld cracked like an axed skull.

The train slowed, he lurched back through the cool white cubes of the vestibules to his own dark compartment, each door opening as if pulling up the shade on a new day. His shoes had still not been returned, and now his luggage had disappeared.

The train was almost at rest. Sam wrapped his feet in Pullman towels and, like some Valley Forge irregular, leapt from the train to the siding between cattlepens, grainchutes and gascapsules.

He was home before midnight by
casually hiring a taxi
reasonably catching a milk train
uncharacteristically hopping a freight
luckily boarding a late bus
illegally hitchhiking
foolishly stealing a truck
programatically renting a car
cunningly chartering a light plane.

No transport can be of vehicular note or particular weight when there're so many ways, uh, to round this world.

The stereo-lounger vibrated him awake near noon.

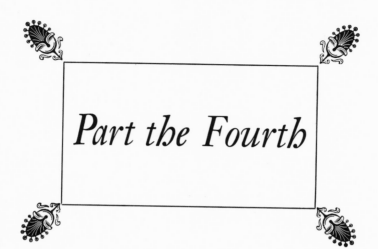

Part the Fourth

27 · Five to Seven, Regrets Only

Everybody was on time. Agapecropolis and his wife who understood each other completely, Wittgenstein and his wife who didn't care all that much, other high functionaries from MC—even Alf and Dorothy Bins themselves, twins in matching plaid tux and culottes—add to this, assorted creative people of the Grassgreens' acquaintance, representatives of our great public media, George Stablefeather who will read a poem commissioned for the occasion, and the guest of honor himself, Aaron, wan in a cape and beret MC had rented for him. Odile had on a new henna peekaboo outfit and a tiara; in one of her ethereal moods Sam noted: her classy stockings bagging at her classic knees. The Dott served the hors d'oeuvres gracefully in a full-length gown and Stargyle managed the bar with aplomb. Sam's recommendations, with Wittgenstein's considerable assistance, had prevailed. The humanistic rebates had gone out to every client, Alf was up for a Nobel, Aaron had got his grant. Product and Process were one.

A dwarfish woman *avec poodle* concatenated her gaze on Sam's stomach. He spoke to her dog politely, and showed them the cigarette box with the dog he had grown up with emblazoned on it.

"I don't really care to make talk about dogs," she said abruptly. "You needn't be polite. I've only come as a favor to Aaron."

Sam blushed and retreated. "God," he thought, "I've got no style left at all. I'm just a dump."

More out of self-therapy than interest, he approached a young man with sideburns braided and tucked behind his ears. A Clone recidivist, it turns out.

"Hi, I'm Sam Hooper. You're one of Aaron's friends, I'll bet."

"You people think you can control everything, don't you?" the boy recited between clenched teeth. "But we got a mammal pride Black Art will never subvert. You may have bought off Aaron but you can't buy all of us. Only need three percent for a revolution, baby. And it's *you* who've brought us to the moral abyss."

Sam frowned, pacing up and down, trying not to look at his adversary, afraid the boy would succumb to his conventional strength, and wanting to try something obvious for a change.

"Listen, young man, when you're living in a filthy flophouse when you're fifty, playing with yourself, and all your friends have cut their throats, we'll still be running things here. And for the same reasons."

The Clone backed away in some terror. "It's what he deserved," Sam reflected, "but I can't keep *that* up the rest of my life."

He went back to the Clone then and took him gently by the arm.

"Lookit man, I'm not trying to put you down or anything. No, that's not it either," Sam thought, "something more formal, with a certain style, but still empathic."

"I'm really most anxious to understand you," he said. "You are clearly a man of intellect with eyes to see. But all of us in this room are protected from destruction by precisely what we want to destroy. And we can't respect ourselves again until we can figure a way out of that. We—"

The Clone said something very obscene to Sam then, but he was not provoked, absorbed as he was in his further plans for the evening.

Aaron's ballet sequence, professionally purchased and mounted by MC's Container Division, had been displayed for the big day throughout Sam's apartment. The ordering, not surprisingly, had been somewhat confused, and a few of the pieces had been hung upside down, but generally Sam had to concede that it was a good showing. The spectators did not seem particularly impressed, however; boggling, shunting, dipping, zooming, they tried fruitlessly to achieve the perspective which Aaron had, at such cost, eliminated. "Now they know what I go through every day," Sam thought. No vantage possible, the crowd retired at one remove, to the bar. Alf Bins was heard to whisper to one of his vice-presidents, "I'm *sorry* Herm, but I just can't get it up hard for them."

"Well, I don't know, Alf," the reply came, "but it sure looks like Black Art to me."

Then they gazed resignedly up at the ingenious miniature replica of the triptych which occasioned MC's lobby, now suspended for the day above Sam's fireplace. The old inscriptions had been replaced, however, with more suitable art aphorisms (18th, 19th, 20th centuries, respectively) from MC's *History of Perception, USA.*

LOVE WHAT YOU CAN'T SEE TWICE
SEE WHAT YOU CAN'T LOVE TWICE
SEE IT TWICE YOU'LL LOVE IT

"Oh, yes," Odile was telling Lorraine Agapecropolis, "Aaron will be going to Rome by himself. He'll be able to work better without the kids, and you know, I've never been able to take Latin men." She laughed defiantly.

"Of course, I understand completely, Adele," Lorraine said as Odile excused herself to greet the host.

"Sam, you'll never guess, wow, what happened." She caressed

his lapel. Her fingers were mustard with nicotine, her teeth glistened.

"Don't take that tone of voice with me," Sam said.

"Oh, but Sam, ever since Aaron knew he was going, well, he's been, well, so active, you know, outta sight!"

"He sure looks like hell."

"That's his asthma, and you know it," she snapped.

"OK," Sam said. "And?"

"And, well, Sam, yes, it was 'yab-yum, yab-yum! Right on! You get me?"

"Does this mean you're a revolutionary now, Odile?"

"Oh Sam, we're *all* revolutionaries now."

"Are you sure it was . . . like *that?*"

"I'm certain of it, Sam. Oh Sam, it was wonderful." She was looking at a point two inches above his head.

"Well, that's great," said Sam. "Then it's not all been for nothing."

"But that doesn't mean we have to stop, does it?" She grinned and shook her head violently to stop the winking. "I mean after all, we both owe you a lot."

Sam gasped and reddened.

"Odile, what are you saying? You know what the deal was. You shouldn't even kid about a thing like that."

"Sam, don't you see, now I can *really* give myself to you. Oh, Sam, you've really got me."

"Get off it, Odile."

"Sam, I couldn't have done it without you." Her lips were pale, her eyes glistening now more than her teeth.

"Wait a minute. Did he use the quad-o-grotus?"

"Of course not!"

"Well, then, it's OK, isn't it?"

She grasped his outstretched congratulatory hand and pulled her fine legs against him.

"Odile, I hardly think this is the time to initiate an affair!"

304

"Samsamsam . . . I don't think I could live without you."

"I'll bet you do."

He turned on his heel and left her there, mouth disfigured, went and locked himself in the bathroom and had a little duet to compose himself. His first objective had been accomplished more easily than he anticipated.

When he came out later, he noticed Wittgenstein and Agape-cropolis across the room, their hemispherical bellies exact replicas, contiguous planets before the bright window, the grope and the gape of MC, grumbling inaudibly:

"Well, Doctor, haven't seen you for a while," Wittgenstein said.

"Yeah. Look, I just happen to have two extra tickets for the—"

"You know better than to try and rope me into *that*."

"Well, our boy Sam enjoyed it, I can tell you. He didn't know quite what to make of it, of course, but he's—"

"You leave that boy alone, Gape. You give him a break, he'll get you accounts you never believed."

"He's a good man. No question about that. He just hasn't suffered enough yet."

"People ain't going to give things up as easy as we did, Gape. That's why he's going to be tough on you."

"His is a perfectly ruthless charm, no doubt about that. He's just still too conscious about what others think of him. He can't handle people yet whom he thinks are less fortunate. He's got to learn to act like a leader, see?"

"For such a shy guy, he sure gets alot of ass."

"Yes, his surveillance folder's as thick as your wrist already."

"Don't know about his folder, Gape, but he's got a wong on him like a nigger's, I can tell you."

"I don't believe we have anything on that. I presumed he was simply highly competitive."

305

Wittgenstein was glaring at the doctor now, and Agapecropolis's throat twitched slightly.

"He's no different than his reports," the doctor stammered, "so opaque, elusive—I wonder sometimes if we can really trust him."

"Shut up," Wittgenstein cut him off. "He's coming over."

"Look at this, Sam," Wittgenstein greeted their host. "There's some lastmen down there throwing things in the lake."

Sam wedged between his two mentors. Sure enough, a group of lastmen in ochre overalls were heaving large objects from a jetty into a widening hole in the ice.

"They look like tools," Sam said.

"Yeah," said Wittgenstein. "There goes a pneumatic drill."

"Do you suppose they're just protesting," said Sam, "or is it a signal for something?"

"Oh Lord," countered Agapecropolis. "They just want to hear the 'plop.' " Then he stalked away.

"You know," Sam said, "I was just thinking. Imagine all the brain power in this room. It's almost disgusting. It's enough to run anything."

Wittgenstein smiled thinly.

"Sam, kid, that's just what you don't know. You may be right that brains aren't used for the right things. And you may be right that there's enough money now to go around for everybody. But there still ain't enough brains to go around. There ain't enough brains to manage any more. We got enough money to tear down this whole place and start over, but we don't have the brains to start over. That's not bein' selfish, it's just a fact. And how you goin' to get around that? Not by bein' a gentleman, I'll tell you, and not by taking just what's offered you."

"You sound like Agapecropolis."

"Nah, we may look alike, but there's one big difference.

306

That's what I been trying to tell you. See, I may be wrong from your point of view, but you know where I stand, and that I'll fight. So you always got the chance of beating me, see? But the doc, he won't fight. He sits and slides, and that's why your kind will never get to him. Now I may be out of style, but I'm the only kind of guy left that can get his kind. And I'll tell you, Samuel, sooner or later, before I'm through, I'll get him. You can bet on that."

Sam tried to ease away, but the broker had lapeled him.

"Before I forget, old buddy, I just wanted to congratulate you on the Peacock deal. I got a call from Palmitz this morning."

Sam feigned curiosity. "Oh?"

"You know damn well," Wittgenstein hissed hoarsely, "there's a frigging sailboat in the middle of Peacock Prairie, that's what!"

"Is that right?" Sam grinned.

"So gloat. Go ahead. It's a brilliant solution. Palmitz went outa his mind. 'A *mystery* boat,' he kept yelling, 'one night a *mystery boat* turns up in your park.' Says it's a miracle. He figures the tourist trade will go up by two hundred percent. Well, old buddy, the housing project's off. You saved it, your lousy grasses. All we got to do now is get a five-minute spot on 'Continuing Images of Greatness' and we're home free."

"It was rather expensive," Sam said quietly. "I'm afraid I had to churn the Denehey account to do it."

"Hey, old buddy, didn't that take guts, didn't it though? How about that? Now that's what really gives me a kick. . . ."

"It doesn't matter," said Sam. "I'm quitting. I'd like you to square things with the Denehey account though. Switch it around somehow. I don't want to leave a bad taste."

"Whoa, waitaminit Sambo, whadaya mean you're quitting, you can't do that *now*!"

"It's not for me, Witty. I've got to get loose and take stock while it's still possible. Oh hell, you know what I mean."

"You mean ta tell me after the job you done, you gonna *quit* on me now—with everything I invested in ya?"

"Witty, believe me, I had my chance. It's just not for me. I've changed or something. It doesn't mean I'm not grateful."

But before Sam could finish, Alf Bins had called for quiet to propose a toast. Aaron was asked to change seats so that the photographers could get him and Odile together. She had just returned from the bathroom with fresh makeup but was still obviously shaken.

"She's so proud of him," Lorraine Agapecropolis whispered to her devoted Chris.

Alfred Bins began to read his statement directly into the videotaper. Behind him, Aaron sat minuscule in the stereo chair, Odile like a staff or sword at his side, Stargyle grinning impeccably behind them.

"This, gentlemen, notches without doubt a benchmark in MC progress, for with this grant to Mr. . . . Grassgreen, we're giving fair warning that MC is going after a new market, that of *total* human fulfillment. To provide through market research better answers to the needs of the research market, in hopes the result will be a more enlightened view of profits by some of our critics, for ventures such as these are the lifeblood of risk-taking enterprise"—nods to Aaron—"and our republic." (Spreads his arms wide.)

Sam tuned out and gently but firmly nudged Stargyle out of the videotaper's range. Agapecropolis had followed them, however.

"Is this the young man you spoke to me about?" he asked ingenuously.

"Uh, yes indeed," Sam said and introduced them helplessly. Stargyle's sullenness solidified as the doctor's jaundiced hand engulfed his.

"I understand Samuel here has managed to get you a job at the Parking Tower."

Stargyle nodded apprehensively.

"Well, we're quite close by, you know, and I'd be delighted if you'd come up and have lunch with me some day."

Stargyle felt behind him with his free hand and grasped Sam's wrist.

"I'm doing this study, you see," Agapecropolis continued, "and I'm sure if you cooperate, there would be something in it for you."

Sam had stepped between them.

"You've had too much to drink, Doctor. Leave him alone."

"Come now, Samuel, maybe we can get this little bugger to let his hair down a little. I'll bet he knows more about what's happening than our illiterate photographer there."

Stargyle relinquished Sam's hand, and snatching free from the doctor, whispered that he had to go to the Parking Tower for his shift. Sam gave him a paternal pat and told the Dott to pack some hors d'oeuvres for him.

"What are you up to, Samuel?" Agapecropolis said, watching Stargyle slip out the door over Sam's shoulder. "I thought we had agreed that you wouldn't have anything further to do with him?"

"I'm not having anything *to do* with him," Sam said quietly, "I'm merely employing him. Anyway, what makes you think you've got a right to see him and I don't? I've got more at stake than you do here."

"You know very well I'm completely disinterested. Any information *I* might get from him would be anonymously quantified. . . ."

"You won't get him to spill the beans, Doc. And anyway, it doesn't matter. I'm quitting, so you've got no way to get to him."

"Quitting? Quitting what? I told you *never* use a synonym with me."

"Quitting, man. Me leave MC. You know, drop out. We're through."

Agapecropolis squinted his fruit-colored eyes.

"Now what could you hope to gain by that?" he mused. "What've you got going for you, a better offer or what?"

"That's all there is to it, honestly, Doc. It's just quits, resignation time."

"You know very well how much you need us—"

"That may be true enough," Sam said softly, "but I just don't *owe* you anything any more."

The doctor's jowls ticked just imperceptibly enough to renew Sam's confidence.

"I finally see *why* it's good to be free," he said firmly. "Now I ought to find out what my strength is good for. Don't you think?"

"You don't work that way, Samuel, and we both know it. You know what you're doing? You think you're better than us because you think we've 'sold out' to MC. Well, let me tell you, there's such a thing as selling out to oneself, and that's what you're doing. You've just sold out to yourself, Sam kid."

Sam heaved a Sunney sigh.

"And don't try and tell me," Agapecropolis continued in a soaring voice, "that those guys throwing their tools away down there right this very minute aren't part of the whole conspiracy!"

"God help you, sir." Sam walked away.

Second objective accomplished.

The Dott had taken over the bar, and they were close to running out of liquor. "Let her go," Sam told her. "Finish it up."

But the time for George Stablefeather's poem had come; the guests managed to seat themselves as the poet subtly dislodged

Aaron from the stereo-lounger. Alfred Bins and other officials gathered respectfully in the foyer to give him the best acoustics possible. Lorraine Agapecropolis and Ruth Wittgenstein were embarrassed to find themselves the only ones talking, but they soon fluttered down upon throw pillows the Dott had thoughtfully provided.

Sam glanced into the bedroom. Wittgenstein was spread-eagled on the bed, hands folded on his Mayan stomach. In spite of everything, he was a lovely man, sweet and tough. Sam realized that Wittgenstein was the only man he really respected. The rest were big American bluffers. And yet he knew he would have to continue to purge himself of those very qualities he most respected in his mentor.

Wittgenstein's gray sideburns burned blue in the coming night. He got up off the bed and stood before the mirror, placing Sam's fedora on his head, posing there, cocking his jowls, concocting new expressions, trying the smallish hat on from every conceivable angle, glancing occasionally at the Purk pennant above the mirror, catching sight of the reddening eyes in his dissolving reflection.

George Stablefeather stood high on the stereo-lounger:

WHO KILLED MOZART?

his skull's in
glass now.

why is not
quite clear

but it's the head
bone we all would

fit to our own
boneless bodies

let us not stoop
to smug or venge

§ *nods deferentially* §
to Aaron

§ *laughs ruefully to* §
himself

311

that head is our
pope's toe.

it hardly matters
whether the vestigial

connection can be   *smiles at MC group*
scientifically enjoined.   *who grin back*
                                       bearishly

no commoner's coffin
for him now.

yet still will
he traffick

with beggars and/   *much applause here*
or suicides. But

will those who set
out with his

body turn back now   *collective coughing*
in the thunderstorms?

the Master none   *nods again to*
theless is being   *Aaron*

poisoned. Not from de   *mild consternation*
bauches or from stay

ing out late but even
his famous canary

now causes him pain.   *oohs and ahs*

the evidence is in
and it points to

his wife.   *Odile smiles*
                                       uncomprehend-
ah Constanze, you   *ingly*
know the symptoms:
                                       bows to
delusions, vertigo   *Odile*
insomnia, gout

312

and the swelling of
hands, feet & trunk.

dropsy, meningitis
nephritis, uremia

& thundering apoplexy.   §§ *Aaron swivels*
                            §§ *uncomfortably* §§

see: Constanze's also
been commissioned by

a "stranger in gray"   §§ *nods to Sam;*
color of mercury   §§ *quizzical glances* §§

the same who comm
issioned this requiem.

is he poisoning
him through her

through their canary

just who is this thin
lipped Salerie

who comes from
court in a cloak

to unburden the   §§ *stares, gestures*
mind of the Master?   §§ *pointedly at Sam* §§

no matter. If he   §§ *brief self-regarding* §§
began the requiem   §§ *applause*

when the Master's   §§ *silenzio* §§
gone, I'll finish it.

It was not immediately clear whether the visual gloss of George's intermediary gestures had enabled Aaron to comprehend the poem's libelous symbology; nevertheless, Aaron had stared with a passionate coldness at Sam throughout the final stanzas, and when the poet's reedy arm had at last scythed past a fidgety Odile to point our protagonist out, the artist permitted himself a moony grin.

Wrapping his rentacape tightly about him, roundtrip Rome airfare in his breast pocket, he gave an uncharacteristic copious bow to the assembled, to Alf Bins he gave the familiar if now passé middle finger, and exeunted with a flourish.

Alfred Bins reassured his circle. "Dream the impossible dream."

(A terrible thought struck Sam at this moment. What if Aaron were really no better than the rest of them, only less powerful, trading on his eccentricities, his work significant only to the extent that it confounded judgment, that he was merely a "reverse negative" of his benefactors? He quickly put it out of mind.)

Wittgenstein shouted something incomprehensible but gleeful from the bedroom door. Tears gutting her mascara, winking like a prizefighter, Odile bolted herself in the bathroom. The Dott held an empty gin bottle nozzle downwards, shrugging the guests away for their wraps. And as soon as the videotaper was off, Sam took George down from the stereo-lounger by his lapels; "What did you have to go and do that for, George?"

"We who speak with tongues must speak the truth," the poet answered with wheezy defiance.

"You didn't have to do that," Sam insisted sadly. "What's it prove?" The poet stared imperiously up at his accoster.

"Are you trying to censor . . . ?"

But Sam had released him loathsomely.

"I'm not sure I get it all, George, but for Christ's sake, I'm not 'poisoning' him. Is that what you really meant? Why exaggerate? And why drag Mozart into it? If you'd just read it straight nobody would have been the wiser. And the least you coulda done was get the references right. You got Salerie and the 'stranger in gray' all mixed up. And for one lousy slant rhyme."

George yanked the ms. from his pocket and began to read it over to himself, counting the syllables carefully.

Sam went after Odile and, finding the bathroom door locked, broke the knob off with the heel of his hand. "If only I was a little older," he thought, "I could take all this better." Odile was sitting in the tub, her legs too long even for its kingsized features, staring fixedly at the ceiling, and breathing without visible success on his fog-pruf mirror.

"Odile . . ." Sam began softly.

"Get the hell outa here," she said wearily, drawing the shower curtain between them.

"It's *my* bathroom," Sam said seriously.

She had started to cry again. He put down the toilet seat carefully and sat facing the scant profile projected on the curtain. All she seemed capable of was softening or sharpening.

"Everything's ruined now," she said, surprisingly calmed. "George's loused up the whole deal."

"Aaron knew before, kiddo, he had to."

"Not him, *you*," she insisted ambiguously, voice cracking. "Aaron's got *his* . . ." but then the tears overtook her again.

Sam waited until the sobs had subsided, then took a new tack, as usual.

"Did Wittgenstein tell you about the Prairie? That it's saved?"

"For all the wrong reasons," she wailed.

"Christalmighty, can't you ever be satisfied with anything? All I promised was I'd save it, and I did!"

"People will come to see the boat, not the grasses. They'll trample them down!"

"They will come," said Sam after some moments, "to see what happens to them there."

Her crying had stopped again; the shower curtain rustled faintly.

"Sam?"

315

"I'm here, kiddo."

"Why don't you quit and let's go away somewhere."

"I have quit, Odile, or more precisely, I've become resigned. Anyway, what do you care? You said that everything was . . . *yab-yum* now!"

Odile accomplished a long theatrical pause with some pathos. Sam wanted very much to join her in the tub, but he clung tight to his reserved seat, stiffening wistfully. Finally she said, "I lied to you, Sam, there wasn't anything like that that happened. I just wanted to give you your out. Seeing I would be alone for a year and everything. I mean you wouldn't have to feel as though you had to do anything. I was just trying to make you feel good and everything. I *do* need you, Sam, but I just don't have it in me to force you."

"Odile, you lovely thing! I know what this is costing you, kiddo, and I appreciate your not putting the pressure on. But I've just got to float now, feint and float, and you don't figure much in that. . . ." Sam could actually feel tears rushing to his head, and his tone of voice was not at all commanding. "It's just too bad we had to take all this so seriously," he stammered, "but I guess it's dead serious. *Isn't* it?"

Her silhouette was blurred with self-hatred, but her voice as calm as all bahamas.

"It really doesn't matter any more."

"I should tell you," Sam said, "that's the only thing I wanted too. I mean, I wanted to get you freed up. In fact, I still do. Odile," he blurted, sooner than he had planned it, "I want to take the kids!"

The curtain shot back. Odile glared at him. Her softness had gone forever.

"Sure! You and the Dott, I suppose."

"Me and the Dott exactly. We've talked it over between ourselves for some time now."

"I just can't believe this." She drew her knees to her chest like a child.

"Then come on."

He helped her from the slippery tub, and gently from the bathroom.

The guests had been dispersed. Sam walked on the cigarettes ground into his carpet as he had once walked on the cookies ground into Odile's. The Dott was busy collecting the glasses. Her heart-shaped buttocks grimaced as she worked. Sam led Odile to the pantry and opened the polished birch doors of the storage cabinets.

"See?" he said. A vast array of canned goods confronted them.

CHEX	rich	great	huge	sweet	quik	STIX
plum	STAX	tart	catsup	heart	PUFFS	honey
grape	topping	JETS	*dreamy*	CRISPI	jelly	pickle
cherry	pudding	*joy*	CRAX	*wonder*	squirt	pretzel
lemon	filling	FLAKES	*supreme*	SHAKES	fudge	noodle
banana	CLUSTER	toffee	custard	sauce	POPS	waffle
DUDS	fluffy	crunchy	strained	creamy	frosty	CHIPS

Third objective accomplished.

"I just can't believe it, Sam." Odile was stricken.

"Lookit, kiddo," Sam said, grabbing a can from Captain Crunch's Library of Good Eating. "You think I'd eat this crap? Yet examine the spectrum of cookies! Every kind there is. Isn't that their favorite brand? Come on now, tell the truth."

"Why, Sam, do you suppose . . . ?"

"So you could go away and start over. And save the kids too. The Dott is great with kids. I've even got the beds ordered. A double-decker. We're going to set it up right in front of the big window and they'll have advantages they never did before."

317

"I just can't believe you're doing this," she whimpered redundantly.

"It'll work, Odile. And with the pressure off, you might make it. The kids like me, don't they? And God knows, they need a father."

As Odile stretched once more to look with disbelief at the larder, Sam noticed that her legs had begun to go. The tub's damp stain on her seat revealed the diamond pattern of her girdle, a new pair of oblate buttocks were beginning to emerge below the originals. A pale network of veins crept down the backs of her thighs, ending in varicose nebulae at the crease of her knees. She had not, truly, much time left to make it.

"Consider the grant an opportunity for yourself as well," Sam said. "Actually it was so conceived."

"You don't want me to move in too?"

"Impossible. The committee has met and rejected your application. You love us for all the wrong reasons. You tried to free yourself through Aaron once, now you're counting on me. . . ."

"You're a bastard, Sam."

"I've kept all my promises, Brighteye; it's a good deal."

But she had flounced out without a word, at least no longer crying.

"I'm quitting," he yelled after her. "I'll have time." But the elevator had sung itself away.

"I've shied away from being cruel too long," Sam ruminated. "Now maybe just being pissed off will see her through."

Sam walked to the window. In its golden reflection he could see the Dott glaring at him, wringing her swollen hands. But before she could speak, he said without turning around, "I know it's late. You better get going. I'll finish cleaning up."

She was gone within the minute, not bothering to change her uniform, frightening a chance couple in the elevator with her

318

moans. They helped her to the front door and even Dean tipped his cap, waiving for once the service exit rule.

Sam extinguished the lights and gazed out across the paralyzed lake. The ice was so hard they were driving trucks out to the Pumping Station. Their headlights blazed over the ice like lasers.

In March or April, Sam knew, the Coast Guard would break a path to the station. It would freeze over nightly but in the morning there would still be a few loons or such bobbing in what airholes remained. Then, one warm wind would unfreeze her like a puzzle, breaking for some arcane reason into octagonals first, the runcinate ribbons of snow which remained giving the distinct impression of frozen waves. Next, the beach's white lip might split into less perfect tetrahedrals, and these most curious lumps would jag finally to just slush, a stolid viscous mantle, breaking from gray to green at the crest of the new rollers a mile or so out.

and *the breakers will smash the last edge of real ice up in one*
crazy day;
the yachts shall swing on their indelicate moorings;
the waterlevel shall drop for a startling instant;
the Smelt will be runnin', and the great Coho a creepin in
the atmosphere shall buckle;
those same yachts busting a few anchor ropes in the ensuing seiche;
the water shall boil at the harbor's grim mouth;
and a model yard high-wide tidal wave shall catch a couple of lastmen's
children in the shallows, turning them up silvery, oh months later
in the chic filters of the Pumping Station:
and at MC, spring shall be seconded.

It was three months since he had met the Grassgreens.

28 · *Human Interest*

Aaron, then, in a huff, a heady *isolatto* pursued by a distraught Odile, except that she is not following him, only going to the same destination, and at roughly the same interval, here comes the Dott, her mind's musts clearly somewhere else, and hardly headed home.

Whatever do they think about? Will Aaron's ugly new knowledge prevent him from taking a well-deserved Roman holiday? Or will a misguided sense of latent manliness serve him to set his career aims aside? Will Sam's common sense overture be misinterpreted by Odile as a *personal* rejection? Or will she use the opportunity to give her children that stiff ingredient their lives have lacked, not to mention a chance for some jollies herself? As for the Dott, will she be the good mother that is so divinely to be wished? Can she conquer her cultural context sufficiently to meet the high standards her understanding boss has imposed?

But let's assume, for purposes of omniscience, that you are in fact that enigmatic lady of the locked thighs who tops out the Management Concern building. What's coming up? Squint now. For across that longitude of Aaron, Odile and the Dott lies another axis: Stargyle, Wittgenstein and X, the latter the figure of Agapecropolis who Stargyle *thinks* is following him, but for the rest of the show, is, you know, rather a counter to the third person Dott, who does not exist in Aaron's mind, even though she is actually proximate. For Agapecropolis is now in a cab with his wife, 'cause they live in the suburbs, and Wittgenstein is not following Stargyle, but only heading, like Odile, for the same destination. In this case, to pick up his large car. A pretty cinematic conspiracy, eh?

So, on your cue, Wittgenstein drops his stub at the collection window of the Parking Tower, it rises pneumatically through a clear tube to the topmost ramp where a sullen Stargyle, finishing off a magnum of champagne, chestnut and bacon hors d'oeuvres patronizing the crown of his mouth, licks caviar and chutney from his fingers, and fumbles with the tube hatch for the slip. His sight is wavering from the threats of Agapecropolis (X), a microphoto of the doctor's gleaming head is stuck in his now definitive mind. Wittgenstein is justifiably impatient, his enormous shoes tap the concrete. . . .

Odile, we must recall, is handicapped for this adventure, her ambivalent high-heeled gait no match for the purposeful strides of Aaron or the Dott. The latter, then, gains on the former couple equally, and finally by "instinct" taking the hypotenuse of Peacock Prairie, cuts the total distance to the apartment roughly in half, passing them both up.

Furthermore, Aaron has stopped, taken by a cloud formation, or to be more precise, the clots of space between the clouds (you can see him there, the one in the cape with the upturned face) and Odile has begun to stagger slightly in her toeless pumps, practicing the toneless rhetoric she will see Aaron off with. The Dott, our mighty caricature, has apparently forgotten her primary mission altogether. She is ascending the stairs of the apartment and Stieglitz, forgetful little bugger, has left the door unlatched. . . .

Stargyle has nearly finished the canapés. He takes the sticky ticket, puts it behind his ear and wanders the floor to match numbers. When he finds the car, he turns on the radio and relaxes in the glove leather, stitched and folded like the contours of the brain, running the electronic aerial up and down to improve reception. But his soul, like an organ, like a mote, is fixed on Agapecropolis (X). Wittgenstein drums his attaché case against a supporting column. Ruth Wittgenstein slumps in the heated reception room, grinding her teeth, enveloped in a chinchilla as big as all outdoors. Her feet appear at its hem like the Mikado's fingernails. She is dreaming of retirement in Mexico. . . .

The Dott opens the door cautiously. The apartment is dark and empty. She goes quickly to the alcove where she unwinds her brief turban and carefully folds her complicated uniform on Odile's best coffee table. She lies down on the cool mattress, staring upward at the ceiling, bubbled with age. Lighting up one of Sam's fine joints purloined from the medicine cabinet, she can feel herself rising. . . .

The clouds are breaking up over Aaron. You can see he has systematically drained himself of all emotion. At the party, Agapecropolis had sought him out and whispered, "Most great men have failed fathers, but then again, most failed men have failed fathers too." He remembers the pensioner's hotel where his father died, his bed surrounded by half-filled Dr. Pepper bottles, light glancing in through the airshaft like a blade. From every side toilets flush periodically, but there is no toilet in his father's room. Most of all, he purges remembrance of Stieglitz or Matthew; he is aware of their fine color, but they quickly merge into the chalky cloud pallor of his father's loathsome body. . . .

Odile has picked up her step. Passersby begin to notice her again. Her ribs hurt her for some reason. Once Aaron is packed and off, she thinks, she will decide about the children. She will reflect *not one iota* of resentment. . . .

Stargyle's body hurts him too. In the chest. He has finished the champagne but cannot wash the fishy taste from his mouth. He studies the complex automatic gearshift for a time, he cannot decided on either drive^1 or drive^2. He makes his selection and the long car leaps out on the runway and plunges down the ramp. Agapecropolis would say he's an autoist. Stargyle presses the horn, accelerator and radio to their maximum. A Communist cello recital rages through the static. His tongue rolls back in his throat from centrifugal force. . . .

Odile finds the apartment door ajar and goes to the rear bedroom calling for her husband and subsequently the childern. She has been getting some pretty weird phonecalls lately and she is nervous. Aaron has left the gas on again and the percolator has burned up. Its bowl is warped, bruised black. Odile feels better as she turns off the gas; she lets her hair down as she sets off to make the beds. . . .

Stargyle, *in machina,* feels for his safety harness. The car lists ominously to the outside of the ramp, horn full blast, leaving flecks of chrome and tomato-red enamel on the wall, he sees only X's as he spirals down. . . .

The Dott feels sleep starting in her ankles, brightness ascends her thighs, the air bubbles on the ceiling exhale. . . .

Wittgenstein stamps toughly to the mouth of the exit ramp and peers upwards at the sounds of the careening destruction. He catches sight of his car's hood ornament in the glistering convex mirrors, and then once again, before he is impaled upon it. The radiator bursts like a camellia, the headlights meet around a supporting column, the drained engine is delivered into Stargyle's lap.

Odile stands for some moments before the bed, mouthing a scream, but her volume is turned off. Ruth Wittgenstein is better at it; with her, it's more spontaneous and hateful.

Odile has not moved by the time her husband enters so magnanimously. The room is redolent of burnt coffee and aluminum. When she does not reply to his chastened invitation to a farewell dinner, he runs up from behind and wraps his arms about her. Over her cold shoulder, through her diaphanous hair, he spies the naked figure on their bed. The fine, flat pectorals of another race, the nostrils flared wide, the corded calves and biceps, and the massive erect organ, black in this case, not pink like the palms and soles as Odile thought they were.

Aaron slowly removes his hands from her shoulders and makes stealthily for the darkroom where his trusty under and over nature camera is always propped in a corner. There are many words ramming up against the rods and cones of Odile's eyes. "Come on, finish it," she thinks, the words are upside down and backwards on her retinas. "Getit overwith!"

Aaron has moved back in behind her steadying his aim with an elbow on the armchair, blitzing the scene with microflashes, telephone receiver tucked effortlessly in a fold of his neck. "Here is an emergency, operator. . . ."

The Dott is posing, Odile is paralyzed, Aaron transfixed, D.O.A. Yet the scene is still blurred—in the eye of you, beholder. Look, can't you just relax? The Dott is not the lengthening shadow of history, Odile no omen, Aaron hardly representative. The pulsations which inform this little stasis are, to your ever-lasting credit, being projected from a point roughly three to fifteen inches from this page. For the Dott, Odile's buttonnose rests a proverbial bullseye atop his dark sight, for Aaron she is the sight for Dott's eye, while Aaron, comptroller of light, is for them merely out of focus. But for you they are, in the end . . . ellipses, that what, nothing more or less than three thumps of the thumb, desperate punctuation of your censored silence. Remember where you are, please. Aaron has put through his second call and Odile is thinking for us all, Come on. Finish it. Come on, finish it. Comeon, she moans, "finish it. Comeon, finishit comenfinishit. . . ."

This is as close as they're going to get. Not because police are already crashing up the stairwell, stumbling on the galoshes, scarifying the dog, detached plainclothes covering the rear with a fifty-caliber watercooled machine gun, but because Odile's pain-ful repetition has made the words near nonsense. Every exquisite murmuring repeated sufficiently ends as a low moan, though any moan has enough mummery in it to get you back the word, the world. Try it with your own won name in bed some night.

29 · Litigation

"That was sure some party, Sam. I'm sorry I lost my head like that. Lorraine gave me hell for it when we got home. She was right, I guess, I deserved it. She's been a wonderful wife to me."

Sam shifted the telephone to his stronger hand, his skin was the color of dust, his teeth mousy. Agapecropolis's early-morning voice confused him.

"What's wrong, Chris?" he finally managed. "*You* never called *me* before."

"Just to warn you, old boy, there's quite a mess down here. You really should have come in. This of all mornings."

"What's up, Doc? I thought I told you I was through."

"Well, for one thing," the doctor said most coolly, "Wittgenstein is dead and for another, that maid of yours tried to put it to our Mrs. Grassgreen. He's in the jug now."

Sam lay back. He was somewhat shocked at himself for being incapable of surprise. He knew then that he had reached his rally point, that he would live out his life alone, keeping the bodies off the street for charity.

"I don't believe the Dott would attack Odile," he said finally. "I know her too well. Are you sure Odile didn't egg her on?"

"You won't think me flip, I hope, but it seems she's a he."

"This is not time for those Clone jokes, Doctor. Good Lord, I thought you beyond that."

"My boy, of this I can assure you. I have just been to the prison hospital, and have noted the fellow's considerable equipment with my own eyes. I have also visited several policemen in the outpatient ward, for whose questionable health your 'clean-

326

ing lady' is responsible. In the end they beat him very badly, but on the whole, he has nothing to be ashamed of. More, he insisted to me that he was the 'fall guy,' that he was innocent, that he was just trying to prove a point."

Sam thought for a moment, *Well sure, it was possible.* "But listen, Doc, I'm positive the Dott wouldn't go after Odile. Maybe he was after Aaron, did you consider that angle? He probably just didn't know how to go about it."

There was a crisp pause, then the doctor resumed at his calmest and most professional.

"Could you substantiate that?"

"Well, there's a lot of circumstantial stuff, I suppose."

"That would redefine the charge, certainly. If one could show that Aaron has had, well, bisexual experience, and have the Dott testify that he went there for that purpose. . . . my God, the worst he could get . . . hell, we might even get them on false arrest. At the worst, trespass." Agapecropolis was clearly excited by this new turn of events. "But how do you feel about turning somebody like that out on the streets again?"

"I don't have feelings either way about that," said Sam. "But he deserves as good a lie in his defense as the one they're prosecuting him with. We need another story, Doctor—he probably doesn't know himself what his motives were."

"OK, OK. We'll put our money on the queer rap. But we've got to show that Aaron's past is susceptible to that sort of interpretation."

"Can't do that," said Sam. "Nope."

"Elaborate, Samuel."

"MC can't be seen as giving a grant to a pederast. To choose art for *your* offices? You've got to be kidding."

"You're right, you know, Sammy-boy. A moral dilemma, then. What's more important—Aaron's art or the Dott's life? You can't weigh them on the same scale."

"You're learning fast, Doctor. Shall we anyway?"

327

"Shoot."

"It's true," said Sam, "that both lives are now tied up inextricably with Management Concern, so it's not just a simple matter of embarrassing MC, because everybody would lose. Only a restructuring of the entire setup can solve that, and the grievances concerned can't wait."

"Could you give me some feedback on that?"

"Surely. In such an insoluable situation, then, it would be well if we both resigned, bringing the full weight of moral pressure to bear—"

"Speak for yourself," said Agapecropolis.

"Well, I've already resigned, and if I got involved with this now, it would just look like you fired me for moral turpitude, that I was just being vengeful, and then the symbolic value of my resistance would be lost."

"You're correct in that assumption."

"And I've got nothing on you, so there's nothing to bargain for."

"You could argue," the doctor said methodically, "that the Dott would be paroled eventually or that Aaron could do without the grant. As a matter of fact, you could make an interesting test case out of either of them."

"Begging the question, Doctor. As you've set it up, one or the other's going to lose."

"Simply delimiting the options, old friend."

"Can't get the Dott off," Sam summed up, "without implicating Aaron, and if you do that, you'll involve yourselves and compromise your effectiveness. Plus, Aaron gets screwed, not to mention his family."

"Ah, his handsome wife and unfortunate children. Yes, I'd forgotten in the excitement," said Agapecropolis. "Sam? Aaron's turned out to be the focal point of all this, hasn't he?"

"Yes, he certainly has gotten us into a bind."

Sam waited in the silence, reflecting on his own intolerable breath.

"Well, offhand," Agapecropolis began judiciously, "I'd say cut losses, Sam. Marry Odile, adopt the kids, implicate Aaron, get the Dott released, employ him fulltime, I mean the Dott, in whatever capacity seems mutually profitable, move up to Wittgenstein's job, pay Aaron out of your salary increase an amount equal to the grant on the sly plus court costs, inasmuch as the defamation won't affect *his* career, force Stablefeather to renege on his unconscionable poem, give a memorial for Wittgenstein, and have lunch with me every day."

"That would hardly be a dignified way out of it, Doctor. I mean lunch every day?"

"Small potatoes, Sam, for what you'd be getting."

(. . . sure, lifting him out of his armchair by the lapels, forcing him to the windowledge, the blank frosted glass is shattered as if by the scream itself, and as the V of fingers is unplugged from the eyeballs, the body rotates dreamily into the tiny traffic, and lord, listen to the horns. . . .)

"Now listen, Christopher, and get this straight. I don't know what the real story is with the Dott . . . we were close, but there's just some people about whom you can't say anything that will throw them into relief . . . don't you see, there was no way for the Dott to love me and be a man. . . ."

The doctor, for once, had no reply.

"I just wanted to see if I could pull on the doctor what he's been pulling on me, you just couldn't resist the irony, could you? You've been playing the game so long you'd bite at even the most absurd contradiction—even if it trivialized everything. Well, what I say may sound ironic, Doc, but *I'm* not."

"You mean that's what you believed all along? That you were just too smart-alecky to say it?"

"I used to believe," Sam murmured, almost as a litany, "not

in MC so much, but in their discipline; a discipline that could manage life so others, like Aaron, say, might be free enough to change it . . . but now it seems they've just reversed their proper roles . . . that's why one thinks the other is Black Art. Well, as of yesterday, Doctor, I've stopped substituting one world for another, and maybe it's not for me to say, but I think I'm for breaking up both . . ."

"Watch it now, I've got this on tape, Sammy-boy."

"Don't lose it."

"You're talking yourself out of that promotion. . . ."

"Oh shit, let's forget it, Chris. Who got Wittgenstein anyway?"

"How'd you know he was killed, just didn't die?"

"Characters like Wittgenstein don't just topple over—"

"Stargyle then, with a car. Smashed his ass. I won't have any trouble getting the info now, boy, not where he is."

Sam allowed another silence to develop, then:

"You know, Doc, I don't think he was after Witty . . . you know, I'll bet he was after you!"

"OK son, you've maybe caught me up once, but not twice. Let's not start that business over again. . . ."

But the doc spake only to the click and silence it had taken his patient a brief lifetime to master.

30 · Recognition

Sam remained in the great bed until he heard the thump of the evening paper against his door. The notice was on the Society Page under a grainy photo of Odile and Ruth Wittgenstein conversing over drinks.

> **HUMAN FULFILLMENT GALA HAPPY EVENT**
> **EXCEPT FOR TWO WOMEN**
>
> The affair celebrating Management Concern's first grant for human fulfillment was successful by all counts save two. These were the unpleasant and unexpected conclusions of the evening for two of its most lovely participants, Mrs. Odile Odets Grass-green, daughter of the Litchfield Odets and wife of the noted photographer (recipient of this year's grant), and Mrs. Ruth Wittgenstein, a member of the Board of Directors of the Mental Health Institute. They were in happy spirits and obviously enjoying themselves, but it was another story when Mr. Wittgenstein, a partner of Management Concern, later stepped before a car. He is survived by his wife as well as a brother, Ralph, of Kenosha.
>
> Mrs. Alfred Bins, known to her friends as Bunnie, wore her hair in her favorite upswept style and both she and her husband were widely complimented on their tans. A Mr. George Steral-fedders read a poem. Mr. and Mrs. Grassgreen, despite rumors of a separation, mixed freely at the affair, but were surprised by a masked intruder upon return to their home. Police, however, apprehended the suspect before he could make off with anything of value. He has yet to be identified.
>
> The party was given in the fashionable lakeside apartment of Mr. Samuel Hooper, also of Management Concern. As an added fillip, Management Concern announced late last evening that young Mr. Hooper would be taking over Mr. Wittgenstein's duties.

Sam scanned back through the paper and caught the item near the comics.

331

The Commissioner of Police reported today that a small sailboat had been mysteriously abandoned in the Peacock Prairie area.

A records check revealed that the boat had never been registered, and a special panel of experts have speculated after chemical analysis that it had probably never been in the water.

While further investigation has produced no clues, the Commissioner has been quoted as saying: "There is no doubt in the Department's mind that this wanton disregard of private property is directly related to the Arte Fair riots and the Loy homicide."

A spokesman for Project Uplift, owner of the tract, announced that the boat would be left in the park for an unspecified time, in the event that the perpetrators return to the scene.

Large crowds were seen converging on the area early this morning.

In the financial section, beneath the headline HIGH-FLYERS TAKE IT ON THE CHIN, exactly in the middle of the Over-the-Counter Market, Sam found his mentor's official memorial:

IT IS WITH SORROW THAT
WE HERE RECORD THE DEATH
OF OUR DEAR FRIEND
AND ESTEEMED PARTNER

Wittgenstein

Management Concern

Interment private.
In lieu of flowers,
contributions
to Purk would
be appreciated.

At the bottom of the exchange, in its familiar classified spot;

Are you fed up with fighting Satan's One percent? Sick to death of the cross-currents between
the Secret Fixers and the Go-Alongs? So is Captain Fuess. A few places on the *Land Voyage of
Sturdy* still open. How you can help, write today.

And finally, the lead piece in *The Family, Leisure, Arts and
Entertainment*:

THE TOP TEN BEST CATCHES
A NEW ADDITION

Calling all girls: Looking for a man with a velvet disposition and
a countenance guaranteed to weaken the knees? A man of recognized taste, the promise of considerable financial security, as
well as that certain aura of *Je ne sais quoi?* Then form a line down
at Management Concern tomorrow, for that's when Samuel
Hooper assumes his partnership, the youngest ever to achieve such
prominence.

Of course, Sam's rise comes as no surprise. Though he had a
reputation as something of a "young hellion," he prepped at
Purk, graduating with highest honors in Economics and Epis-
temology and a letter in Greco-Roman wrestling. He's also a whiz
on the Mayans and post-Tang porcelains, but he doesn't hit you
over the head with his erudition. Well, maybe a little. He's probably the only bachelor in the city with a computer in his bedroom.

While not exactly a shrinking violet, Sam sports an independent
nature and not much is known about his socializing. Since his
return to the city after his parents' unsolved double murder, he
has cultivated a small circle of friends who are most willing to
honor his passion for privacy. Yet, for all his sophistication and
international travel, Sam seems to be that rare homebody, the
kind of man with whom marriage would be more than just sharing
a bathroom. Given the fascination and demands of his job, his
main hobby is "keeping in shape," though he's also hip to the
policological scene.

Altogether chummy and possessing a whippy sense of humor
while on display, Sam is still something of a mystery man, and
will require a self-sustaining woman who can play both hostess
and confidante, a high-speed honey with an intellectual streak.

If he can be found anywhere, it's at the International Club
before the ballet, where he is fond of taking nonbusiness ac-
quaintances. He's the one in the shaped but sincere clothes,
curly hair, and no jewelry but a chronometer.

So if you don't sleep in hair curlers or wear furry slippers, you
may be the girl.

Beneath was a photo of him striding purposively down the aisle at the Opera House, taken apparently from the front rows. It was a clear warning: Agapecropolis had released the unclassified portion of his dossier, and Aaron was somehow in cahoots.

Sam dialed Odile at once, and she answered the phone matter-of-factly.

"Odile, I've got to know. Do I get the kids or not?"

"You're lacking a housekeeper, I believe," she said all-too-brightly.

"Doesn't matter. I've quit! I'll be home alot."

"Might I have them back when the grant expires?"

"We'll just have to wait and see. But I tell you frankly, it's a matter of the utmost importance that I know immediately. You and Aaron go your separate ways. I'll hold the fort."

"Sam," she interrupted him, "did you see Hooper's early morning show?"

"No, why?"

"He gave a review of Aaron's ballet retrospective."

"How was it?" Sam asked dully.

"Well, Aaron claims *he* didn't understand it, but *I* thought it was basically favorable. The only problem was, Hooper said, 'Where can Aaron go from here?' Sam, that isn't the point. He must have been at the party!"

"That's impossible."

"But, *Sam*, he had to—"

"For chrissake, Odile, *I* would have recognized him, don't you think? I only watch him every night. I know damn well he wasn't there."

"Well, maybe they'll do a rerun tonight."

"Look, Odile, will you please just give me an answer about the kids? You don't realize how much depends on it."

"All right, wiseguy, just to force your hand, I think we'll take

334

this little item up, right now. Sure, what the hell, let's clear the air."

She slammed the phone down, he could hear her rancorous voice in the background, but he could not make out whether the ensuing shouts were in his favor or not. When Odile finally returned, however, her voice was unsteady. He heard another shout and then the door slam in the background.

"Sam?"

"What's the problem?"

"I shouldn't upset you. I don't even know what he means."

"Aaron?"

"He said," she began to cry, "he said he was going to *fix* you! Fix you good, once and for all." Sam was silent. "Oh, Sam," she wailed, "be careful. Don't hurt him."

"You think he means it? Should I protect myself?"

"I don't know, Sam, he seems capable of anything now. Oh, I've really messed things up. I should never have brought it up!"

"Well, it sounds like he's serious. I'd better do *some*thing."

"I know you won't let him kill you, Sam," she shrieked.

"Don't make too much of this, Odile; I'll be in touch."

He cut her off, yanking the phone from the wall. He went immediately to the closet and fetched Stargyle's gun, but there was no ammo. Then he went to the buffet where Mother's knife lay in its velvet case. Unsheathing this, he stalked the apartment, calculating the logistics of defense. He tried to lift the stereo-lounger for a blockade, but found it would swivel against any obdurate pressure.

But then as his initial panic subsided, he began to assess the options that even Agapecropolis had not envisioned. He knew then what Fuess must have felt as the corn lapped closer to his house; a wave inedible, unsalvageable, unmarketable. Work and

335

Grammer! "All that is necessary is to *remember* that other man, *remember* him always, and that will be enough for you. . . ."

Sam's omnicompetence, all his brave protestations to Agape-cropolis dissolved. The doctor was right; he needed them. His life had been wasted in mastering all other styles in order to compete with them on their own terms, and in truth he was nothing without their resistance. He realized that as he had so cunningly increased his freedom to choose, the possible choices had decreased, almost, it seemed, in inverse proportion, until only two alternatives remained—one of which, victory, was already banal. He felt himself slipping back into the very comforting irony he so detested; that in order to go out a winner, keep his record intact, it was necessary to cast off all power, abandon every prerogative, resist probability to the utmost. Sam was getting monotonous, he would have to go. He went out on the balcony to think and get some air.

But the wind was from the south and hideously filthy. Large toxic glistering snowflakes embalmed with soot plummeted by. A large one landed on the left lens of his glasses, and the cityscape pooled into a concatenation of iridescent rainbow.

He did not feel the cold nor did he shiver. The knife slipped from his hand and disappeared into the thickening night.

31 · Last of the New

Odile's rib cage still ached. She wondered if she were pregnant again. She went to the bookshelves and took down the second volume of Leibniz, where she kept her fertility chart. She found, however, that she had disguised her peaks and troughs with such an elaborate coding system, against the day when Aaron might find it, that it was impossible to determine where she was. She could only remember that she kept Sam in blue and Aaron in pink, should it ever be necessary to determine parentage. It struck her that she should have kept such a chart from the very moment she had become a woman—a disconcerting halftime of a field hockey contest. With its many-colored braid of standard deviations, a seismographic mural of her poor old life, she would be spooled in it when she died. She imagined that the graphs of these truly great women could be purchased with public funds, their bodies cremated, their ashes scattered from helicopters, their murals unfurled from telephone pole to telephone pole, city to city.

She put two TV dinners in the oven for the children, set the Magic Eye to broil and hold; clipped on the last complete earrings of the late Mina Loy, and set out with vague thoughts of heading off Aaron.

Aaron at the moment, however, was engrossed in conversation with a delightful ravenhaired reservations clerk in a foreign airlines office. He paid in cash, taking care not to dislodge the heavy metallic lump on the inside of his new houndstooth sportcoat. The girl later complained that the "little lecher" had tried to proposition her.

We know that he took his time from this point on; Leonardo remembered him taking an early gargantuan supper at the International Club, paying with a hundred-dollar traveler's check; a cabbie recalled taking a rather furtive ("hairy" was the way he put it) individual to the Esplanade Apartments after midnight.

Odile waited in the blizzard for the express bus. *Sturdy* rode the storm well at Peacock Prairie, its foreshortened masts already tinseled with the excrement of gulls, ice-encrusted panic grass billowing at her prow.

The bus loomed greenish-white like a turbot out of the storm, disgorging her twenty minutes later in a rivulet of slush at the corner of the Esplanade. It had sleeted over and now seemed only an extension of the frozen moonless lake. The wind tore travel posters from the bulletin boards and whipped the snow into gray latticework on the thermopane walls. Large drops of condensation formed in the air pockets between the glass.

Dean the doorman recognized a forlorn Odile and moved to assist her, but at the last moment, only ten yards away, she seemed to break stride, and pirouetting against the wind, moved diagonally across the esplanade toward the estuary. The pain in her ribs made her face nothing but a knot. Dean would recall to his grandchildren how remarkable it was that she did not slip or falter on the icy overpass. The traffic shuffled peremptorily below her. Dean called out to her, but stopped when he realized he had forgotten her name.

The lake was jammed solid against the breakwater, iron pilings sheathed with ice. The traffic and the wind were one as Odile traversed the estuary. Slag heaps of frozen foam formed vast suspended waves on either side of her. Gulls limped meekly out of her path; she picked one half-frozen staggering bird up; it did not resist her; but it felt precisely like a fish and she dropped it. It skittered along the ice like a mullet on a chute, wings finally dragging it to a halt just at the edge of the abyss. It hung by a single wing as if nailed there. Odile suddenly remembered something she had seen at four or five, a jay dashing its beak against its reflection in the hubcap of her father's Packard. When people asked her mother what kind of car they had, she always said she didn't know, but it was the finest one made.

She had reached the end of the estuary. Her eyelashes stuck to her cheeks when she blinked. Her quiet body stirred expectantly. She whipped her head back and forth to stop the winking and put down her handbag. Then, balancing for an instant on the edge, tears streaming down her smiling face, but nonetheless holding a dignified pose, she leapt.

But the ice did not give, she went to her knees. She was so cold already that the sight of blood brought her no pain. The two star-shaped gashes above her knee sox quickly coagulated in the wind, and she raised herself up. She could not see the top of the estuary in the dark, but she calculated she could not have fallen more than a few feet. She turned herself three times around and walked north, looking for water.

The snow grew whiter and purer as she walked. Her knees were warm; once when she throught she heard a joyful crackling and looked down expecting to see the ice dividing beneath her, she saw only her own footprints; effluvial wounds on the perfect ice. She had suspected she would grow tired, though she did not wish to go to sleep like Arctic explorers. She desired no trace save the handbag. Dean would sing her disappearance as he had announced her arrivals. "It was the war that kept *our* marriage together," her father had told her when she had first gone home with Stieglitz.

She was excited by the cold and her pace quickened. Occasionally she glanced over her shoulder—something her mother had told her never to do. A cloak of soot clung close to the shoreline—above it she could see the myriad lights of towers. The snow began white against the stars and planets, becoming invisible as it joined the city's vapors. The windows of the towers were filled with couples. Had Dean sounded an alarum? She counted the luminescent stories, thirty-two up, thirty-one over, but there was no light from Sam's balcony. She suspected Aaron of bluffing; Sam would not run out. But there were more couples at their windows than the odds would allow at any one moment, and she began to run.

Her ears were filled with her heart, her mouth with mucous. She felt the ice throb mechanically beneath her, a blessed heaviness in her legs. Suddenly, the wind died out and Odile was aware of being shielded. A pulsating drone circumferenced her. She had the sensation of watching herself from a calm vesicle of her own heart. "When that fellow pushed in front of me to get a cab," her mother had once confided to her, "I knew I was out of the market."

The reverberations increased in intensity; then all of her senses were annealed. Before her loomed the black hulk of the Pumping Station.

As she approached it through the whorling snow, the drone ceased imitating her heart and became a thin insistent syncopation. She put her hand to the metal—at once frozen and greasy—and left a patch of skin upon it as she pulled away in horror. (Her brother had once gotten his tongue stuck to a frozen street light.) Gradually, curiously, she wandered the utility's circumference, fighting to stay upright on the windward side. At any minute she expected to be sucked momentously into the filters, but the ice abutted every juncture of the station.

At the end of her circuit she found a ladder. She took it expertly, two rungs at a time, hauling herself up onto the flanged catwalk near the top. Through the frosted portholes, she could see the control room, fully automatic, unmanned, bathed in the half-light of computers, dials and circuitry. The catwalk gave off

340

to a trapdoor which admitted her to the interior. Here a crescent balcony led across a great domed space to the control room. The oval skylight was clotted with snow. Below her were situated two massive hemispherical pumps and filtering pools, the waters seething gray-white beneath the floodlights. She was impressed with how clean everything was.

There was no place to sit in the control room; Odile dragged herself up on the master panel and hung her wet things across the dials and switches. Then she lay on her side, something like a Titian contessa, head propped on her hand, staring vacantly out of the porthole at the city. There was hardly a light in Sam's tower now; numerals of time-weather flashed intermittently about the MC Lady. An airliner circled contentedly in an approach pattern.

The master panel warmed Odile. It soothed her protracted flesh. Her dampness and odor filled the room. The dials worked feverishly beneath her body. The pain in her stomach subsided. A tremor caused her to arch languorously, her thighs became moist. But she refused to regard herself.

Eye unblinking on the city, she resisted sleep.

32 · Kudos

Sam worked fanatically to finish the Christmas Memo. He had
not eaten since the party and had been drinking from dusk. The
extramural dictaphone balked at his heavy breathing, the
scanner light glowed and dimmed like an expiring nebula.

It is difficult at this time to calculate an upside objective for the market,
for deterioration in its structure still exists. The downside risk appears
significant as a certain softness in prime areas has been noted recently,
and in-and-outers have been unloading once favored issues. We now face,
at the least, an area of intense resistance, and support does not appear
forthcoming. Some respected analysts believe that if we do not have a
prompt rally, we are in jeopardy of considerable unfavorability.

Ordinarily, we would advise caution to our clients until we get a clearer
picture. And in any case, for those who now own, it is most likely too
late to sell. Further, those simple linear relationships which were thought
to underlie our activity no longer seem sophisticated enough for their
purposes. The issues we have dealt with can no longer be said to have
fundamental or intrinsic value, but are only assigned such by the random
operation of the market.

Therefore, as it remains unclear whether the reliability of the information justifies the cost of getting it, we advise our customers to select future
issues at random—imputing to them no intrinsic value, nor evaluating
them by past behavior—with the expectation that profits will at least
be equal to those achieved under what, in retrospect, seem rather mystical,
nostalgic, not to say cruel, circumstances. . . .

A final word of thanks to those odd-lotters, *Mr. Go-Along*. We in
Management forget at our peril that the constancy of our profit is governed
directly by the consistency of your error. In such perplexing times, it is
some solace that at least your ignorance remains predictable.

As for the individual who wishes to diversify with only small holdings, he should remember that the load-cost of incorporation with other rational profit-maximizers offsets, on the average, any increase in leverage, and he may as well go it alone. We urge you all, then, in this festive holiday time, to seriously consider withdrawing your portfolio from Management Concern and take that random walk.

Sam coded the message for immediate worldwide distribution to all employees and customers, and the scanner light gave him its banal twinkling OK. By morning the information would be disseminated. It should take more than routine effort to discount that, he hoped.

Then he switched the dictaphone to his private channel, connected to the memo cord on his office desk.

KNOW YE ALL MEN BY THESE PRESENTS that Samuel J. Hooper, enjoying good health and being of sound and disposing mind, but calling to that mind the blatant certainties of this life, hereby makes his last will and testament.

I devise and bequeath my estate in the following manner, and nominate and appoint Christos E. Agapecropolis the executor herein.

Should any beneficiary named herein die as a result of the same calamity or accident that shall cause my death, I direct that the bequest allotted him shall pass under the laws of intestacy.

To Agapecropolis, Christos E., my colleague and erstwhile advisor, I leave my complete file of back issues of *The Meliorist*, my report cards, and all other correspondence and papers (including the Fuess Formula) to be preserved within the MC Data Bank— I do not begrudge him this information and provide it freely. May he piece it together and make use of its concealed patterns as I have failed to do, though I am aware that such information has no "intrinsic value" and is probably useless for predictive purposes.

For your information, I consider my life neither a waste nor strict warning; simply the culmination of some large evolution that's begun to bite its own tail. I tried to live up to what the market assigned me; I have not failed the market, nor could it be said to any purpose that the market failed me. At this point there's no use in speculating about my misappropriation, or forcing apologies. I was a frontman. I practiced the Second Vesicle of Liberation. I too tried to be modern. And I was one of the few who got up to zero. But everything that keeps you privately alive seems to get so destructive in the marketplace.

There are those who will say that I gave the secret-fixers necessary ammunition, but I would prefer to think of myself as—if nothing else—a damaging statistic. The measure of my life is that I lived without blaming the market for my own inadequacies. But that sort of pride has incalculable consequences these days; it leads one off in too many directions, it turns your training against your strength; it makes of your love just a pity. The truth is, had I been able to beat the market I just might have stayed with it—and it's likely, with such momentum, that I would have forgotten all about that *other man*. As it stands, the potential profit seems so marginal that there's no reason for us all not to have a hand in it. That's what's become of Humanities I these days.

So sometimes it's quitting, it's stopping the action that counts. My deepest regret is that I couldn't talk about the market without reference to myself. I guess that's the real problem—information gets disseminated, discounted so fast, you don't know who's doing the talking—truthtelling becomes largely a matter of personal style. Maybe it's just as well. Aside from that, the funniest thing is, I never did find out who that "other man" is. I mean remembering him certainly isn't enough when you never knew him in the first place. I think, honestly, the problem is that I detest him, wherever he may be. Not because he had what I wanted, but because he seemed satisfied with so little. No, I didn't want to get to know him, just *help* him; and that, Doctor, is the purest sort of hatred. That's something more than an irony, wouldn't you say? Silly to become a martyr for someone you don't even know, y'say? Ah, friends, just another way of keeping one's distance.

I can't say how good a description of reality this is over the long term, but I'd wager the market's next move is unpredictable. Oh, don't worry about another Big Creamer; we may be oversold, folks, but no convenient apocalypse is going to get *you* out of it. . . .

anyway,

To Odile Odets Grassgreen, I leave the sum of $1,000 for the purpose of choosing a mate to her contact lens and pursue such periodic ocular checkups as may be necessary until the exhaustion of this fund and/or her. I further hope that she will take to heart the final advice I have urged upon my other clients. No more excuses, eh, Princess?

To Aaron Grassgreen, I leave the *objets d'art* in my apartment, my wardrobe, travel accoutrements and men's accessories, if he will have them.

To Stieglitz and Matthew Grassgreen, I leave my vast and unnatural love, my king-sized bed (unless Aaron claims it as art), my Strat-O-Mocs, basketball, clock-radio and such other of my personal effects not yet accounted for, which might amuse them. I refer them specifically to my medicine cabinet.

I further instruct my executor to liquidate my auto, stereo-lounger and insurance, and use the not inconsiderable proceeds to form a non-profit corporation the purpose of which shall be a "Free the Dott Defense Fund" in perpetuity, or as long as this matter is subject to litigation. Should this issue be resolved leaving an excess of capital, I bequeath all remainders to Wittgenstein's *Club* in his memory.

Finally, I leave the bulk of my estate, all MC stock options and pension funds to the *People for the Preservation of Peacock Prairie Association*, providing they fulfill the following proviso: that upon my decease, my handsome body be placed in the boat which now occupies that property, and that it, together with all surrounding vegetation, be burned to the ground.

As Sam finished this he smashed the circuitry of the dictaphone as he had the telephone. Nauseous from the cigarettes and bourbon, he stumbled for the bathroom. Lungs congested, head in his hands, elbows on knees, the old knot bobbing from his throat to his bowels and back, he sang in a low tremolo those lyrics from that funny foreign opera he loved enough to memorize but still did not know the meaning of:

> *Io son pure il tuo fedele!*
> *Alcun non dubiti di me!*

But there was no response. The ripe but opaque words dissolved away in the ducts. Only their echoes, pure phonics, buzzed back at him from the tiles; his elbows left red rings on his knees.

After several more bourbons, Sam put on his pajamas and crawled into the cool stereo-lounger; he turned on the TV, but could get only an image—the sound system had been somehow disrupted in smashing the dictaphone—yet Sam Hooper[2] jarred and boggled forth upon the screen, his fine mouth fluttering about a ghostly text. He was indeed reviewing Aaron's work; a facsimile of one of the ballet photos was propped against his chest. The camera zoomed in on it upon his command, but work's outlines were smeared, its texture annealed; the screen gave it a fluid quality—withered or bloated, Sam could not tell which. Ignorant of what part of Miss Julie Rowen he was touching, Sam[2] traced a finger along the hollows and shadows like those mad astronomers who perfunctorily dissect the heavens' model with a flashlight. Sam could not tell whether the wavering of the photo within the coarser image was due to an

346

imperfection of the machine or his own bourbonized myopia; he leaned forward, extending a limp index finger along his sightline until it met, for an instant, the moving finger of Sam[2].

The entry light on the console flashed.

"He's here," Sam thought, "at last," and pressed the lobby door off-duty release mechanism. Then he switched off the tube and its myxedemic finger, not wishing to be finished in their presence, and quickly scanning the MC Cultural Programming Guide, chose appropriate background music for the occasion.

"The Sound of Genius," the Guide informed him, "the great themes excised from their often interminable former formal corpi, compiled and collaborated in suitable units for the listener's historical as well as aural interest."

Sam found the station on his handy portable, positioned the earphone, and hung the instrument about his neck.

He recognized the first eighth of *Eine Kleine Nachtmusik*, four bars of some Vivaldi bassoon concerto, a trill from the Chopin "Polonaise in A-Flat," a snippet of "Clair de Lune," the coda of St.-Saëns's organ concerto; the masters following each other like dogs in heat in the dark, throwing their foreshortened bodies against the present, then going down forever beneath the inevitable equal essence of next genius, please.

Uniform gaps of imperfect silence announced their deaths and renewals, the hushed shard of posterity grinding with precisely the same intensity, amplifying only the sound of its own monotonous, lubric touch. Every speck of dust, each scratch, treated just as lovingly as the great themes themselves, filtered just as precisely, the first and last thing one ever hears, those inane intervals which themselves make time, always through the great themes you can hear it, no matter how fine or expensive the equipment, that penultimate synapse of fire on water.

Through the congeries of melodies, Sam heard a fumbling at his door. He started, horrified; he had forgotten to remove the

347

chain. The door opened rudely and the chain clinked straight as a pike. Sam heard the small cry of disbelief. But he could not stir himself to remove the chain, disgusted that the last vestige of his will to win had betrayed him. Nevertheless, Aaron's wily wrist had already spun through the aperture, and closing the door against his minimal arm, his fingers flicked the chain free. He backed into the room, more coquettish than apprehensive, trying to suppress a shy grin. "Thought I might have to come down the chimney."

Sam tried to focus bravely—his astigmatism gradually canceled out, but his face twitched under the pressure. He had very much wanted to appear resigned, it was a mistake to have drunk so much. Sam fully expected that he would be treated to an orgasmic recapitulation of his predictable life in these last moments, or failing that, at least a mysterious personage with a rehearsed announcement—little girl that he had made up to carry down the plaza, little girl he had seen falling once, the one who watched him when he *did it*, maybe even that "other man"—but nothing came through save the old dream of himself, determinedly coasting the tricky whip-currents of America, a true and perfectly adapted fishbird, feinting, floating, who feeds, digests and excretes in one single marvelous instant, passing the world repeatedly and whole through his transparent system.

They were apparently out to breakfast in the control room, for the recording was convulsed in its final redundant groove. Sam turned the volume down.

"Go ahead," he said softly. "Get it over with."

He put his head back and rotated the axis of the lounger to improve the angle. Aaron advanced quickly, cocking a new velour Borsalino with a partridge feather in the band over his brow. But for Sam, Aaron was only an ageless blur now; he could barely make out his adversary's hand stuffed within his lapel, over his heart.

348

"Baggage all checked," the grantee intoned. "Night flight leaves in an hour. Two meals an' a snack included."

"I should have sided with one or the other of you," Sam offered, his voice catching.

But Aaron only bit his lips and produced a dark muzzle as from within his own body, requiring both hands to steady his aim.

"Don't make too much of this," Sam said and lay back easily, blind but whole.

(Oh shit, he thought, they'll never burn that boat or me.)

"Ya know, Sam," Aaron said, closing the viewfinder about the open face, "I always thought you was a better person than me. But let's see, hey, what ya look like now!" he snarled.

The flash cauterized Sam's lids, his hands flew involuntarily to his temples. He could hear Aaron's footsteps but not the shots. Sam's torso luffed like a sail; he sensed for an instant his own smell.

. . . *the code flashes from the windows of the darkened tower. But even from her new vantage, Odile cannot decipher . . .*

Aaron circled the chair fearlessly. His new custom-made walking shoes gleamed in the intense shadows.

"I don't got much time," he said, "so I wish you'd cooperate."

Sam lifted his head slowly, his unmatched eyes rolled red. He was aware of his spasmodic double defecation in the chair. He managed to raise his eyebrows and felt a smile settle in his mouth. The flipside of *The Sound of Genius* came on strong.

"That's better," said Aaron. "Be yourself."

Aaron encouraged him programmatically, shading the portrait lens with his palm, throwing the blackened flashbulbs over his shoulder.

"Thata boy, that's right . . . thata boy . . . thata boy! Hold it! *There* we go. Thata boy . . . thata boy . . ."

349